Terri Reed
and
New York Times Bestselling Author
Lenora Worth

Police Protector

Previously published as *Protect and Serve* and *Truth and Consequences*

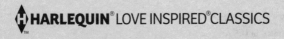

HARLEQUIN® LOVE INSPIRED®CLASSICS

 LOVE INSPIRED BOOKS

Recycling programs for this product may not exist in your area.

ISBN-13: 978-1-335-06125-6

Police Protector

Copyright © 2019 by Harlequin Books S.A.

First published as Protect and Serve by Harlequin Books in 2016 and Truth and Consequences by Harlequin Books in 2016.

The publisher acknowledges the copyright holder of the individual works as follows:

Protect and Serve
Copyright © 2016 by Harlequin Books S.A.

Truth and Consequences
Copyright © 2016 by Harlequin Books S.A.

Special thanks and acknowledgment are given to Terri Reed and Lenora Worth for their contribution to the Rookie K-9 Unit miniseries.

www.Harlequin.com

Printed in U.S.A.

CONTENTS

Terri Reed's romance and romantic suspense novels have appeared on the *Publishers Weekly* top twenty-five and Nielsen BookScan's top one hundred lists, and have been featured in *USA TODAY*, *Christian Fiction Magazine* and *RT Book Reviews*. Her books have been finalists for the Romance Writers of America RITA® Award and the National Readers' Choice Award and finalists three times for the American Christian Fiction Writers Carol Award. Contact Terri at terrireed.com or PO Box 19555, Portland, OR 97224.

PROTECT AND SERVE

Terri Reed

For God has not given us a spirit of fear,
but of power and of love and of a sound mind.
—*2 Timothy* 1:7

To my family and my critique partners for your encouragement, love and support. And to my editors Emily Rodmell and Tina James for inviting me to write this book and for believing in me. Thank you!

ONE

"Georgiiiinnnaaa!"

Gina Perry froze midstride in the center of her bedroom. An explosion of panic detonated in her chest. She recognized the unmistakable singsong tone of her brother.

Oh, no. No, no, no. Tim had tracked her to Desert Valley, Arizona.

Frantic with alarm, she whirled around to search the confines of her upstairs bedroom. The sliding glass door to the terrace stood open, allowing the dark March night air to fill her house.

Where was he? How had he discovered where she'd been hiding? Had she made a fatal error that brought him to her door?

She stumbled backward on shaky legs just as her brother stepped from the shadows of her closet.

Light from the bedside table lamp glinted off the steel blade of a large knife held high in his hand. His face was covered by a thick beard, his hair stuck out in a wild frenzy and the mania gleaming in his hazel eyes slammed a fist of fear into her gut.

Choking with terror, she turned and fled down the stairs.

She couldn't let him catch her or he'd make good on his threat to kill her. Just as he had their father two years ago.

Her bare feet slid on the hardwood steps. She used the handrail to keep her balance.

Tim pounded down the stairs behind her, the sound hammering into her like nails on a coffin.

Her breathing came out in harsh rasps, filling her head with the maddening noise. She made a grab for her phone on the charger in the foyer but missed. Abandoning the device, she lurched for the front door and managed to get the lock undone and the door opened.

Without a backward glance, she sprinted into the night, across the small yard to the road. Rocks and debris bit into her bare feet, but she ignored the pain. *Faster!*

Dear God, help me!

The Desert Valley police station was only half a mile down the quiet residential road on the west side of town. Street lamps provided pools of light that threatened to expose her. She ducked behind the few cars parked along the curb and moved rapidly through the shadows.

She had to reach the police station. Only there would she would be safe.

There, Tim couldn't hurt her.

"Sisssster! I'm coming for you!"

He wasn't far behind. She'd never make it to the station before he caught her. But the K-9 training center where she worked was closer. If she could get inside, she could call for help.

Grateful the moon hid behind cloud cover on this spring night, she stayed in the shadows and prayed she'd make it to safety. Just a little farther now. Her lungs burned from exertion. Her heart pounded in her chest.

Not daring to glance back to see how close Tim had gained on her, she ran for the training center and dove behind the bushes growing along the fence of the small outdoor puppy-training yard. She sent up a silent plea to God above that Tim wouldn't find her in the bushes.

"You can't hide from me," Tim shouted, his voice taking on the manic tone she knew all too well. A tone that had always sent her into hiding when they were kids.

Her body trembled with fear. She curled into herself, hoping to make herself smaller, less of a target for him to spot. The unmistakable sound of his heavy breathing as he passed by her hiding place tormented her. She bit her lip, drawing blood, the coppery taste making her gag. She clamped a hand over her mouth.

"You betrayed me, Gina. For that you'll pay. I'm going to kill you as soon as I find you."

His voice sounded farther away now. He'd moved past the yard and was nearly at the end of the next building. She breathed a small sigh of relief. But she couldn't relax. She wasn't safe yet. She had to get inside the training center.

Cautiously, she made her way along the training yard fence in a low crouch. The gate to the yard was open. Odd. All the trainers were careful to keep them closed and locked in case a dog escaped from the center and made it outside. It was as much for the dogs' protection as the general public's.

She rounded the corner and froze.

Someone lay faceup on the ground, half in, half out of the gate.

Moving closer, Gina recognized Veronica Earnshaw. Gina's boss.

Panic crawled up Gina's throat and she gasped for air. There were two gaping wounds in Veronica's chest. Oh, no. No! Had Tim done this? Had he come to the training center first and, when he'd failed to find Gina, hurt Veronica instead?

Gina scuttled closer. *Please, Lord, don't let her be dead.* "Veronica?"

With a trembling hand, she put two fingers against Veronica's neck.

No pulse. Gina's heart sank.

It seemed, once again, God had ignored Gina's plea. Just as He had when Gina witnessed her brother murder their father.

She choked back a sob. Tears blurred her vision. It should have been her lying in the dirt, not Veronica.

A scrape of noise echoed in the stillness of the night. Her brother retracing his steps?

She scuttled back to the bushes, burrowing in deep and drawing her knees to her chest. A line of Scripture wove through the shock numbing her mind. She clung to it like a lifeline. *The Lord is with me, I will not be afraid.*

The litany echoed through her head, mocking her. Because she was afraid. Deathly afraid.

Officer Shane Weston and his canine partner, a German shepherd named Bella, walked along Desert Valley Road. The cool Arizona night air smelled of the fragrant western honey mesquite trees that had started to flower as spring arrived.

It was dark, nearly ten o'clock, but Shane couldn't remain cooped up inside the condo he was staying in, one for out-of-town trainees. He was restless, anxious to see where he'd be assigned. He'd put in a request for his hometown police department of Flagstaff, but no one could guarantee he'd get his choice or even that he had a choice.

This past Friday, he'd completed his twelve-week

training session at the Canyon County Training Center, a pilot project for the state of Arizona that trained new police recruits to be K-9 officers.

Not every candidate who applied was selected for the K-9 program. Shane had been thrilled that he'd made the cut. Once he was accepted, he'd been placed with a group of other rookies, and they'd attended the police academy together in Phoenix before coming to Desert Valley for the K-9 training.

Upon the start of every twelve-week session, the trainers matched each officer with a dog based on master trainer Veronica Earnshaw's research into the rookies, along with questionnaires the recruits filled out prior to the start of the program.

Shane had gleaned that all the trainers used their instincts and knowledge of dogs to help with the pairing of officers to canines. The center was a well-run operation, highly respected throughout the state and a model for other centers.

Shane couldn't be more pleased with his pairing to Bella.

He knew, however, that once the training began, if a dog and rookie officer hadn't jelled for whatever reason and the trainers' attempts to intervene failed, then the officer and dog were reassigned to work with new partners to finish out the program.

Thankfully, he and Bella had meshed from the moment they were introduced.

Now that training was complete, the officers and their canines would be allocated to various police stations throughout Arizona, and the training center would then be reimbursed by the police stations. A win-win for everyone.

Shane sent up another quick prayer that his request

would be honored and he'd be assigned to the Flagstaff PD, where he could prove to his brothers and father that he wasn't weak. He wasn't a failure.

He planned to be the best officer he could be, with ambitions to one day make captain, or even chief. One day he'd be the one in charge, and then he'd finally earn his family's respect.

Shane waved a greeting to an older man taking out his trash.

Very few people were out on this Saturday night, and those who were made a point of acknowledging him and Bella. Shane liked that the community of Desert Valley embraced the K-9 officers and their canine partners. He couldn't say the same of bigger cities, where law enforcement was usually viewed with fear, suspicion and malice.

Bella stopped abruptly, her ears perking and her nose lifting to smell the air.

Unease tightened Shane's shoulder muscles. She'd been alerted to something. "What is it, girl?"

Bella took off. Keeping the beam of the flashlight aimed ahead of him, Shane ran to keep up, his feet pounding noisily on the pavement. The lead connected to the dog's collar pulled taut, and Shane pressed himself to move faster. They headed toward the training center. Had something happened to one of the dogs? The trainers?

Bella led him past the veterinary clinic and skidded to a halt at the outdoor puppy-training yard.

Shane stopped and kept Bella at his side. He swept his flashlight over the scene before him. Dread crimped his chest. He sucked in a quick breath.

Veronica Earnshaw lay twisted on the ground with her dark hair and striking face coated in dirt. Her open eyes stared at the stars above. And what appeared to be two gunshot wounds marred her chest. Bile rose in his throat.

His priority as the first officer on the scene was to determine if the victim was alive or dead.

Bella tugged at the leash. He gave her the hand movement to sit and stay. She obeyed, but her gaze was riveted to the bushes along the fence.

Was the perpetrator hiding in there?

Wishing he had his sidearm, which he'd left locked up in the condo, he shone the flashlight on the thick shrubbery. He let out Bella's lead. She made a beeline for the greenery and sat staring at the dense foliage.

Caution tripped down his spine. There was no coverage for him to use. If the person who'd shot Veronica was in the bushes with the gun, he might well be the next victim.

"I'm a police officer. If someone is in there, you better come out," he said with authority.

"Shane?"

He knew that voice. "Gina?" It was the junior trainer from the Canyon County training facility. A sob came from the bushes, then Gina crawled out. He reached out to help her and she flinched. Her long auburn braid was coming undone. The hazel of her eyes was nearly gone because of her enlarged pupils.

He held up his hands, palms out.

Was Gina's shock real or fake? Had she committed murder? Or was she a witness?

Cautious, in case there was a gun he couldn't see, he crouched beside her, noting blood on her hands and smeared on her khaki pants and pink sweater. "Gina. Are you hurt?"

"No." She took a shuddering breath. "She's dead. Veronica's dead. He killed her."

A witness, then. He refocused his attention on Veronica. There was no discernible movement of the upper part of her abdomen, indicating her breathing had stopped or was too shallow to be observed.

He checked for a pulse and found none. He shone the flashlight into her eyes—no response.

There was no question in his mind.

Gina was correct.

Veronica Earnshaw was dead.

His chest tightened; his lungs seized. An itch scratched at his throat. He put his hand on the inhaler in his pocket, but he refused to let the asthma take hold. There were procedures to follow. A crime to investigate. He had no time for an asthma attack right now. And as the first responder, he had a responsibility to make sure no element of the scene was disturbed any worse than it had already been.

Instead of his inhaler, he took out his cell phone and called the police department. When the dispatcher answered the call, he said, "This is Officer Shane Weston. I need assistance at the side yard of the Canyon County Training Center. One gunshot-wound victim. One potential witness."

He hadn't ruled out perpetrator. Not yet.

"I'll let the chief and Officer Hayes know," she responded before the line disconnected.

Slipping his phone back into his pocket, he made mental notes of the scene since he didn't have a notepad and pen. When he left the condo, he hadn't expected to end up working a crime scene.

He hadn't heard the report of a gun, much less two shots, so he knew this tragedy hadn't happened recently. Unless…a noise suppressor had been used.

The thought stuck in his mind like a thorn.

Because if that were the case, then Veronica's murder was premeditated.

He did a quick visual search with the flashlight for the weapon but came up empty. A dark trail of what he assumed to be blood led from Veronica to the training center doors. Had Veronica been dragged out of the building or had she managed to crawl to the gate seeking help?

As he waited for the Desert Valley police, he turned his attention to the woman sitting on the ground by the bushes. She'd drawn her knees to her chest and had begun rocking. Compassion tangled with suspicion. As much as he didn't want to think ill of Gina, she certainly had a reason to dislike the lead trainer.

"Gina, can you tell me what happened?"

She didn't acknowledge him but kept rocking, her gaze locked on something only she could see. He gently touched her shoulder.

She started and scrambled away from him. "No, please, no," she cried and curled into a tight ball.

He backed away, giving her space. "Gina, I'm not here to hurt you."

She raised her teary gaze to meet his. She blinked as the glazed fog lifted. "Oh, Shane. We're not safe. He's here. He found me."

A knot in his chest tightened. He? "Who are you afraid of?"

A visible tremor ran over her. "My twin brother, Tim."

"Wait, you have a twin?" He'd had no idea.

"Yes. Two years ago he escaped police custody in Mesa and disappeared." She rubbed at her temples. "I moved to Desert Valley to hide from him. I had hoped he wouldn't find me here. But he has. And now…"

Concern arced through Shane. They had an escaped criminal on the loose. Gina's twin brother. Had he killed Veronica thinking he'd shot his sister? Or was this a contrived story to cover Gina's crime? Was there really a brother, much less a twin? He didn't know her well enough to know if she had a sibling. "What happened to Veronica?"

"I'm not sure. I found her like this. I checked for a pulse." She looked away. "There isn't one."

He winced. She'd already contaminated the scene—if she wasn't the perpetrator. "Don't touch anything else or move again until the chief arrives, okay?"

She nodded on a shuddering breath.

"Why do you think your brother killed Veronica?" Shane asked her.

"Isn't it obvious?" She stared up at him. "He came here looking for me and instead found Veronica. He killed her out of rage because I wasn't here."

"You didn't see it happen?" Though her explanation was plausible, there were holes. "How would he know where you work?"

"I don't know. He's smart."

"But you don't work here anymore, right?"

"What?" Her voice held a note of confusion.

"Didn't Veronica put you on indefinite probation?" It had been a spectacle. Veronica had turned her mean streak onto Gina yesterday right in front of the newest class of graduated rookies. Veronica had loudly and very publicly claimed Gina had used the wrong training technique and declared Gina was on probation indefinitely.

Shane had attempted to talk to Gina after the incident because he'd felt bad for the pretty trainer, but she'd hurried home and he hadn't seen her until now.

Gina's shoulder rose and fell. "She did. But in typical Veronica fashion, she called me this morning to apologize."

"That's surprising," he said. "She didn't strike me as someone who would own her mistakes easily."

One side of Gina's mouth curled. "Oh, it wasn't a humble gesture. She does this almost every session. She gets mad for some perceived infraction and makes a scene." Gina blew out a breath. "Veronica needed me to return to the center to process the intake of three new German shepherd puppies donated by Marian Foxcroft."

"So you were here today."

"Yes. This morning." She wiped her forearm across her forehead. "I would have been at the training center this evening if I hadn't already committed to serving at the community church's Saturday-night potluck dinner."

He hadn't known she attended church. He hadn't seen her there these past few Sundays. "Do you mean the church's singles' potluck?"

She nodded.

For some reason the idea of her mingling with other singles rubbed him wrong. Which was so out of left field and inappropriate at the moment. Irritated at himself, he pushed the thought aside to focus on Gina.

Fresh tears rolled down her cheeks. He hated seeing her cry. Yet there was a jaded part of him that wondered if the tears were real. Were they a ploy to gain his sympathy?

"Veronica wasn't pleased that I couldn't be here tonight," she said. "But she agreed to microchip the new puppies and expected me to take over their care and training first thing on Monday morning."

However, that didn't explain how Gina came to be here now. Something about her story felt off.

The sounds of Desert Valley Police Department's finest arriving drew Shane's attention. Since the station was so close, several officers came on foot while the chief of police and the lone K-9 officer of the department drove to the training center.

"Is that…?" Louise Donaldson, the first officer to reach the scene, clamped a hand over her mouth and turned away.

Officer Dennis Marlton put a hand on her back and bowed his head as if the sight were too much to bear.

Officer Ken Bucks staggered back several steps. Though it was too dark to see his expression, Shane imagined that seeing an acquaintance murdered like this must be a shock, to say the least.

The last murder victim in the community of Desert Valley had been the wife of K-9 officer Ryder Hayes five years ago. A murder that had never been solved.

Shane glanced at Ryder, his face hidden in shadows created by the many flashlight beams directed toward the victim. Sitting at Ryder's side was his canine partner, a handsome yellow Lab named Titus. Shane had seen the pair around but hadn't really had a reason to interact with the Desert Valley Police Department's only official K-9 officer.

Chief Earl Jones, a tall, imposing seventy-year-old man with thick graying hair, knelt beside Veronica and checked for a pulse, apparently to confirm Shane's pronouncement that the master trainer was dead.

When he lifted his head, tears shone in his gray eyes. He stood, his hands fisted at his side. He was clearly struggling to contain his grief and anger. "Who did this?"

"Gina believes her brother, Tim Perry, did," Shane said, noting that Gina hadn't moved, just as he'd instructed her. "She didn't see it happen, though. I haven't asked her how she came to be here tonight."

"Hmm, her brother, huh?" Earl scrubbed a hand over his jaw.

"Apparently he's a wanted criminal in Mesa," Shane added. Did the chief know Gina had a brother who was in trouble with the law? Or had she kept that information hidden? The thought made him wonder what else she could be hiding. Was Gina capable of murder? Was the story about her brother a convenient way to deflect blame?

TWO

"All right, everyone." The chief's voice held a sharp edge that swept over the group outside the Canyon County Training Center's side yard. "We have a crime scene and a potential suspect. Let's work this for Veronica and bring her killer to justice." His voice broke on the last word.

Shane felt for the man. It was no secret that the chief and Veronica had had a special relationship. Though they weren't related, Chief Jones regarded Veronica as the daughter he'd never had.

And despite complaints from other trainers and rookies that she was too harsh, critical and demanding, Chief Jones's philosophy was if you couldn't handle working with Veronica, how could you handle all the stress of being a cop or training police dogs and their handlers?

Chief Jones barked out orders for Marlton to fetch standing lamps and Bucks to call the coroner and start documenting the scene. "Donaldson, gather forensic evidence."

Officer Marlton left and returned a few minutes later with two huge freestanding lamps. Within moments, pools of sharp glaring light replaced the darkness.

Shane and Bella stepped out of the way as Ryder and

his dog moved past. Shane could only imagine Ryder was remembering his wife's murder. But in this case they had a clear suspect. They would solve Veronica's murder.

Chief Jones pinned Shane with a questioning look. "Have you cleared the building?"

"No, sir, I was waiting with Gina."

Earl turned to Ryder. "You good?"

Taking a deep breath, Ryder nodded. "Yes, sir."

"Clear the building," the chief instructed. "And, Ryder, be careful."

"Yes, sir." Ryder and Titus headed toward the training facility door, keeping a wide berth around the dark, bloody trail.

The chief ran a hand over his graying hair. "I'll need to let her brother, Lee, know. He's the only family she had left." He shook his head with sadness.

"Is he here in town?" Shane asked. He hadn't known Veronica had a brother.

"No, he's in the state prison. He was convicted of larceny a few years back."

Shane bit back his surprise as he turned his attention to Gina. Seemed she wasn't the only one with brother issues.

Officer Donaldson squatted down in front of Gina. "Honey, I need to swab your hands for gunpowder residue."

A stricken look crossed Gina's lovely face, making her already pale complexion even more so. "I didn't shoot her. I don't even know how to handle a gun."

"It's procedure," Officer Donaldson explained as she worked. "Our department isn't large enough to employ a crime scene technician, so all of us officers have been trained to do basic forensic collection." She bagged the pad that she'd swiped over Gina's hands and face.

"I touched Veronica to see if she—" Gina turned away.

"I'll send everything gathered to the lab in Flagstaff. As long as the particle count is twenty or less, then you're fine. Cross contamination happens."

"But even if you don't find any sign of gunpowder on Gina, the lack of forensic evidence could be explained away," Shane said. "Someone wearing gloves when they pulled the trigger wouldn't have any residue on their hands. There could be some blowback on the perpetrator's clothing."

Gina whipped her attention to him.

"True," Officer Donaldson said. "The lab won't be able to process Gina's clothes until she's able to surrender them."

The flash of a camera burned Shane's eyes. Officer Ken Bucks snapped shots of Veronica's body.

"Marlton," the chief called to the older officer standing off to the side, observing.

"Yeah, Chief," Dennis Marlton answered, but didn't step closer. He had his arms folded over his potbelly as if protecting his paunch. He was shorter than his coworkers and had gray, thin hair and watery blue eyes that squinted at the chief.

"You and..." Earl frowned as he glanced around. "Where's Harmon?"

Dennis shrugged. "Late as usual."

The chief harrumphed. "Bucks, go with Marlton to canvass the area. See if anyone saw anything that might be helpful."

Bucks looked at the chief, his face glowing a pasty white in the light of the lamps. "I'm taking photos." He pointed to the trail of blood. "You said to document everything before we lose any evidence."

"Right. Stay on it." Earl turned his sharp steely eyes

back on Officer Marlton. "You can handle the interviews alone."

Officer Marlton sighed heavily and unfolded his arms. "Fine." He trudged off, mumbling about having to do everything himself.

Shane watched him. His father, a police chief in Flagstaff, would never have stood for such disrespectful behavior from his men. First Harmon not showing up, then Bucks defying an order and Marlton making it clear he wasn't happy doing his job.

There was a rumor going around that Chief Jones would be retiring soon. Perhaps that was why the chief wasn't strict with his employees. Or it could be the grief and shock of Veronica's death.

"I've gathered what I can from Gina," Officer Donaldson remarked as she held on to the evidence bags.

"Thank you, Louise. We'll get Gina's clothes bagged. Would you track down Harmon and then start a search for Tim Perry? Build a profile. I want to know where he's been and what he's been doing."

Louise nodded, her usually serious expression even more grim on her pale face. "On it."

Earl squatted down in front of Gina. "When was the last time you saw your brother?"

Her hazel eyes looked too large for her petite face. "Do you mean before tonight?"

Shane frowned. "So you did see him tonight."

She kept her gaze on the chief. "When I returned home from the potluck, he was in my bedroom. He had a knife. I ran downstairs hoping to get to the phone but he was too close so I escaped out the front door and ran this way, hoping to make it to the station, but then I found…" She closed her eyes.

"Why were you hiding in the shrubs when Bella and I arrived?"

Her eyelids popped open. "I was afraid you were Tim."

Or was she hoping she could slip away undetected?

A car pulled up. Shane yanked his gaze from Gina to see Sophie Williams, another trainer at the center, emerge from behind the wheel. Tall, earthy and willowy, the former K-9 cop's normally confident demeanor was lacking as she hurried over.

Her shoulder-length blond hair was tied back in a messy ponytail, and her hazel eyes were anxious as she took in the scene. She and Veronica had clashed many times during Shane's weeks of training. He watched Sophie closely. Was her shock real? Could she and Gina have come up with a plan to off their boss?

Sophie halted beside Shane, but her gaze was on Veronica. "Oh, no. Is she…?" She clamped a hand to her mouth. Tears leaked down her face.

"Sophie, what are you doing here?" Earl asked, clearly puzzled by her presence.

"I heard on the police radio that something had happened at the center," she explained. Her teary-eyed gaze moved to Gina and widened. "Oh, no, Gina. Are you all right? Were you attacked, too?"

Before Gina could answer, Earl filled Sophie in on the details. It was clear by the way his voice shook that he was hanging on to his composure by the tips of his fingers.

A few minutes later, Randolph Drummond, the mortician who doubled as the coroner, arrived wearing a subdued black suit, white button-down shirt and black tie. He carried a medical bag. He stopped a foot away from Veronica's body to don gloves and booties, then he squatted beside her.

Bella whined. Shane stroked her head. She let out a loud bark just as a commotion broke out near the doors. Two small German shepherd puppies raced out of the center, followed by Titus and Ryder. The older dog circled the puppies, unmistakably in an attempt to corral them.

"Oh, no," Sophie said.

Gina jumped to her feet. "The puppies are loose. How…?"

Shane snagged Gina by the elbow before she could chase after the puppies. "We need your clothes."

She blinked at him, then grimaced. "Of course."

Shane turned to the chief. "Veronica was microchipping the puppies tonight and was supposed to come over to the condo afterward to work with James and Hawk." K-9 rookie officer James Harrison and Shane shared the furnished condo used by out-of-town rookies. "I'll call James and let him know what's going on. Maybe Hawk will be helpful." James's bloodhound, Hawk, specialized in crime scene evidence.

The chief held up a hand. "Have him clear Gina's house before you take her home to change. Bring back her current clothing in an evidence bag."

"Sir," Shane spoke up. "Shouldn't she be taken to the station for questioning?"

Gina let out a small gasp. "You can't really believe that I…"

The stricken hurt in her eyes stabbed at him, but he couldn't rule her out as the murderer, not until forensic evidence cleared her. "You had a very good reason to want to hurt Veronica."

"So did many other people," she shot back.

"True." Including the other trainer, Sophie. Could the two women have conspired to murder their boss? Though Sophie had once been a cop, that didn't mean she couldn't have colluded with Gina. Hmm. Something to talk to the chief about later.

To Gina, Shane said, "Veronica humiliated you on Friday. And from what I've heard, she stole the fiancé of one of your best friends." He hated throwing the rumor in her face but it went to motive.

"It's true Veronica did steal Simon from Jenna just to prove she could. It broke Jenna's heart and caused her to resign and leave, not only the training center but Desert Valley." Gina squared her shoulders. "And yes, I may have loathed my boss, but I never wished Veronica dead."

He wanted to believe her. There was something about the young trainer he found very attractive. Even now, she was standing up for herself but not in an over-the-top display of hysterics or viciousness. He respected her quiet confidence in the face of hardship.

Yet his father had always told him that the evidence never lied, only people did. Was Gina lying?

And Dad had said to never make a judgment on innocence or guilt until all the evidence came in. "If your brother is truly after you as you've stated, then you should be where you can be protected."

Earl narrowed his gaze on Shane. "She's been questioned. She's innocent until proven guilty. But you're right, she's in danger and needs protection. That'll be your job, Weston."

Oh, man. He hadn't expected to be given a protection assignment. What did he know about being a bodyguard? He'd trained to be out on the streets, catching criminals and thwarting the schemes of bad people. Surely the chief would want someone with more experience to protect Gina. "Are you sure—"

Earl arched one eyebrow as he cut Shane off. "Yes."

There was no room for argument in his tone. Then Earl turned his gaze to Gina. "Don't leave town."

Gina lifted her chin. "No, sir, I won't."

Sophie and Ryder joined them. They'd managed to corral the puppies and now each had one in their arms.

"Where's Marco, the third pup?" Gina asked.

"He's probably inside," Sophie said. "I'll round him up and put him in the crate with these two."

"I didn't see a third puppy when I was inside," Ryder said. "Just these ones."

For a moment no one said anything. Then Shane asked, "Could the killer have taken the puppy?"

Shane thinks I could have killed Veronica! Standing beneath the bright glare of the flood lamps that illuminated the crime scene in garish detail, Gina curled her fingers into fists and pressed them into the sides of her thighs. She stared at Shane as he stepped away to call another rookie—his roommate, James Harrison—and wanted to scream. How could he think she'd do something so horrible?

But it wasn't as if he knew her, despite their having spent every day together the past twelve weeks. She knew he took his job very seriously, but really?

She inwardly scoffed. What did it matter anyway? So what if the handsome officer had invaded her daydreams over the past weeks. She couldn't, wouldn't, allow herself to develop deep feelings for him. There was too much risk involved. And risky behavior was something she avoided. Besides, now that his training had ended, he'd be moving on. As he should.

Forcing her mind away from what Shane thought of her, she tried to focus on the missing puppy, Marco. But the fear of Tim and where he might be made it difficult.

His presence loomed, a dark shadow at the edges of her awareness.

"Maybe Marco got out of the yard," she said, careful to keep her gaze from where Veronica lay in the dirt. Even though the coroner had covered her body with an opaque plastic sheet, Gina didn't want to look. The image of Veronica's lifeless eyes, so like Gina's father's after Tim had killed him, would haunt her nightmares for a long time to come.

Instead, out of habit—or out of self-defense, as her therapist would most likely observe—she shifted her gaze to the wooded area behind the training center. "The puppy could be in the woods."

So could Tim. A shiver chased the thought across her flesh.

She turned to look down the residential street flanking one side of the center. "Or in someone's backyard. Maybe he ran out and someone took him in?"

"Good thought," the chief said. "As soon as Harmon arrives I'll have him start searching for the pup. The woods will have to wait until daybreak since we don't have the manpower to spare."

"The puppy has a distinct black circular marking on its head, between its fawn-colored ears," Gina told them. "He's a very sweet puppy. They all are."

"Is there a way to check if Veronica chipped the dogs? That would give us a better time line for when she was… killed." Ryder nearly dropped the wiggling pup. "Hey, settle down."

"That's Ricky," Gina told him. "Mrs. Foxcroft insisted on naming the puppies. Marco was named after one of her relatives who founded Desert Valley. The other two are Ricky and Lucy. She loves the *I Love Lucy* show."

Sophie stroked Lucy's head. "I can check to see if

they're chipped. It will only take a moment. But we'll have to go inside."

The chief asked Ryder, "Did you find the scene of the crime?"

"Yes, sir," Ryder replied. "The trail of blood leads to the clinic."

"That's where Veronica would have done the chipping," Gina interjected, sick at the thought of Veronica facing down Tim alone.

"Any sign of a struggle?" Sophie nuzzled Lucy. The pup squirmed in her arms, clearly wanting to be set free again.

Ryder shook his head. "Not in the clinic. My guess is she knew the killer. Otherwise, Veronica would have fought. She's— She was a fighter."

Gina's heart thumped. "She didn't know Tim."

No one in Desert Valley even knew she had a brother.

She'd been careful to keep her past buried. She hadn't wanted the attention. She'd tried to keep a low profile. With her brother on the loose, having escaped police custody and out for vengeance after she'd turned him in for killing their father, she'd hoped and prayed he'd never find her. But he had. How? What had led him to Desert Valley?

"But if he came in asking for you and she didn't think he was a threat…" Shane said, rejoining them and pulling her from her thoughts.

Gina frowned, hating that he was right. Tim could be charming when he wanted to be. He could have surprised Veronica, not given her time to defend herself. Gina's insides twisted. How had Tim found her? How many more lives would Tim ruin before he was stopped? Cold sweat broke out on her neck.

Ryder eyed Gina's fellow trainer and friend Sophie

with a speculative gleam in his blue eyes. "Where were you tonight?"

Sophie's gaze hardened. "Home. Alone. As I said, I heard over the police radio that something was going on here."

"Which means the press will have heard, as well," the chief interjected. "No doubt a reporter from the *Canyon County Gazette* is on the way. Let's secure this crime scene pronto." He looked to the coroner. "Randolph, what do you think?"

"My preliminary examination supports that the scene of the crime was elsewhere. Rigor hasn't set in yet, so estimated time of death is within the past hour. There are two visible wounds in the chest, consistent in size and shape to what one would expect to see from a bullet. No exit wounds. Once the…"

He faltered as he straightened. In such a small town as Desert Valley, it was conceivable that Randolph had known Veronica. Since Desert Valley didn't have a crime lab, everything including the victim's body would be transported to Flagstaff and processed there. Gina considered that a blessing for the visibly shaken coroner.

Randolph removed his gloves and tossed them into a plastic bag before plucking his thick glasses from his nose. His dark eyes were sad. "Once the autopsy is performed you'll be provided a conclusive cause of death."

Ryder gestured to the dark trail of blood. "What I can't determine is if Veronica was dragged out here or if she crawled out on her own steam before she died. Even with the lamps it's too dark to see impressions in the dirt. In the morning we'll have a better idea of what happened."

"She might've been trying to find help," Gina said. "Though why wouldn't she use the phone? Either the center's landline or her cell?"

"Good questions," the chief said. "Ryder, I want you to take the lead in this investigation."

Clearly surprised, Ryder nodded. "Yes, sir. I'll do everything possible to find Veronica's murderer."

"What's the story with your brother, anyway?" Shane asked Gina, drawing everyone's attention. "Why was he in police custody?"

Gina bit her lip, loathing to air her sordid family history in public. She'd purposely kept her personal information vague when asked, but with everyone staring at her, waiting for an explanation, she had no choice but to explain.

"He suffers from schizoaffective disorder. Our father enrolled him in an experimental program two years ago, but Tim didn't want to go. He was in one of his manic phases and had a psychotic break. He killed—" Her voice wavered. "He killed our father with Dad's own service weapon. The police arrested him, but he escaped custody and fled. He blames me for calling the police and turning him in. Now he's here and has made it very clear he wants to kill me, too."

"That's rough," Ryder said. The puppy in his arms licked his face.

Earl put his hand on her shoulder. "We won't let anything happen to you."

Shane's gaze was skeptical. He didn't believe her. And that hurt.

Sophie snuggled Lucy closer. "If Tim has Marco, do you think he'd hurt him?"

Gina put a hand over the pain exploding in her heart. "I hope not." She gave a helpless shrug. "He has killed before, so I'm not certain of anything when it comes to Tim."

"James is headed to your house," Shane said. "As

soon as he gives the all clear, we'll head over so you can change."

Gina looked at Sophie and admitted softly to her friend, "I'm afraid to go home."

"Weston will accompany you." The chief squeezed her shoulder.

Her stomach somersaulted. For the past twelve weeks she and Shane had danced around each other and the attraction that, at times, was so strong between them she grew light-headed. Like she was now as she stared into his emerald gaze.

But apparently the attraction had been one-sided.

Just as well. She had homicidal tendencies floating in her genetic soup. A fact she couldn't deny, nor would she burden anyone else with it.

Besides, Shane was leaving town as soon as he was given his assignment. She'd be a fool to ever let herself become attached to him.

"You'll be safe with Harrison and Weston." The chief's voice was reassuring and confident, yet did nothing to assure her.

Would she be safe with them? Would they be safe with her? Or would they become two more victims of Tim's rage?

She didn't want to go anywhere with Shane if he thought she could be a murderer.

A taunting thought screamed through her. *You share the same DNA as Tim. Why wouldn't he wonder if you're capable of murder, too?*

THREE

Giving herself a mental shake, Gina tore her gaze away from Shane and focused on Sophie. She liked the other trainer; they got along well. Veronica had intimated that Sophie had somehow failed as a cop, but Gina had been careful not to ask many questions about what had brought Sophie to Desert Valley. Not that Gina wasn't curious, but she'd figured she'd better not probe if she didn't want anyone probing into her past. "Can you take me?"

Sophie winced. "I'm going to need to stay here and see what else might be missing besides our little Marco."

Gina blew out a frustrated breath. "I understand. You should also check the vet's prescription drug supply next door. If Tim needed money, he could sell the dog and any drugs he stole." She glanced at Shane as he answered his ringing phone.

After a moment, he hung up and said, "Officer Harrison says your house is clear."

She was boxed in with no other option. "Okay, fine. Let's go."

She hurried away. Each step that took her closer to her house pounded another shard of fear into her. What if Tim had slipped past them and was waiting for her to return home? What if he was there now hurting James Harrison? She shook her head to dislodge the horrid thought.

"Hey, wait up," Shane called as he hurried toward her, Bella trotting at his side.

She slowed, keeping her gaze alert for any sign of Tim. Having Shane and Bella close did help keep the terror from overwhelming her. She whistled for the puppy. "Marco!"

Shane fell into step beside her. Bella stayed at his heel on his other side. He swept his flashlight over the bushes and at the trees. "Marco, here, boy."

Worry for the pup churned in Gina's stomach. Predators such as coyotes, mountain lions, bobcats and bears roamed the area. Though most stayed clear of the town, there had been enough sightings for Gina to know the small puppy wouldn't stand a chance on his own in the wild.

She knocked on every front door between the training yard and her house, but no one had seen Marco. He must have run in the opposite direction. Or toward the woods at the back of the training center.

Though the moon was high and the clouds had moved on, there was no way to track the puppy at night. She shivered, grateful for Shane's presence. His calmness helped to ground her fears and keep her coherent as she woke her neighbors with her questions about the missing puppy.

As they neared her house, Shane said, "For the record, I don't want to believe you killed Veronica."

"For the record, I didn't kill her," Gina shot back with frustration. "I may have had my issues with her, but I would never hurt another living soul."

At least she prayed not. But the fear was always at the edge of her consciousness. "I can't imagine how Marian

Foxcroft will react to learning one of the puppies she do-nated to the center has gone missing."

"Ellen's mother, right?"

"Yes." Ellen Foxcroft was another graduate from the same training session as Shane. "Marian has a purebred German shepherd." Acid burned in Gina's tummy. "I pray we find Marco. I can only imagine how upset Marian will be."

"It was very generous of Mrs. Foxcroft to give the puppies to the training center," Shane commented.

"Yes. Very generous. However, Veronica was certain Marian's intention wasn't pure benevolence." A wave of sadness washed over her. Veronica had had her faults, but she hadn't deserved to die.

Shane stopped walking and drew her into the shadows of a mesquite tree. "How so?"

His closeness sent her senses spinning. She backed up a step and bumped up against the tree. "I'm not sure. Veronica could be so caustic at times that I rarely paid any attention to her snide remarks. But she'd said something to the effect that Marian holds her donations over the center and expects something in return."

"Like what?" He braced a hand on the tree near her head, surrounding her in a warm cocoon.

Her brain became a muddled mess. "I have no idea."

"What's the story with Mrs. Foxcroft?"

Needing distance from him and the confusing effect he had on her, Gina sighed and pushed away from the tree. She really hated telling tales out of turn. But if doing so helped her to earn Shane's trust, then so be it. She stepped back onto the road. "I don't know all the details. Her husband left about five years ago. As far as I know they never divorced. Marian's family dates back to the founding of the town, though I'm not sure where her wealth came from."

"I find it interesting that Ellen became a police officer," Shane said, falling back into step with her. "How did her mother take it?"

"I don't know. Ellen doesn't talk much about her mom." Gina wrinkled her nose. "Marian Foxcroft is…" She struggled to come up with a polite term for the town's feisty matriarch.

"Intimidating?" Shane supplied.

"Yes, exactly."

A car horn beeped. Shane waved a hand. James Harrison, another of the rookies from the most recent graduating training session, pulled up alongside them in his truck. His bloodhound, Hawk, poked his droopy-faced head out of the open passenger window.

James leaned over. "Hey, I was headed to the station." He turned his focus to Gina. "Your house is in shambles. But there was no sign of the intruder."

"That's good," Shane replied.

Gina detested hearing her house had been violated. Obviously, Tim had doubled back just as she'd thought. He could have easily sneaked past them through the woods. And he'd taken out his rage on her home. The thought knocked the breath from her lungs.

If she hadn't been quick enough to get out of the house, if he'd overtaken her at any point, she could very well be dead at this moment. Like Veronica.

Gina clenched her jaw tight to keep from throwing up.

"Is it true? Veronica's dead?" James asked, openly stunned.

"Yes," Shane replied.

James ran a hand through his hair. "That's shocking. I mean, I just saw her this afternoon at the station."

"You'll need to give your statement to Ryder," Shane said. "That'll help with the time line leading up to her death."

"Yeah, sure," James said. "Should I head over there now?"

"Not yet," Shane said. "The chief wants us to stick close to Gina." He turned to her. "Which is your house?"

"The one on the corner." She pointed to the end of the street, at the small yellow-and-white two-story cottage that had been her safe haven for two years. She'd had the house painted yellow because the color had been her mother's favorite.

James nodded and turned his truck around before heading back to Gina's and parking in the driveway. As Gina, Shane and Bella approached, James let Hawk out. Bella and Hawk greeted each other.

Shane filled James in on what had happened both here at Gina's house and at the training center.

James whistled through his teeth as he climbed out of his truck. "Wow, this is a lot to process. Veronica had insisted she needed to come to the condo tonight to show me some pointers she thought would be helpful with Hawk."

"That's strange," Gina said. James had done well with his and his bloodhound's training. "What kind of refresher would you need?"

The tall blond and blue-eyed man shook his head. "I have no idea. I thought it was weird, too, but…" He shrugged.

Dismissing the mystery of what Veronica had been thinking, Gina stepped through the open front door of her little house. She stopped at the sight of her living room. Everything was smashed and broken.

A deep sense of violation and helplessness spread

through her, choking off her air. The destruction was senseless.

"The upstairs is just as bad, if not worse," James informed her, with sympathy tingeing his words. Hawk, James's bloodhound, let out a long wail that echoed through the house. Stark fear grabbed Gina by the throat. Had Tim managed to sneak in after James's walk-through?

But the dog turned toward the front door. Something outside the house had him on alert.

Was Tim out there?

Gina moved closer to Shane. He stepped slightly in front of her. The protective gesture melted some of the animosity she'd been feeling toward him.

A woman and a dog entered. Gina let out a relieved breath at the sight of rookie Ellen Foxcroft and her large golden retriever, Carly. After a quick nod of acknowledgment to James and Shane, Ellen turned to Gina. Her normally bright blue eyes were clouded with anxiety. "Are you hurt?"

"No. I'm fine," Gina was quick to assure her. "I'm glad to see you, but why are you here?"

"Mom received a call that something was going on at the training center and then on the way here I heard dispatch say officers were responding to a break-in at your house. I wanted to make sure you were okay."

Gina's stomach twisted as she related the night's events to the rookie.

Visibly shaken, Ellen touched Gina's arm. "That's terrible. And you think your brother killed Veronica?"

"I don't know for sure, but who else could have done it?" She could feel Shane's intense gaze on her. Was he studying her, assessing if she was telling the truth? "Anything's possible with Tim. He never took responsibility for his actions, always blaming his mental illness even though he refused to take his meds."

"That's hard," Ellen said. "I've heard that many times people who go off their medications act out in ways they wouldn't if they were staying on their regimen."

Gina appreciated the other woman's understanding. "Right. But there comes a point when accountability rests with each of us. Tim was cognizant enough of his actions to know right from wrong. And he blames me for calling the police when he killed our father."

Empathy softened Ellen's features. "I'm so sorry for your loss."

"Thank you. It still hurts."

"No matter what degree of loss we experience, it's painful," Ellen said. "But we have to remember that God will never leave us nor forsake us."

Her words wound through Gina. She really wanted to cling to the hope, but sorrow and pain kept her from grabbing on with both hands. She righted a chair.

Ellen glanced at the chaos. "You can't stay here. I'll call my mom and see if she'll mind if you stay with us."

Though Gina was touched by the offer, the thought of going very far from the safety of the police station made her heart race. "I appreciate the offer, but I need to be close to the center."

"You could bunk in the empty bedroom at the condo," James said. "It's only a few blocks from the police station. You'll be safe there with us."

Gina's gaze flew to Shane to see what he thought of the idea. His mouth pressed into a firm line, but he didn't comment.

Hmm. "Shane, would you be okay with that?" she asked.

"It's a good idea that you stay with us," Shane said. "The chief did assign your protection to me."

Gina stared at him. If he thought it a good idea, then why did he look as if he'd just swallowed a lemon? Shaking her head over the perplexing man, she said, "I'll go pack a bag."

"Ellen, would you mind accompanying Gina upstairs?" Shane asked.

"Not at all." Ellen and Carly escorted Gina to the second floor.

Seeing the damage to her beautiful bedroom brought Gina to tears. The curtains she'd sewn had been ripped off the rod and shredded. The porcelain doll that had once been her mother's lay smashed on the floor.

James hadn't been kidding when he'd said the upstairs was as trashed as the living room. In what hours ago had been her sanctuary, Tim had taken a knife and shredded everything, including the clothes hanging in the closet.

Deep sadness welled from within. She didn't understand how Tim could be so out of control and mean. Whatever God's purpose was, it was lost on her, which was why she couldn't bring herself to attend church services. How could she worship a God who allowed such travesties?

It was hard enough socializing at the Desert Valley Community Church's singles' potluck and pretending to feel a closeness to God that was absent.

She wasn't even sure why she went every month. Okay, that wasn't true. She went because some part of her hoped to fall in love. Yet she turned down any offers of dates, too afraid to allow someone into her life. Nuts, right?

What was that saying by Albert Einstein? The definition of insanity was doing the same thing over and over again and expecting different results.

She snorted. Maybe she was more like her brother than she wanted to admit. Carly's wet nose nudged her hand. Absently, she stroked the dog's head.

It wasn't as if the town of Desert Valley, located in the northwest part of Arizona, was big enough for her to meet someone new. After living in the small community for nearly two years, she knew most everyone on a first-name basis.

The revolving door on the K-9 training center didn't lend itself to finding romance. The rookies arrived for their twelve-week session then left, taking assignments that took them all over the state of Arizona. Most of them held little interest for her.

She mentally scoffed. Who was she kidding?

Shane Weston had caught her attention. But he wasn't staying. He'd made that clear from day one.

Maybe she was a glutton for torturing herself or maybe subconsciously she wasn't really as interested in becoming half of a whole as she professed. Was she deluding herself? Wasn't that a sign of mental illness? She'd have to do some research. Maybe check in with her old therapist.

"You okay?"

Ellen's soft question brought Gina's focus back to the closet. She wouldn't find the answer to her life's questions in her destroyed dresses and pantsuits.

"Yes." She stuffed her thoughts away. Taking clothes that Tim had left untouched from the hamper, she quickly changed out of her soiled outfit, then handed it to Ellen, who put the clothes into the evidence bag.

Ellen's gaze raked over the sliced and diced garments barely hanging on the hangers. "Whoa."

Gina waved a dismissive hand. "This can all be replaced."

"If you need to go shopping in Flagstaff, I'm always up for a trip to the city," Ellen said with a sympathetic smile.

Carly left Gina to go stand beside her mistress.

Appreciating Ellen's attempt at levity, Gina returned her smile. "Thanks. I'll keep that in mind."

Gina grabbed her suitcase from beneath the bed, gathered her toiletries and dumped them in the bottom of the suitcase. "Your mother must be very proud of you for having completed your training."

Ellen made a noise halfway between a laugh and a scoff. "Mom's never been behind me being a police officer."

"I'm sorry to hear that. I think you'll make a great one." Gina pulled the rest of the clothes from the laundry basket, figuring she'd wash everything at the condo. Her pulse skipped a beat as she thought of sharing a living space with Shane. She ruthlessly squelched her reaction.

And James, she reminded herself. She wouldn't be alone with Shane. And she'd have her own suite. Thankfully.

"Thanks. But it's the story of my life." Ellen's gaze took on a faraway look. "There's a lot that Mom and I don't see eye to eye on."

Sensing something painful behind the other woman's words, Gina put a hand on Ellen's arm to offer what comfort she could. "But you have her and you two love each other." Gina would give anything to have her mother back. Even for just a moment.

Ellen nodded, but doubts lingered in her blue eyes. "Yes. You're right. But I'm looking forward to being assigned far from Desert Valley. You know that old saying, absence makes the heart grow fonder. I'm hoping that will prove to be true."

Gina hurt for the apparent rift between Ellen and Marian.

"Ladies?" Shane called from the bottom of the stairs. "Do you need some help?"

Gina rolled her eyes. "Impatient much?" she muttered.

Ellen smiled. "It's a guy thing."

"Or just a Shane thing," Gina quipped as she zipped the suitcase. She'd noticed during training that he wanted things to progress at a swifter pace. She'd had to remind him training was a process that couldn't be rushed. She supposed he was anxious to get back to the city. Apparently country life wasn't to his liking.

Gina picked up her suitcase and followed Ellen and Carly down the stairs. She retrieved her cell phone from the charger sitting on the hall table. The one she hadn't had time to grab before running for her life.

Once they were out of the house, Gina thanked Ellen for her help. She climbed into James's truck along with Shane. The two dogs hopped into the canopied truck bed and lay down. James latched the tailgate in place but left the windows open for airflow.

Sandwiched between the two men, Gina could hardly believe her life had taken such a drastic turn in such a short amount of time. Her brother had attacked her, her boss had been murdered, and now she'd been displaced from her home and put under the protection of two handsome men. One who made her heart flutter despite how much she tried to quell her attraction.

Could her life get any more complicated?

A loud *thunk* echoed inside the cab of the truck, sending a jolt of fear through Gina. "What was that?"

FOUR

James brought the truck to an abrupt halt and jumped out, leaving the driver's-side door open.

Shane's heart hammered in his chest. He gripped Gina's hand. His gaze raked over her. "Are you hurt?" He had to yell over the frantic barking of the two dogs in the truck bed.

Her hazel eyes were wide and her pretty face pale, but otherwise she appeared unharmed. "No. I don't think so."

Ellen's vehicle pulled up behind them, her headlights shining through the window.

James jumped back in the cab of the truck. "An arrow," he said as he hit the gas. The truck shot forward.

The two words sent a shiver down Shane's spine.

James drove quickly to the police station, with Ellen close behind, and parked in front of the doors. Shane jumped out and hustled Gina inside. Bucks was manning the desk.

"Keep an eye on her," Shane told the officer before running back outside just as James dropped the tailgate and both dogs jumped out. Bella ran to Shane's side.

Shane moved closer to see what had struck the truck. Protruding from the front of the truck bed, just below the rear window, was indeed an arrow. But not the kind found in archery. This was steel, a long bolt with yellow fetching. The kind meant for killing.

The blood drained from Shane's head. He gripped the edge of the truck bed. A couple of inches higher and the bolt would have gone through the window, right into Gina's skull.

Or the projectile could have easily hit one of the dogs. But thankfully, both were uninjured.

Was this the work of Gina's brother? Why would he change weapons from a gun to a crossbow? Hadn't Gina said he'd had a knife, too? They had a well-armed fugitive in their town.

James hooked Hawk to his lead. The bloodhound lifted his nose to the air and howled. "We're going hunting. The keys are in the ignition if you need to move the truck. Hawk and I will meet you at the condo."

"Be careful," Shane advised.

"Roger that." James and Hawk took off, trailing a scent, and disappeared from view.

Ellen approached from where she'd parked her vehicle. "Did you see the shooter?" Shane asked.

"Shooter?" Her blues eyes darted to the arrow then back to him. "Is Gina okay?"

"Yes, she's inside." Shane moved back to the cab and ran a hand over the back of the seat. Applying a little pressure on the backrest, he could feel the sharp tip of the arrow where it had gone through the metal of the truck. So close. He breathed out a prayer of thanksgiving.

Another inch and the arrow absolutely would have skewered Gina in the back.

Clearly someone wanted her dead. It seemed her story about her brother was true.

Gina came out of the police station with Bucks hot on her heels. "Someone tell me what's happening."

Shane glared at Bucks.

He raised his hands. "Hey, I couldn't stop her."

Gina spotted the arrow sticking out of the back of the cab and gasped. The moon's glow shone on her face, creating shadows in the contours of her cheekbones. "Do you think… Did Tim do this?"

He wouldn't sugarcoat the truth. "Unless there's someone with a vendetta against the trainers, which I doubt, I can't think of anyone else who wants you dead. Can you?"

She wrapped her arms around her middle. "No. And I didn't kill Veronica. Tim must have. Don't you see that?"

"Come on, let's get you back inside." Shane placed his hand to the small of her back. He didn't like her standing outside, making herself an easy target if her brother had followed them to the station. "I'm sorry I jumped to a hasty conclusion."

Gina's glance lanced across his face like a laser. "So you believe me now?"

Innocent until proven guilty. The evidence to suggest she was the culprit was circumstantial at best. It was more likely that her brother had killed Veronica. "Yes."

Some of her tension visibly released.

Once they were all in the lobby of the station, Ellen logged in the evidence bag filled with Gina's clothes and then said good-night before heading home. Keeping Gina close, Shane asked Bucks to dust the arrow for prints.

"Hey, I don't work for you," the older officer grumbled.

The chief stepped out of his office. "What's the trouble?"

Bucks shot Shane a venomous look. "He'll explain." He marched off.

"On our way here from Gina's house a bolt from a

crossbow pierced the cab," Shane explained. "I asked Officer Bucks if he'd dust the arrow for prints."

Chief Jones's jaw hardened. "Seems your brother is determined."

"Yes, sir," Gina murmured as she sank onto a bench. Bella went to her and put her chin on Gina's knees.

"Thank the Lord above none of you were hurt," Earl said. He'd seemed to age in the past few hours. The lines around his mouth and eyes were deeper, adding to his haggard look. Undoubtedly, Veronica's murder was hitting the man hard. "This has been a horrific night for our town. We've seen more crime in the past six hours than we've had in five years...since Melanie Hayes's unsolved murder."

Ryder Hayes's wife, Melanie, had been gunned down on a wooded path near the couple's house on the eve of the big annual Canyon County Police Dance and Fundraiser. Robbery was the suspected motive, since Melanie's purse had gone missing.

Shane had also heard about two other mysterious deaths. Each on the night of the annual dance and fundraiser event, and each a year apart. But both fatalities had been deemed accidents.

The chief rubbed his chin. "Tonight makes retirement that much more enticing."

Back home in Flagstaff, this night would have seemed tame to Shane's dad and brothers. "Did the canvass around the training center yield anything useful in determining who killed Veronica?"

Earl held up a hand. "So far no one heard any shots fired or saw anyone come or go from the center."

"Has anyone turned in the missing puppy?" Gina asked.

"Unfortunately, no," the chief replied.

Gina's arms wrapped around her middle as if holding herself together. The tender skin beneath her eyes appeared bruised from fatigue and her face was pale.

Empathy twisted in Shane's gut, despite his need to stay emotionally detached. First being attacked in her house by her crazed brother, then stumbling upon Veronica's dead body. It was obvious she loved the animals she worked with and they loved her, if Bella's actions were any indication. No doubt the thought of the little German shepherd puppy running loose outside where wildlife could prey on it weighed heavily on Gina's slim shoulders.

"Was Sophie able to determine if the other two puppies were chipped?" Gina asked.

"They were," Earl replied. "Chipped and registered to Veronica with the training center's address just as we'd expect."

"Hopefully, someone will pick up the pup and take him to the vet," Gina said. "If Veronica was able to get him chipped then the vet will find the chip and contact the center."

"I'll give the vet a heads-up," the chief said.

Bucks returned a few moments later. "I got a partial. I'll run it through IAFIS."

Shane hoped the FBI's national fingerprint database would provide a visual of Tim Perry. Or whoever had handled the arrow. Shane struggled to believe no one had known Gina had a brother to begin with, let alone one who was a criminal. Was the shooter the same person who'd killed Veronica? Or was there more than one villain running around Desert Valley? That seemed too much of a stretch.

"Let's finish our discussion in my office," Earl said, ushering Shane, Bella and Gina inside.

The chief had just settled into his chair behind his desk when there was a knock on the doorjamb. James and Hawk entered the office, looking grim.

Shane gave him a questioning look.

James shook his head. "Hawk tracked a scent but lost it on a street two blocks away from Gina's house. The shooter must have jumped into a car and taken off."

"Did you get a look at the archer?" Earl asked.

"No, never caught a glimpse of him," James said.

Earl looked at Shane. "But you're sure it was her brother?"

"Hard to say without confirmation," Shane said. "But without any other suspects…"

The chief considered him a moment. "Okay." He focused on Gina. "Where will you be staying? Obviously you can't return to your home until we have your brother in custody."

"Sir, Gina is going to move into the empty room at the rookies' condo," Shane stated. He met Gina's gaze. She arched one delicate eyebrow. Okay, maybe he shouldn't have answered for her.

Earl nodded approval. "Good." He settled his gaze on Gina once again. "We'll find your brother. Or whoever did this. No one can hide in Desert Valley for long."

"Thank you, sir." Her voice was tight. She turned her gaze on Shane. "I'd like to keep the puppies with me if possible."

The anxiety in her hazel eyes tugged at him. If having the two pups close comforted her, then… "Of course. We'll swing by the training center and pick them up."

She gave him a grateful smile as she stifled a yawn.

"You all go and get some rest," the chief said. "You won't do anyone any good if you're too exhausted to be of use."

Shane escorted Gina from the station. They took James's truck to the training center. Sophie had crated the puppies and had locked up the center for the night. Gina used her key card to enter the building.

They gathered the puppies and their crates, along with their beds, water and food bowls, and put them in the back of James's truck. Gina held both pups on her lap during the ride to the condo.

James parked in the carport stall reserved for the rookies' unit. He grabbed her bag from the back and led the way to the front door. Shane carried the pups' accoutrements and brought up the rear with Gina and the puppies between them.

Once inside, Shane showed Gina to the room at the end of the short hall. He arranged the crates side by side along the far wall beneath the window facing the queen-size bed covered with a deep burgundy comforter.

Gina set the puppies down on their respective beds and left the crate doors open. They immediately went to sleep, obviously tuckered out from their run in the yard and the move to the condo.

"Shouldn't you shut the crate doors?" Shane asked.

"I will when I'm ready to go to sleep, but for now I want them to feel safe inside their crates and safe to leave, as well. The crate needs to become their safe haven. Locking them in too soon can be traumatic."

Her concern for the puppies was touching. Given she'd just lived through a very dramatic and dangerous situation, she was holding it together really well. Assuming she was telling him the truth, which seemed more likely with every passing moment. His admiration and respect for her increased. How had he questioned whether she could be guilty of hurting Veronica?

"The place comes furnished," Shane explained, to battle the discomforted way she made him feel. "Each room is a suite. Housekeeping launders all the linens between the training sessions. The bedding's clean and there are towels in the bathroom cabinet."

"Thank you," Gina said. "I appreciate all you're doing for me and the puppies."

Her teeth tugged on her bottom lip. She looked so vulnerable. Blood surged through his veins and his gut tightened. It was all he could do not to step closer and gather her in his arms. He'd been attracted to her from the beginning, but this was more intense and focused. The disturbing urge had him backing away. The last thing he wanted was to become emotionally attached to this woman. It was one thing to guard her and help her feel safe, and another entirely to want to make her feel cared for.

"I'll say good-night." He stepped out of the room and shut the door, blocking her from his view. Now if he could only block her from his thoughts as easily.

Gina stared at the door. Confusion swirled through her mind. For a moment, she'd seen something in Shane's expression that had her heart fluttering and her pulse skittering. Interest. There'd been definite interest in his green eyes. Answering attraction flared within her. But then his gaze had shuttered and he'd retreated, leaving her wondering if she'd only imagined the look.

What did it matter? There was no sense in letting herself feel anything for him. For anyone. With her brother back in her life, she was intensely aware that she, too, had the propensity for evil. She shared Tim's DNA. DNA that could be passed on.

She'd never have the family she longed for. What man in his right mind would want to saddle himself with her?

With sadness filling her heart, she filled the dogs' bowls with water and placed them on the bathroom floor, and she sank down on the edge of the bed. She dropped her head into her hands.

What a nightmare her life had become. Tim was attempting to follow through on his threat to kill her. She didn't understand what purpose Tim had for wanting her dead. It wouldn't change the fact that he was wanted for murdering their father.

That he hadn't succeeded in killing her so far was a blessing.

It hurt her heart to believe Veronica had died because of her. She had no doubt Tim had killed her boss. What other explanation could there be?

"Oh, Lord, please. I…" She didn't know what to say or how to pray.

She wanted to ask God to stop her brother, yet the words wouldn't come. They felt like rocks stuck in her throat. Would God even hear her? She was so used to being disappointed she was afraid to try anymore.

She lay back, wishing the oblivion of sleep would take her away, but her mind was buzzing with all that had transpired. The image of Veronica's lifeless eyes staring at the sky tormented her. Worry for the missing puppy scraped her nerves raw.

"Please let us find Marco, Lord," she whispered, finally finding some reserve of faith. She curled on her side. The sleeping puppies looked so peaceful. So vulnerable. They needed her now. She had to be strong for their sake.

Her mouth felt like cotton. She needed water. She rose

to check the bathroom for a cup and found none. She left the bedroom to pad barefoot to the kitchen in search of a glass. As she passed the living room, she noticed Shane sitting on the couch, brushing Bella, who sat at his feet, obviously enjoying the attention to her coat.

Light from the gas fireplace played in the dark strands of Shane's hair, making them appear more blue than black. Once again the pull of longing lurched at her and attraction flickered through her. He was so handsome and capable. And she appreciated the fact that he'd apologized for jumping to an assumption of her guilt before knowing all the facts. She figured it was probably hard for him to admit he was wrong. But he'd owned up to his mistake and that meant a lot to her.

Plus, she had enjoyed working with him during their training. Even if he was a bit impatient with the progress, he'd never once taken that impatience out on Bella or Gina. But Gina had seen the frustration in his eyes and the tension in his shoulders. She wasn't sure what had driven him. Wasn't sure she wanted to know. Getting too close to her protector wouldn't be smart.

She paused, contemplating turning back. But then Shane's gaze lifted and met hers.

He swiftly rose, the brush dropping to the floor. "Are you okay?"

The concern in his tone caused warmth to flow through her. Bella cocked her head and stared at Gina as if waiting for her answer, as well.

She smiled. "I'm fine. I just wanted a glass for water."

He nodded and resumed his seat. "Glasses are in the cupboard to the right of the sink."

Bella lay down at his feet, apparently reassured that all was well.

She filled a glass from the tap. She drank the cool liquid and then refilled the glass to take to her room. She halted on the threshold of the living room. "Why are you still up?"

"Someone has to stand guard. Just in case."

A shiver of dread skated over her flesh. She felt bad that he was losing sleep to keep watch over her. However, she did appreciate his sacrifice. "Have you heard if anyone has reported finding the puppy?"

He shook his head. "No. I'm sure the chief will let us know if he turns up."

Heaviness burdened her heart. Her hand tightened around the glass. "What if no one finds him? What if he's hurt? Or worse?"

"Don't go there. You can't give up hope. We'll find him."

He sounded so confident. She wanted to believe him.

"Tell me about your brother," Shane asked, surprising her. "You're twins. Who's older?"

She moved to sit on the edge of the recliner facing Shane. Warmth from the fire curled around her. "I am, by two minutes and forty-five seconds."

"How long has Tim been…?" His voice faded with uncertainty.

She bit out, "It's okay, you can say it. Mentally ill."

"Right." He sounded uncomfortable. Which was how most people reacted when they learned of Tim's condition. "Mentally ill."

Memories crashed over her, making her heart ache. "The professionals had a hard time diagnosing him. His symptoms were all over the place. No impulse control, inattentive, hyper. But then, as we got older, his mood swings became more erratic, violent even. Our mom was the only one who could handle him." Her heart burned with grief. "She died when we were fifteen."

"I'm sorry. How?"

She appreciated the sympathy in Shane's voice, but she dared not look at him or the tears would break through. Instead she focused on the blue-gold flames in the fireplace. "A car accident. She hit a patch of black ice and slammed into a concrete barrier."

Shane made a sympathetic noise in his throat. Bella shimmied closer and put a paw on her foot as if sensing her sorrow.

Gina leaned down to run her hand over Bella's soft coat. "Tim took Mom's death really hard." Her heart squeezed tight and she straightened. "It was hard on all of us. I miss her every day. Dad did the best he could. But being a cop and a father of two teenagers was a lot for him to handle."

"That's right, you'd said your dad was a police officer. So is mine. And my grandfather was and both brothers are."

"Ah." That explained his drive. He had a family legacy to live up to and he was anxious to get going on his career.

"My dad would be lost without my mom," he said softly.

"Yeah, Dad had a rough time of it. Especially as Tim's behavior became more unpredictable. He hung around some bad influences and started down a very destructive, criminal path. Dad forced him to see a counselor, who passed Tim on to a psychiatrist. But Tim wasn't interested in getting help. I can't blame all of his behavior on his mental illness. He made his choices of his own free will."

"And you? How are you?"

She could feel Shane's gaze on her. More than curiosity drove his question. She understood. This wasn't the first time and it wouldn't be the last someone asked if she, too, had a mental illness. As soon as anyone learned of Tim's disorder, she became suspect, since they were twins. "I saw the same psychiatrist, just in case."

"And?"

"He said I didn't display any of the markers. But no one can guarantee I won't develop a mental disorder one day. It runs in my mother's family." A constant fear that hung over her life like a dark cloud threatening to wash her away and kept her from risking her heart. She wouldn't subject anyone to that uncertainty.

"Did the psychiatrist have any idea why your brother would be affected and you seemingly aren't?"

She shrugged. "Even non-twin siblings have a ten-percent chance of developing the same disorders."

"That's a pretty low percentage. Chances are you'll never suffer the same fate."

She wished she could count on his words to be true. "But there is still a chance. No one can make any guarantees one way or the other."

"One of God's many mysteries."

She met his gaze, expecting to see wariness, pity even. Instead, his expression was open and sincere.

"I often wonder why God chose to afflict Tim," she told him. "Dad would say God never made mistakes and that, for reasons we may never know, God made Tim the way he is for a purpose." She couldn't keep the bitterness out of her tone. "I love my brother but I fear him, and have for as long as I can remember. Maybe I inherently knew something wasn't right with him. As for a purpose? That I can't wrap my mind around."

"I agree with your dad. God has a purpose for Tim.

For you. I don't know what that purpose is, but He does have one. You have to trust Him."

She cocked her head and studied Shane. She hadn't realized he was a believer. But then again, it wasn't something they'd had reason to discuss during class, and she'd been very careful to keep things work-focused despite how much she wanted to spend time with him outside class. "My dad would have liked you."

The green of his eyes was highlighted by the firelight. "I wish I'd had the chance to meet him."

So did she. A wave of sadness washed over her. She missed her dad so much.

Bella jumped to her feet, her ears back. She let out a loud bark.

A shaft of anxiety tore through Gina. "What's wrong with her?"

Shane rose. "I don't know."

They heard scratching and a long howl. Hawk. James opened his bedroom door. The bloodhound raced through the living room and halted at the sliding glass patio door. Bella joined Hawk, her deep growl ricocheting off the condo's high ceiling. James came into the living room wearing sweats and a T-shirt, his expression sharp with concern and his service weapon in his hand.

From her bedroom, the puppies' excited barks rang out. Even the pups sensed danger. A shiver of dread ran across her flesh.

Shane touched her shoulder, startling her. "Go to your bedroom and lock the door." He and James moved toward the sliding door.

Gina nearly dropped the glass in her hand. Someone was on the patio. Deep in her heart she knew the trespasser was her brother. Hating the thought of anything happening to Shane or James, she said, "Be careful. You know how dangerous he is."

Shane met her gaze. "I know. Now go."

She hesitated for a second then hurried to her bedroom, locked the door and gathered the pups in her arms. "Oh, Lord, please," she whispered.

There was only one thing for her to do.

Leave Desert Valley and hope this time Tim wouldn't find her.

FIVE

Shane tempered the adrenaline swamping his system with the knowledge that Gina was safely tucked away behind the locked door of the third bedroom of the condo. They'd made the right call in bringing her here.

He only regretted that he hadn't been the one to suggest it, but the idea of having her underfoot had left him feeling a bit off-kilter.

With the threat of her brother lurking so close, Shane knew his own discomfort had to be relegated to unimportant.

It didn't matter that he found Gina attractive and interesting and that he admired how well she was holding up considering she'd been chased from her home, had discovered her boss's dead body and was being stalked by her evil twin. Not a good day.

Shane reached the kitchen drawer where he'd stashed his service weapon. He grabbed it along with a heavy-duty flashlight, then followed James out the condo's back sliding door.

The dogs ran for the tall fence separating the oblong-shaped patch of grass behind the building and the empty lot beyond. Both dogs sniffed the ground near a spot in the fence where a loose board had been pushed aside.

The acrid odor of tobacco hung in the chilling air. The temperature had dropped as it often did at night in the northwest part of Arizona.

Shane swung the flashlight's beam in sweeping arcs. The light revealed a freshly lit cigarette abandoned on the cement patio floor; a wisp of smoke curled from the smoldering tip in the cool breeze.

How long had the intruder been standing outside? Had it been Gina's brother? Of course. Who else could it have been?

James inspected the fence. "Our guy pried the nails loose."

Which spoke of Tim's determination. Tension knotted Shane's neck muscles. "We need to reattach the board ASAP. And bag and tag this cigarette butt."

James joined him on the patio. "Agreed."

"He's not getting her," Shane vowed. He could feel James's gaze on him but was powerless to keep the fire out of his voice. "I won't let him."

"She's one of the good ones," James observed quietly. "A keeper."

Shane closed his eyes for a moment. "It's not like that."

"Whatever you say." The mocking amusement in James's voice grated on Shane. "I'll get a baggie for the evidence."

James whistled for Hawk and the two went inside, leaving Shane and Bella standing on the patio.

Bella nudged his thigh.

He scrubbed her behind the ears. "It's okay, girl. We'll get him next time."

Because, unfortunately, Shane knew there would be a next time. He knew in his gut that Tim wouldn't give up. "We'll keep Gina safe."

It was his job to protect her. But he had a feeling he'd

have a hard time walking the tightrope between doing his duty and letting himself care too deeply.

He wasn't staying in Desert Valley, and becoming attached to his beautiful charge would only complicate his life in ways he couldn't—wouldn't—allow.

His focus had to be on his career. Distractions like love and romance were for way down the line. He wasn't ready to open himself up for a relationship. Even if the sweet and special dog trainer made his heart pound with longing to amend his plan.

Gina paced the floor of her suite in agitated silence. Three steps right, pivot, three steps left, pivot, repeat. She'd calmed the two puppies, now both chewing on bones she'd grabbed from the training center earlier.

Every noise beyond the confines of her room sent a jolt of alarm through her, making her heart pound and her blood rush. She was terrified to think Tim had somehow found out where she was so quickly.

Had he been watching, and trailed them to the condo? Would Shane and James capture him? Or would Tim hurt these two brave men who'd promised to protect her? Had Tim put an arrow through Shane? Was Shane even now bleeding and dying because of her?

She squeezed her eyes tight against the onslaught of horrible scenarios that played through her mind. Awfulizing was destructive, as her therapist had advised on numerous occasions. She wasn't even sure that was a real thing but she understood the sentiment behind his caution.

Letting herself spin awful outcomes that hadn't happened as if they had happened only led her to a place of fear. She'd been doing so well here in Desert Valley. All that peace she'd been experiencing had been an illusion, shattered by her brother's reemergence into her life.

"Please, Lord, this time, please don't let anything bad happen to Shane and James."

A soft tap on her door brought her to an abrupt halt. The puppies rushed toward the sound. She stared at the portal, half-afraid to answer the knock.

"Gina?"

Shane's voice echoed inside her head and relief swept through her, making her knees weak. He was alive. That was something to celebrate. But was he hurt?

On shaky limbs she hurried to unlock the door. She scooped up one pup, scooted the other away with her foot and swung the door open. Shane stood there, tall and proud, with worry in his green eyes.

A profound gladness to see him in one piece with no sign of harm washed over her and she nearly launched herself into his arms. To keep from making a fool of herself, she nuzzled the puppy closer to her chest as if doing so would temper her exploding heart. "Did you… Was it Tim?"

Shane shrugged his broad shoulders. "Not sure. But whoever it was—they're gone now."

Letting her chin rest on Lucy's tiny head, she took a deep, calming breath. "Good." She shook her head. "But he won't stop until I'm dead."

Shane stepped into the room and gently took the puppy and set it on the floor. Then his big hands settled on her shoulders. "I'm not going to let anything happen to you."

Warmth from his palms seeped through her light-weight sweater and heated her skin. She gave him a tremulous smile. His concern was so sweet and his determination admirable. But she couldn't put him or anyone else in harm's way, Tim's way, again.

Veronica had paid the ultimate price with her life at Tim's hand. Gina couldn't bear it if another person died because her brother couldn't get to her, especially someone she cared for. "I know you would, but the best thing for me, for everyone, is for me to leave. To disappear again. To start over somewhere else, hopefully somewhere Tim can never find me."

Shane's brows drew together. "You can't run. If you do, you'll be running your whole life. That's no way to live."

"What choice do I have?" she implored, needing to make him understand. "I don't want anyone else to die because of me."

"No one else will," Shane argued. "Now that we know there's a threat out there, we'll all take precautions. Tomorrow we'll put out your brother's photo. Someone in town will have seen him. Desert Valley is a tight-knit community. Any stranger will draw attention."

She moved out of his grasp to where she'd set her suitcase. She held it in front of her like a shield. "I have to leave Desert Valley. There's no other way to keep everyone safe." She glanced at the puppies rolling around on the floor in a cute wrestling match. Her heart hitched. "Will you make sure the puppies are cared for?"

For a long moment, he stayed silent. A muscle in his jaw jumped as he paused, clearly digesting her words. She had no doubt he'd come to the same conclusion that her leaving was the best idea.

Then he shook his head, dispelling her of that notion. "No, leaving is not an option. If you don't trust me to protect you, I'll talk to the chief and have him assign someone else."

"No!" The objection shot from her before she could

formulate any coherent thought. "It's not that I don't trust you. I don't want you to get hurt. It's too dangerous."

He smile was tender. He took the suitcase from her and set it on the floor. "I appreciate your concern, but I signed up for danger the minute I applied to the police academy. I'm more troubled by the thought of you fleeing and giving your brother the power to chase you away from the life you've made for yourself here in Desert Valley."

His words rattled through her, stirring up the resentment and anger she'd spent so many years stifling. "I don't want to give Tim any more power over my life. He's taken too much away from me as it is."

"I can't imagine the losses you've suffered."

Empathy dripped from Shane's words, prompting her to say, "For as long as I can remember, he garnered most of the attention from our parents with his bad behavior. There were times when I felt invisible."

"Because they were busy dealing with Tim." His words weren't a question but a statement that pegged the situation exactly.

"The majority of their energy went into helping Tim, keeping him from the destructive behavior he was prone to."

"Which left little time for you."

"Right." He seemed to understand so well. Why was that? "I learned to be self-sufficient. Mom would always say I was more responsible and wiser than most kids my age."

"I'm sure she appreciated that she could rely on you."

Guilt clawed through Gina. Tears pricked her eyes. "And I failed her. The night of her death she'd asked me to keep an eye on Tim while she attended a church function. She'd thought he'd taken his meds that kept him calm, but he hadn't."

Shane enclosed her hand within his. "What happened?"

She curled her fingers around his. "Tim had an episode. He went totally ballistic. I was so afraid of him. Dad was on duty and couldn't be reached. So I hid in the closet and called Mom, begging her to come home. She never did."

Shane squeezed her hand. "I'm so sorry."

"If I hadn't called her…if I'd been able to handle Tim on my own, then Mom wouldn't have been driving so fast and wouldn't have lost control on the black ice, slamming into the concrete divider."

"Her accident wasn't your fault."

She retracted her hand from his grip. Guilt and sorrow settled around her like a veil, dulling her view of the world. "Yes, it was. And now Veronica's dead, too, because of me. I have to leave before Tim kills someone else."

"Gina, listen to me." Shane gripped her shoulders. "Stop being a martyr. You are not responsible for your brother's actions."

Defensiveness reared through her. "That's what you think I'm doing? Being a martyr?"

His expression softened and his voice gentled. "Yes. You're smarter and stronger than you let yourself believe."

The compliment bounced off her as indignation took hold. How dare he say she was being a martyr? He didn't know her well enough to make that kind of assessment.

Yet something inside of her stilled. Was she being a martyr? Maybe that was how her mental illness would surface. She shuddered.

"Leaving isn't the answer," he insisted with grim determination tingeing his tone. "You have the whole Desert Valley Police Department behind you. Let us do our jobs. We'll protect you. And arrest Tim and put him away where he can't hurt anyone ever again."

"But you're leaving come Monday morning. You won't be here to protect me."

A frown pinched his eyebrows together. "Ryder will be here and the chief. They are good and dedicated police officers. They will protect you. But hopefully, we'll catch Tim by Monday morning."

Against her will fat tears welled in her eyes. She desperately wanted to believe in Shane. Believe he could triumph over Tim. "But what if he hurts you or someone else?" She laid her hands on his broad chest. His heart beat strong beneath her palms. "I couldn't take it."

"We have to trust God."

Staring into Shane's green eyes, she dug deep for faith and trust and hope. From the far reaches of her soul she found the courage to nod. She blinked to clear her tears.

She'd stay and stand her ground. She'd let the men and women of the Desert Valley Police Department protect her. She'd trust Shane.

And she'd pray every single moment for their safety.

Because if another person died because of her, she would shrivel up and die herself.

By Monday morning, Tim hadn't surfaced. He was still on the loose and Gina's nerves were stretched taut. Shane and Bella escorted Gina and the puppies to the training center to begin the puppies' training. As they entered, Gina noticed the caution signs indicating the linoleum floors had recently been mopped and were slick. She scooped up Lucy, holding her in a cuddling position against her chest. She said to Shane, "Can you carry Ricky? Their nails will slip on the wet floor."

"Of course." He picked up Ricky and held him like a football. She suppressed a smile. Dressed in jeans that hugged his muscular legs and a short-sleeved, colorful checked button-down shirt, he and the puppy made a handsome pair. One would never know he was an officer of the law, except for the service weapon holstered at his hip on the belt encircling his trim waist and the gold shield butted up next to the holster.

Though she'd dressed in her normal work attire of lightweight stain-resistant pants and a pink T-shirt, she sort of wished she were dressed a little more attractively. She nearly groaned at her silliness. She wasn't trying to attract the handsome rookie.

They moved farther into the center, past the bathing stations and the room they used to chip the canines. The place where Veronica had faced her attacker.

Thankfully all traces of the devastating violence that had occurred here were gone. Mopped up and wiped away. No doubt the chief had a crew of crime and trauma scene decontamination come in from Flagstaff and take care of the aftermath of Veronica's death once the Flagstaff crime scene unit had finished collecting evidence.

Gina's stomach lurched as the horrible scenario of Veronica being shot by Tim played inside her head, like a movie clip. Her mouth went dry. Tears burned the backs of her eyes. Lucy licked her face, breaking the hold her imagination had on her mind.

"You okay?"

Shane's gently asked question forced her feet to move. "I will be when Tim is caught."

In the common space, Gina was grateful to see the other trainer, Sophie, was already at the center.

"Hey, I didn't expect to see you here today." Sophie

leaned on the mop in her hand and dressed in blue coveralls. Her blond hair was twisted up in back.

Heart beating in her throat, Gina managed to say, "You didn't clean up…?"

Sophie's eyes widened. "Oh, no. That's not in my job description." She visibly shuddered. "I was keeping busy by cleaning the indoor yard and mopping out the bath station."

A job they rotated doing. Gina blew out a relieved breath. She'd hate to think her fellow trainer had had to be responsible for the cleanup of the crime scene.

"Did you get any rest?"

Sophie's question didn't surprise Gina. She'd seen the dark circles under her eyes in the mirror. There wasn't much she could do to hide them. "I managed to get a little sleep. You don't mind that we're here, do you?"

"Not at all." Sophie scratched Lucy behind the ear. "You can let them in the training yard. It's clean and ready for use. I'm just surprised you're ready to be here."

They moved into the indoor training yard. The large space was filled with agility equipment placed strategically throughout. Against one wall was a set of cabinets that housed treats and toys; lining another was a row of benches with cubbyhole storage for the trainers and the handlers to use for their personal effects. She set the puppies down. Bella ran roughshod over the two rambunctious pups.

"We had a bit of trouble," Shane told Sophie, who'd followed them into the yard. "Someone, presumably her brother, broke through the fence to spy on the condo late last night."

Concern darkened Sophie's gold-tinted eyes. "But you're all okay?"

Gina nodded. "Yes. Shane and James and Bella and

Hawk chased him off." She couldn't keep a shudder from rippling down her spine.

"The chief has called a meeting over at the station," Shane said, his reluctance to leave obvious.

"It's customary on the Monday after a training session ends for the chief to hand out the rookies' new assigned police station," Gina told him. The thought of Shane leaving bit into her, making her admit to herself she didn't want him to go. Because he was protecting her. Not because she liked him.

Okay, she did like him, but her feelings didn't go any deeper than that.

Shane's green eyes grew troubled. "Right, but I don't feel comfortable leaving you here."

"Sophie's armed," Gina pointed out. "I'll be fine. You go. Find out if anyone has found Marco."

"Don't worry, Shane," Sophie added. "I'll make sure the door is locked behind you."

"You have your cell phone?" Shane asked Gina.

She tugged the device from the training pouch at her waist. "Right here. And you're on speed dial. So is the station."

"Maybe I should leave Bella with you," Shane said.

As sweet as that offer was, she couldn't let him. "She's your partner, you can't leave her behind," Gina said. "I'll be busy training Ricky and Lucy. We'll be fine."

She let out a soft whistle to draw the two puppies' attention. They raced over. Ricky chewed on the laces of Shane's black boots while Lucy sniffed the floor, following a scent toward the treat cabinet. Lucy obviously already had the instinct to track. Good.

Gina looked forward to working with her. It would take more effort, however, to figure out the correct specialty for Ricky. He seemed more inclined to chew and play than work. But she had high hopes for him.

Just as she did for Marco. Her heart ached with worry.

However, it'd be one to two years before any of the dogs were ready to begin the rigorous K-9 training demanded of the canine officer and his handler. First the pups needed to learn basic commands as well as potty training. As demonstrated when Ricky lifted his leg.

"Hey!" Shane exclaimed and jumped out of the way.

"I'll mop up the mess," Sophie said through suppressed laughter.

Shane shook his head and moved away from the puddle. "I'm glad Bella came with manners already in place."

Gina scooped Ricky up. "He'll learn. He's still very young, you know. I hope someone finds Marco soon."

"I talked to the chief this morning," Shane told her. "He gave the vet a heads-up in case anyone brings Marco to her and sent Officer Donaldson out to search again."

She was sure the veterinarian, Tanya Fowler, would be quick to act if anyone brought the lost little puppy to the veterinary clinic. "I'd like to help search for Marco."

Shane shook his head. "We can't risk you being out in the open. You're safer here."

Though he was right, it chafed that she had to be basically a prisoner in the training center until her brother was caught. She sighed. "You better get to your meeting."

He nodded. "Lock the door behind me."

She followed him to the training center exit.

He paused halfway out the door. Bella stopped next to him as she'd been taught to do. "I won't be long."

"We'll be fine." She waved him and Bella out. When she slid the lock in place, the noise echoed inside her head. For a second she had the strangest urge to run after

Shane. His presence made her feel safe and cared for. Without him close, she felt exposed, vulnerable.

She was being ridiculous. She couldn't allow herself to become too reliant on him. He would be leaving for a new town, a life that didn't include her.

Squaring her shoulders, she reminded herself there was no way Tim could get inside the training center. She was safe. And had a job to do.

Holding Ricky up at eye level, she stared into his dark eyes. "Okay, you, time to get busy. I have lots to teach you and your sister."

Shane entered the Desert Valley police station to find the department's secretary balancing a tray with a coffee carafe and a stack of hot cups in one hand and a laptop in the other.

"Here, let me," he said, taking the tray. This wasn't the first time he'd offered to help the woman who seemed to have a propensity to juggle many things at one time.

The quiet, plain woman smiled at him. "Thank you, Shane."

He nodded and racked his brain for her name. "Is this for the rookies' meeting?"

"Yes." She gestured down the hall. "This way."

He followed her to a conference room. Bella's nails clicked on the tile floor beside him.

The secretary moved to a corner where there was a shelf. She opened her laptop and appeared ready to take notes.

After setting the tray on the conference table, Shane took the empty seat next to fellow rookie Tristan McKeller. His dog, a yellow Labrador named Jesse, who specialized in arson and accelerant detection, lay behind his chair. Bella mirrored the other five dogs already in the room by lying down behind Shane's chair.

"Hey," Shane said to Tristan.

"Morning," the former soldier greeted him and then reached for a cup and the carafe. Tristan's tall, muscular frame dwarfed the chair. He wore his brown hair military short. There was no mistaking the worry in his blue eyes. Shane didn't know the full extent of Tristan's story but did know he was raising his teen sister, which was why he'd rented a small house for the duration of their training.

The chief walked in. On his heels was a diminutive woman in a tailored charcoal-colored pantsuit. She wore horn-rimmed glasses over intense dark brown eyes and her auburn hair was cut short at her strong jaw.

Marian Foxcroft.

Shane recognized her from the times she'd come to observe their training at the center. Shane glanced at Ellen Foxcroft at the far end of the table. She had her brown hair pulled back in a braid. She sat ramrod-straight with her eyes on the chief. Shane imagined it was hard for the rookie knowing her mother disapproved of her chosen field.

The chief's gaze scanned the men and women present. Not only were all of Shane's fellow rookies present, but so were the officers of the Desert Valley Police Department.

Shane wasn't sure why the DVPD officers had been included in this meeting to hear where the rookies would be assigned. He sent up a quick prayer that his request to be sent to the Flagstaff PD came through. The sooner he escaped from the feelings Gina stirred, the better.

"Ladies and gentlemen," the chief intoned in a grave voice. "As you all are aware, Veronica Earnshaw was murdered two nights ago."

From the expressions of some of those sitting around the conference table and leaning against the back wall, not everyone mourned Veronica's passing. But some did. The sadness in Ellen's eyes matched the look in the chief's.

"I know some of you had issues with Veronica in the past," the chief went on to say.

"You got that right," Officer Ken Bucks mumbled.

Chief Jones narrowed his gaze on Bucks. "Whatever problems any of you had with her must be put aside to find her killer."

Bucks had the good grace to flush a bright red.

"Mrs. Foxcroft has generously endowed the department with the funds to hire all five graduating rookies for the foreseeable future. You'll remain with the Desert Valley Police Department until we bring Veronica's killer to justice."

"What?" Ellen exclaimed. "Mother?"

Marian Foxcroft spared her daughter a quick look but made no comment.

Shane exchanged a stunned glance with James. They'd all expected to be assigned to police departments throughout Arizona. Shane wanted to be sent to Flagstaff to become the city cop his family expected him to be, not that he'd been guaranteed the assignment of his choice. None of them had any say in where they ended up. Even still, Shane had made the request at his dad's insistence. Dad wasn't going to be happy about this turn of events— he was already champing at the bit for Shane to take his place in the family business, so to speak.

But as Shane searched his heart, he found he was a bit conflicted, confused even, by how the news didn't stir anger or outrage or even disappointment. Odd.

He shrugged off his lack of reaction and refused to

consider its origin. They knew who killed Veronica and would track down Tim Perry soon enough, and then Shane's plan to join the Flagstaff PD could be realized.

"We already have a strong suspect in Veronica's murder," Shane said. "It shouldn't be too difficult to find and arrest Tim Perry."

The chief nodded and picked up a stack of paper from the head of the table where he stood. "This is the only photo the Mesa PD had of our suspect. Tim Perry is Gina Perry's twin brother. Though there's hardly a resemblance. He is mentally unstable as well as bent on revenge against his sister for turning him in after he shot and killed their father. A Mesa police officer." The chief's gaze settled on Shane. "I trust Gina is at the training center with Sophie."

Shane straightened. "Yes, sir." He trusted the ex-cop to keep Gina safe.

Marian stepped forward. "This latest murder has been very upsetting. I can appreciate that you have a suspect, but other murders have gone unsolved. Veronica bragged to me that this latest batch of recruits were the best and brightest of all her training years."

Her gaze swept over the stunned rookies, lingering slightly on her daughter before she continued. "The county sheriff, the mayor and the governor have given me their assurances that all of you will be given every resource possible not only to bring Veronica's murderer to justice but to solve the cold case murder of Melanie Hayes."

All eyes turned to Ryder. He lifted his chin. "Solving my wife's murder would mean a great deal to my daughter, Lily, and me."

Marian nodded. "No doubt it would. But Melanie's

untimely demise isn't the only unsolved crime in Desert Valley."

Shane frowned. He hadn't heard of anything more serious than some robberies.

"What are you referring to, Mother?" Ellen asked.

"The deaths of two rookies in the past five years are suspicious."

Officer Bucks waved a dismissive hand. "Those were ruled accidents."

Tristan sat up. "I never believed Mike Riverton fell down a flight of stairs on his own. He was an expert mountain climber and very agile."

Chief Jones inclined his head in Tristan's direction. "As you've so vocally proclaimed since the day you arrived."

"And I know Brian Miller, who lost his family in a house fire, wouldn't have lit a candle in his home," Whitney Godwin said. "His death has never made any sense to me."

"Well," the chief said, "this will be your opportunity to dig into each death and prove once and for all whether Riverton's and Miller's deaths were indeed accidents or the result of foul play. The five of you will be assigned to Desert Valley until Veronica's murder, at the least, is solved. Then you'll receive your permanent assignments."

Shane let the chief's words about the murders sink in. Four deaths. Two unquestionably murder, and two suspicious accidents. Was this a pattern?

No. Veronica had simply been in the wrong place at the wrong time. In between a rampaging Tim and his sister. Veronica's death had nothing to do with the previous ones.

Desert Valley wasn't nearly the peaceful small town

Shane had originally thought. It seemed death and danger hung over the sleepy community like a shroud.

Foreboding whispered across his nape, raising the fine hairs. Would someone in the room be the next victim? Or would Gina?

SIX

Gina sat on the floor of the indoor training yard with a treat in her hand. The large space built with opaque skylights in deference to the Arizona sun was reserved for more advanced training of the K-9 officers and their handlers, but Gina hadn't wanted to go outside to the smaller puppy-training yard. Her palms had grown damp at the thought.

Not only would going outside leave her exposed, but the idea of once again seeing where Veronica had died left her queasy. She knew one day she'd have to face the training yard, but not today.

Sophie had understood when Gina told her she and the puppies would be staying inside. The ex-cop had offered to work in the arena rather than the office, but Gina had insisted she'd be okay. Just knowing Sophie was within screaming distance alleviated some anxiety.

Besides, the training center had two exits, one door leading to the fenced yard that was locked tight and the other only accessible from within the center. Still, she wished Shane were here with her.

For safety reasons. Not because she missed him.

Though she kind of did, if she were to be honest with herself. She missed the way he listened to her and made her feel special, cared for, even. It had been a long time since she'd felt either emotion.

Lucy sniffed Gina's closed fist, eager to get at the morsel of goodness inside. Ricky, on the other hand, wandered away, completely uninterested. That one was definitely going to be hard to train.

"Sit," Gina told Lucy while holding her closed fist to the dog's nose and moving her hand upward. Lucy's nose followed Gina's fist, tilting her head up while her hind end lowered to the ground. The second Lucy's behind made contact with the Astroturf covering the concrete floor, Gina released the treat. "Good *sit*."

Lucy gobbled the treat up.

After several more practice sits, Gina picked up Lucy for a quick snuggle. "You are a brilliant little pup. Now it's time to work with Ricky. Where's your brother?"

She set Lucy down. The puppy followed at her heels as she went in search of Ricky. No doubt Lucy smelled the treats stuffed into Gina's training pouch belted around her waist. She found Ricky in one of the agility tubes used during the K-9 training. The puppy had fallen asleep. She gently roused him. "Okay, Ricky, your turn to learn how to sit."

Ricky raised his head and quirked his ears, but not at her.

The sound of the interior door opening scraped across Gina's nerves. Her heart hammered a sporadic beat. She whipped around to face the threat and breathed in to prepare a scream.

Shane and Bella walked in. Shane held up his hands, palms out. "Whoa, it's just us."

Lucy trotted over to sniff Bella. Even Ricky emerged from his resting place. With a yip, the dog jumped from the agility tube and tumbled into a somersault before springing to his feet and racing to his sister's side.

Gina's shoulders sagged and she let out the breath trapped in her lungs. "I'm a bit jumpy."

He nodded. "Understandable."

Though a different sort of jittery feeling replaced the spurt of fear. She smoothed a hand over her hair, hoping she didn't look too messy.

She walked to Shane, and though her legs held her upright, they shook from the adrenaline rushing through her system. She hoped he didn't notice. And she told herself she was shaky because of fright, not because of Shane. "How did the meeting go?"

He lifted a shoulder in a half shrug. Bella lay down at their feet, and the puppies wandered off. "Okay. Last night's canvass of the area didn't turn up any witnesses to Veronica's murder, but the chief is sending Harmon back out. The Flagstaff crime scene techs didn't find any conclusive evidence to link your brother to Veronica's murder."

She frowned. "But we both know he's guilty, right?"

His grim expression didn't bode well. "Knowing it and proving it are two different things."

She blew out a breath. "Maybe when you capture him, he'll confess."

"That would be helpful." He rubbed a hand over his square jaw, drawing her gaze. Her fingers curled with the urge to touch the strong lines of his face. "No one has come forward with the puppy. Once word gets out that he's missing, hopefully that will spur some action."

She was anxious for little Marco to be found. It was so upsetting that someone hadn't already reported finding the stray pup. If someone had picked him up they might not know Marco had a home. "We should put up flyers. I took pictures of the puppies before giving them their shots yesterday."

"Good idea."

His approval warmed her cheeks.

"Your brother, however, is still in the wind and that bugs me." The grim look in his gaze spoke to his frustration. "The Mesa PD sent over a mug shot of him and we'll be out canvassing the town to see if anyone has seen him or knows where he's hiding."

Confused by his words, she asked, "But aren't you and the other rookies leaving town for your assignments?"

Departments all across the state vied for the newly trained K-9 officers and their canine partners. Each K-9 team would go where their specialty was needed. Though Shane had said he'd requested to join the Flagstaff PD, where his family members served. For his sake, she hoped his dream came true.

"Not yet," he said, running a hand through his hair, making the spiky ends stand up a little taller. "Marian Foxcroft has been in contact with the mayor and the governor and talked them into signing off on her idea of keeping the five of us here. She has generously provided the necessary funds to employ all of us until Veronica's murder is solved—as long as it takes, apparently."

A flutter of delight tried to take flight but Gina quickly squelched its attempt. He was staying only long enough to solve Veronica's murder. Letting herself get all dreamy about him wasn't practical. Or smart. "I'm sure you'll be able to leave by the end of the week. Tim can't hide out for long."

His green eyes were troubled. "With the additional manpower, Mrs. Foxcroft has also requested that Melanie Hayes's murder be reopened and the suspicious deaths of two rookies be reexamined."

It took a moment for Gina to process the information. "I never met Ryder's wife. However, I did some training with Brian Miller and Mike Riverton. Their deaths were such a shock, but both were ruled accidental." Though her friend Whitney questioned the fire investigator's finding that there was no proof of foul play.

"Mrs. Foxcroft wants fresh eyes on the cases," Shane said.

"So you could be here for a while?" That giddy flutter resurfaced beneath her rib cage and this time it wouldn't be quieted. Shane would be in town for longer than expected. She wasn't sure what that would mean for her, but she had to admit she hoped to spend more time with him—as friends, of course—once Tim was caught and she could relax again.

Though a small voice whispered in her head, *To what end?*

The unspoken question smashed the flutter like a wet wool blanket. She didn't have an answer. Was there really anything wrong with some pleasant evenings? If they led to heartache, then yes, there was. As much as she longed for a family, she had to accept the reality that she couldn't, shouldn't, ever go down that road.

"Maybe. It could take time to satisfy Mrs. Foxcroft." Shane didn't look happy about being stuck here. "I'm sure my dad will push to have me released sooner."

"And that's what you want, right? To join the Flagstaff PD," she blurted, even though he'd already made it clear he was out of here as soon as possible.

A little V appeared between his eyebrows. "Yeah." Bella must have sensed a shift in her master, because she rose to all fours. However, her posture didn't raise any alarms. Her tail wagged.

Keeping her attention on Shane, Gina cocked her head.

"That doesn't sound very convincing." Did he want to stay? Why? Her ego puffed up a bit in hopes his reluctance to leave was due to her. But that was ridiculous. She was silly for thinking there could be something between them. He'd never even hinted that he felt anything more than friendship and responsibility toward her. Which was just as well, considering she couldn't let herself seek more than a platonic relationship. Anything else would be unconscionable. Irresponsible even.

The emerald color of his eyes fascinated her. He was such a handsome man, but not in a pretty-boy way like some of those guys who graced magazine covers. No, Shane's good looks weren't classic, but rather made him more attractive because of the planes and angles to his face that weren't quite symmetrical.

Thick dark brows winged over almond-shaped eyes and added prominence to his cheekbones and a sturdy jaw. She forced herself to look away and concentrated on the dogs. The last thing she needed or wanted was to be entranced by this man even if he made her heart pound and her pulse jump.

"I'm more concerned about finding your brother at the moment than I am about returning to Flagstaff," he finally said.

His statement reminded her that he was here for the job, not her. Reining in her attraction to him, she offered a small smile. "And for that I am grateful."

"I'm going to head to the coroner's office to see what the autopsy revealed," he said. "Do you want to come with me?"

She shuddered. "No, thank you. I have no desire to lay eyes on Veronica's corpse again."

He inclined his head. "Got it. I'm more interested in learning if she was truly shot by a gun or a crossbow."

Gina's gaze snapped to his. "Last night you were sure it was a gunshot wound."

"After the attack on the truck, I'm not so sure. It was dark. The coroner will confirm one way or the other."

"You'll let me know what you discover?"

"Of course." Shane reached out to push a stray strand of her hair behind her ear. His finger grazed her skin and sent a quiver through her.

She couldn't remember the last time she'd felt such attraction. Discomfited by the contact, she stepped out of his reach.

His eyes were unreadable as he tucked his hands behind his back. "I saw Sophie on the way in. She's trying to make some sense out of Veronica's bookkeeping."

"I don't envy her that," Gina replied with a dry chuckle. "Veronica had her own way of doing things and not all of them made sense."

He tilted his head to study her. "She was a tough boss for you."

Gina let out a wry scoff. "That's an understatement. I'm sorry she's dead, but I can't honestly say I'll miss her." As soon as the words left her mouth, guilt swamped her. "That's a horrible thing for me to say, isn't it?"

Shane shook his head. "No. You're being honest. Veronica had a very abrasive personality. I think she earned more enemies than friends."

Gina made a face. "That's true." In the early days, just after Gina had taken the job with the training center, she'd questioned her sanity for staying. Not just because of the genes that ran in her family line but because Veronica could be so nasty and mean. Who in their right mind would willingly accept her abuse? Right up to the day Veronica died, Gina had been butting heads with her. Sometimes Gina wondered if Veronica had felt threatened by how easily Gina made friends with the other trainers and the rookies who had come and gone. "Has the chief mentioned a memorial service?"

"Not to me. Though he did mention Veronica has a brother in prison."

"I'd heard that, as well, but I've never met him. He was incarcerated just before I arrived in town."

"What about Veronica's ex-husband? You ever meet him?"

"I know of him," Gina admitted. "He's a doctor at the Desert Valley clinic. I've never met him. I do know there was no love lost between him and Veronica. I had the distinct impression there was some infidelity, but I couldn't say for sure or by whom."

He stroked his chin. "Interesting. I'm sure the chief has let the doctor know about Veronica's death."

Gina wondered if anyone besides the chief would mourn Veronica. She'd alienated most everyone in her life, though she'd never lacked for male company. She'd played loose and free with her love life.

Had Veronica thought she could charm Tim out of killing her? Gina's heart ached as once again the scene of how the event had transpired played through her mind. Even though Veronica had been mean-spirited and unkind at times, she hadn't deserved to die at Tim's hands. And Gina could do nothing to bring her back. "I should focus on the puppies."

"Right. I'll let Sophie know I'm leaving so she can stay alert."

The fact that he was taking her protection so personally sent pleasure through Gina. His concern for her well-being warmed her from the inside. "Thank you for keeping me up-to-date on the investigation."

"No problem." He smiled, flashing his white, even

teeth. She felt the impact of his smile all the way to her toes as they curled inside her rubber-soled shoes.

"Come on, Bella," he said. "Time to go."

The puppies followed them to the door. Gina bent down to grab each pup by the collar until Shane shut the door behind him. Releasing them, Gina leaned her back against the wood for a moment. She'd better get a grip on herself. Crushing on Shane wouldn't do anyone, especially her, any good.

She glanced at the clock on the far wall. Nearly noon. Deciding she'd work with Ricky for a little bit before returning them both to their crates so she could eat lunch, she scooped him up and carried him to the cabinet in the corner where the training treats were kept. Lucy trotted along at her heels. Since Ricky apparently wasn't interested in the beef and sweet potatoes treat she'd used with Lucy, she'd let him pick his favorite.

Inside the cabinet were four bins filled with different flavors of treats. She set Ricky down and scooped up Lucy. Then, with her free hand, she took one of each flavor and set them on the floor in a line. Whichever one he gravitated to first would be the one she'd use.

The puppy ambled over to the treats and sniffed each one. Apparently the little guy was a picky eater, unlike his sister, who squirmed to be released, no doubt wanting to get at all the treats.

Ricky stopped to lick one. Gina thought maybe they had a winner with the buffalo-flavored treat, but then he abandoned it to gobble up the one on the end.

"Ah, you're a fish lover." Gina picked up the dismissed treats in one hand before releasing Lucy.

Gina grabbed a handful of the salmon treats and waved her hands beneath the puppies' noses. "Come."

Then she walked toward the center of the arena with both dogs trailing behind her.

She stopped and turned her focus to Lucy. "Sit." The little pup sat, her sweet eyes expectant. "Good dog, sit." Gina fed one of the treats in her hand to Lucy then stuffed all but one into her pouch.

Ricky let out a protesting bark. Glad to have his attention, she held out her hand with the salmon-flavored morsel so he could smell the treat, and then slowly raised her hand as she'd done with Lucy.

Ricky, however, didn't cooperate. He backed up and barked.

Hmm. She plopped down on the ground and held out both hands in closed fists. One concealed a treat and the other was empty. "Which hand?"

Ricky barked and cocked his head.

"Which hand, Ricky?"

Ricky ventured closer and sniffed, then lifted a paw to scratch at the hand that held the treat. "Very good!" Delighted that he'd picked correctly, she slipped the treat into his mouth. It was a good sign that he could be taught to alert on a scent. He may prove to be a good tracker, cadaver dog or drug detector.

While he chewed, she stood and walked away a few feet, then filled one hand with another treat and held out her fists. "Which one?"

Ricky ran toward her.

The overhead lights went out, throwing the arena into murky gloom. The skylights allowed ambient light, but not enough to illuminate the cavernous arena.

Gina stilled. *It's just a shorted-out fuse.*

But deep down she didn't believe it. Terror flooded her veins.

A whisper of noise jolted through her. She ran and

crouched down behind the agility tube. She grabbed treats from the pouch at her waist and held out her hands palms up, hoping to lure the puppies to her. Ricky found her right away. She clutched him to her chest. Where was Lucy?

A cold wet nose nudged her arm. With a dose of relief, Gina scooped up Lucy with her free arm. The two puppies squirmed and she stuffed treats in their mouths in the hope they wouldn't bark to be released.

Gina peered around the edge of the agility tunnel. The neon red glow of the exit light outlined the silhouette of a man standing in front of the closed door. Tall and slim. Unmistakable.

Tim.

She shuddered and jerked back out of sight. Her cell phone vibrated on her hip. She prayed Tim hadn't heard the muffled sound. She didn't dare answer. She'd have to release one of the dogs to get it and then the light from the display would pinpoint her location for Tim, ensuring that he found her.

Her breath came fast and shallow. Somehow, someway, Tim had located her whereabouts. How had he infiltrated the center? Shane and Sophie had made sure the place was locked up tight.

Oh, no! *Sophie!*

Gina's heart lurched. *Oh, Lord, please don't let Sophie be dead, too!*

As Shane walked down the sidewalk of Desert Valley's main street, he scanned the faces of the other pedestrians, searching for Tim Perry. Colorful awnings provided shade, though on this mild late-March day the sun's rays weren't blistering the way he knew they would be come summer.

Both sides of the road were dominated by storefront businesses, restaurants and hotels with stucco or brick facades.

There was an eclectic mix of old-world charm and newer, modern architecture. Shane had heard that Marian Foxcroft had poured money into the town to bolster the economy as well as to entice more tourists to the small community.

Up ahead was the brick mortuary where the coroner, who was also the town's mortician, worked. As Shane reached the entrance his cell rang. He glanced at the caller ID. Sophie. With a spike in his pulse rate, he quickly answered, "Sophie?"

"Hey, so I somehow locked myself in the supply closet. I called Gina but she's not answering her cell."

He frowned, confused and alarmed. A twinge of constriction zinged through his chest. "Did she leave the center?"

Gina knew the seriousness of the situation. Why would she leave? Shane did an about-face and stalked back toward the training building, keeping his gaze alert for any sign of Gina or her brother.

"I'm sure it's nothing. Gina's phone is on silent since she's working with the puppies."

"Oh, okay." That made sense. Yet a large knot formed in his gut. He picked up his pace. "I'm almost there. How did you lock yourself inside the closet?"

"The door slammed shut. I'll have to check the springs on it."

That knot expanded and put pressure on his lungs. He worked to control his breathing. Doors didn't just slam shut on their own. Something was wrong. He sent up a plea that he reached Gina in time.

Anxiety tightened Gina's muscles and full-blown panic built in her chest.

No! She couldn't panic. She had to stay calm if she hoped to survive.

She needed to reach the other exit, the one leading to the puppy yard. In a low crouch, she shuffled toward the agility tire jump, though the freestanding frame wouldn't provide much protection.

"Sissster." Tim's voice echoed off the walls. "I'mmm hhhheere."

Fear snaked down her spine. She struggled to keep hold of the puppies while she increased her pace. Thankfully neither dog made a sound. She'd sent up a fervent prayer for protection, promising she'd start going to church again, read her Bible and pray more if only God would make Tim go away.

Struggling to keep terror from overwhelming her, she forced herself to keep moving toward the exit. Afraid to let the puppies go, she had to juggle their weight while moving in a low run. She caught her elbow on the edge of the frame of a regulation jump and nearly lost her grip on the dogs.

Only a little farther.

The interior door of the arena banged open. The bright glow from a high-powered flashlight filled the space, forcing the shadows to abate enough that Gina was exposed. But so was Tim. A crossbow hung across his body and long bolts stuck out of a pouch on his back.

"Halt! Police!" Shane shouted.

Gina nearly cried with relief. How had he known to come back? God had answered her prayer. Though she couldn't see Shane behind the glare of the flashlight, his very presence made her knees weak. He was putting himself in harm's way.

Tim whirled to face Shane. He grabbed the crossbow, bringing it up as he reached over his shoulder for a steel-tipped bolt.

"No!" Gina screamed. "Shane, watch out!"

A whirr of movement caught Tim by surprise. Bella launched herself at him with a deep growl. Tim used the crossbow like a club to knock the attacking dog away. Bella yelped and fell in a heap at his feet. Tim turned and ran for the door at the back of the arena. Gina scuttled quickly out of his reach as he passed her.

Shane raced after him. "Stop or I'll shoot."

Not heeding the warning, Tim kicked the door open.

Gina held her breath as sunshine flooded the room, dispelling the gloom and washing Shane in a bright light. He had his service weapon aimed at her brother's retreating back. Her heart stalled. He pulled the trigger just as Tim disappeared through the exit. The bullet shattered the edge of the door frame and filled the arena with a deafening echo. Shane ran for the door and skidded to a halt, clearly debating giving chase.

Gina's stomach tensed with a more pressing question. "What about Sophie?"

A loud crash sounded from somewhere inside the training center, then Sophie ran into the arena, holding her gun in a two-handed grip. "I heard a gun go off. I finally managed to kick open the supply closet door."

What? Gina didn't understand—clearly her hearing was off from the retort of the gun.

Standing poised on the threshold of the exit, Shane glanced over his shoulder. "Stay with them," he instructed Sophie, and then he stormed out after Tim.

Gina released the puppies and rushed to where Bella lay on the ground. The dog's eyes were open and her breathing was labored. Tears filled Gina's eyes. She struggled to get her phone from her waist pouch. She dialed the police station. Though her ears hurt and the world was muffled, she managed to quickly tell the dispatcher what had happened, just in case Shane hadn't had a chance to before he came to her rescue.

Shane returned a moment later. "Tim got away." His grim tone echoed with anger and frustration. He knelt beside Bella. "You'll be okay, girl. You have to be okay." He bowed his head. "Please, God. Let her be okay."

SEVEN

The acrid odor of burned gunpowder filled the arena. Shane barely noticed as worry chomped through him. Though he hadn't given Bella the command to attack, she'd done what she had been trained to do. And Tim had hit her pretty hard with the edge of his crossbow.

Shane's gut tightened. Too bad he hadn't aimed for Tim's back instead of firing a warning shot. By the time Shane had run out of the center, Tim had made it to the corner at the end of the road and disappeared. When Shane had reached the corner, there was no sign of the man.

On the way back to the center, Shane had had to use his inhaler. The first time in a long time.

Now he laid a hand on Bella. She lay on the floor panting. "You're a brave dog," he told her, hoping Bella understood how proud he was to call her partner.

Sophie tucked her weapon into her waistband at her back. Her training uniform was damp with sweat. Her honey-blond hair was no longer in a twist but hung in a braid, secured with an elastic rubber band. She touched Gina's shoulder. "Are you okay?"

Gina's slight smile showed appreciation for the other

woman's concern. "I'm good. Shane returned just in time."

Sophie frowned. "What happened?"

"Tim. He somehow gained entrance to the center," Gina said. "He came after me but…"

"But?" Shane pinned her with his gaze.

Gina wrapped her arms around her middle. "He could have easily just killed me. Instead, he seemed more interested in terrorizing me."

Sophie knelt next to her and put an arm around her shoulders. "I'm glad he didn't hurt you. I'm so sorry I let my guard down."

"You did nothing wrong," Gina countered. "I'm just glad he didn't hurt you."

Unlike Veronica. Or Bella. Fury burned in Shane's abdomen. He looked at Sophie. "You being locked in the closet was no accident."

Sophie nodded. "So I'm gathering. When I heard the gunfire, I kicked the door down. I should have done that in the first place."

Chief Earl Jones barreled through the open exit. Right behind him came the town vet, Tanya Fowler, a medium-built woman with strawberry-blond hair and light blue eyes. Shane had met her the first week he'd been in town when she'd come to the training center to meet the dogs and their handlers. She'd been politely reserved with the handlers and gentle and loving with the animals.

Chief Jones skidded to a stop beside them. "Is anybody hurt?"

Shane quickly related the events while Tanya knelt down beside Bella and checked her vitals.

The chief called for Officer Harmon to come secure the scene. Then to Shane he said, "You'll need to come to the station and surrender your weapon and file a report."

Shane frowned. "Are you taking me off protection detail?"

Jones shook his head. "No. I want you to shadow Gina even more closely from now on. Your service weapon will be returned to you as soon as possible. No later than tomorrow morning. But protocol and policies need to be adhered to."

Shane understood. He knew the drill. He could remember days when his dad stayed home from the job because he'd discharged his weapon while on duty. His brothers had loved those days, but not Shane. Dad would regale them with horrible tales of the gritty side of law enforcement while devising some new exercise drill or obstacle course to put his sons through.

Mitchell and Jeremiah thrived on the challenge. Shane had wanted to earn his father's approval, too, but his asthma would knock him out of the competition quickly, much to the amusement of his elder siblings and his father's disdain. What would his father think to learn Shane had discharged his weapon and missed on purpose? Shooting a man in the back hadn't seemed right.

Jones turned his attention to the vet. "How is she?"

"Heart rate's up. Her pupils are slightly dilated." Tanya's light blue eyes sought Shane's. "Did she lose consciousness?"

"If so, only for a second," Gina interjected. "She went down hard. She's tried to get up, but she's obviously struggling."

Tanya nodded. "She probably has a mild concussion. I'd like to take her to the clinic for a full exam."

Shane lifted Bella into his arms. "I'll carry her over." He glanced at Gina, his chest tightening again. He didn't want to leave her unprotected. "You're coming with me."

She gestured to the puppies now rolling around together wrestling over a toy. "I better put them in their crates."

"I'll take care of them," Sophie said. "Once I get them settled down, I'm going to examine every inch of the center and figure out how your brother gained access and plug whatever hole he crawled through."

The fact that Tim Perry had somehow managed to breach the facility gnawed at Shane. He'd better step up his game. Maybe he wasn't cut out for police work, as his father had declared on more than one occasion. The fire inside of Shane burned a little hotter. He'd underestimated Tim's determination to get at his sister. It wouldn't happen again.

If Sophie hadn't had her phone at the time she was locked in the supply closet, it could have been Gina's body Shane was carrying out the door.

The thought made him break out in a cold sweat.

Gina stepped out into the mild late-afternoon sunshine that should have been enough to chase away her shivers. She was thankful for her sweater. The northern Arizona spring temperature was barely over sixty degrees. But her chill was more from her scare than the weather. She kept her gaze alert for any sign of Tim.

The chief insisted on keeping her on his left, using his big frame as a shield. Tanya hurried ahead to prepare an exam room for Bella while Shane carried his canine partner tenderly in his arms. It was clear how much the man cared for his partner. The bond that formed between canines and humans never ceased to amaze her.

A familiar yearning tugged at her. She wanted to have that kind of bond, wanted to find a man to love and who loved her. But fear kept the dream from becoming a reality.

Inside the clinic, the receptionist, an older woman with jet-black hair peppered with gray, rose and came around the desk. To Shane, she said, "Dr. Fowler will meet you in exam room three." Turning to Gina and the chief, she held up a hand, stopping them from following. "You can wait out here."

For a moment Shane hesitated. Gina didn't have to be a mind reader to know he didn't want to leave her side. The thought both warmed and chilled her. The confusing reaction made her heart beat hard in her chest.

"I've got her," Jones said, clearly picking up on the same vibe as Gina.

Mollified, Shane nodded and followed the receptionist to the exam room. Once he and Bella disappeared, the older woman headed back to them. "Care for some coffee, Chief?"

"Thank you, Gladys." Jones tipped his chin to her. "Much appreciated."

Gladys sent Gina an inquiring look.

"No, thank you." She had enough acid reflux going on. Adding to it would only exacerbate the malady. She took deep, calming breaths and tried to block the terror that lingered in her veins.

Twenty minutes later, Shane and Bella walked out of the exam room followed by the vet. Delighted to see Bella up and about, Gina knelt to give the dog a hug.

Bella licked her face. Emotion clogged Gina's throat. She lifted her gaze to Shane. "She's all right?"

"She's tough," he said with obvious pride in his tone.

Tanya smiled. "She'll need to rest for a day but she'll be fine. I found no permanent damage."

Chief Jones's cell phone rang. He answered, listened and then said, "We'll be right over." When he hung up, he tipped his head toward the door. "We need to get to the station."

"Did someone capture Tim?" Gina asked.

Jones shook his head but didn't say anything more before striding toward the exit.

After thanking Tanya, they hurried to the station. Once there, the chief motioned for Shane and Bella to follow him. "Gina, you can wait in the break room."

Trying not to be hurt by the dismissal, she took a seat at one of the round tables in the space reserved for the officers' breaks. Her stomach growled, reminding her she hadn't eaten lunch. She'd left her purse at the center so she had no money to feed the vending machine. Instead she made a cup of tea from the communal box on the counter.

The rapid click of heels on the linoleum echoed in the stillness as Carrie Dunleavy entered the room and stopped abruptly when she saw Gina. Gina didn't know the police department's secretary well. In fact, she couldn't remember having a conversation with her that was more than a few sentences of polite chitchat.

Not in the mood to move beyond politeness right now, Gina smiled a greeting and resumed her seat at the table. She held the warm cup between her hands.

"I heard what happened to you," Carrie said as she glided forward, her brown eyes concerned behind the frames of her horn-rimmed glasses. "It's just awful. You must have been so scared."

Gina wasn't sure exactly what Carrie was referring to considering all that had happened in the past twenty-four hours. So she let her answer encompass all of it. "Yes, very scared."

"I heard Bella was hurt?"

"She'll be okay." Gina stared into her cup of Earl Grey as guilt for the dog's injuries choked her.

Carrie moved to the refrigerator and withdrew a white box. "I made cupcakes. Would you like one? Double chocolate."

Gina's mouth watered. Normally, she'd pass on sugary sweets, but today she'd make an exception. "Yes, please. That's so kind of you to offer."

Carrie used tongs to pluck a large cupcake from the box and put it on a napkin in front of Gina. The big round cupcake was encased in a flowery paper holder and the top was piled high with creamy chocolate frosting sprinkled with colorful confetti candy pieces. Gina bit into the confection. Rich, creamy, moist and oh, so delicious. She couldn't remember the last time she'd tasted anything this good. "Wow, this is fabulous."

"I love to bake," Carrie confessed with a shy, pleased smile. "It's my therapy."

Gina shot her a startled glance. Was she making fun of Gina? Did she know mental illness ran in her family? But Carrie's gaze held no laughter or mockery. Relaxing slightly, Gina remarked, "Probably more cost-effective than retail therapy."

Carrie laughed softly. "I'm definitely not much of a fashion horse."

"Me, neither. Dogs don't care what I wear as long as I have treats available."

"That's true."

Gina munched on the sweet in her hand, savoring every morsel. "I hear plans for the upcoming Canyon County Police Dance and Fundraiser are coming along nicely." A few ladies at the singles' potluck had been talking about the event held every year in May, though Gina hadn't been able to bring herself to attend. The event was too big with too much attention drawn to the attendees. She'd needed to stay out of the limelight, too afraid the publicity would attract her brother's attention.

So much for having to worry about that anymore.

Carrie shut the bakery box lid. "I'm on the food committee."

Wistfully watching the box of treats disappear back into the fridge, Gina remarked, "Makes sense for you to be on the food committee since you like to bake, right? I imagine everyone will want to taste whatever you make."

"Hope so. I should get back to my desk. See you later." She left the room as quickly as she'd entered.

Gina enjoyed the last bite of cupcake and washed it down with a swig of tea. Thinking about the upcoming dance made her wonder if Shane would still be in town come May. And if so, would he attend?

She couldn't stop the flurry of excitement tying her insides into knots. Maybe this year she would go. Maybe Shane would ask her to dance.

Her palms grew slick with anticipation. And worry. If he did ask, how in the world would she ever do the smart thing and say no?

Shane settled into a chair in the chief's office with Bella sitting at his feet. Chief Jones took his seat behind his desk. Ryder Hayes folded his frame into the seat next to Shane, his dog, Titus, moving stiffly to lie down next to Bella. The Lab nudged Bella with his nose, prompting Bella to also lie down. She set her chin on her paws.

The chief opened a folder. "The medical examiner in Flagstaff rushed Veronica's autopsy and faxed over the report confirming the cause of death as two gunshot wounds." He ran a finger down a page as he read. "Stippling at the entrance sites suggests the killer was within a foot of Veronica when the trigger was engaged. Two .45-caliber slugs were retrieved. The crime scene techs in Flagstaff ran the bullets through the National Integrated Ballistics Information Network but no hits."

Meaning the gun in question hadn't been previously used in a crime. At least not one that had been inputted into the database that the Bureau of Alcohol, Tobacco and Firearms maintained to provide federal, state and local partner agencies with an automated ballistic imaging system. NIBIN partners used the database to discover formerly impossible-to-identify links between firearms-related violent crimes and to identify firearm users or "trigger pullers."

"Fingerprints on the slugs?" Shane asked, thinking the perpetrator might have left behind a trace of evidence when loading the weapon.

"None viable. Nor on the casings recovered in the training center last night," the chief said. "I have Harmon and Marlton out searching every garbage can, crevice and potential dumping spot for the weapon."

The chief set the folder aside then pinned his gaze on Shane. "For the next twenty-four hours, you'll be relieved of duty while we investigate this morning's shooting."

Though he'd known this was coming, the order still rankled. "Yes, sir." Shane withdrew his sidearm and placed it on the desk.

"Ryder, take Donaldson to the training center. Find the spent bullet and casing. Make sure no innocent bystander was harmed because of Officer Weston's weapon."

Ryder stood. "Will do." Titus struggled to his feet, ready to work.

"And, Ryder, check in with Sophie. See if she found out how Tim Perry gained entrance to the center." The chief steepled his fingers and rested his elbows on the desk. "Go over her alibi again."

For a moment Ryder hesitated, then nodded. "On it." He and his partner left the office.

Once the door closed behind them, Shane met the chief's gaze. "I'll take Gina back to the condo. She and Bella both could use some downtime."

"Good idea," the chief said. He reached for a paper on his desk and handed it to Shane. "Call the people on this list and check alibis. In some cases, double-check their alibis. If anyone seems the least bit fishy, flag them and we'll bring them in for a formal chat."

Glad to be of service, Shane took the list. A quick perusal showed the names of many people in town, including Veronica's ex-husband, and a few who'd left town, like Gina's friend Jenna Cruz, a former employee of the training center. He folded the paper and put it in his breast pocket. "Gina asked about a memorial service for Veronica."

Jones leaned back in his chair and scrubbed a hand over his unshaven jaw. "Arrangements will need to be made once the Flagstaff ME releases Veronica's body. I'll have Carrie talk with Randolph Drummond about a service."

"Has her next of kin been notified?"

"I'll drive out to the state prison and tell her brother, Lee." Jones heaved a heavy sigh.

Shane didn't envy the chief the task of notifying Lee Earnshaw of his sister's murder. Giving notifications was one of the harder parts of the job.

The quick rap of knuckles on the office door had the chief calling out, "Enter."

Officer Ken Bucks stuck his head in. "The rookies are all set up with desks."

The inflection in his tone when he said *rookies* set Shane's teeth on edge. It was clear the officer wasn't happy to be sharing space or duties with the newly graduated K-9 officers. Too bad. From what Shane could tell, the officers of Desert Valley needed help.

Jones inclined his head. "Thank you, Ken." Ken remained in the doorway. "Was there something else?"

Ken shrugged, not exactly eager to leave. "Nope." He backed away and clicked the door closed behind him.

The chief huffed out a breath. "That boy. Sometimes…"

Shane wouldn't qualify Ken Bucks as a boy. He was older than Shane by at least ten years. "Sir?"

"Sorry. Ken's my stepson. Ex-stepson, to be exact. I raised him through the teen years."

Shane hadn't known they were family. It was on the tip of his tongue to commiserate with the chief, but then he thought better of it. Time to change the subject before he said something he might regret. "Gina had the idea of putting up flyers for the missing puppy."

"Good idea." Jones's tone was rife with approval. "Have her give the information to Carrie to make the flyers. While they work on that you can file your report on the OIS."

Filing a detailed account of any officer-involved shooting was standard procedure. It would be Shane's first. He rose. "I'll do that."

He and Bella left the chief to find Gina in the break room. She sat at a round table by herself, staring into her cup. She'd retied her long red hair back into a neat braid that trailed down her back. Her T-shirt and light-colored cargo pants still looked fresh despite the trauma of her brother trapping her in the training arena. She looked up. Her pretty hazel eyes had lost some of the sparkle she'd had during his training sessions. He missed that sparkle. He'd liked that sparkle. He liked her.

"Everything okay?" she asked.

"Yes." He explained about his temporary leave of duty and that the chief had given him a list of potential suspects to contact. "He also suggested you work with Carrie, the police department secretary, to make flyers about Marco."

"Great." She pushed back her chair and rose. "I'll go find her now."

"I have to write up a report on the incident this morning. Then we can start hanging the flyers."

She touched his arm. "I'm sorry for all the trouble my brother has caused."

He covered her hand with his own. Her skin was cool and yet warmth spread from the point of contact to the vicinity of his heart. "Stop that. Your brother's actions aren't your fault. He's chosen this destructive path. He's the only one to blame."

Her smile trembled. "You're a kind man, Shane Weston. I appreciate you and all you're doing for me."

Staring into her gold-flecked eyes, he found himself wanting more than her appreciation—he wanted her affection. Yearning pulled at him so strongly, like an invisible hook, dragging him toward her. The distance between them shortened as he leaned close. Her lips parted. She made a little noise in her throat.

His gaze jumped to hers. Was she distressed?

What was he thinking? Kissing Gina? So inappropriate, unprofessional and dumb. Stricken by his loss of self-control, he jerked back.

But Gina's hand fisted the front of his shirt and tugged him closer.

He'd mistaken her response as upset, but apparently it was consent. His pulse skittered.

Their lips touched. Hers were soft, pliant, and yet there was a hint of desperation in the kiss that made him want to weep for her. Gina was reacting to the danger and terror she'd suffered.

She was reaching out for contact as a way to assure herself she was whole and intact.

Shane's head knew this, but his heart cracked just a little as he disengaged. Reading more into the kiss than simple human need for connection would only hurt him, and her, in the end. A fate he hoped to avoid.

EIGHT

Two hours later, Gina and Shane left the police station in his Jeep and headed for the center of town. From the back compartment that was separated by a tension gate, Bella moved from window to window, her vigilant gaze sweeping the main thoroughfare. Gina hoped the dog would alert on Tim long before either she or Shane saw him.

There was a measure of comfort in the dog's presence, but she knew they couldn't become complacent. Tim was out there somewhere and he wanted to hurt her, terrorize her and eventually kill her.

Gina was glad for a task to take her mind off her brother. She and Shane were armed with a stack of colored flyers displaying a cute picture and details about Marco as well as a plea to please contact the Canyon County Training Center or the Desert Valley Police Department with any information regarding the missing puppy. A staple gun and a roll of tape sat in the console between them.

Shane parked the vehicle so they could jump out and take the flyers into the businesses. He also had a photo of Gina's brother and showed it to every person they encountered.

Unfortunately, no recognized him.

Moving quickly, she and Shane managed to tape up

flyers in most of the front windows of the businesses along Desert Valley Road while Whitney and James tackled the telephone poles and trees lining the street. By the time they were done, it was after five, and most of the citizens of Desert Valley were closing up shop and heading home for dinner with their families.

The setting sun painted streaks of vibrant yellows, oranges and pinks across the western sky, backlighting the dense forest of mesquite trees and ponderosa pines that surrounded the town. Normally, Gina would find the view calming, but her pulse still hadn't settled down to a regular rhythm after the brief kiss she'd shared with Shane.

She must've had a momentary flare of insanity, because she'd practically forced Shane to kiss her!

Okay, he'd leaned in, yes. But then he'd clearly reconsidered the wisdom of kissing her and started to back away. And she, well, she'd acted. Brazenly. Boldly. And so recklessly.

Though she regretted her impulsiveness, she didn't regret the moment. His kiss had poured through her like warm chocolate over ice cream, melting her all the way to her toes. That her legs had kept her upright was a surprise.

She'd never had a kiss so potent before.

Not that she'd done a lot of kissing. Kind of hard to find someone to kiss when she rarely went on a date, let alone allowed herself to become emotionally attached enough to warrant a kiss. Because she was too afraid to fall in love, to believe she could have a normal, happy life.

There'd been one guy before she had been forced to flee Mesa to hide from her brother. She'd met Roger Clay at a dog-training facility.

Both he and the rottweiler he'd brought in for training had taken a shine to her, making her feel special. Roger had been kind and caring, funny even. They'd gone out three times. He'd kissed her on their last date and she'd been left feeling let down and disappointed by the lack of chemistry.

Not so with Shane's kiss. The second their lips touched, energy flowed between them, thrilling in its intensity. But then he'd pulled away, leaving her wanting more.

She was in so much trouble. It had to be the stress of Veronica's murder, the missing puppy and her brother stalking her. Letting her attraction to Shane rule her head wasn't a good idea. She needed to keep him at an emotional distance. She could be friendly but professional. Yes, that sounded like a good plan.

Then why did she feel so out of sorts?

"It'll be dark soon," Shane commented. "We should head to the condo. I'm starved. We have steaks I can grill."

"Food would be good." Though she wondered if she'd be able to eat with her nerves jumping. Every time he got close, agitated butterflies took flight in her tummy and her lips ached for attention. "I need to stop at the training center to get the puppies. I don't want to leave them there alone all night."

"Of course."

As they approached the center, Gina glanced down the side street to her little house at the far end of the road. She sighed and wished she could go home. She had no idea if or when that would happen. It wasn't that she was ungrateful to Shane and James for letting her share the condo, but her house had been her sanctuary. Only, now it wasn't. Tim had violated her home and forced her out.

A horn beeped, drawing her focus to the Desert Valley Police Department vehicle. Chief Jones sat at the wheel. He rolled down his window. Gina did the same.

"I'm heading to the state penitentiary to talk to Lee Earnshaw."

Gina winced with sympathy for Veronica's brother. Gina knew Veronica and her brother hadn't been close, but they had been family. Gina imagined Lee would be angry and hurt by the loss of his sister. It was kind of the chief to drive out there himself rather than rely on the prison warden to inform Lee of his sister's demise.

"Stay safe, sir," she said. Desert roads could be treacherous at night.

The chief regarded her with kindness. "You, too, young lady. Stick close to Weston, and if either of you need anything, call Hayes. I left him in charge."

Shane leaned farther across her toward the window to say, "Will do, Chief."

Every point of contact on her body felt like a live wire. Electrical impulses zinged through her blood. His musky scent was a heady mixture and made her feel weak-kneed. She was glad she was seated or she might have had trouble staying upright.

With a nod, the chief drove away.

Shane slowly resumed his position in the driver's seat and proceeded toward the training center.

As darkness descended, the temperature plummeted. Nighttime in the desert, especially in the northern part of the state, usually came with a drastic change in temperature. At least that was how she attributed her sudden lack of warmth. Certainly it wasn't from missing contact with Shane.

As they rolled past the closed gate where Gina had found Veronica's body, Gina couldn't help but stare. Crime scene tape blocked access to the center through the puppy-training yard. The gruesome reminder had her bowing her head. She sent up a silent plea for understanding.

Why had Tim done this horrible thing? Why was he

so bent on killing his own sister? And why had he killed their father? Why had God made Tim with a mental illness?

But she knew she couldn't blame all of Tim's actions on his mental condition. Tim had free will, as did everyone. It saddened and sickened her that her brother chose to act with such malice and violence.

"Are you doing okay?"

Shane's softly asked question forced her to lift her chin. She didn't want him to see her as weak or overly emotional, even though he'd already seen her in a state of shock after she'd found Veronica and today cowering behind the agility equipment when he'd rescued her from whatever madness her brother had planned for her in the training center.

She wasn't sure why it was so important that she appear strong to Shane. Maybe if he believed she was strong, she could believe it herself? Believe she was strong enough to overcome the DNA flowing inside her.

"I'm good," she replied and started walking again. "We'll need to go around to the front entrance."

At the door to the training facility, Shane swiped his card over the reader and the lock popped open. Inside the building, lights blazed. Sophie stepped out of the men's restroom with a hammer and a bag of nails in her hands.

"Hey, I was going to call you," Sophie said. "I found how your brother entered the building. The lock on one of the men's bathroom windows was busted. I nailed all the windows shut. No one's getting in here again without permission."

"Thank you." Gina appreciated Sophie's take-charge attitude. "I'm going to take the puppies with me."

"Are you sure? Because I don't mind taking them home," Sophie said.

Gina felt a sense of responsibility to the puppies. And, if she were honest with herself, she needed the distraction and comfort of taking care of them. "I'd like to take them with me."

Sophie nodded with understanding. "They'll be in good hands, then."

As they were readying the pups to leave, Shane's cell phone rang.

He answered the call. "Weston."

Gina watched his face. He frowned, then his eyes widened with surprise.

"Where? We'll be right there."

He hung up but seemed lost in thought, his green eyes troubled.

"Shane, what is it?" Gina asked as worry flooded her system. Had her brother been apprehended? Was someone else hurt? Marco?

"That was Ryder," Shane said. "A maintenance man at the train depot found a gun in one of the trash bins."

"Put the puppies back in the crates," Sophie instructed, clearly excited at the prospect of finding the weapon that had killed their boss. Having once been a cop, she obviously still felt the thrill of discovery. "Let's go over there. I'll drive."

After recrating the puppies, Gina climbed in the backseat of the training center's SUV and wondered why Shane was so bothered by the development. He was quiet as Sophie drove toward the north side of town where passenger trains passed through on the way to their final destinations in midwest Illinois or Los Angeles.

The train depot housed not only the ticket booth for the passenger trains but the tourist visitor's center that Marian Foxcroft had insisted on building to supply the station with maps and town highlights. The building reminded Gina of a Tudor cottage more likely to be seen in an English countryside village than northwest Arizona. More of Marian Foxcroft's influence, no doubt.

Two official Desert Valley police cars waited with red and blue lights flashing, creating a strobe effect over the grim faces of the officers gathered on the platform.

Sophie brought the SUV to a halt. Shane shifted and turned to Gina. "You should stay here, out of sight."

She wanted to argue but knew he was right. Whatever was going on would provide a distraction that might allow her brother an opportunity to grab her or, worse yet, kill her. "Fine."

He and Sophie climbed out. Shane released Bella and had the dog jump onto the back passenger seat with Gina. "Even though she's not 100 percent today, she'll protect you. I'd rather have Bella at 50 percent than not at all," he said before firmly shutting the door and walking toward the train platform.

Sophie electronically locked the vehicle doors, effectively trapping Gina inside the SUV.

Burying her hands into Bella's thick fur coat, Gina fought off the anxiety pulling at her mind.

At least she was safe.

But for how long?

As Shane approached Ryder and Officers Bucks and Harmon, the fine hairs at the back of his neck tingled. His gaze swept the area and though he saw no visible threat, that didn't mean there wasn't one.

He glanced back at the black SUV where Gina waited. He couldn't see her through the tinted windows but he imagined he felt her gaze on him as surely as he still felt her kiss on his lips. That had been unexpected. She'd surprised and pleased him when she'd followed through on what he'd decided was a bad idea. Not so bad at all.

Except he knew pursuing anything the least bit romantic with this woman would lead to potential hazards he'd rather not face. He may be sticking around Desert Valley for the foreseeable future, but that didn't mean he should toy with Gina's affections. Or leave either of them open to heartache when he eventually left.

Shane addressed Ryder. "Where is it?"

Ryder nudged his dog, Titus, and the two stepped aside to reveal a large plastic bag laid out on the platform. Resting in the middle of the bag was a handgun.

Not just any handgun.

A SIG-Sauer P220 fitted with a suppressor can. Exactly like the weapon Shane's grandfather had given Shane before he'd passed on. A weapon that was secured in a lockbox in the bedroom closet of the condo where Shane was staying.

How could there be two of the same weapon in Desert Valley?

Shane's grandfather had purchased the weapon new in the early 1970s when the Swiss company first produced the pistol for the Swiss army. It was one of a handful of sidearms that Grandfather Weston had bequeathed to his grandsons.

Shane lifted his gaze and met Ryder's. "That isn't mine."

Officer Ken Bucks snorted. "It sure looks like the one you were showing off at the church picnic a few weeks ago."

Shane wanted to wipe Bucks's smug expression on the ground. "Mine is locked up in the condo."

Ryder's expression held no hint of his thoughts. "I'll need to see it."

"Of course. I have nothing to hide," Shane said.

"Did you find prints on this one?" Sophie asked.

"It's been wiped clean," Ryder state flatly. "We'll have the crime lab in Flagstaff test fire it and compare the ballistics to the slugs taken from Veronica's body."

Shane understood what Ryder wasn't saying. If the two ballistics tests matched, then Shane could be facing a murder charge.

Concern darkened Sophie's eyes. "Who found the weapon?"

Ryder gestured to Officer Marlton, who was interviewing a man dressed in blue coveralls. Next to him was a pushcart filled with trash bags. "He said both the gun and the suppressor were lying on top of the garbage inside this can." He pointed to the nearest trash receptacle.

"Which suggests someone wanted the weapon found," Sophie said.

But why? Shane chewed on the question as acid burned in his gut. What purpose would framing him serve?

"Ken, bag the evidence," Ryder instructed. "You and Harmon drive it to Flagstaff. I've already been in touch with the techs. They're expecting it."

"Hey," Harmon protested. "Shouldn't we wait for the chief to give us instructions?"

Ryder's expression hardened. His blue eyes turned to ice. "I'm in charge until he returns."

Harmon shoved his hand into his pants pockets. "Aw, man, Mary's not going to be happy if I'm not home tonight."

Shane didn't doubt that Eddie Harmon's spouse would be upset. With six kids at home, Shane couldn't imagine how the woman managed. He gave an involuntary shudder. It wasn't that Shane disliked children. They were fine at a distance. He had no experience with them and no desire to remedy that anytime in the distant future.

Once Bucks and Harmon left with the evidence, Shane and Sophie returned to the SUV. After securing Bella back in the safety of the crate, he slid back into the front seat. Gina's curious gaze bored into him. There was no help for it; he had to tell her what was happening.

"The janitor found a handgun in the trash can. A gun eerily similar to the one my grandfather left me upon his death."

"That's bizarre," Gina said. "I'm sure it will turn out that your grandfather's handgun is where you say it is and this is some strange coincidence."

"From your lips to God's ears," he said. But her belief in him warmed him almost as much as the kiss they'd shared. He hoped there would be more kisses. Whoa! What? Immediately, he pushed the thought away. No sense going down that rocky lane. Kisses, romance, emotions. He wasn't ready or willing to tread there. His career had to come first.

He sent up a silent plea that Gina's prediction came true and this was all an uncanny coincidence. Problem was, Shane didn't believe in coincidence. Anxiety stiffened the muscles across his shoulders and up both sides of his neck. His jaw ached.

He forced himself to unclench his teeth as Sophie brought the vehicle to a halt outside the training center. Shane jumped out and opened Gina's door. She and Sophie hurried inside to get the puppies.

"Do you mind if I come along?" Sophie asked once they had the puppies in the back of Shane's Jeep with Bella.

"Not at all," Shane said though he was too preoccupied by the turn of events to care about much at the moment.

Gina slipped into the Jeep's passenger seat while Sophie went back to the SUV to follow them.

"Don't worry." Gina laid a hand on his arm. Her touch was soft and comforting.

"That's like asking me to put toothpaste back in the tube," he stated. "Not going to happen."

They parked just as Ryder pulled up behind them. He climbed out of the car and grabbed a black bag from the back passenger seat.

Sophie stopped the SUV behind Ryder.

"What are you doing here?" Ryder asked with a scowl. "This is police business."

"Support," Sophie said and stepped past him to reach Gina's side.

Shane appreciated that Gina had a friend willing to incur Ryder's displeasure and not flinch.

Ryder shook his head and released Titus. Bella and Titus greeted each other before following their human partners to the condo. Once inside, Gina and Sophie took the puppies outside to the small backyard area.

Shane led Ryder to his room. "I haven't opened this side of the closet since before Veronica was killed."

He opened his closet and crouched down in front of the biometric handgun safe on the floor. Incredulous anger flared. Deep grooves marred the front panel and edges of the door where something sharp had been used in an effort to pry open the safe's door.

"Don't touch it," Ryder said, kneeling down next to Shane.

"The safe opens by my fingerprint," Shane told him.

Ryder pointed at the gouge marks. "How long have those been there?"

"Last time I used the safe was a week or so ago and those were definitely *not* there," Shane curtly informed the other officer. "But there's no way anyone breached the security lock. They'd have to have my fingerprint."

From the black bag, Ryder withdrew a fingerprint kit, complete with colored powder and various shapes and sizes of dusters. He went about the task of checking for prints on the outside of the safe. He checked all sides and found none. "Whoever attempted to break in wiped the safe down." He dusted inside the print scanner and with a piece of magnetic tape lifted one print. He scanned the print into a handheld computer device.

"It will be mine," Shane said.

"Let's see." Ryder held out a fingerprint inkpad and a three-by-five index card.

Shane pressed his finger to the inkpad and then onto the card. Ryder scanned Shane's print in, as well. The device beeped.

"A match to you," Ryder confirmed. "Go ahead and open the safe."

Shane stuck his finger into the slot and pressed down so that his fingertip flattened for the biometric reader. The locked popped open. With his breath trapped in his lungs, Shane swung open the lockbox door. Confidential papers, his passport and a hunting knife were the only contents.

His stomach dropped. Dread flooded his veins. "My grandfather's handgun is gone."

"It's gone?" Gina's incredulous voice came from the doorway.

Shane's gaze jerked to her. Her hazel eyes were wide with stunned disbelief. Beside Gina, Sophie stood quietly, taking in the scene.

"No, it's on its way to Flagstaff," Ryder amended. "Unless there are two of that make and model here in

Desert Valley, which would be a huge coincidence." He gathered his supplies and rose.

Shane stood and squared his shoulders. His gaze held Gina's. "I didn't kill Veronica."

"Do you have an alibi?" Ryder asked.

"I was here with James until nine twenty." Which would have given him time enough to make it to the center and kill Veronica by nine forty, the estimated time of death. Acid burned in his gut. "Then I went for a walk."

"Did anyone see you?" Sophie asked, her tone hopeful.

Shane let out a relieved breath. "Yes. I saw a couple of home owners taking out their trash."

"I know you already surrendered your sidearm after today's discharge," Ryder said. "But until we can confirm your alibi, you'll need to stay away from the station."

His pronouncement grated on Shane's nerves. He hadn't intended to go to the station tomorrow. He'd planned to check the alibis of the people on the list the chief gave him from the training center. Even so, having Ryder say he wasn't allowed at the station, in front of Gina no less, made Shane's gut burn even worse.

"Could anyone else have opened the safe?" Gina's tone held a good dose of wariness. With the "evidence" at hand, he didn't blame her for doubting him. Especially after he'd practically accused her of Veronica's murder.

The dread in his veins bubbled hot when he realized whatever trust he and Gina had built in the past twenty-four hours had crumbled.

NINE

Gina stared at the square safe on the floor of Shane's bedroom closet and wasn't sure what to think. Shane had been so certain his gun was locked up tight inside the metal box. He'd been wrong. Had he used it to kill Veronica? What possible motive could he have? And why would he then leave it somewhere it would be easily found? That scenario didn't make sense.

Shane wasn't a killer. He was a smart man who liked order and logic.

But more than that, he was a man of integrity. She was as sure of his honor as she was her own name. Shane wouldn't have killed Veronica. That was Tim's doing.

She lifted her eyes to Shane. The distress on his handsome face was real and assured her he wasn't being deceptive.

Yet, she couldn't shake the unease spreading through her despite her conviction that Tim was the killer.

Not Shane. Or anyone else.

But then who took Shane's handgun? And had it been used to kill Veronica? If so, how on earth had Tim gained control of it?

Shane held her gaze. "Apparently, someone accessed the condo while James and I were out."

"Everyone knows there's a spare door key in the police station," Sophie said.

Gina nodded, grasping on to that thought. "That's true. And I don't believe the locks have ever been changed. At least not in the two years I've been working at the training center with rookies who've lived here."

"Someone who has stayed in the condo before could have kept a copy of the key," Ryder said.

"That's a lot of people," Sophie remarked dryly.

"So a lot of people could have done this." Shane shook his head in puzzlement. "Though why would someone want to frame me? And how would some past rookie even know about my grandfather's handgun or this safe? And how could they get my fingerprint to open the safe?"

The questions hung in the air like dark clouds threatening thunder and lightning. Gina didn't have answers, and, apparently, neither did the others.

A sound in the front of the condo had Shane, Ryder and Sophie visibly tensing. Gina moved closer to Shane.

A moment later, James, his T-shirt and running shorts drenched from his run, halted in the doorway. He blinked at them, obviously noting their tension. His eyebrows rose as he scanned them. "What's up?"

Shane explained the situation.

James frowned. "You don't think I had anything to do with this, do you?"

There was a heartbeat of silence before Shane shook his head. "No, I don't."

James turned his gaze to Ryder and arched an eyebrow.

"I'm not ruling anyone out," Ryder replied.

Sophie made a disparaging sound in her throat. "That's apparent."

Ryder widened his stance and stared Sophie down.

"Do you have a problem with the way I'm conducting this investigation?"

Gina hated how the situation was pitting them against each other. And from the manner in which Sophie squared her shoulders and met Ryder's glare with one of her own, Gina had no doubt things were only going to get worse.

"I don't like being repeatedly interrogated," Sophie ground out.

Needing to defuse the tension, Gina stepped forward. "This animosity isn't helping anyone. We know that my brother most likely killed Veronica and wants to harm me. He could have stolen the handgun hoping to get Shane into trouble. We know he was lurking outside the condo. I mean who else could it have been?"

Sophie cocked her head. "Well, there is the other murder to consider."

Ryder glanced at her sharply. "It's doubtful Melanie's murder is connected to Veronica's."

"Are you sure?" Sophie challenged. "I know you've been asked to reinvestigate her death as well as the other two rookies' accidents. And if those weren't accidents but murders…?"

"But the marks on the safe," Gina pointed out. "Tim could have succeeded in prying it open."

"Your logic is flawed." Shane's gentle tone inserted itself through the tension mounting in the room. "How would Tim even know about the gun? Even peeping through the curtains, there's no way he could have seen into the closet, let alone been able to get my print to open the safe. And we know he wasn't in Desert Valley when the other deaths happened, right?"

"No, he wasn't here. Tim was in Mesa when—" She

faltered, not wanting to cause Ryder pain at the mention of his wife's murder. "The other incidents occurred."

"Time to change the door locks and maybe even add a dead bolt," James said. "The idea that anyone could come and go as they please creeps me out."

"I agree," Ryder said. "I'll have Carrie make the arrangements."

"I can take care of it," James offered.

"The department will pay for it," Ryder said. "But it will need a signed work order."

James shrugged. "Okay. Whatever you say—you're the boss."

"Only temporarily while the chief's away," Ryder reminded him. He walked out of the room. In a line, they followed him to the living room.

Bella, Titus and Hawk lay near the sliding glass door. Both puppies played with chew toys nearby. Gina wished she'd had a camera handy because the animals made a cute picture. That would be even better if little Marco were here to complete the trio. A deep hurt burned inside of her. Where was Marco? Why hadn't someone come forward with him? *Please, Lord, let the little puppy be alive and safe somewhere.*

Ryder whistled. Titus struggled to his feet and trotted to Ryder's side. Once again Gina noticed Titus's odd gait. She exchanged a concerned glance with Sophie. Ryder may not want to acknowledge that Titus was getting on in years, but the dog definitely was having some hip trouble. Hip dysplasia wasn't uncommon in large-breed dogs. Now wasn't the time for her to discuss with Ryder the fact he would soon need a new partner.

Bella and Hawk stood, their gazes trained on their respective partners, as if waiting for the call to action. Gina was gratified to see both Shane and James use the training technique she'd taught them as each gave the hand motion that let the dogs know they weren't going to work.

It was the same hand motion that Veronica had objected to. She'd thought the signal would be too confusing for the dogs and the handlers because it closely mimicked the halt command and the separate lie-down command.

However, Gina didn't think combining the two signals with an added motion was confusing, and obviously the dogs and their partners didn't either.

With his hand on the doorknob, Ryder said, "Shane, I'll follow up on your alibi. Then we'll talk again." His gaze swept over the rest of them, lingered a moment on Sophie, and then he gave a slight nod before leaving the condo.

Sophie blew out a breath that sounded full of frustration. Gina refused to believe Ryder thought Sophie had anything to do with Veronica's death. Though Sophie did benefit with Veronica gone, since the chief had appointed Sophie as the lead trainer.

The position came with the use of the training center's SUV and an apartment above the facility, which Sophie didn't need since she had her own place.

However, she had no hesitation about the SUV and had started it using the morning after Veronica's murder. Though the thought of Sophie being a suspect didn't settle well with Gina. She refused to think badly of her friend. Tim had killed Veronica. There was no other explanation that made any sense.

"I should go, as well." Sophie touched Gina's arm. "You have my number. Call me if you need anything."

Grateful for her friendship, Gina nodded. "Thank you, Sophie. I will."

Left alone with Shane and James, Gina sought something to neutralize the strain filling the air. "You said something about steaks?"

Shane ran a hand through his hair. "Yes. I did."

"I'm going to the store," James announced "Do either of you need anything?"

"The makings for a salad," she said, thinking they needed something besides protein for dinner. "I'll get some cash."

James held up a hand. "I've got it." He whistled for Hawk and the two left the condo.

Shane moved to the kitchen to prep the steaks. Gina hesitated, torn between retreating to her room and wanting to be with Shane. She could only imagine the blow it must be to think someone had used his grandfather's handgun to kill Veronica.

Until the ballistics test proved conclusively that was indeed the case, Gina would keep hoping for the best.

However, the need to comfort Shane moved through her in a strong wave, and she found herself wanting to ease his worries.

But did she really want to get too involved with him?

Who was she kidding? She was already involved. He was her guardian protector until Tim was caught. And they'd kissed. Not that kissing signified a deeper connection, but whether she wanted to admit it or not, her heart was caught up with Shane. That was pretty involved, right?

She had to remember not to let things between Shane and her become personal. Or do anything that would lead to more kissing, no matter how much she'd enjoyed the one they'd shared. She knew he was only temporarily in her life. Once the cases were solved, he'd leave. Shaking her head at her preposterous thoughts, she pivoted and went in search of the pups.

After making sure they had sufficient water and food, Gina stepped into the kitchen, determined not to let Shane affect her. They were living in the same domicile for the moment; she had to overcome her awkwardness. Shane stood with his hands gripping the edge of the sink, his head bowed and his lips silently moving.

No doubt praying. Empathy swamped her. She hated seeing him so vulnerable. She started to back away but he lifted his head and turned toward her.

Reminding herself she had to keep things impersonal, she asked, "Can I help?"

Assisting him with something in the kitchen would distract her. After a beat of time, her words' double meaning made her press her lips together as heat spread up her neck and into her cheeks. She'd meant with the food, not with his emotional struggle. But to point that out would make too big a deal out of it, not to mention would be embarrassing.

His jaw tightened. The desolate expression in his green eyes tugged at her heart. She clasped her hands together to keep from reaching out to offer comfort.

He shook his head and pushed away from the counter. "Not much to do. I have the steaks marinating. I'll get the barbecue fired up."

He brushed past her, the air swirling with the force of his masculinity. He towered over her, yet she never felt intimidated by his size. Comforted, that's what she felt. Comfort and safety. Which were good, considering she was putting her life in his care.

She followed him to the patio with the puppies at her heels. Her gaze swept over the yard. The grass was dry and brittle but short, as if someone had recently mowed. James, she thought, since she and Shane hadn't been apart much all day.

Well, except for when she was in the training center and he'd been in a meeting with the other officers. She'd noticed earlier when she'd let the puppies out that one of the planks in the fence had been replaced with a newer one and nailed tightly down. Shane had said that whoever had been spying on them had broken one of the boards loose. She hoped the fix prevented any more unwanted visitors.

From her place at the counter, she could see Shane preparing the grill. His body language was anything but relaxed. His wide shoulders were hiked up and the muscles in his back bunched beneath his shirt. His movements were jerky as if he was struggling to go through the motions. Seeing his obvious upset overwhelmed her with the desire to ease his suffering. Her defenses were wobbling. One strong blow would bring them down for good.

But even if she could make him feel better, if she could rewind time and banish the situation, doing so would only leave her exposed and vulnerable.

She had to dig deep for the strength to resist the powerful draw she felt for Shane. Or they would both end up hurt in more ways than she wanted to think about.

After dinner, with Gina secured in her bedroom and Bella lying at the foot of her bed, Shane and James agreed to take turns on guard duty in case Tim Perry showed up at the condo.

James took the first shift. Shane tried to rest on his own bed though he remained fully dressed, but his mind wouldn't cooperate. Too many scenarios played in his head. Ones where he was charged and found guilty of a crime he hadn't committed. But the worst were of failing Gina.

When he did finally drift off, his nightmares were

filled with him being unable to protect her. Tim dragged her away. Terror contorted her face as she reached out to Shane and called his name.

Shane jerked awake, drenched in sweat, adrenaline fueling his fear as if he were still within the dream. But the cacophony of chaos assaulting his senses revealed his nightmares had followed him into reality.

Dogs barked. Glass shattered. Gina screamed his name.

James shouted, "Halt, police." This was followed by the sound of an engine roaring to life and tires screeching on pavement.

Heart pumping with panic, Shane jumped up and raced out of his room. He kicked open Gina's bedroom door. The sight that met him squeezed the air from his lungs.

Her room was on fire. Or rather her bed. Three arrows pierced the thick bedding and flames licked at the comforter, threatening to engulf the whole room if Shane didn't put them out quick. Smoke and ash filled the room along with a sugary sweet scent that was out of place.

Gina struggled to free the puppies from their crates. Her long red hair flowed down the back of her pink robe. Her bare feet stuck out beneath.

Shane let out a relieved breath to see her unharmed. But he needed to put out the fire. He grabbed a decorative blanket Gina used as a throw from the back of the corner chair and beat at the flames.

One of the puppies got loose. Bella grabbed the pup by the scruff of the neck and carried him out while Gina hugged the other pup to her chest. For a moment she stood still, her gaze fixated on the flames.

"Get out of here!" Shane shouted.

She turned and fled. A moment later James ran into the room with a fire extinguisher. He sprayed the remaining embers with white foam. Smoke billowed out of the broken window.

Once the flames were completely out, Shane inspected the bolts. Two had the remnants of steel scrubbing pads wrapped around the tips. The third arrow, not a bolt, had a charred, gooey substance melted on its end and on the bedcover.

"There were two perps," James informed him. "They got away in a car a block down the street. I didn't get a good look at them or the vehicle. They'd broken out the street lamp."

"It had to be Tim Perry and he's got himself a buddy," Shane said. He touched the sticky mess on the bed and brought a sample to his nose. "What in the world? Marshmallow?"

"I know, right? The exterior wall took two marshmallow hits," James said.

"Can you call this in?" Shane asked. "I'm going to check on Gina." He found her in the living room, hunkered down on the floor in front of the couch with Bella and the puppies. He crouched down beside her. "We put the fire out. It's okay."

She lifted her gaze. Her eyes were wide and her pupils large. "Tim tried to burn me alive."

Shane gathered her in his arms. "But he didn't. No Gina flambé today. Though the marshmallows were a nice touch."

She slapped at his arm with a snort. "Thanks a lot."

"Hey, it could have been worse."

She trembled in his arms. "The first arrow broke through the glass and landed near my feet and woke me. I jumped out of bed before the other two arrows came through the broken window."

He hated to think what would have happened had the

bolts found their target. He kissed Gina's hair. He was grateful she was alive and uninjured. But it could have gone so wrong. He banished the terror from his nightmares turned reality and vowed he would not fail Gina. Her brother would not succeed in hurting her, not on his watch.

The next morning Shane and Bella escorted Gina to the training center. They were both exhausted. Neither had slept after the flaming arrows. They'd disposed of the burned bedding and mattress after Ryder and Harmon had collected and bagged the arrows. The chief surmised that Tim had used a battery attached to his bow to ignite the steel scrubbing pads. No one had any answers as to why Tim and his cohort had shot burning marshmallows at the house.

First thing that morning, Shane had Carrie, the station secretary, order a new mattress and bedding for the condo. Now Shane carried with him the list of potential suspects in Veronica's murder that he needed to call, since yesterday's efforts had been a bust. Not that he thought anyone but Tim Perry was the culprit. Still, he'd been given a job to do. The few people he'd been able to get ahold of yesterday had alibis, which he verified. But no one had been overly upset about Veronica's death. How sad was that?

Granted, he didn't get along great with his family due to his inability to fit into their idea of the perfect path a lawman should take. Still, he hoped he'd be mourned a little more deeply when his time came.

He planned to work inside the training center while Gina did her thing with the puppies. That way he and Bella could keep her under their watchful eyes. There was still no clue about Marco's whereabouts, and he knew the fate of the missing puppy weighed heavily on Gina. On all of them. He sent up a quick prayer for the pup's safety.

Sitting on a bleacher near the door where he had an unobstructed view of her and the two high-spirited puppies, he used his cell phone to make calls. The first name on his list he'd been unable to reach yesterday was Dr. Pennington, Veronica's ex-husband.

The chief had already conversed with the man, but wanted Shane to follow up to see if there was any change in the doctor's alibi.

In most murder cases the spouse, or ex-spouse as in this case, was first on the list of suspects. Despite believing Tim Perry was the murderer, the police department had to do due diligence.

Shane watched Gina work while the phone rang. She had such a lovely and lively face. She was more relaxed when she was with the puppies. More like she'd been in their training class.

Today she wore a kelly green long-sleeve top with tan-colored pants. Her long red curls were tamed back with a ribbon. He liked it when she let her hair hang loose about her shoulders. It looked so soft. He tightened his hand on the phone, fighting the urge to go to her and release the ribbon.

"Hello?" The deep male voice boomed in Shane's ear.

Shaking his head to clear his focus, Shane asked, "Is this Dr. Pennington?"

"Yes, it is. Who is this? I don't usually receive calls on this line."

"This is Officer Shane Weston with the Desert Valley police," Shane began. "We—"

"I've already talked to Chief Jones," the doctor stated firmly. "I have an alibi for the time of Veronica's death that Jones was supposed to substantiate."

Shane looked at the chief's note. "Yes, I see that you were in the emergency room at the Canyon County Medical Center at the time of Veronica's murder, and a nurse and another doctor have corroborated your story."

The doctor certainly didn't seem too upset by his ex's death. He could have hired someone to kill Veronica. But that didn't explain Shane's missing gun. He prayed it wasn't the one used to murder Veronica.

"It's not a story, it's the truth." The doctor's voice shook with rage. "Clearly, I need to speak with the chief."

"You could do that, sir, but he's awfully busy solving a murder. Your ex-wife's," Shane added. "We will leave no rock unturned in our investigation."

Dr. Pennington sniffed. "Well, I'm sure you'll be turning over many rocks and uncovering many lizards in Veronica's past. But I wasn't involved and would appreciate if you'd leave me alone." The doctor hung up.

Shane put a check mark beside Pennington's name. The next couple of calls were to Veronica's hairdresser and her dentist. Both had alibis, which Shane verified, and both at least had expressed some sympathy for the deceased.

"Hey," Gina said when she came over to sit beside him. "I completely forgot that I have a commitment this afternoon at the library."

Shane tensed. "Cancel."

"I knew that was going to be your reaction." Her hazel eyes took on a determined gleam. "You told me not to let my brother have power over me. If I cancel, then I'm giving Tim power over my life by flaking out on my commitment."

Not liking to have his words come back to bite him, Shane pinched the bridge of his nose. He appreciated and

admired her desire to fulfill her commitments. But…
"What is it you have to do?"

"Today is story time in the children's wing of the library."

He tucked his chin in confusion. "And you want to go listen to fairy tales?"

She laughed. "No, silly. I read the stories to the kids. I've been doing it every week since I arrived in town. It's my way of giving back to the community."

He hadn't known she did that. Knowing her wish for a family, her time with the kids must be precious to her. His respect and admiration for her increased. But he couldn't allow it.

"Take today off," Shane said. "You don't want to put all those kids in jeopardy."

A little V appeared between her brows. "Of course not."

"There you go."

The sparkle in her eyes dimmed. She scratched Bella behind the ears. The dog nearly climbed in her lap.

"You're right, of course. I want this to end. I want Tim caught so I can resume my life."

He hated to see Gina's disappointment and could sympathize with her. No one like having their freedom restricted, especially when it was taken away in such a dramatic fashion. He wished there was a way to make her smile again. His gaze snagged on her lush lips. Smooth and soft. The remembered feel of them against his own mouth reared through his brain. Suddenly the collar of his shirt was too constricting. He gave it a good tug but that didn't alleviate his discomfort.

Her cell phone rang. She brightened as she glanced at the caller ID. "Whitney," she said aloud to him before she pressed answer. "Hi, Whitney." She listened for a moment then glanced at Shane. "I think so. Let me clear it with my shadow."

Shane made a face at her teasing jab, which elicited a smile, and the impact speared through him like a ray of sunshine, heating him from the inside out.

Covering the phone's mouthpiece with her hand, Gina explained, "Whitney has a meeting with the chief, and her babysitter is not feeling well. She'd like for me to watch Shelby for an hour or so. That okay with you?"

He appreciated her asking and he knew she was chafing at having to ask permission for something that she'd normally agree to without any reservations. "We could meet her at the station and watch the baby there."

Gina gave a small roll of her eyes. "My shadow says we'll meet you at the station. I'll bring the puppies." Gina laughed at something Whitney said. "Okay. See you then." She hung up, tucked her phone away and then rubbed her hands together in apparent glee. "I get some baby time."

The sparkle in her eyes nearly undid him. His chest constricted. His breathing hitched, but the cause wasn't his asthma—it was the woman in front of him. She took his breath away.

He cleared his throat in an attempt to calm his racing pulse. "I'll call Ryder to let him know we're heading over."

"Great." She pirouetted away to herd the puppies out of the training room. "I'll ask Sophie if we can take the center's vehicle," she said over her shoulder.

He jumped to his feet and followed her while dialing the nonemergency number for the Desert Valley police station. He watched her coax the puppies into the crate with treats and then step into Sophie's office out of his line of sight. His breathing finally eased.

Carrie Dunleavy answered the station phone. Shane asked for Ryder.

"One moment, please," Carrie said and then music filled the line and tension flooded Shane.

A moment later Ryder was on the phone. "Weston, I was just about to call you. The Flagstaff crime scene techs will be doing the ballistics test today," Ryder informed him.

Shane's stomach dropped. If the ammo in his grandfather's handgun matched the .45 slugs taken out of Veronica's body... Acid burned beneath his breastbone. "How soon...?"

"They said they'd have results by this evening."

Shane clenched his jaw. It took effort to ask, "Were you able to confirm my alibi?"

"As a matter of fact, yes."

Shane rested a hand against the wall for support as relief rushed over him. He sent up a silent prayer of thanksgiving. "That's good. Gina and I are headed over to the station now. Whitney needs someone to watch her little girl while she meets with the chief."

"Ah. I'll see you soon then."

Shane hung up, feeling the weight on his shoulders lighten. Gina stepped out of Sophie's office.

Concern dimmed her smile. "Is everything okay?"

"Yes." He straightened and shoved his phone into his pocket. "My alibi checked out."

He needed to make sure she knew, though why it was important to him to dispel any doubts she might have about him was a mystery. He told himself it was because, as her protector, he needed her to trust him. And knowing he wasn't a viable suspect would go a long way toward building that trust again.

"I knew your alibi would prove you innocent," she

stated with certainty, and stepped close to unexpectedly hug him.

His heart thumped as he slipped his arms around her. Holding her felt so right, so natural. The fresh floral scent of her shampoo teased his nose and her hair felt silky against his cheek. He didn't want to let her go, but he did. Stepping back, he shoved his hands into his pants pocket.

She ducked her head, but he noted the pink brightening her cheeks. She bent to scoop up the puppies and handed him one. The fluffy ball of fur licked his face before he could tuck the squirming bundle under his arm. Gina's laugh invaded his heart and stole his breath once again.

He had to concentrate to force his legs to move. He carried the puppy and followed Gina out of the building.

"Tim killed Veronica to get to me. You had nothing to do with her death." She placed her free hand on his arm. Her touch sent a ribbon of warmth curling through him.

He covered her hand with his own. Their fingers entwined. He lifted her knuckles to his lips. "Thank you for believing in me."

"Always." She sounded breathless.

Did he do that to her? He leaned closer, wanting, needing to kiss her. Her lips parted in silent invitation. His breath grew erratic as he slowly touched his lips to hers.

One of the puppies yelped, breaking the enthralling moment. He jerked back. She gave a nervous laugh and turned away. Disappointment fisted in his gut. He'd have liked to continue kissing her. Her lips were so soft and tasted like the cherry ChapStick she wore.

He helped secure the puppies in one crate then secured Bella in the second and tried to pick up the conversation where they'd veered off. "Though my alibi checked out I'm not in the clear yet. If my grandfather's gun was used to do the deed the chief would have to investigate whether I hired someone else to kill her."

She walked around to the passenger side and stopped to let him open the door. As she slid into the vehicle, she said, "Yeah, that's a sticky wicket, isn't it? But I know it will work out in the end. You'll be proven innocent."

"Yes, it is, and I pray you are right." Anger at whoever took his gun churned within him as his chest bound up, making his lungs feel too big. He paused, breathing in and out through his nose in an effort to regain some calm.

There wasn't anything he could do about the person who'd stolen his gun until they apprehended the culprit.

Giving the anger any room only set him up for more stress. He shut the passenger door and walked around to the driver's side. His gaze snagged on movement near the tree line. The vague shape of a person shifted in the shadows.

The instinct to give chase was strong. From the back compartment of the SUV, Bella let out a loud series of barks. Clearly, the dog had seen the same thing as Shane. But he had to fight the urge to release Bella and go after the person trying to hide in the trees. Keeping Gina safe was his priority.

He yanked open the driver's door. "Get down," he instructed Gina as he slid onto the seat, keeping his gaze trained on the dark woods. There. Yes. Someone was in the woods skulking around. He grabbed his cell and dialed 911.

The dispatcher answered. "What is your emergency?"

"This is Officer Weston. Requesting backup at the Canyon County Training Center. I may have spotted Tim Perry, suspect in a homicide case, in the woods behind the center."

"I'll send officers to your location."

TEN

Gina hunkered down on the passenger side of the Canyon County Training Center's SUV. Her heart hammered against her ribs, creating a thunderous beat that banged through her body. Had Shane really spotted Tim? Would Tim show himself again so soon? Was her brother more bent on hurting her than concerned about being caught?

Beside her, Shane slid down, making himself less of a target. The thought of Tim shooting a crossbow bolt into the vehicle filled her with dread. She'd been spared the last time by the grace of God. The bolt hadn't pierced all the way through the back of the truck's cab and embedded itself in her flesh. Her muscles tensed and she fisted her hands.

Please, Lord, have mercy on me. On Shane, she silently pleaded with God. *Again.*

She remembered the promise she'd made to God when she'd been quivering with fear in the training center, sure that Tim would find and kill her. She'd promised she'd resume going to church, would study her Bible and spend time in prayer.

Shame washed over her. Not once since then had she thought about her promise. She didn't want to call on God only in times of distress. Where was her praise and thanksgiving when life wasn't fair or neat and tidy? Why did she wait to reach out to the Lord when her life was on the line? She was like David from the Bible. God constantly provided and protected David and yet his faith had been weak and he doubted God at every turn.

She vowed to keep her promise. She just needed to live long enough to do it.

Within moments, the screech of sirens announcing the arrival of the Desert Valley Police Department echoed through the SUV, stirring the puppies into a barking frenzy. She longed to comfort them. They were scared by the chaos. So was she.

"Stay out of sight," Shane advised before sliding out of the vehicle.

She couldn't stand not seeing what was happening. Mindful of Shane's warning, she inched up enough to peek over the top of the dash. Shane conversed with Officer Bucks and Officer Ryder Hayes. Sophie came out of the training center and joined them.

A second later, Ryder and his yellow Lab, Titus, hurried toward the woods with Bucks and Sophie trailing behind them. Gina noticed Titus's odd gait as if his hips were bothering him. Something she'd have to mention to the officer. It wouldn't be good for Titus or Ryder if the dog couldn't perform his duties because of his hips.

Shane returned to the SUV and slid down as best he could, despite the steering wheel in his way. "We'll sit tight while they secure the area. I doubt your brother stuck around, but Ryder wants to be sure."

Her legs were beginning to cramp and the door handle dug into her back. She wasn't sure how much longer she could stay crouched on the SUV's floor. She shifted, trying to find a more comfortable position.

At Shane's curious glance, she said, "I'm cramped and freaked-out and angry."

With a gentle hand, Shane smoothed back a chunk of her hair that had fallen over her eyes. Her skin tingled where his fingers lightly touched her forehead.

"It won't be much longer," he said. "I promise."

She wanted to believe him, though she knew he was referring to being trapped on the floor of the SUV. She wanted to believe the police would find and arrest Tim quickly. But so far he'd evaded capture. And as long as he was out there, she wasn't safe.

A knock on the window startled her. She let out a small yelp.

"It's Ryder," Shane said as he straightened and popped open the door.

Relieved, she crawled out from under the dash. Sophie went back inside the training center while Bucks leaned against the police-issue cruiser to wait for Ryder.

"Nothing," Ryder said. "Titus didn't alert on any scent either. And the ground's too dry for footprints. Are you sure you saw a person?"

"Someone was in the woods." There was no mistaking the frustration and disappointment in Shane's tone, because the same emotions choked Gina. "It had to be Tim Perry."

"If it was, he's gone now," Ryder stated.

A muscle in Shane's jaw flexed but he didn't respond. She was proud of Shane. No good would come from him arguing with Ryder. They were on the same side. She leaned toward the open driver's-side door to see Ryder. "Thank you, Ryder."

Ryder nodded at her. "No problem." He and Bucks left.

Shane slid back behind the wheel. "Sorry about that. I know what I saw."

She laid a hand on his arm to show her support. "I believe you."

The muscles of his forearm flexed as he gripped the steering wheel. "I'm not sure Ryder did."

"He has no reason to doubt you."

"Right." He started the SUV and she buckled up. As they drove through town toward the police station, Gina noted with gratefulness that the police presence didn't decrease. Ryder followed close behind in his vehicle.

"I'm a little on edge," Shane admitted.

Understatement. "Aren't we all? A lot is going on. Veronica's murder is hanging over all of us. Your grandfather's special handgun is in question and my brother could be lurking around any corner," she pointed out. "But I appreciate your diligence."

"Thanks." He sent her a smile full of gratitude that curled around her heart.

She lifted a shoulder, trying not to let on how much she cared about him. "It's true. I didn't even think to look at the forest. But it makes sense that Tim would use the cover of trees to hide in. It's been his thing for some time. He'd take refuge in the park after a particularly bad manic episode. Dad had tried to interest him in wilderness training, but Tim was more interested in archery. Hence the use of the crossbow. He traded up from the harmless target archery set Dad bought him to the very deadly weapon that has become so popular in recent years."

"The woods. I wonder if he's holed up in the Desert Pines campground."

"I doubt he'd be somewhere that public, but maybe."

"It's worth having the campground ranger take a look around. I'll ask Carrie to send the ranger Tim's photo."

"Good idea." She appreciated Shane's proactive way.

At the station, Shane backed into the parking stall near the side entrance. Gina put a harness around each pup and held tight to the leash as both sprinted for a patch of grass. Bella followed the puppies, herding them to keep them from straining at their leads. It was so sweet the way the older dog's natural instinct was to protect and guide the two younger canines.

Officer Louise Donaldson pushed open the door to the side entrance. Tall and solidly built, she wore her short-sleeved, navy-colored uniform, complete with utility belt.

A badge pinned over the left side of Louise's chest gleamed in the spring sun. Her short brown bobbed hair had streaks of silver that glinted in the sunlight. If not for the graying hair, Gina would believe Louise to be younger than her sixty-plus years.

"Hey, I was heading out on a coffee run," Louise said. "You two want anything?"

"I'm good," Shane replied.

Gina smiled at the older woman while coaxing the puppies to the entrance. "No, thank you. Do you know if Whitney has arrived yet?"

Louise shrugged. "Haven't a clue."

Gina managed to get both puppies to the door. Lucy sniffed at Louise's shoes while Ricky chased his tail, twisting the leash around Gina's hand.

Louise's gaze softened on the puppies. "They sure are cute. But I'm glad I'm not the one taking care of them. They seem like a lot of work."

Gina didn't mind the work. "They are well worth the time and energy."

"If you say so." Louise slipped past the dogs and headed toward town.

Once inside the police station, Gina and Shane found Whitney with her four-month-old, Shelby, already in the break room. A stroller was pushed into the corner with a bright pink diaper bag hanging from the handle.

Whitney bounced Shelby on her knees. The baby giggled. The sound rippled through Gina, making her heart ache for a child of her own to love.

"You both came," Whitney said as they entered the break room. "Thank you so much." Her gaze went to the puppies. "They are so cute!"

The curious puppies sniffed the floor at Whitney's feet where a blob of spit-up had fallen. Gina gently steered the puppies from the mess with the lure of a treat. She gave the hand motion for the pups to sit and was gratified when both obeyed. So smart.

Bella also sat and strained her nose forward. Gina rewarded all three with a treat. Ricky took it in his mouth then dropped it. His sister swooped in and gobbled it up.

The baby giggled at the dogs' antics.

"I'll clean that mess up before I head to my meeting." Whitney stood and handed Shane her baby.

The surprise on Shane's face made Gina's chest constrict. He held the squirming cherub by the torso and at arms' length as if he didn't quite know what to do with her. He obviously had little experience with babies. Whitney seemed not to notice his discomfort as she grabbed paper towels.

Shane's panicked gaze met Gina's. He extended the baby toward her. "Here."

Laughing, she used her free arm to secure Shelby close to her body while handing him the puppies' leashes.

His grateful smile devastated her senses. He gazed at her with tenderness in his eyes. "You're a natural with her."

A blush crept into her cheeks. "Thanks."

Whitney tossed the soiled paper towels into the garbage. "I so appreciate you two doing this for me. My regular babysitter, Marilyn, is sick and I want to protect Shelby from catching a bug."

"Not a problem," Gina took the seat Whitney had vacated. Settling Shelby on her lap with her back pressed against her abdomen, Gina felt a contentment she'd rarely experienced before. Motherhood was a concept that seemed so far out of her reach.

Whitney said to Gina, "I'll just be down the hall if you need anything." She kissed Shelby on the forehead before hurrying from the room.

"Can you check the stroller for a toy or a book?" Gina asked Shane.

He found a set of plastic keys and several board books. "Here you go."

As she took them from him, their fingers brushed. His skin was warm and the contact sent a charge of attraction zipping along her arm. Strange how even such a harmless touch from Shane could set her nerves on high alert. She'd never had that happen with anyone else.

Shane pulled a chair close and sat while he motioned for Bella to do the same. The puppies wandered within the limits of their leashes, which kept them from getting too far out of reach.

Taking one of the board books, her own childhood favorite, *Goodnight Moon*, Gina held it up for Shelby to see.

Focusing on the book, she began to read. Awareness of Shane watching her intently made her stumble over the words. A flutter of nerves hit her without warning. She had to stop herself from touching her hair to make sure she looked good.

Giving herself a mental shake, she stared at the page, but she couldn't remember if she'd read the page already or not.

As she tried to make sense of the words, her heart beat erratically. She chanced a quick peek at Shane. He raised his eyebrow slightly and smiled encouragingly. She couldn't stop her own smile. Man, oh, man. She'd never been self-conscious when she'd read to kids in the past. At the library there would be thirty or so children and parents attuned to her every word and not once had she'd lost her focus. But for some reason Shane messed with her ability to concentrate.

Clearing her throat, she flipped the page and forced Shane from her awareness, though every cell in her body was hypersensitive to his perusal.

She needed to get a grip. Now. Letting herself get all fluttery over Shane wasn't a smart idea. But she had a feeling that controlling her response to him was going to be about as easy as finding shade in the desert.

Nearly impossible.

Shane settled back in the hard plastic chair of the Desert Valley police station's break room with Bella and the puppies lying at his feet. The puppies fell asleep while Bella kept her alert gaze on Gina and the baby as if she, too, were fascinated with the pair. Shane couldn't take his eyes off Gina.

She looked so complete and natural with the baby on her lap. The little girl's chubby legs kicked in apparent joy as Gina read. Her voice was both alive and yet so soothing.

A strange yearning filled Shane as he drank in Gina. It wasn't anxiety, which usually brought on the feeling of constriction in his midsection. His inhaler wouldn't banish what was causing his insides to compress and expand. Affection bloomed within him. She really was a special lady.

He thought about her fear of becoming like her brother. Shane didn't know the physiological or the psychological implications of her twin's mental illness, but he couldn't see her ever making the choice to hurt another person.

She wasn't wired like that. Nurturing was in her nature, a part of her makeup. Despite whatever stray component of DNA that made Tim Perry the man he was, Gina hadn't been afflicted with it. She was good, kind and compassionate. It hurt Shane to think she didn't know that or believe it.

A foul odor filled the break room. Shane's gaze dropped immediately to the puppies, but both were curled up next to Bella fast asleep.

"It's Shelby," Gina said with a wry twist to her lips. "She's soiled her diaper. Can you grab her bag for me?"

"Of course." He jumped up and fetched the pink bag.

Gina pushed the baby into his hands so she could dig through the bag for a diaper, wipes and a changing cloth. His eyes watered at the baby's stench but the happy little girl didn't seem to notice the smell. She twisted her head to look at him with her bright green eyes. She babbled as her legs kicked. She really was a cutie.

After spreading out a padded changing cloth, Gina took the baby from him and laid her on her back on the pad.

"Whew," he said. "That's toxic."

Gina's laugh curled around his heart. "Have you never changed a baby's diaper?"

"That would be a negative," he answered with a shudder, but he watched with fascination as Gina made quick work of the task.

"What a good baby you are," Gina crooned. "I love your bright green eyes." She cocked her head. "Hmm. They remind me of someone."

"Whitney?" Shane threw out. He couldn't remember what color the other rookies' eyes were.

"No," Gina said, her voice puzzled.

"The baby's daddy?"

Gina pursed her lips. "Whitney has never named the father as far as I know but…" She shrugged. "It's none of my business." She wrapped the soiled diaper in a plastic baggie. "Can you watch her while I dispose of this and wash my hands?"

"Uh, sure." His heart raced. "What do I do?"

"Pick her up and sit with her on your lap, like I was doing. You can do it, I have faith in you." She walked from the room, taking the dirty diaper with her.

Good thing someone had faith in him. He stared at the sweet child and shook his head. Taking care of a baby wasn't what he'd expected to be doing in Desert Valley. Nor had he expected to be assigned to protect such a caring and loving woman as Gina.

Feeling inept, he lifted the baby and held her at eye level. Shelby cooed little bubbles of spit that made him laugh. "Hello, Miss Shelby." He sat back in his chair and turned the baby to face outward, setting her on his lap and drawing her up against his chest. Warmth spread through him. This wasn't so bad. He held out the plastic ring of keys for her tiny hands to grasp. A nursery rhyme his mother used to sing to him and his brothers when they were kids played through his head.

He softly gave voice to the words.

He sensed Gina's gaze and looked up to see her standing in the doorway. Her hazel eyes were soft with tenderness and joy. She was so beautiful it made his chest ache. He was happy to see delight on her face rather than the fear he'd seen earlier. He never wanted her to fear again.

But that wouldn't happen until Tim was apprehended. In the meantime, Shane would keep Gina safe. But would his heart stay as safe?

The next morning, Gina awoke to two whining puppies who needed to go outside. She slipped on a pair of sweatpants and a pullover hoodie sweatshirt and opened the bedroom door. The scent of rich coffee permeated the air. Shane was talking in an intense tone. She hesitated, not wanting to interrupt him, but before she could close the door the puppies raced down the hall. She hurried after them.

Shane stood in the kitchen, talking on his cell phone. He had on drawstring cotton pants and a white T-shirt. His hair was a spiky mess and he needed a shave, but she thought he'd never looked better. Her pulse sped up and she quickly smoothed a hand over her own hair, wishing she'd taken a moment to run a brush through the thick strands.

Still on the phone, Shane reached the sliding door before she could and opened it. The puppies ran outside to the fenced yard. Bella, who'd been lying on the carpet in the living room, rose and followed the puppies into the backyard. He left the slider open so the dogs could enter when they wanted.

"Dad, I gotta go," Shane said into the phone. "Give Mom my love." He hung up and laid the phone on the counter. He closed his eyes for a moment as if in pain.

Concern lanced through her. "Everything okay?"

Shane opened his eyes and met her gaze. "Yes. That was my dad. He's not happy about my extended service here in Desert Valley. He's trying to pull strings to bring me to Flagstaff."

"Which is what you want, right?"

"I did." He frowned. "I do." He ran his hand through his tousled hair. "I don't know."

He'd been so sure during the training sessions. All he could talk about was joining the Flagstaff PD to serve under his father. What had changed? A little flutter of hope wanted to think maybe he didn't want to leave her. But she quickly shot that thought down. But they'd kissed. Twice. That had to mean he had feelings beyond obligation for her, right?

"I need coffee," he said, distracting her from her wayward thoughts. "Would you care for some?"

"Yes, please." She filled the dogs' bowls with food and set them out on the patio.

"Did you sleep okay?" he asked as she returned to the kitchen.

"I did, surprisingly," she answered. Though it had taken her a bit to fall asleep, once she had, she'd slept hard without dreaming. She took a seat on one of the bar stools. "Thank you again for helping me with Shelby yesterday. I think she was taken with you and Bella."

"And the puppies," Shane said with a smile as he grabbed two mugs from a cupboard.

"Yes, they were a hit."

"It was fun," he said in a tone that suggested he was surprised.

"You were good with her," she remarked.

One side of his mouth lifted in a self-effacing smile. "That was the most time I've ever spent with a baby."

"Really?" She wouldn't have guessed that. "You did a great job."

"Thanks. You were magnificent with her. A natural. I, on the other hand, felt very afraid I'd drop her."

"That's not unusual the first time you hold a baby, but you get used to it. Don't sell yourself short," she said.

"You handled Shelby beautifully. You'll make a great father one day." Her heart spasmed. But who would be his children's mother?

"Yeah, I don't think so."

She frowned. "You don't want a family?"

He paused. "Normally, that would be an automatic no. But now after taking care of Bella…" He shrugged. "Maybe." He poured coffee into a mug. "After watching you with the puppies and little Shelby, I know you'll make a great mother."

His words brought a pang to her heart. She wanted children, a family to call her own. But the risk of passing on the faulty DNA that afflicted her brother would prevent her from ever fulfilling that dream. Shane's words reverberated through her mind. *Stop being a martyr.*

She wasn't. She was being realistic.

"Remember that day last week at the training center when you and Whitney were talking about children? You want five kids, right?"

He'd overheard their conversation. Embarrassment rushed up her neck in a wave of heat. "Doesn't hurt to want." She slipped off the bar stool to grab the loaf of bread. "Toast?"

"So do you?"

"Want toast? Yes." She popped two slices into the toaster. "You?"

His look said he knew what she was doing and wasn't going to let her get away with distracting him. "I mean do you want five kids?"

She settled back on the bar stool and set her elbow on the counter. Resting her chin in her hand, she sighed. "I don't think it's realistic of me to want kids of my own."

"Excuse me? Why would you say that?"

"Bad genes, remember?"

The toaster popped and he moved to retrieve the toast. As he buttered the slices, he said, "That sounds like a convenient excuse to me."

Irritated by his comment, she straightened. "It's a valid consideration."

"Maybe, maybe not."

"I told you, mental illness runs in my mother's family. I don't want to perpetuate it."

"You can't be sure you would."

"My mother's sister was also diagnosed with schizoaffective disorder. She was institutionalized when she was twenty-five. She killed herself on her thirtieth birthday."

"That's rough." Sympathy tinged the green in his eyes. "But your mother wasn't afflicted. Right? Heredity may be a factor, but fearing that something might happen when you really have no control over *if* something will happen is no way to live your life. I think this is where faith comes in. You need to believe God is in control."

She wanted to trust God, to let Him be in control of her life, but it was hard to do. The fear seemed too big, too overwhelming. How could faith banish the fear? A memory surfaced, long buried beneath the anguish and grief of losing her family. "'God has not given us a spirit of fear, but of power, of love, of a sound mind.'" She repeated the words she'd once heard her father recite to her mother.

"Exactly," Shane said with a pleased smile. "Second Timothy, chapter one, verse seven."

"You know your Bible."

He nodded. "Mom took us to church every Sunday, and summers there was vacation Bible school, then day camps and eventually overnight camps. Some far away. The best were the weeklong camps in the milder climate of South Lake Tahoe in the Sierra Nevada Mountains of California."

They'd had such different upbringings. "I volunteered at the animal shelter during school breaks, though we attended church on Sunday mornings as a family. I would have liked to go to the mountains. We didn't travel or even get out of the city much." She sighed. "I keep meaning to explore around here. Just haven't made time." Or felt like going alone. But she couldn't admit that to him.

He reached across the bar to take her hand. The warmth of his skin shot through her, making her overly hot.

"Once this is all over we can plan a day hike," he said. "We can take the dogs."

She blinked back sudden tears. She longed to take him up on the offer. "That would be nice, if you're still in Desert Valley…"

"Good." Shane withdrew his hand, taking his warmth with him. She wrapped her hands around the full mug of coffee he'd set in front of her. He moved to the refrigerator and took out a carton of eggs. "Do you like your eggs scrambled or fried?"

"Whatever is easiest." She was unused to having someone cater to her needs. It felt strange to sit idle while he cooked.

Wanting to take the focus off her, she said, "You mentioned you have brothers. I didn't think to ask, are they younger than you?"

"No. They're older. Mitchell is thirty-five and Jeremiah is thirty-one. Both are single and both are on the job in Flagstaff."

"So you're the baby of the family."

"Yep. And a disappointment to my dad."

That was out of the blue. "What do you mean?"

He scrubbed a hand over his jaw. "Whoa, I can't believe I said that out loud."

"Why do you believe you're a disappointment?"

"Unlike the other men in my family, I didn't make it in the military."

That was surprising. "What happened?"

"Asthma."

"You have asthma?" She'd seen no indication of a breathing problem while working with him and Bella.

"I do. It flares up occasionally. Stress can trigger an attack and so can allergens. But the military won't take someone who's had an asthma diagnosis after the age of 13."

"I didn't know that. But asthma didn't prevent you from completing the police academy."

"No, it didn't. Thankfully." He set a plate of fluffy scrambled eggs in front of her.

"Your dad has to be proud of you for becoming a police officer like him," she reasoned.

He shrugged. "I suppose. Though he'd rather I went the traditional route of patrol, then detective. Being a K-9 officer wasn't what he had in mind."

"Did you always want to be in law enforcement?"

He shook his head. "No. When I was a kid I wanted to be a veterinarian."

"Really? Why didn't you become one?"

"Because I went the way of expectations. I wanted my family's approval. And their respect."

Her heart hurt to realize he wasn't living the life he wanted. "If you don't want to be a police officer then you shouldn't be. You need to find what makes you happy and not worry about what your family wants. They'll respect you for being your own person."

He paused, cocking his head to the side. "The strange

thing is, I like police work and I want to excel at it. For me, not just for them."

That statement made her feel somewhat better. "You and Bella work well together."

"Thanks." He grinned. "We had great training."

She laughed, pleased by the compliment.

His cell phone vibrated against the counter, drawing not only their attention but Bella's, as well. She entered through the open slider with the puppies following closely behind. Gina liked how the older dog was teaching the younger ones. Bella sat at the ready as Shane answered the call.

"Weston."

He visibly tensed. "We're on our way." He signed off quickly. "That was the chief. Apparently someone has taken the clerk at the Sun Break minimart hostage. The perp fits the description of your brother."

Her breath caught. Oh, no. A hostage. *Please, Lord, don't let Tim hurt the person.*

Could they finally capture and arrest Tim? Would she finally be free of his threats? She slid off the stool. "I'll be ready in five."

He nodded. They both hurried to their respective rooms to change. The Sun Break was a small mom-and-pop convenience store on the outskirts of town. She sent up a plea that God wouldn't allow Tim to hurt anyone else the way he had Veronica. And that her brother would be caught once and for all.

ELEVEN

Shane brought his vehicle to an abrupt halt at the perimeter of the barricade around the Sun Break minimart made by three Desert Valley police cruisers. Officers Harmon, Bucks and Marlton crouched behind the vehicles with their weapons aimed at the minimart's front door.

Chief Jones and Officer Ryder Hayes and his partner, Titus, were off to one side. Both men wore flak vests with the initials DVPD across the front and back. They had a blueprint of the store spread out on the back end of the Desert Valley K-9 Unit vehicle. Ryder had his cell phone to his ear.

"Stay here and lock the doors," Shane advised Gina. Since everyone had been called out, there was no one left at the station in a position to adequately protect her. He didn't want her in the line of fire. If Tim caught sight of her, he might take a shot at her.

"I might be able help," she countered. "Tim may let the hostages go in exchange for me."

"That's not happening," Shane practically growled as a tight fist of dread clasped his heart and squeezed. "There's no way I'm letting you sacrifice yourself. We'll get him out without anyone getting hurt."

"Though I love your optimism, you can't guarantee someone won't get hurt." She popped open her door. "I'd rather it not be an innocent bystander."

"Gina!" Shane made a grab for her, but she was too quick. She was out of the vehicle and hurrying toward the chief.

Infused with frustration, he exited the Jeep, briefly touching the butt of his sidearm, thankful the chief had released it back to him. He released Bella from the back, quickly leashing her before following Gina to where Chief Jones and Ryder stood. Shane was glad they'd taken the time to drop the puppies off with Sophie, though he could tell the ex-cop had wanted to ride along with them.

Chief Jones glanced their way. "He's barricaded the door. We've tried to reach him on the store's landline, but he won't answer. So we've resorted to the bullhorn." He held up the white horn.

Gina stepped up. "Chief, let me try to talk to him."

He handed her the horn. "It's worth a shot."

Her nerves shook, making her hand tremble as she held the bullhorn up to her mouth. "Tim, it's Gina. Please pick up the phone. I want to talk to you. I want to understand."

A face appeared in the window. A man or woman? Shane's gut tightened. He remembered a hostage situation his father had once told him and his brothers about. A man had taken his neighbor's family hostage because he believed they'd talked the man's wife into leaving him.

And every time the hostage negotiator reached out to the kidnapper, a hostage was killed. Dad had finally ordered his men to breach the house, which resulted in the kidnapper's death but spared two children their parents' fate. Shane sent up a silent plea to God not to let this situation turn into a killing spree.

"Try the phone again," Jones instructed Ryder.

Ryder nodded and dialed. He put the call on speaker so the sound of the ringer echoed through the air. After a moment the line was picked up.

"What?" a deep voice demanded.

Gina frowned and met Shane's gaze. She whispered, "That's not Tim."

"Who am I speaking with?" the chief asked.

"I'm not talking to you," came the terse reply, though the words were slightly slurred. "I want to go home." The way he drew out the last word reminded Shane of a child having a tantrum.

"You want to go home. I can understand that," the chief said. "Where's home?"

"Santa Fe. I need money for the train to take me home. Nobody was supposed to get hurt."

Shane winced. That didn't sound promising.

"You want enough money to make it to Santa Fe. Of course you didn't mean to hurt anyone." Sweat trickled down the chief's brow. He wiped the back of his hand across his forehead. "Could you let the injured leave? We can take care of them out here while we work on getting you home."

The chief impressed Shane. He was mirroring the kidnapper's words and showing empathy, which would hopefully go a long way toward building trust with the kidnapper.

"You'll help me?" Doubt echoed in the man's voice. "Robin Hood said I shouldn't believe anyone. He's coming back. He'll help me."

Shane shared a stunned glance with the others. A sinking feeling settled in the pit of his stomach. Was Robin Hood Tim Perry? Was this guy the same one who had been with Tim when he shot the flaming arrows into Gina's bedroom?

"Sure, we'll help you," the chief assured him. "There's a train bound for Santa Fe tonight. We could get you on it."

"No. You won't let me go," the kidnapper said. "Robin Hood said you'll hurt me if you catch me."

The chief put his hand over the phone's microphone and addressed Ryder. "You and Weston go around back. See if you can get in while I keep him occupied on the line."

Shane was pleased the chief trusted him with the assignment. But he didn't want to leave Gina. If Robin Hood was her brother, then according to the guy on the phone, he was coming back. Shane needed to be here to protect her.

She put her hand on his arm. "I'll stay right here with the chief. Be careful."

Touched by her concern and by the knowledge she'd known what he was thinking, he squeezed her hand. He met the chief's gaze. The older man nodded, a silent promise to protect Gina. Relinquishing control wasn't easy, but Shane knew he had to trust the chief to keep Gina safe. Urging Bella into action, they followed Ryder and Titus in a wide arc that took them behind the minimart.

At the back door, Ryder easily turned the knob and the door swung soundlessly open. Shane and Bella hung back, allowing the senior officer and his partner to enter first.

Nerves stretched taut, Shane stepped inside with Bella at his heels. The corridor took them past a small office space and stacks of inventory. They came to a set of swinging doors with square windows. Ryder pressed his back to one side of the door while Shane mirrored him on the other side. He peered through the window. Tall shelves full of packaged goods obscured the view.

Ryder eased open one side of the door and slipped into the store. Shane followed suit. Ryder gestured to Shane to approach the front from the left while Ryder would take the path to the right.

Though a bout of nervous anxiety zinged through Shane, he had trained for this—he knew what to do. He took a calming breath and set his mind to the task at hand. In a low crouch, he headed for the far left aisle and peered around the shelves. He had an unobstructed view of the cash register, where a thin man stood holding a sawed-off shotgun in one hand and the store's phone pressed against his ear with the other. Shane saw only the one kidnapper.

The man's slurred voice rose and fell in agitation. He shifted from foot to foot, clearly amped up. From adrenaline? Or were drugs involved?

Stringy brown hair spilled over the collar of a worn leather jacket. The jacket was too heavy for Arizona, even at this time of year. On the left shoulder, a patch snagged Shane's notice. A Native American symbol by his guess, but one he wasn't familiar with. A black arrow pointing upward with three black feathers at the bottom and beneath the arrow's tip was what looked like a skull. The man had said he was from New Mexico; perhaps the symbol had meaning in the other state.

A mirror above the man's head provided a panorama of the store and revealed Ryder and Titus herding a group of kids and a lady out the rear exit. Shane prayed the kidnapper didn't look up, but that was a risk they had to take to get the hostages out safely.

Shane hustled Bella across the aisle to another tall

shelf, grimacing as her nails clicked on the linoleum floor. He peered around the corner along the refrigerated cases. A man and two teens huddled together in the middle of the aisle. Shane waved them toward him. The trio hurried to his side.

"Stay out of sight," Shane whispered.

The man nodded, putting his arms around the boys as they hunkered down at the end of the aisle.

Shane and Bella moved toward the front of the store. When they reached the end of the shelving rack, he chanced a peek at the kidnapper. The man cradled the phone against his shoulder and grabbed the store clerk, a middle-aged woman with a riot of black curls, by the back of her collar. He pressed her against the front window with the shotgun pointed at her head. The woman let out a terrified yelp.

It took everything in Shane not to rush to her aid. Not yet. If he moved too soon, it might spook the kidnapper and cost the woman her life. The priority was securing the clerk's safety. Shane said a quick prayer of protection and for success. In the mirror above the register, Shane saw Ryder and Titus return, along with Officer Bucks.

Catching Ryder's eye in the reflection, Shane pointed to himself then to the man holding the shotgun. Ryder nodded. Taking that to mean Shane was clear to make a move, he unleashed Bella and stepped from the aisle with his gun drawn. "Police! Drop your weapon!"

The kidnapper whirled toward Shane. A bag of marshmallows dropped from beneath his jacket. The store clerk lunged away. Bella sprinted forward and leaped at the man, latching on to his forearm, forcing him to relinquish his hold on the shotgun. It clattered to the floor.

With a scream, the kidnapper dropped the phone and pummeled Bella with his fist.

Titus's barks ricocheted off the linoleum floor as Ryder grabbed the man's flaying arm and bent it back behind him.

"Release," Shane instructed Bella. The dog immediately complied but kept her alert gaze on the suspect as Ryder subdued the man by pushing him to the floor and slapped cuffs on his wrists. Shane clicked the leash back on Bella once the man was secured. He toed the bag of marshmallows. Had they planned on more letting loose more flaming arrows?

The sales clerk sank to her knees in tears. Her name tag read Ronda.

Bucks and Ryder led the kidnapper out of the store. Shane and Bella helped the clerk to stand. "Are you hurt?"

She shook her head. "No. Scared. That man's crazy. I think he was high on something."

"There was another man with him," Shane said. "Where did he go?"

"He ran out as soon as he heard the sirens."

Frustrated disappointment camped out in his chest. He needed to get back to Gina.

Ronda scrunched up her nose. "They both smelled horrible. When they came up to the counter and demanded money, I thought I was going to gag from the stench."

"Was anyone else hurt?" Shane hadn't seen any injured hostages but he had to ask to be sure.

"No. That one kept waving that shotgun around but he never fired it," Ronda said. "Thankfully, we weren't too busy this morning."

"That is a blessing," Shane agreed. Though he doubted those who'd been trapped inside the store would define the situation in that way. The blessing was that no one was harmed. Shane escorted Ronda and the other customers out the front entrance. Officers Marlton and Harmon rushed forward to take the hostages' statements.

A crowd had gathered around the perimeter, and Shane sought Gina out. She stood where he'd left her by the chief's side, looking lovely with sunshine bathing her in a warm glow and making her red hair spark. He headed toward her with an urgency that confused him.

The relief in her eyes twisted him up inside.

She'd been really worried.

About him?

He was surprised by the ribbon of warmth twining through his chest.

She cared? It scared and pleased him at the same time. A romantic relationship with the lovely trainer wasn't in his future, yet there was a part of him that yearned to see where a romance with Gina could lead. Boy, he was in deep trouble.

The chief stepped into his path before he reached Gina's side. "Good job, Weston." The chief slapped him on the back.

"Thank you, sir. But Bella's to be commended. She disarmed him."

The chief nodded. "Of course. It's gratifying to see the Canyon County Training Center is so effective."

"It is, sir," Shane assured him. "Gina and Sophie are excellent at their jobs."

Chief Jones's gaze narrowed. "So was Veronica."

"She was, sir," he was quick to agree, though he hadn't technically worked with Veronica. She'd had a more hands-off approach, letting Gina and Sophie do the work and then taking the credit for herself. But Shane kept that quiet, not wanting to disparage Veronica to the chief. "Sir, the store clerk confirmed there was another man with our suspect, but he escaped before we arrived. I'm sure it was Tim Perry."

The chief ran a hand over his jaw. "Then we definitely need this suspect to talk. He may be the lead that breaks the case."

"Yes, sir." Shane hoped so.

After seating the suspect in the back of Bucks's cruiser and leaving Bucks to keep an eye on the man, Ryder and Titus walked over.

"Our guy's in bad shape," Ryder said. "High as a kite. Barely lucid. He's got track marks on both arms."

"Did he say anything more about Robin Hood?"

"Nothing useful. Just keeps blathering on about his merry band of men and that he was only allowed to shoot marshmallows."

Had Tim enlisted more than one junkie to help his cause? Shane had figured something like that. "Did you get an ID on him?"

"Yes, he's in the national criminal database. His name's John Krause, from Santa Fe, New Mexico. He's got a rap sheet a mile long. Mostly misdemeanors for possession of illegal substances, a few assault charges, and breaking and entering. He's done jail time. Last known address puts him in Tucson. Not sure how he ended up here and he's too far gone to be coherent."

"Take him in," Jones instructed. "Call Dr. Pennington and have him come to the station to do a blood draw and tox screen. I want to know what this guy is on. And where it came from."

"Yes, sir," Ryder said and led Titus back to the cruiser.

The chief turned to Shane. There was a haggard look in the chief's gray eyes. The past few days had taken a toll on the man. "You'll need to come to the station to give your statement, as well."

"Will do, sir," Shane said.

Chief Jones strode away, his gait even but slow. He climbed behind the wheel of his Desert Valley police car and drove away.

Gina walked over. "That was intense."

To say the least. "I'm glad no one was hurt." He steered her to his Jeep. "I have to give my statement at the station. I'm not comfortable dropping you off at the training center."

"I'll go with you," she said as she slid onto the passenger seat.

As he shut her door, he admitted he was glad to have her company and relieved to have her close. With the adrenaline fading, he found himself needing Gina's soothing presence. Something he knew he had no business needing, let alone wanting. He really had to put some distance between them; however, as long as she was his to protect, distance wasn't an option.

Instead, he had to find a way to regulate his response to her. His father would tell him to stop his bellyaching and compartmentalize his feelings. Emotions had no place on the job. Emotions interfered and could result in tragedy.

Way easier said than done. But for Gina's sake, Shane would do whatever was necessary to keep her safe. To keep them both safe.

At the police station, he and Gina entered through the side door just as Ryder was escorting the suspect to the cells.

The man, John, lifted his eyes to stare at Gina. His muddy gaze widened. He lunged toward her. "Are you Maid Marian? Robin Hood is going to rescue you. And me. I'm Little John." He grinned, revealing yellow stained teeth.

Gina shrank back from the man. Shane urged her away. "What was that about?"

With a sigh, Shane told her about Robin Hood.

"Tim's delusional now," she said. "That makes him more dangerous."

"He's not getting anywhere near you," he assured her.

They stopped at the cubicle that bore his name. He sat at the desk he'd been assigned and wrote up his account of what had transpired inside the convenience store while Gina sat nearby quietly petting Bella. Her presence was distracting. It took him several tries to get the words written in a coherent fashion. So much for compartmentalizing.

When he was finished, he handed the report to Carrie, who'd add it to the case file.

"Ready to go?" Shane asked Gina while resisting the urge to offer her his hand.

"Definitely," she answered as she rose from the chair. "Do you mind if we stop for coffee before picking up the puppies?"

He could use a jolt of caffeine. "Not at all."

"I wish we knew where Marco was," she said as she hitched her purse higher on her shoulder. "Maybe we could check in with the store owners along Main Street and see if anyone has mentioned finding the puppy?"

"If anyone had, I'm sure we'd know. But when we get back to the training center I can make some calls." And just because her brother had escaped from the minimart didn't mean the man wasn't still out there waiting for an opportunity to strike. Shane and Bella had to be on their A game at all times.

A tall, distinguished man in his midforties entered the station, nearly running Gina over. Shane snaked an arm around her waist and drew her out of the way. Which proved a good tactic to keep her from being bowled over, but played havoc with his senses.

"I was summoned by the chief," the newcomer bit out in an impatient tone. He had neatly styled graying dark hair and rimless eyeglasses that distorted his dark eyes. He carried a black bag with the initials W.P.

Taking a guess, Shane held out his hand and said, "Dr. Pennington. I'm Officer Weston. We spoke the other day."

Ignoring his outstretched hand, Pennington said, "Where's the chief?"

"Right here," Jones said as he came out of his office. "Good of you to come, Doctor."

Pennington's lip curled. "Did I have a choice?"

Shane had the distinct impression there was no love lost between the two men. No doubt the animosity was due to their respective relationships with Veronica Earnshaw. Pennington had divorced the woman the chief had considered a daughter. Granted, Shane didn't know the full story of what had happened between Veronica and the doctor.

"We have a suspect in custody I'd like you to do a tox screen on," the chief said, ignoring Pennington's snide question.

Pennington huffed. "You mean a junkie." He made a face of disgust. "What a drain on society. They clutter up the clinic and keep us from helping those who really need medical care."

"Yes, well." The chief's voice hardened. "The clinic *is* for everyone, is it not, Doctor?"

The two men locked gazes in a battle of wills. Shane exchanged a curious glance with Gina. She gave a slight shrug, clearly unnerved by the power clash in front of them.

Finally, Pennington let out a loud breath. "Show me where you've stashed the criminal."

"This way." The chief led the doctor through a set of double doors leading to the jail cells at the back of the building.

"I sure hope his bedside manner is better when he's with his patients," Gina commented.

Shane touched his hand to the small of her back and led her out of the station. "I can't imagine him and Veronica as a couple. Two abrasive people together…" She shuddered.

"It does seem like a strange pairing," Gina replied. "If I weren't so sure that my brother killed Veronica, I'd wonder if the good doctor didn't have something to do with her murder."

"Spouses and ex-spouses are usually the first suspects in a murder case. But I checked, and the doctor has an alibi."

"Oh, well, then I guess he's innocent. Just not very nice."

After Shane, Bella and Gina were in the Jeep, Shane asked, "How about we grab lunch with our coffee?" His stomach growled.

"That works," Gina said. "I'll call Sophie and see if we can bring her lunch."

"Good idea." Shane headed for the Cactus Café downtown while Gina made the call.

At the café, Gina ordered Sophie a turkey on whole wheat sandwich and a chicken salad on a sourdough roll for herself. Shane ordered a roast beef on rye and a side of fries. They each ordered a coffee to go.

While they waited for their food, they sat on a bench outside the café while sipping from their to-go coffee cups. Bella lay at their feet with a bowl of water provided by the café owner.

Shane surveyed the small community of Desert Valley, feeling a kinship with the people he'd come to know over the past three months. A couple of teenage girls on bicycles rode past. The postman, Charlie, waved from his truck as he drove through town. Bill Baxter swept the sidewalk in front his hardware store, The Tool Corral. A mother and her adult daughter, arms linked and smiles on their faces, entered the Brides and Belles shop.

It seemed like such a peaceful little town. Quaint, even, with colorful storefronts sporting awnings to provide shade from the heat of the Arizona sun. Though today was a mild spring day, he knew in a few short months the weather would turn scorching.

"Do you like living in Desert Valley?" he asked Gina.

"I do." She let out a small sigh. "It's been a nice place to be these past two years. The way the community is so tightly knit. It's a good place to raise a family, too. The schools are good, with high test scores."

He noted her wistful tone and ached for her. He wished there were some way for him to convince her that she shouldn't give up her dream of children out of fear. "You know you could adopt."

She slanted him a quick glance. "True. Or foster. I've toyed with the idea. I think I could provide a stable and loving home for children in need." A small smile touched her lips, drawing his gaze. "I need to stop being a martyr and explore other possibilities. I'll give adoption and/or fostering more serious thought once Tim is no longer a threat to me. Or anyone else."

Pleased to know she hadn't taken too much offense by his blunt comment, he returned her smile. "I think you should. Desert Valley seems perfect."

"Normally, there's not much crime," she said with a grimace. "People tend to look out for each other. At Christmas, the town goes all out with decorations and most everyone attends the community church's pageant." Her voice ticked up in enthusiasm. "There's an Easter parade with kids and adults alike dressed in their Sunday best. Then in May, there's the annual Police Dance and Fund-raiser."

She slanted him a glance, then quickly darted her gaze away. The offer to escort her to the event tripped on his tongue but he wasn't going to set her or himself up for disappointment. Surely by then Tim would be arrested, the cold cases would be resolved one way or another and all the rookies would be on their way to their assignments.

"But I enjoy summer the most," Gina stated firmly. "With the rodeo, the Fourth of July parade and a street fair in August with artisans from all over the state displaying their wares."

He could hear her excitement and love for the town in her voice. It made him ache with longing. He doubted he'd be here to see any of the things she described. And he doubted she'd be willing to leave.

Whoa. Where'd that thought come from? He wasn't about to ask her to uproot her life, leave behind a good job and friends to go with him wherever he was assigned. Once her brother was behind bars, she'd be free to really put down her roots here in Desert Valley, a place she obviously loved.

The café's door swung open and the waitress stepped out with their bag of food. "Here you are," she said with a smile.

"Thanks, Patty," Gina said as she took the bag.

"Enjoy," Patty said, and ducked back inside.

They walked to the Jeep. With Bella secured once again in the back, they settled in the front seats, and Shane headed toward the training center. He turned onto Desert Valley Road. The screech of tires against pavement was the only warning Shane had before a car shot out from the side street and plowed into them.

TWELVE

Gina looked out the passenger window and locked eyes with the maniacal stare of her brother behind the wheel of a silver sedan coming straight at her. She barely had time to brace herself before the Jeep was shoved sideways.

The sickening sound of metal colliding, crushing and collapsing reverberated through her, drowning out her screams of terror as she was thrown left then right like a rag doll.

A loud *whoosh* within the Jeep confused her until the dashboard exploded in her face at the same instant the side curtain air bag deployed, slamming into her shoulder. Rough pillows of material nearly smothered her as the Jeep tipped up and then crashed back to earth, landing on all four tires with a jarring bounce.

Her head collided with the side passenger window. The air bag minimized the impact so the window didn't break, but not enough to keep pain from exploding behind her eyes in a shower of bright stars. The world spun. The seat belt dug into her chest and shoulder, pinning her back. Her face flamed and her nose burned from the air-bag residue. Bella's frantic barks punctuated the horror rolling over Gina.

Shane muttered as he worked valiantly to keep the

Jeep from rolling. Blindly, she reached for him, but found only air.

Finally, the spinning subsided and the vehicle came to an abrupt stop in the middle of the intersection. Tim's car shot forward and rammed into a light pole.

Eerie quietness stole her breath. Bella! Shane! Were they okay? Her vision danced in and out of focus. Something wet and sticky ran down her face.

Then a hand landed on her shoulder. "You're bleeding."

She swiped a hand over her eyes and forced herself to focus on Shane's face. His green eyes were full of panic as he grabbed his cell and called dispatch. He swiveled to look at Bella. Gina followed his gaze. The dog appeared unharmed. Her ears were standing up, her attention focused on something outside the Jeep. She let out a loud growl followed by a barrage of frenetic barks.

The sudden sound of the passenger-door handle rattling startled Gina. With a yelp, she shrank from the door. A face peered at her. Tim. *Please, Lord, no!*

He bared his teeth and continued to yank on the door handle, but the metal had been crushed and refused to budge.

Shane kicked open the driver's-side door and rounded the front of the Jeep, drawing his weapon. "Get down on the ground!"

In the back of the Jeep, separated from the front seat by a metal barrier, Bella barked and clawed at the window in a frenzied effort to get to her partner. Shane needed Bella.

Gina tried to pry loose the seat-belt latch, but her hands were too slippery with blood. She wiped her hands on her jeans and reached again for the latch. This time she managed to release the buckle. The seat belt retracted quickly, the metal buckle hitting her in the chin, adding another blast of pain to her already bruised and battered body.

Ignoring the many agonizing places that burned for attention, she scrambled into the driver's seat and out of the Jeep. She hurried to release Bella...but the hatch was stuck. She'd have to figure out another way to free the dog.

She raced to the rear driver's-side door but was momentarily distracted by Shane. He'd holstered his weapon and had her brother down on the ground in the middle of the road. Shane's knee was planted in the center of Tim's back and Shane seemed to be searching his utility belt for something. His handcuffs were missing. Had they dislodged from his utility belt during the crash?

In the fraction of a second it took her to debate whether to continue her goal of freeing Bella or search for the handcuffs, Tim burst into action. He reared up with a loud roar and bucked Shane off. Shane stumbled back and landed on his rear while Tim shoved to his feet and ran. Before Shane could regain his feet, Tim had reached the crowd of bystanders that had been drawn to the accident.

The shrill cry of sirens filled the air. Too late. Her brother was escaping. They needed Bella. Gina pivoted, intent on crawling in the Jeep.

"Gina!"

Tim's shout froze her in place. She met her brother's crazed stare. Even from this distance, malice gleamed like a flame in his eyes. Her heart thudded in her chest. Her brother, her twin, hated her. Her mind couldn't grasp the concept. His mental illness may be driving him but at some point he had to take responsibility for his actions. They were connected by blood, yet were so far apart in every other way that he was a stranger to her.

A stranger with a desire to kill.

And she was his target.

She staggered back a step. A piercing wail sounded in her head. Pain exploded in her chest, making each breath difficult. She pressed a hand over her heart.

Two police cars arrived and skidded to a halt. The sudden silence released Gina from her panic. Chief Jones and Officer Bucks exited the chief's vehicle while James Harrison and Ellen Foxcroft climbed out of another with their canine partners.

Tim turned and raced toward the woods and quickly disappeared into the shadows of the trees and brush. Shane jumped to his feet with his weapon out, but there were too many people between him and Tim.

Shane quickly explained to the chief and officers what had happened.

James's lip curled. "We'll get him this time." He tugged on the leash attached to his bloodhound, Hawk. "Let's go, boy."

The two headed for the woods with Officer Bucks following closely behind. Gina sent up a quick prayer of safety for the trio.

Shane glanced toward the Jeep. Meeting his gaze, Gina rushed to yank open the Jeep's rear passenger door. Anchoring herself with her back against the driver's seat, she grabbed the metal tension grate, tugging on it with all of her strength. Finally it gave and she was able to push it aside to allow Bella to jump out. The dog raced to Shane's side and Gina followed, stopping next to him.

He holstered his weapon and then gripped her by the shoulders. "Are you hurt?"

She laid her hands flat against his chest. His heart hammered beneath her palms. She searched his face, wincing at the dark bruise forming on his cheek. "No. Thankfully. You?"

"A bruised ego." A muscle ticked in his strong jaw. "I can't believe I let him escape."

"You stopped him from getting to me. That's all that matters." Staring into his handsome face she was inundated with relief that they were both alive and unharmed. The strong urge to kiss him slammed into her. Her breath caught and held. Did she dare? It would be reckless and foolhardy, but the need was nearly overwhelming. Instead, she dropped her head forward to hide her flaming cheeks. "I owe you my life."

Shane's arms slipped around her and drew her close. She clung to him, grateful to God above that they both were alive.

Ellen hurried to Gina's side with gauze pads and pressed them to her forehead. "An ambulance is on its way."

When it arrived, the chief insisted Gina and Shane go to the hospital to be checked out by a doctor.

Gina wasn't thrilled to ride in the back of the ambulance, but when Shane and Bella jumped in, she had no complaints. They sat side by side on the bench usually reserved for the paramedic, with Bella at their feet. He slid an arm around Gina again, pulling her close. She laid her head on his shoulder, concentrating on the feel of his solid grip holding her tightly as a way to keep the aftermath of the trauma from turning her into a sobbing mess.

When they arrived at the hospital, the orderly led them to the emergency room. Shane grasped her hand as they walked. The pressure of their palms pressed together soothed her more than any medicine could. Though she had to admit her head throbbed and her body ached from being thrown around during the crash.

"Officer Weston, we'll take you over here." A stout nurse gestured to an open curtained room.

"No." The protest was out before Gina could stop it. She didn't want to be separated from him. He was her anchor. She was afraid that without him by her side she'd succumb to the hysteria that had built up inside of her during the ordeal.

Shane squeezed her hand. "It'll be all right. Bella will stay with you."

"This way, Miss Perry," another nurse urged.

Reluctantly, Gina let go of Shane's hand to follow the nurse. Bella's nails clicked on the tiled floor as she kept pace with Gina. *Breathe*, she told herself. *Just breathe. You're safe now. Tim can't get to you here.*

The nurse handed her a gown. "Put this on. The doctor should be with you soon. Do you need help?"

She clutched the gown to her chest. "No, I can manage."

When the nurse left, Gina finally succumbed to the horror. She staggered to the exam table and leaned against it as the full impact of what they'd just survived hit her like a rogue wave. Her chest grew tight. Her breathing constricted. Her mind replayed what had happened. Tim had crashed a car into the side of Shane's Jeep in an attempt to kill her. He wanted her dead. There was no mistaking his intent.

But he hadn't succeeded.

Would he ever stop trying?

Bella nudged her in the thigh as if sensing her dark thoughts. Grateful for Bella's presence, Gina squatted to hug the dog, a liberty she only dared take with the police dog because she had trained her. It was kind of Shane to let his partner come with her; he obviously understood that Bella would ease Gina's fears. His compassion touched her deeply. He was a good and honorable man. A man she was swiftly falling for. How crazy was that?

After hurriedly donning the gown, Gina waited for the doctor.

Shane. He'd become such an important part of her life in such a short amount of time. She knew the trauma and tension of the past few days had had an effect on her judgment, but she couldn't discount the very real attraction and affection she harbored for the handsome rookie.

If things were different, if she were different, she could see herself giving Shane her heart. As it was, she struggled to keep her emotions in check. The last thing she needed was to become attached to Shane. Not only was he leaving, but she couldn't ever saddle anyone with the danger of her DNA. Tonight had brought home once again that faulty genes and bad decisions ran in her family.

With a sinking sense of doom and a heart that felt as if it were cracking open wide, she reminded herself that Shane deserved better than that. "You were fortunate, Officer Weston. You and Miss Perry both," claimed the doctor, who'd introduced himself as Dr. Ruskin. He was older, with a shock of white hair and pale blue eyes that seemed to see right through Shane.

Shane didn't believe in luck. God had put a hedge of protection around him and Gina, preventing Tim from doing more damage beyond totaling the Jeep. They'd been blessed, that was for sure. If only Shane hadn't let Tim take advantage of Shane's momentary distraction when he'd realized his cuffs were missing. Inexcusable.

His father would be mortified. And he could just hear the jabs his brothers would aim at him. *Loser. Weakling. Mama's boy.*

Shane shoved away the echo of his brother's taunts and concentrated on the doctor. "Can I go now?"

He needed to see Gina, to assure himself that she hadn't suffered any major injuries.

"Yes," the doctor replied in a tone that had Shane waiting for more. "I'd advise you both to rest for the next twenty-four hours at least. The bruises you sustained to your ribs need to heal before you are too active. And the same goes for Miss Perry. Though she's a bit more banged up than you are."

Shane winced with concern. He'd seen the laceration on her forehead from the air bag deploying. He wasn't sure what other injuries she'd sustained during the crash.

He changed back into his uniform and went in search of Gina and Bella. Every moment away from them ratcheted up his tension.

He found them waiting at the administration desk. The stark white bandage wrapped around Gina's head glared in contrast to the tumble of red waves cascading over her shoulders. Her hazel eyes were clear, but her smile appeared strained. She looked tired and scared and pretty all at the same time.

The rush of relief at seeing her caught him by surprise. As he moved toward her, he tried to analyze what he was feeling. But his emotions were in a jumbled mess, so dissecting his feelings wasn't happening.

She closed the distance between them and he automatically opened his arms for her to step into his embrace. It felt like the most natural act in the world. Holding her close, tucked within the shelter of his arms—that was where he wanted her. Always. A pipe dream, but for now, he wouldn't fight his emotions. After the ordeal they'd been through, he just didn't have any fight left.

"Hey, you two," James Harrison said as he sauntered

through the hospital double doors and halted beside them. Hawk, his bloodhound, greeted Bella. The police dogs all had a special place in their hearts for their former trainer. "Thought you might need a ride home."

"We do," Shane said. "Did you track down Tim Perry?"

James's jaw tightened. "I'm sorry, I didn't. The guy's slippery. He had another vehicle stashed not far away. The one he used to ram into your Jeep was stolen from a house down the block."

"He must have followed us from the Cactus Café," Gina said.

"Yes, and anticipated we'd be crossing that intersection on the way back to the training center." Shane hated to admit it, but Tim was smart. An evil genius. But one of these days he'd make a mistake that would land him in jail for good. At least Shane prayed so.

James drove them back to the training center. As soon as they entered, Sophie hugged Gina. "I freaked out when I heard what happened. Are you okay, for real?"

"I'm a little banged up, that's all." Gina hugged her friend back. "The seat belt did a number on my ribs." She touched the bandage around her head. "Not to mention the stitches on my forehead and in my scalp where I hit the window."

Shane hadn't realized she'd banged her head, as well. He was surprised she didn't have a massive headache. Must be the pain meds that would eventually wear off. He wanted her home before then.

"Thank God above you two are safe and relatively sound," Sophie stated.

"I'm sorry to leave you with all the work here," Gina said.

"Nonsense," Sophie replied. "For now I can handle

the center. Until we can open back up for training sessions, there isn't much for me to do. Though I have had two breeders call to say they have dogs old enough for training. I told them we aren't offering sessions but that I'd take the pups and start working with them to get them ready for when we do offer police training sessions again. And I've also put out a call to departments all over the state for refresher courses. When you're ready to come back there will be plenty of work but until then rest and recover from the crash."

Shane noted the way Gina grimaced. He touched her arm. "See, nothing to worry about here."

Gina sighed. "I know. I just feel responsible for everything that has happened. So many people's lives have been affected."

"You're not to blame," Shane told her, but he could tell by the look in her pretty eyes she still held herself accountable for her brother's evil acts.

"He's right," Sophie said. "Don't beat yourself up for your brother's actions. When he's caught, life will get back to normal and we'll open back up for training."

Which would mean Shane would be gone, assigned to another department, either in Flagstaff or somewhere else in the state of Arizona. Somewhere far from Desert Valley. The thought left a bitter taste in his mouth.

"In the meantime," Sophie continued, "I've organized the supply closets, gone over the accounts and scrubbed every square inch of the place." She frowned. "Except for Veronica's apartment upstairs. I can't bring myself to go in."

"I don't blame you," Gina said with a visible shiver. "I'll be back tomorrow to help you if you'd like."

He admired her willingness to be there for her coworker, but she needed to look out for her own well-being. "The doctor said you need to rest for at least twenty-four hours," he reminded Gina.

Shane scooped up the puppies and escorted Gina out. James dropped Shane, Gina and the puppies off at the condo while he and Hawk went back to the station.

"I'll take care of these two while you rest," Shane told her as he set the puppies on the floor. They immediately ran for the back patio door.

"There's no way I can sleep right now," she countered. "Can we watch a movie?"

Her question socked in him in the gut. An image of the two of them snuggling on the couch like a couple in love marched through his mind. His pulse picked up. As tantalizing as that thought was, they weren't in love. They weren't a couple. They were just two people who'd endured a harrowing event and needed some downtime to decompress. He could handle that. "Sure, but first I'm going to put these two out back and then make us something to eat."

Ten minutes later, with the puppies chewing on bones and Bella lying on her bed, Shane and Gina settled on the couch. A lunch of cold cuts and cheese, bread slices and two apple ciders was laid out on the coffee table. Gina picked a movie from the On Demand function on the cable box as she nibbled at the food. Shane wanted to urge her to eat more, but refrained. The last thing she needed was him bossing her around. Before long, she abandoned the food to curl up next to him.

His chest grew tight. The image he'd had earlier was coming true. He should move away from her, stop this madness right now, but it felt too good having her so close. And as he settled his arm around her, he knew there was no way he'd break this moment for anything.

She rested her head on the soft plane between his

chest and shoulder, fitting perfectly within his embrace. Warmth spread through him and he couldn't help but feel protective of this sweet woman. He knew there were other emotions floating through his system—affection, caring, attraction. As much as he wanted to deny that he was growing attached to this beautiful woman, he couldn't.

It was going to be torture to leave her behind when he left. But he would leave and she would stay. That was the way of their jobs.

And he needed his focus on his career, not on a woman, if he hoped to earn his father's and brothers' respect.

Though that driving need that had propelled him through his life didn't have the same intensity it once had. Being here in Desert Valley, away from the influence of his family, he found himself questioning his needs. Questioning his path in life.

As Gina's breathing evened out, he glanced down to find her sleeping in his arms. For a long time, he held her, savoring the feel of her against him. When the movie ended and he had no legitimate reason to keep holding her, he lifted her and carried her to her room. Bella followed.

Awkwardly juggling Gina, he pulled back the blankets and then laid her down. He slipped off her shoes, then settled the covers over her. Bella rested on the floor at the foot of the bed. The puppies trotted in and headed for their crates. Afraid the two young dogs would wake Gina, Shane dragged them and their beds into the hall. They'd sleep in his room tonight.

Shane paused at Gina's bedroom door and gave the hand command for Bella to come with him. She stood and came to him but then turned to look back at the woman on the bed. Bella sat and nudged him in the thigh.

Was she trying to tell him she wanted to stay with Gina?

Seemed his partner was as smitten as he was.

Leaving the dog there added another measure of safety. He crouched down so he was at eye level with Bella. "Okay. You stay here and protect Gina," he whispered.

Bella immediately moved back to the end of the bed to lie down. She settled her chin on her paws and closed her eyes.

Marveling at Bella's intellect, he left the door slightly ajar in case Gina awoke and needed him.

His heart spasmed as the thought seared clean through him. He wanted her to need him. No one had ever needed him. But Gina did and that made him feel invincible. And foolish.

How was he going to say goodbye when the time came?

Gina awoke to find Bella standing beside her bed. The dog cocked her head and then walked to the door, which was cracked open. Bella glanced back at her, clearly wanting out, but also wanting her to follow.

Blinking the sleep from her eyes, Gina realized she was fully clothed. She must have fallen asleep on the couch with Shane and he'd put her to bed. And he'd left Bella with her as protection.

Tenderness filled her. Shane's thoughtfulness set her heart beating. He was such a caring man. Honorable and committed. The type of man every woman hoped to find.

That they'd been thrown together by danger only added to his appeal, because he could have refused the assignment of guarding her. He could have been cold and distant in dealing with her but he wasn't.

He was personable, concerned for her comfort and

safety. She knew he would protect her at all costs. He'd taken an oath to protect and serve. And yet she hoped his actions stemmed from more than just duty. Could he care for her beyond an assignment? Did she want him to?

And did she care for him?

Of course she did. He'd put his life on the line for her. But what she felt went beyond gratefulness and that scared her because she knew there could be no future for them. Her shoulders slumped. She had to protect Shane as much as he was protecting her. She needed to keep things between them from turning personal. They could be friends but nothing more.

She slipped from the bed, every muscle protesting, and opened the door all the way. Bella waited for her and walked at her side into the living room. Shane was in the kitchen with his back to her. His broad shoulders filled out his dark blue T-shirt nicely. The puppies came running, tumbling over themselves to get to her. She knelt to receive their love. Bella headed for the back patio door. Shane hustled over to open it for his partner.

"How are you this morning?" Shane asked, his green-eyed gaze searching her face.

"I feel like I was in a car accident," she replied as she gingerly sat on a stool at the counter. The puppies lost interest in her and chewed on their toys.

He gave her a lopsided grin that made her breath catch. "Yeah. Me, too."

Forcing herself to breathe evenly, she said, "Thank you for last night."

Heat flooded her cheeks as she remembered how she'd snuggled up next to him on the couch. She'd been so worn-out and emotionally drained she hadn't had the mental fortitude to stop herself. "I mean for leaving Bella to watch over me through the night."

"You're welcome."

Best to put last night behind them. "So I guess today we stay here."

He nodded. "Doctor's orders."

She smiled, thinking there were worse ways to spend a day than with a handsome man, two puppies and a guard dog on duty. Just as long as there was no more snuggling. Or kissing. Even if she yearned for more.

She knew this forced proximity was necessary, and she'd enjoy it while it lasted. But she'd have to put a lock on her emotions if she hoped to make it through this situation unscathed. The wounds to her flesh were nothing compared to the potential wound to her heart.

THIRTEEN

Though they'd been housebound for the day, Gina decided the best use of their time, and the best way to keep things between her and Shane on a more professional level, was to continue working with the puppies while reviewing Shane and Bella's training.

There'd been some hysterical moments where they'd both ended up doubled over with laughter at the antics of the puppies. Bella had even proved a good teacher for the two rambunctious pups by using her herding instincts to keep Lucy and Ricky in line.

All in all a good day. And after dinner, when it was so tempting to curl up on the couch with another movie and a potential opportunity to snuggle with Shane, Gina opted for reading in her room. She told herself that wasn't disappointment she'd glimpsed in Shane's eyes when she'd wished him good-night.

When she'd awoken this morning, she'd found Bella sleeping in the hall outside her bedroom door, which had melted her heart and made her seek out Shane to thank him.

"Hey, I'd like to take credit," Shane said with a smile. "Once you went to bed last night, she took a position in front of your door and wouldn't budge."

That made her feel so loved. At least by the dog. She ignored the tiny, mopey voice inside of her that wished Shane loved her.

Time to get back to work.

James dropped Gina, Shane and Bella off at the training center on his way to the station with Hawk. He and the other rookies would continue helping in the investigation into the two previous rookies' mysterious deaths and the cold case of Melanie Hayes's murder.

If Shane was disappointed not to be more involved in the investigations because he had to protect her, he didn't say so. Gina felt bad regardless. If her brother hadn't come to Desert Valley with murder on his mind, then the rookies would now be far away at various police departments around the state, and Marian Foxcroft wouldn't have had to so generously endow the police station with the funds to keep the rookies on staff.

Strange how life had a way of changing so dramatically, so quickly. Her father would have said God takes the bad in life and uses it for good. She wasn't so sure that was true, but at least now Ryder could solve his wife's murder, and the questions that surrounded the two other mysterious deaths might be answered. She prayed so.

Her cell phone rang as they entered the training center. Shane set the puppies free while she grabbed her phone from her purse. Her ribs ached with every movement but she forced herself to ignore the pain. The doctor had said only time would heal the sprain in her rib cage from the seat belt locking so tight across her torso. She'd taken off the bandage covering the few stitches on her head, opting to let the wound breathe now that it had stopped bleeding.

She stared at the caller ID and didn't recognize the

number. Fear tightened her throat. Would Tim call? She met Shane's gaze. "I don't know who this is."

"Put it on speaker."

She did as he instructed. "Hello?"

"Is this Gina Perry?" A woman's crisp voice spoke through the speaker.

"Yes, this is Gina."

"Marian Foxcroft here. I understand you've been caring for the two puppies, Ricky and Lucy."

Relaxing, she nodded. Then quickly answered, "Yes, ma'am."

"I take it there's been no word on where little Marco is?"

Gina's stomach clenched. "No, there hasn't. We've put up flyers, we've gone door to door as well as searched the area surrounding the training center."

"I will offer a reward for the puppy's safe return. Surely that will galvanize the person who took him to come forward."

"That's very generous of you." Gina couldn't stop the spurt of excitement. If someone had found Marco maybe they would want the money more than the puppy. She sent up a quick prayer that puppy would be found alive. That he hadn't become food for a predator.

"I'd like to see the other puppies," Marian said, interrupting Gina's prayer.

"Of course. I'm with them now at the training center. We'd love for you to visit us."

"No. I want you to bring them to me. I'm sure their mama would be happy to see them."

Gina raised her eyebrows. Though the puppies had stayed with their mama long enough for the mother dog to remember them, Gina doubted the dog longed for her puppies. Dogs didn't have the same emotional attachment to their offspring as humans do, even if this litter was the mama dog's first.

More likely Marian Foxcroft was lonely up in that big house of hers. Though Gina knew Ellen lived at home, the young rookie wasn't often there, preferring to work rather than deal with her mother. Empathy for the older woman had Gina agreeing. "Yes, of course I can bring the puppies to you. We could be there in an hour."

"Thank you, Gina. I appreciate that." Marian hung up.

"Why did you say you'd take the puppies there?" Shane asked with a frown. "We need to keep a low profile. Stay here or the condo. After yesterday, I don't want you out and about."

As much as she wanted to agree with him that staying in safe places was the smart thing to do, she didn't want to be a prisoner to her brother's madness. "We can borrow the training center's SUV. I'm sure Sophie won't mind. Besides, Marian Foxcroft isn't someone we can say no to. She funds the center as well as your salary."

He blew out a breath. "Fine. But I'll let Ryder know where we're going in case we run into your brother again."

Gina's tummy twisted at the thought, but she refused to live her life in fear. They would take the necessary precautions. Besides, God was on their side.

Between the two, she, Shane and the puppies should be all right. Shouldn't they?

The Foxcroft home sat on a five-acre rise east of Desert Valley in an exclusive and secluded neighborhood. It was rumored some of the houses in the area belonged to celebrities. Gina wasn't sure she believed the rumor, since she'd never seen anyone she recognized from television or the big screen around town. But whoever owned the sprawling homes out here definitely had money, just like Marian Foxcroft.

On the way in, with Shane driving, they'd passed some big spreads, but the Foxcroft house was by far the most impressive to Gina. After entering the code Marian had texted them earlier, they passed through an ornate wrought-iron gate and drove up the long drive.

Though maybe not as big as some of the other mansions they'd passed, Marian's butter-yellow multilevel Victorian-style house sat back from the road like a regal queen. Dormer windows and a curved veranda with large bay windows added character. Smaller multipaned windows graced every wall, no doubt providing a panoramic view of Desert Valley and the scenic landscape in all directions.

Gina smoothed the front of her slacks as she climbed out of the training center's SUV, suddenly wishing she'd changed into something more presentable than her work clothes. It wasn't every day she was invited to visit Marian Foxcroft.

She harnessed and leashed the two puppies before they could dash off to explore unfettered. She let the dogs have a quick break before tugging on the leash to corral them in as she and Shane headed up the walkway.

At the foot of the cedar stairs that led to an ornately carved, knotty pine front door, his cell phone rang. She paused with a foot on the stair as he stopped to check the caller ID.

"It's the chief," he said. "You go on in, I'll be right there."

She nodded and urged the puppies up the steps. On the wide porch, the puppies sniffed the edges of the colorful flowers and greenery growing in the numerous clay pots.

From inside the house a dog's deep bark could be

heard. The mama dog sensing intruders? Or greeting her puppies?

Gina rapped her knuckles against the solid wood door. The force of her knock pushed the door open. It hadn't been closed all the way. The fine hairs on her arm rose and a shiver tripped down her spine.

Caution tightened her shoulders as she strained to listen. The only noise she heard was the now frantic barks of an adult dog.

After a heartbeat, she called out, "Mrs. Foxcroft? It's me, Gina Perry. I have the puppies with me."

No answer. Gina glanced back at Shane. He had his back to her as he talked with the chief. For a moment indecision warred within her. Did she go in and investigate or wait for Shane? But how long would he be?

The puppies leaped up the short doorstep, pushed the door wide and took off, practically dragging Gina behind them. She dug in her heels in an effort to stop them, but that even as their trainer, she'd only been working with them a few short days and was no match for their combined weight and power.

Hurrying to keep up, Gina followed the puppies across a gleaming cherrywood-floored foyer to a vaulted ceiling great room at the back of the house. In the corner was an extralarge kennel housing a beautiful adult German shepherd. The puppies' mama.

But it was the woman lying prone on the plush white area rug that forced the breath from Gina's lungs.

Marian Foxcroft.

Gina's legs buckled. She went to her knees. *Not again. Oh, please, God.*

A dark, crimson stain marred the light-colored fibers beneath Marian's head. Her eyes were closed, her complexion nearly matching the carpet.

"Shane!" Reeling in the puppies so that they didn't contaminate the scene, Gina crawled to Marian's side. With a tight grip on Ricky and Lucy's leash in one hand, Gina pressed the shaky fingers of her free hand against the pulse point on the older woman's neck and braced herself for another tragic death.

But Marian had a pulse. Weak, but definitely there. Gina's shoulders collapsed with relief. Marian was unconscious but alive.

"Shane!" Gina yelled again, putting all her strength into her voice.

Who would do this? She fumbled to grasp her cell phone from the bottom of her waist pack as the question rattled around her brain. Why would anyone want to hurt Marian? Gina couldn't see her brother doing this. Why would he?

As she yanked her cell out, a baggie of treats dropped to the ground. The puppies lurched for it, each taking a corner.

Gina dialed 911 and then wedged the phone between her ear and shoulder while she wrestled to get the baggie from the pups. The last thing she needed was the bag to tear open and dogs treats to go flying all over to contaminate the scene, making it harder for Shane to do his job. She pulled the dogs farther away from Marian.

When the dispatcher answered, words gushed from Gina. "We need an ambulance at the Foxcroft house." She spit out the address from memory. "Hurry, please. Marian's bleeding from a head wound."

The dispatcher assured Gina the paramedics were en route.

"Hang in there, Marian," Gina whispered to the center's benefactor. "Help is on the way."

The pounding of feet on the hardwood floor announced Shane had heard her cry. Marian's German shepherd burst into another volley of barks at the newcomer as Shane burst through the archway into the living room with his weapon drawn. His gaze landed on her then bounced to Marian. Surprise crossed his face before a shuttered look overtook his features.

Slowly, he holstered his gun and stepped closer.

"What happened?"

Not liking the wariness in his tone, Gina grew defensive. "She was like this when I came in."

A muscle in his jaw jumped. He moved to check her pulse.

"Alive," she was quick to assure him. "Barely. I've called 911. An ambulance is on its way."

"Good." His gaze swept the room. "Don't move or touch anything. I'm going to clear the house."

He pivoted with his hand on his weapon and stalked out from the room. He couldn't really believe she'd done this, could he?

A sense of déjà vu hit her hard. Shane's first reaction when he'd come upon her and Veronica had been to suspect Gina of murder. But they were long past that now, weren't they? What would she have to gain from hurting Marian?

Nothing. And if Shane didn't know her well enough by now to know she wouldn't do this...

But hadn't she been telling him she had her brother's blood in her veins? That she and Tim shared the same genes? That somewhere in her DNA malice lurked, waiting to be released? So why wouldn't his reaction be suspicion?

She slumped. That it hurt was her problem. A problem she had to get a handle on fast.

She may be many things, but a masochist wasn't one

of them. From this point on she would guard her heart with every ounce of energy she possessed.

Letting herself care about Shane, about his opinion of her, was detrimental to her well-being. If she hoped to resume her normal life once her brother was captured, she had to remain detached, unemotional.

She could feel a hardening taking place and she prayed God would understand. Somewhere in the recesses of her mind, she remembered reading once that the quickest way to distance oneself from God was to have a hard heart.

But to protect herself from the pain of a broken heart that was exactly what she needed to do.

Shane moved from room to room, checking closets and under beds. No sign of an intruder except for the rear patio door. It stood wide open. Bingo.

He stepped out onto the back patio. There was no sign of the intruder. The large dog run to the left was empty. And no one lurked on the lush lawn, which extended to the edge of the property and opened to a long stretch of desert before converging with the outer rim of the forest that dominated one side of the valley.

Marian's attacker was long gone.

Was it Gina's brother?

No, that didn't make sense. Why would Tim Perry want to hurt Marian Foxcroft? How would he even know about her?

Something else was going on here. What it was, Shane didn't have a clue.

He retraced his steps back to Gina's side. She glanced at him, her hazel eyes clouded with anxiety. He could only imagine how horrible this was for her.

After everything she'd been through these past five days and then to add more trauma to the mix by finding

Mrs. Foxcroft rendered unconscious by obvious foul play, it amazed Shane that Gina wasn't hysterical. He certainly wouldn't blame her for having a meltdown. She was due.

Anger churned in his gut. He'd come so close to capturing her brother and ending this ordeal for Gina. And it chafed his ego and pride that he'd allowed Tim the opportunity to escape. Shane had been distracted when he'd realized his handcuffs were gone. If only the handcuffs hadn't dislodged from his utility belt during the crash, Tim would be in custody and Gina would be safe and… Shane frowned as he realized Gina would still have found Marian unconscious and bleeding.

If Shane truly believed Tim wasn't the culprit here, then who was?

He touched Gina's shoulder. "The ambulance should be here any moment."

She moved away and picked up her phone from where it lay on the ground. "I should call Ellen."

"I can do it," he offered, wanting to make this easier for her.

"That's okay." She scrolled through her contact list. Her hands shook so badly that Shane thought she might drop the phone.

He covered her hands with his own. "Let me do this."

She relinquished her hold on the phone and scrambled away. "Okay." The sound of sirens had her rising to her feet. "I'll meet the ambulance. And put these two in the SUV."

As he watched her hurry out of the room, taking the puppies with her, he had the strangest feeling she was trying to get away from him as much as she was anxious to bring help to Marian.

He pressed the number under Ellen Foxcroft's name. She answered on the second ring.

"Gina?"

"Actually this is Shane. Gina's with me. We're at your house." He sought the right words to say. "We found your mother unconscious when we arrived."

"I heard. I'm almost there," the other K-9 rookie stated, the tension in her voice tugging at Shane. Despite the rocky relationship between mother and daughter, Shane had no doubt Ellen loved her mother.

He hung up as the paramedics hurried in with Gina close behind. Shane moved out of the EMTs' way and stepped to Gina's side. They watched in silence as the medics tended to Marian's wound and put her on a stretcher.

A few moments later Ellen Foxcroft rushed in as the paramedics wheeled Marian toward the front door. Ellen clasped a hand over her mouth. Gina hastened to put an arm around Ellen.

"Who would do this?" Ellen asked. She reached out to touch her mother's hand.

Gina shook her head. "I don't know. There was no one else here when we arrived. She'd called me and asked if I'd bring the puppies out for a visit."

Ellen visibly got ahold of herself. "We have to find the person who did this."

"Can you tell if anything is missing? Maybe this was a robbery gone bad," Shane suggested gently.

"What else could it be?" Ellen's voice rang with anger. She walked to the fireplace in the corner and pointed to an empty spot on the mantel. "There's a statue missing. A silver poodle that was a gift to my mother from the mayor."

The German shepherd in the crate whined at Ellen. She put a hand on the kennel door. "Gina, would you mind taking Amber to the training center? I'll come get her later."

"Of course I will," Gina quickly answered.

"Ma'am, we need to get your mother to the hospital," one paramedic said. "Do you want to ride with us?"

"Yes, thank you." Ellen left with the paramedics, passing Chief Jones and Officers Bucks and Harmon as they entered.

Shane explained the situation to the newcomers.

The chief tilted his head and addressed Gina. "When you approached the door, there was no sign of a break-in?"

"None, sir," she said. "The door was unlatched. I called out for Mrs. Foxcroft but there was no answer. I stepped in and found her there."

"I cleared the house and found the back patio door open, as well, but there was no sign of tampering with the locks on either the front or the back door," Shane supplied.

Officer Bucks elbowed Harmon and said in a low voice, "Isn't this the second body she's discovered? A little too coincidental, don't you think?"

Gina gave a little gasp at the accusation.

Shane whipped his attention to Bucks. "Hey, don't go disparaging Gina. She didn't hurt Mrs. Foxcroft or kill Veronica."

Bucks held up his hand. "Whoa, there, boy. Didn't mean to rile you up over your girlfriend."

Anger and dislike spread hot through Shane, and he ground his teeth together as he stepped toward Bucks. The craving to plow his fist in the older man's face was strong.

"Enough." The chief's voice brought Shane to a halt. "Bucks, Harmon, I want this place dusted for prints now."

"Yes, sir." Harmon held up a black box by the handle. "I anticipated the need."

"Brownie points for you." Bucks sneered. "Come on, let's get the front door first."

Shane blew out a calming breath and met Gina's wide-eyed gaze. Red stained her cheeks. He hated that she had to hear Bucks's inflammatory remarks and that she'd witnessed Shane nearly losing it. He wasn't usually so easily provoked, but the snide way Bucks talked about Gina had set something primeval off inside of Shane.

Chief Jones shook his head. "I'm not sure what I'm going to do with those two." He shrugged. "Sorry about that, Gina."

"I didn't do this," she said. "I didn't hurt Marian."

"Of course you didn't," Shane said, upset that she'd even have to defend herself. "And anyone who could think such a thing doesn't know you."

Her lower lip trembled. Confusion swirled in her hazel eyes. "Thank you, Shane."

Afraid she'd break down and cry in front of their boss, Shane gestured to the mantel, hoping to direct the conversation back to the assault. "Ellen said a silver statue is missing. Most likely the weapon used on Marian."

The chief rubbed his chin. "If it wasn't a break-in, then Marian knew her attacker. And if the statue was used, then perhaps Marian had invited the person into the living room. They argued and the perpetrator reached for the nearest heavy object and bashed Marian over the head."

"And left her for dead," Shane pointed out. "If we hadn't happened to have an appointment with Mrs. Foxcroft it could have been many hours before Ellen came home and found her."

"Do we think this could be the work of Tim Perry?"

The chief's question echoed Shane's earlier thoughts. "Sir, I don't think so. First, I can't imagine Mrs. Foxcroft inviting him in, and second, there's no reason for him to go after her. It's his sister he wants to harm."

"Right." The chief heaved a beleaguered sigh. "The assault on Marian is a separate deal. We need to dig into what Marian has been doing lately that would motivate an attack like this."

Officers Bucks and Harmon reappeared in the archway of the living room.

"Both doors have been wiped clean," Officer Harmon announced.

"All right, people," the chief said. "Let's clear out. I'm calling the Flagstaff crime lab to come in and do a full forensic search of the house and grounds. Hopefully there's a clue waiting to be discovered. I hate the thought of two maniacs running loose in Desert Valley."

Shane couldn't have agreed more. Suddenly the previous deaths that Marian Foxcroft had asked the rookies to look into took on a more ominous meaning. Had Marian's attacker been lurking in town for the past five years? Had the request to solve the cold cases been the motivation for the assault on Marian? And what lengths would the person go to in order to keep the past mysteries unresolved?

FOURTEEN

At the police station, Gina and Shane were separated as part of standard procedure in an investigation where there was more than one witness. Each was sent to a room to write out their account of finding Marian unconscious in her home.

Alone in an interrogation room, Gina tried to recount every detail she could remember about the visit to the Foxcroft home. Her hand shook so hard, her writing looked like that of a kindergartener.

The horror of finding Marian lying unconscious and bleeding twisted Gina up inside. She couldn't grasp why someone would hurt the older woman. She was so generous to the town, to the police department and the training center. Though not the most personable woman in town, Marian's roots were deep in the community.

Poor Ellen. She had to be beside herself with worry.

Gina understood the heartache of losing a parent.

She knew the agony of watching her father die at her brother's hand. That night would forever be etched in her mind. The terror of seeing her brother grab their father's service weapon from his holster, seeing the shock on Dad's face as he realized what Tim was doing.

Dad had tried to talk Tim down. He'd reasoned, cajoled and demanded, but Tim's manic state only worsened. He'd felt threatened and claimed Dad was trying to keep him from his full potential. But Dad had only wanted to help his son.

And Tim had killed him for it.

With a shudder, Gina pushed the memories to the recesses of her mind and finished the report. She stepped out of the room and headed toward the chief's office. No one was there.

She wandered farther down the hall to the conference room. Through the interior window she could see a meeting in progress. All of the rookies and the Desert Valley police officers were sitting or standing around an oblong conference table listening intently to what the chief was telling them from his place at the head. She hesitated, not wanting to disturb them.

"Are you done?"

Startled, Gina whirled around to find Carrie Dunleavy, the police department secretary, standing behind her. "Oh, Carrie. How are you?"

"Good, thank you." Her gaze went to the papers in Gina's hand.

"Yes, I'm done. What should I do with this?"

Carrie held out her hand. "I'll take it and add it to the file."

"Thank you." Gina handed over the report.

Carrie patted her arm. "Just so you know, I don't believe you hurt Marian, despite what anyone else thinks."

A knot formed in the pit of Gina's stomach. It seemed Officer Bucks had made his opinion well-known very quickly. "Uh, thanks."

Carrie walked away, her shoes clicking on the linoleum.

Gina remained in the hallway, unsure what to do next.

She peeked into the conference room again in hopes of catching Shane's eye, but he was focused on the heated conversation taking place. If Carrie were to be believed, Gina was the topic of discussion.

Just then Whitney Godwin glanced toward the window, meeting Gina's gaze. The sympathy in the rookie officer's expression curdled the breakfast in Gina's stomach. Needing to get away from the station and the sense of accusation permeating the air, Gina headed for the side exit. She drew up short.

The door had a warning sign that it was an alarmed exit and to please use the main entrance to come and go from the building.

She spun around, intending to go back to the front of the building, but who was she kidding? She couldn't leave. Not without Shane.

Her brother was still out there somewhere.

She felt trapped and condemned. She veered from the exit and entered the women's restroom. After slipping off her waist pack and setting it on the wooden bench, she splashed water on her face.

Tears leaked from her eyes to mingle with the water running down her cheeks. How could anyone believe she had attacked Marian Foxcroft?

Shane didn't. He'd defended her when Bucks made his outrageous claim that she was responsible for Marian's injury.

And he hadn't corrected the officer when he'd stated she was Shane's girlfriend. Because the accusation was so ridiculous that Shane hadn't felt the need to set Bucks straight? Or because there was some part of Shane that wanted her to be his girlfriend? Wishful thinking on her part.

She gripped the side of the sink and willed herself to

stop crying. She wasn't weak. She wasn't crazy and she wasn't capable of hurting someone else. She wiped at her eyes and stared at her reflection in the mirror.

She may share Tim's DNA but she wasn't like him. She was like her mother.

And her fear was just that—fear. She'd allowed fear to rule her life for too long.

Not anymore. Shane had shown her how to be brave.

Shane believed in her. More than she believed in herself. He made her want to allow love into her life. He made her want to be strong. Strong enough to know that she was done hiding here in Desert Valley.

Yes, her brother wanted to kill her. She wasn't a martyr and she wasn't suicidal. But once he was caught and jailed, then she would leave Desert Valley. She'd start over somewhere else. She'd done it once. She could do it again.

With Shane?

Sorrow twisted in her chest. No, not with Shane. He was committed to staying in Desert Valley until the mysterious deaths of the two rookies and Melanie Hayes's cold case murder were resolved. And now with Marian Foxcroft having been assaulted, all the men and women of the Desert Valley police force were needed.

She could wait for him. Then they could leave together.

However, she had no idea if he felt the same.

The same?

How did she feel about Shane?

She'd come to rely on him. She trusted him in a way she'd never trusted anyone else. She respected him and cared for him.

Was there more?

Her heart thumped against her ribs. Yes, she felt more

than she'd been willing to admit. She'd fallen for him. With her whole heart. She loved him.

She leaned her forehead against the cool surface of the mirror. Now what was she supposed to do?

Survive long enough to be able to leave Desert Valley. With or without Shane.

Despite the ache in her heart.

"There's no proof Gina Perry isn't guilty of attacking Mrs. Foxcroft. She had motive and opportunity," Officer Bucks stated with a smirk on his thin lips. His pale blue eyes sparked with animosity.

"Come on, really? She didn't have motive." Fisting his hands, Shane couldn't keep his exasperation from showing. Bella leaned into his leg. The dog had to sense his upset.

Shane had written out his report detailing the events at the Foxcroft place before joining the others in the conference room. He swept a look over the rookies and the established officers seated at the large table or standing against the wall of windows running along both sides of the conference room, giving the space a fishbowl feel.

Shane and the other rookies had each been issued a dark blue Desert Valley police uniform that matched the other officers'. Until now Shane hadn't really felt like part of the police force, even though he wasn't wearing this uniform. His assignment of protecting Gina had kept him isolated from the collective.

He was relieved to see the incredulous expression letting him know they weren't buying Bucks's outrageous claims either. Shane sent an imploring look to the chief, seated at the head of the table. "Chief, you can't believe what Bucks is spouting? Gina did not hurt Mrs. Foxcroft." Shane shot Officer Ken Bucks a seething glance.

"She went in alone and had time to crack Mrs. Foxcroft over the head before you went in," Bucks volleyed back with distain. "Maybe she and her brother are in this together. Like some twisted version of Bonnie and Clyde."

It was all Shane could do not to throttle the older officer. How on earth could the man think she and Tim were in cahoots? The man had a screw or two loose. "Are you nuts? Tim Perry is trying to kill her."

Shaking his head with frustration and anger, Shane didn't understand why Bucks was pushing so hard to throw Gina under the bus. "Gina had no reason to hurt Mrs. Foxcroft."

"Maybe Mrs. Foxcroft asked to have the puppies back?" Bucks said, folding his arms over his chest. "Gina seems pretty attached to the mutts."

"Of course she's attached." Whitney Godwin spoke up, her voice hard-edged. Her canine partner, a tan-and-white Pointer named Hunter, lifted his head to stare at her. "She's the puppies' trainer. That's her job."

"Maybe she was hoping with Veronica gone, she'd be lead trainer," Bucks said.

"That's ridiculous." Shane fought to keep from shouting. "And certainly not motive to hurt Mrs. Foxcroft. We already have a suspect in mind for Veronica's murder— Tim Perry."

"Has the statue been found?" Ryder asked quietly, drawing the room's focus. He sat at the far end of the table opposite the chief. Titus, his yellow Lab partner, lay panting on the floor. A bowl of water was beside him.

Officer Eddie Harmon shifted in his seat to face Ryder. "No. Marlton and I searched the house and the property. There was no sign of any silver poodle statue or any fingerprints beyond Mrs. Foxcroft and her daughter, Ellen."

"Whoever assaulted Mrs. Foxcroft took the statue with them," James said. "Hawk followed a scent to the edge of the property line where there were tire tracks."

Shane threw his housemate a grateful glance.

"Same tread as the tracks found after Tim Perry crashed the stolen sedan into Shane's Jeep?" Tristan McKeller asked, referring to the place where Hawk had lost Tim's scent. Jesse, Tristan's canine, lay under the table at Tristan's feet. At the sound of his partner's voice, his tail thumped against the floor.

James shook his head. "No, these were different."

"We'll know who attacked Marian when she awakes." The chief pinned a dark look on Bucks. "Ken, no more disparaging talk of Gina. She's not a suspect." He rubbed a hand over his weary face. "Where are we on the investigation into Veronica's murder?"

Ryder laid his hand on a file folder in front of him. "The ballistics report on the bullets used in Veronica's murder came back."

Shane's gut clenched in dreadful anticipation.

"They matched the striations on the weapon found at the train depot."

Confirming Shane's grandfather's SIG-Sauer P220 was indeed the weapon used to kill Veronica.

Air left Shane's lungs in a rush. His chest tightened. He reached for his inhaler inside the pocket of his pants but didn't bring it out as he willed his breathing to even out. So not the news he'd wanted to hear. He still didn't know how someone had gained his fingerprint, enabling them to open his safe and take the weapon. Whoever had killed Veronica had done so with willful intent.

But what did this do to the theory that Tim Perry was Veronica's murderer?

"Wait a minute," Tristan said, straightening in his chair. At his feet his partner stirred, obviously sensing Tristan's tension. "Are we still going with the assumption that Tim Perry killed Veronica when he couldn't find Gina at the training center?"

All eyes turned to the chief. But it was Ryder who answered, "I'm inclined to say Veronica's killer wasn't Tim Perry."

A stunned silence met his calm and grim pronouncement.

"We won't know for sure until we capture Tim Perry and question him," the chief said.

Shane wasn't so sure it would be that cut-and-dried. He had a very bad feeling that things were not as they seemed.

"Was Shane's handgun used in any other crimes?" Bucks asked Ryder. "Like your wife's murder."

Shane clenched his jaw tight. The man had no tact. "No. There's no way my grandfather's handgun was used in another crime. My grandfather was still alive and in possession of the weapon five years ago."

"Shane is correct," Ryder stated. "Veronica's murder is the only crime on the handgun."

"And where are you on Melanie's murder?" The chief's tone, though not gentle, was at least respectful, unlike Bucks's.

"Sifting back through evidence," Ryder stated.

Shane couldn't imagine how hard that had to be.

Chief Jones gave a short nod then turned his attention to the others. "The Riverton and Miller cases?"

"The same, sir," Tristan answered. "Combing through the reports and evidence files of both cases."

Though Whitney didn't verbally respond, she nodded an affirmative to Tristan's statement.

"Okay, good. Let me know if you come across anything that might have been missed or could be further explored," the chief said. "Weston and Harrison, I want your focus to be on the Perry situation."

"Yes, sir," Shane and James said in unison.

"Then we'll adjourn." The chief stood and walked from the room.

Bella rose to all fours, her head tilted to the side. Her ears perked up in alert mode.

Unease slithered down Shane's spine. The last time she'd exhibited this same behavior had been the night they'd found Gina with Veronica's dead body. He put his hand on Bella's neck. "What is it, girl?"

Hawk also scrambled to his feet and lifted his nose to the air. He let out a guttural growl that turned into a howl.

Shane had a bad feeling. He needed to find Gina.

A scrape of noise behind the closed door of the stall next to the exterior wall made the hairs at Gina's nape rise in alarm. She'd thought she was the only one in the restroom.

The two-foot by two-foot sash bathroom window was open. Unease threaded through her, making her break out in a cold sweat. Had that been open when she entered the restroom? She couldn't remember.

She glanced under the stall doors but saw no feet indicating there was another person in the restroom with her.

This is a police station. You're being silly. With a rueful shake of her head, she turned back to the mirror. Hadn't she just decided she wasn't going to let fear rule her life? And yet she was jumping at the slightest provocation.

The last stall door on the end burst open and her brother charged out.

She yelped with a burst of terror and lunged for the door, but Tim grabbed a handful of her hair and yanked her backward. His sweaty palm clamped over her mouth, stifling the scream that finally broke loose.

"Shut up!" He whispered the harsh command into her ear. "I'll kill you here and now if you make any noise."

Her mind scrambled to make sense of the situation. He'd climbed through the window, just as he had at the training center. No one had anticipated he'd try to get to her inside the police station. It boggled her mind that he'd be so bold. Had he been waiting inside the stall? How could he have known she'd enter the bathroom? Had he been watching her? But how?

"Do you understand me?" He tightened his hold on her hair, ripping strands from her head.

She nodded as tears of pain and panic crawled up her throat and burned her eyes.

"Good." He met her gaze in the mirror. Eyes the same shade of hazel as hers stared at her, but the malice in Tim's gaze sent terror zinging through her like a pinball.

Twigs and dirt clung to Tim's dark auburn hair. He smelled of body odor and damp earth. His crossbow clung to his back, the fletching of arrows sticking out of a pouch attached to the bow. His clammy hand made her skin crawl as he slowly lowered it from her mouth to wrap his fingers around her throat. "We're going out the window."

Not in this lifetime.

He was going to kill her anyway, right?

Better to die knowing she'd put up a fight. Maybe someone would hear and come to her rescue, because if she let him take her from here, the next time anyone saw her would be when they stumbled upon her remains out in the desert.

Fierce anger filled her. She was ready to do what needed to be done to stop him.

He dragged her to the window and shoved her hard. "Climb out."

She braced her hands on either side of the window, her fingers clutching the window jambs. She planted her feet where the wall and floor met. "No."

Tim drove his shoulder into her back in an effort to force her out the window. Pain in her kidneys nearly took her out but she breathed through the pain and let loose a loud scream that reverberated off the tiled walls.

Fisting her hair in his hand once again, he dug the tips of his fingers into the soft flesh of her throat, pressing against her esophagus, cutting off her scream and choking her. "Fine. We'll go out the side door. And just to be clear, after I kill you, I'll go after every cop I see. I'll take down as many as I can before they get me. Those deaths will be on you."

She swallowed the bile burning a hole through her, and she sent up a silent plea to God above. *Help me stop him, Lord. Please.*

Keeping his hand gripped in the soft tissue at her throat, he opened the bathroom door with his other hand to peer into the hall. It was empty. He opened the door and pushed her through. The exit was steps away.

Hopeful anticipation rumbled through her.

Once he pressed the metal bar running across the center and the door opened, the alarm would sound.

He'd bring the police running on his own. She'd have to make sure he couldn't use his bow to hurt anyone.

But would she be strong enough?

* * *

Shane's heart beat in his throat as Bella led him past the empty interrogation room where he'd last seen Gina. Where could she have gone?

Bella sniffed the floor. Shane prayed she picked up Gina's scent. Bella moved away from the interrogation room and headed down another hallway that led them past the backside of the conference room.

The sudden, jarring sound of the alarm system jolted Shane's heart into high gear. Bella barked and strained at her leash. Letting out the lead, he raced after her as she ran, the tapping of her nails drowned out by the siren. She led him down a short corridor that ended with an emergency exit. The door was slowly closing.

"Gina!" Shane shouted. He couldn't hear anything over the alarm.

Shane and Bella rushed for the door. Hitting it with his shoulder, Shane burst out of the police station and into the side parking lot. Bella put her nose to the ground. Making a zigzag line, she crossed the lot to an empty space where a car had been. His heart dropped. Gina was gone.

FIFTEEN

A band of panic pulled taut across Shane's chest as he surveyed the empty parking spot where a car had once been. Bella had led to this spot. Where was Gina? What had happened to her?

He didn't believe for a second she'd left of her own accord. Her brother had somehow infiltrated the police station and kidnapped her. Or killed her and taken her body away.

The thought made him stagger back a step. *Oh, Lord, please no.*

No, he couldn't let his mind go there. She had to be alive. There had to be a chance of saving her.

Shane had promised Gina he'd keep her safe. He'd failed.

Bella whined as she paced in a circle, clearly as upset at losing Gina as Shane. They'd both fallen for the lovely trainer. Shane's breath hitched. He'd fallen in love with Gina. The ramifications of the realization rippled through him. But now was not the time for examination or analyzing. Gina's life was in danger.

"Shane!" Whitney Godwin called from the side exit to the police station. "We found something."

Something? Not Gina. Please not Gina. He and Bella

hustled back inside and followed Whitney to the women's restroom. He crowded inside. James and Ryder were there. The window in the exterior wall was open. On the bench beside the sink lay Gina's training pouch.

His stomach sank. She wouldn't have willingly left this behind. Pulling on gloves, he lifted the pouch and checked inside, confirming what he feared. Her cell phone lay nestled among the treat bags.

Tracking her through her phone wasn't going to happen.

"Everyone back to the conference room," Ryder said. "We need to come up with a plan to find Gina and Tim Perry."

"Her one hope is if the canines can trail her scent." Though Gina's scent would be on her pack, it would be muddled by the dog treats and whoever else had handled the pack. Shane grabbed James by the arm. "I'm going back to the condo to get Gina's pillowcase. Her scent will be the strongest on that."

"Agreed." James handed over the keys to his truck and then glanced toward the conference room door. "I'll cover for you."

Grateful to his fellow rookie, Shane accepted the keys, and he and Bella hurried out of the station house. At the condo, Shane rushed to Gina's room and stripped her pillowcase off the pillow. He held the material to Bella's nose. "Gina. We have to find her, Bella. Gina. Find Gina."

They jumped back into the truck. When they returned to the police station James and Hawk were waiting. Shane released Bella then handed James the pillowcase. James offered its scent to Hawk. The dog let out a woof.

Bella gave an answering bark.

Ryder and Titus stepped outside, followed by Whitney and Hunter, and Tristan and Jesse. The pillowcase was handed off to each handler to let his or her K-9 partner have a good whiff of the special scent that was Gina.

Chief Jones and the other officers filed out, as well.

The chief pinned Shane with a tense look. "The next few hours are critical. We'll fan out and start searching."

Shane nodded. If Tim Perry was as bent on killing Gina as he seemed, he'd do the horrendous deed within the first couple of hours. And then he'd be in the wind.

Rage like he'd never experienced before engulfed Shane. When he found Tim Perry, Shane intended to make the man pay for all the terror he'd caused his sister.

"Ken and Harmon, you ride with Tristan and Jesse. Start at the train station and run the tracks. Whitney and Hunter, you'll ride with me. We'll head back to the training center and work from there. Marlton, you go with Ryder and Titus. Start your search in town and move south," the chief instructed. "James and Shane, you and your partners work together from here." He encompassed them all with a sweeping glance. "Watch each other's backs."

The officers of the Desert Valley Police Department headed off to start their search for Gina Perry.

As Shane gave Bella another whiff of Gina's pillowcase, he prayed they were on a rescue mission and not a recovery one.

The old beater station wagon chugged along, bouncing over every rut and pothole on the fire road cutting through Desert Woods. After Tim had forced Gina into the back of the wagon, he'd tied her hands behind her back and toppled her over, demanding she stay down or he'd run anyone she tried to contact over.

She'd stayed lying sidewise on the bench backseat for as along as she could, but once they'd gone off the road, she'd worked her way to a sitting position. Without the use of her hands, though, she was unable to brace herself as the wagon took another jolting hit. Her teeth snapped together with the impact. The wagon groaned. The thing was on its last legs. She expected the transmission to drop out any second.

In front of her, Tim sat in the driver's seat, clutching the steering wheel and staring out the dirty front window with singular concentration.

"Tim, talk to me," she said for the umpteenth time. "I don't understand what you want. What do you hope to accomplish?"

He continued to ignore her. She wiggled closer to the door and tried as subtly as she could to grasp the handle, but it was just high enough to be out of her reach. Frustration washed over her and she barely refrained from kicking the back of Tim's seat.

That he hadn't killed her outright was a blessing, but she had no doubt he had some nefarious plan for her demise. The farther they drove away from town, the more worried she was that Shane and Bella wouldn't be able to find her. She didn't even have her cell phone, so they couldn't use that to locate her. Despair crept into her consciousness but terror remained prominent.

She licked her dry lips, thankful the windows were open to offer some relief from the stench of the vehicle, though the dust swirling through the interior clogged her throat and nose, making her cough.

Looking out the window, she tried to gauge where they were, but since she hadn't taken the time to explore Desert Woods, she wasn't sure how far away the Desert Pines campground was or if they were anywhere near it. Maybe they were closer to Valley Lake at the other end of the woods, or near the water, which was an arm of the

Colorado River. The area was massive and the landscape alternately treacherous and beautiful. How was Shane going to locate her?

She was going to have to find a way to escape and get help for herself. If she could alert someone, then they could call for help. But so far they hadn't passed anyone after leaving the town.

Tim made a sharp left turn. Gina slammed up against the door, her shoulder taking the worst of the hit. "Hey!"

The way became even more jarring as they bounced off the fire road and blazed a trail through the woods, barely missing a tree. He finally slipped the station wagon behind a large tangle of bushes and cut the engine.

A cloud of dirt enveloped her through the open windows. Her body was racked with a coughing fit as she tried to expel the dust from her lungs.

Tim got out and walked away.

Gina twisted in the seat, trying to keep him in her sight. What was he up to?

He disappeared around the tangle of bushes. She studied the dense foliage and realized the bushes weren't a naturally occurring bramble. Tim had forged out a fort of bushes, tree limbs and rocks. So this was where he'd been hiding the past few days. How long had he been here?

With him out of sight, she tried again with less subtlety and more awkward groaning since her hands were tied behind her back to get the door unlocked and opened. Finally the lock released and the door popped open. She practically fell out of the wagon. She rolled the rest of the way out, tucking in her chin and landing on her back, smashing her hands beneath her.

She sat up and wiggled to get her feet beneath her. Afraid Tim would return, she searched for the way they'd come in but couldn't discern the path they'd taken. Didn't matter. She needed to move. To escape. Better lost in the woods than meekly awaiting her fate at Tim's hand.

She darted behind a tree and glanced up through the branches and leaves. Maybe she could navigate her way back to town using the sun to set a course. If she kept the ball of fire at her back, then she'd be heading west. Or was it east? Or did she need to move toward the sun, which would mean she'd be traveling south? She wished she'd paid better attention to her astronomy class in college. She just had to pick a direction and pray it was the right one.

She pushed off from the tree and sprinted away.

"Oh, no, you don't!" Tim screeched from somewhere behind her.

She didn't dare look back. Keeping her focus on the way in front of her, she hopped over an exposed root, only to land on her foot wrong. She went down. Without her hands to break the fall, her head hit the dirt with a thud. She scrambled back up despite the pain exploding behind her eyes. She had to keep moving.

A hand grabbed her arm and hauled her off her feet. Tim threw her down on the ground. She screamed and kicked at him but he danced out of her way. He huffed as he towered over her. "I'm not done with you yet."

He yanked her to her feet. She let out a yelp at the sudden pain in her shoulder. He dragged her stumbling back to his fort and shoved her inside the makeshift shelter. She fell heavily onto her knees but the pain barely registered. Tim came in behind her and plopped down on a cot.

The space had the cot, a small cooking stove and pint-size generator for electricity. A light had been strung up and a laptop computer sat on the dirt floor. A pile of filthy clothes was stacked in the corner. How could he live like this?

Her gaze met his. The malice she'd seen before was gone. He looked tired, regretful. He'd come down from his mania. Maybe there was still hope he'd let her go.

In a gentle tone that she'd heard their mother use with him, she said, "Tim, why are you here?"

"For you."

"How did you find me?"

His lips spread into a grim smile. He pointed to the computer. "No one can hide from the mighty internet."

She struggled to comprehend what he meant. She didn't have any social-media outlets and was careful not to let herself be photographed.

"There was a publicity shot of the center. You were in the background," he said. "I knew you couldn't stay away from dog places. I combed the Internet looking for you. I'd know you anywhere."

Her heart sank. Veronica had set up the publicity event. Gina knew the shot he referred to, but Gina had had her back to the camera. She'd been so sure no one would be able to recognize her. But Tim had. And the photograph had brought him to the center. Where he'd hoped to find her but instead had found Veronica. "Why did you kill my boss?"

Tim tucked in his chin. "I didn't kill her. I locked her in the closet. If she died while in there that's not my fault."

"What?" Oh, he meant Sophie. "No, I mean when you first came to the center last Saturday night. I wasn't there but you found my boss, Veronica. The lady that was in the photo you saw. You killed her when you couldn't find me."

He shook his head, his gaze confused. "No, I didn't. I did go to the center that afternoon and saw you there. But you left before it got dark and went home then to the church where you were serving food." He giggled. "You spilled gravy on the floor and that guy slipped. That was funny. I decided to wait for you at your house. I didn't kill anyone."

His words slammed into her. She had spilled some soup and Carson Lloyd, a banker in town, had slipped. She'd been aghast. He'd asked her out and she'd declined.

"I wasn't going to grab you at the church, though." Tim wrinkled his nose. "I don't want to bring down the wrath of God on me."

Gina's mind tried to make sense of what he was telling her. He'd followed Gina to church and then went to Gina's home to wait for her to return. He hadn't killed Veronica.

Then who did kill Veronica?

The same person who assaulted Marian Foxcroft?

Mysteries Gina hoped she lived to see resolved.

Right now she had to find a way out of here. "Tim, I have to go to the bathroom. Can you untie me? Let me go, please?"

"There's a can in the corner," he said.

She clenched her jaw to keep her temper under control. "Why are you doing this?"

"You're my sister. We need to be together."

"You've been trying to kill me the past few days!"

"Yeah, sorry about that." He stood. "Want something to eat? I caught a squirrel. They aren't too bad."

She gagged at the thought. "No, I'm not hungry. Tim, please let me leave. I won't tell anyone where you are. Just let me live my life in peace."

"No!"

"You need help," she said. "Don't you see that?"

His face hardened and that malicious gleam returned. He moved swiftly to stand in front of her and poked her in the chest with his finger. "Don't you dare be like Dad or you'll end up dead like him." He grabbed her by the arm and forced her up and into a camping chair. He tied her feet to the legs. "Now, shut up. I'm tired."

He lay on the cot and rolled onto his side, away from her. After a few minutes, his snoring filled the shelter.

Unbelievable. If she weren't so terrified, freaked-out and scared, she'd laugh with hysteria. Instead, she set to work on trying to free her ankles from the leg of the camping chair. She sent up a prayer that help was on the way and it arrived before her brother changed his mind and killed her.

SIXTEEN

Shane jogged behind Bella, with James and Hawk just off to his right side. The dogs had found a scent in the air and they were trailing it through Desert Woods. Shane had already had the campground ranger check all the cabins and campsites, but he'd come up empty. Had Tim somehow slipped past the ranger?

Bella and Hawk were leading them not to the campground but to the fire road, which gave the forestry service access to the lake and the river whenever there was a fire in the region. There were tire tracks in the dry earth. Shane couldn't tell if they were recent or not.

Bella lifted her nose to the air and swerved to the left. Hawk kept moving forward then doubled back and hurried after the other dog. Shane shared a curious glance with James as they veered left to follow the dogs.

All the dust and dirt of the forest floor made Shane itch and tightened his lungs. He fingered his inhaler, yet he was unwilling to stop to use it. The panic he'd been keeping at bay edged closer, crowding out his focus. But he had to stay on task and detached so he could be an effective officer.

Losing it wouldn't do Gina any good.

Both dogs stopped and sat in front of a large tangled

mess of bushes and branches. Not a natural structure. Heart beating in his ears, Shane drew to a halt. He gestured for James to go left around the crude shelter while he and Bella would go to the right. There had to be an opening. Would he find Gina inside? Alive or dead?

Pain craved a hole in his heart. He sent up a prayer that God would see them through this.

Bella sniffed the air and the ground as they rounded the rudimentary lodging. An old-style station wagon, battered and dirty, was parked on the back side of the snarled mass of debris. Bella alerted in front of a makeshift door fashioned from branches and chunks of moss. Anxiety twisted him up inside.

James joined him with Hawk. Shane withdrew his sidearm; James followed suit. Shane counted down with his fingers. On three they breached the manmade lodging.

"Halt, police!" Shane shouted as he rushed inside. He took in the scene, quickly cataloging that Gina was half out of a chair with one ankle tied to a leg. She blinked up at him in stunned surprise.

Tim scrambled up from the cot with a large knife in his hand. Tim's gaze darted between Shane and Gina. Shane understood the other man's intent just as he lunged for Gina.

"Don't!" Shane shouted. Bella barked. Hawk howled. James aimed his weapon at Tim's head.

Tim ignored the order and wrapped one hand around Gina's arm, yanking her close. The knife hovered over her throat. "Back off!"

Not willing to risk hitting Gina with a bullet, Shane used the best weapon available. "Attack!" Shane gave Bella the command.

The dog didn't need any more encouragement. She

leaped at Tim, her teeth sinking into his hand that held the knife. Bella's paws landed on the chair beside Gina's head. Tim screamed, the knife dropped to the side to land on the ground, and he released his hold on Gina. She scrambled away from her brother as best she could with her hands tied behind her back. James moved in and subdued Tim.

Shane holstered his weapon to gather Gina in his arms. He quickly untied her hands and her ankle. His pulse thundered in his veins; his heart pounded. "I feared I wouldn't get to you in time."

Relief washed over him as he captured her lips before she could say anything and kissed her with all the pent-up anguish, longing and love he could pour out.

James cleared his throat, snapping Shane back from the brink of losing himself in Gina.

"You want to call Bella off?" James asked with a wry twist of his lips.

The dog still had Tim's hand in her teeth.

"Release." Immediately she did. Then she jumped down and came to Gina and licked her face. Gina hugged Bella.

"I'll just take him out and call the chief," James said with a grin. Then he pushed Tim out of the shelter. Hawk followed them.

Gina gazed up at Shane with eyes bright and full of tears. "I was so scared but I knew in my heart you two would find me."

"I've never been this frightened before," he admitted. He cupped her cheek. "I don't know what I would have done if I'd lost you."

She turned her head to place a kiss in his palm. "Thank you." After a moment, she looked to him. "Can you help me to my feet?"

He jumped up and lifted her off the ground, then slowly set her on her feet. He pulled her close for a hug and kiss, thanking God that she was safe. A few minutes later they walked out of the shelter hand in hand.

They were crowded into the conference room. Shane stood behind Gina's chair, his hands warm on her shoulders. She couldn't stop herself from reaching up to place her hand over his. That he'd found her in the middle of the woods was a feat she'd despaired wasn't possible. Her relief at seeing Shane and Bella had been overwhelming. Seeing Bella in action had been amazing. Though she'd trained many dogs over the years to take down a suspect, she'd never seen a dog in action during a real crime. Now her respect for the K-9 officers and their partners had tripled. Her job was important, and the officers and their canines were critical in the field.

And now with her brother in custody, the adrenaline and fear seeped from her, leaving her feeling weepy and joyful and exhausted all at the same time.

But what had her heart still thumping in her chest was the way Shane had tended to her. He'd been gentle, loving. His kiss lingered on her lips, making them tingle. They hadn't had a moment alone since they'd walked out of Tim's makeshift shelter, so she hadn't told Shane how she felt. She wasn't sure she was brave enough to.

"Thank you, Shane and James," the chief said in a voice choked with pride. "You will be receiving commendations for your service in bringing in the prime suspect in Veronica's murder."

"Uh, sir," Gina spoke up. "Tim didn't murder Veronica."

All eyes swung to her. The room filled with stunned silence.

Shane's hands flexed against her collarbone. "What are you saying?"

She looked up at him. "I asked him why he killed her but he said he didn't."

"Of course he'd deny it," Officer Bucks spat out. "He's a criminal. He's not going to confess to murder so easily."

She shook her head and turned her gaze to Chief Jones. "Sir, I believe Tim. He found me from the publicity shot that Veronica had had taken for the center. He came to the center and followed me home and then to the church, where he spied on me before he returned to my house to wait for me. He was trashing my house at the time of Veronica's death. Veronica's murderer is still out there."

Everyone started talking at once. The chaotic noise filled Gina's head, making her temples throb.

"Excuse me," Carrie Dunleavy called from the doorway.

The chief held up a hand, calling for quiet. "Yes, Carrie?"

"Chief Weston of the Flagstaff PD is in your office. He'd like to speak to you and Officer Weston."

Gina's gaze jumped to Shane. What was his father doing here? His jaw tightened and his green eyes glittered with concern. Her heart squeezed tight. She prayed the elder Weston wasn't here with bad news.

He leaned down to whisper in her ear. "I have to go talk to my dad. I'll be back."

She nodded as he removed his hands from her shoulders, leaving cool spots that sent a shiver racing through her.

"Okay, folks," the chief said. "We've jobs to do. Ryder, you take point on questioning the suspect."

Jones tipped his chin toward Shane. "Officer Weston, after you."

The two men left the room with Bella at Shane's side. Gina remained seated while the others filed out of the conference room. Carrie Dunleavy moved to stand next to Gina.

Gina glanced up at Carrie with a questioning look. "Is everything okay?"

"I just wanted to say I'm glad you're okay," the station's secretary said. "We were all worried about you."

"Thank you," Gina replied, touched by Carrie's sentiment. Gina decided she needed to make more of an effort to befriend the woman.

"Too bad Weston will be transferring out sooner than expected," Carrie said. "I was under the impression you two had a thing going on."

Gina swallowed back the surprise bubbling up inside of her. So that was why his father was here, to insist that Shane be released to join the Flagstaff PD. Her shoulders slumped with disappointment because she knew that was Shane's goal—to work with his family. She didn't even have the fortitude at the moment to correct Carrie's assumption that there was more going on between Gina and Shane than there actually was.

"Carrie, I hear the phone ringing," Whitney Godwin said as she plopped down in the chair next to Gina, her canine, Hunter, at her feet.

"Oh, thank you." Carrie turned and hurried away.

Whitney touched Gina's arm. "I can't imagine how hard this has been for you."

"It's been an ordeal," Gina confirmed. "Tim needs help. I hope now he'll get it."

"And what about you and Shane?" Whitney wagged

her eyebrows. "Is Carrie right? Do you and the handsome rookie have a thing going on?"

Needing to confide in someone, Gina faced her friend. "I've fallen in love with him."

Whitney's eyes widened and a smile spread across her pretty face. "I thought so. You two are so good together. I could tell you both had feelings for each other during the training."

"Well, it doesn't matter, because he will be leaving," she replied. "Whether it's now or later."

"Then go with him," Whitney said in a tone that suggested the thought was a no-brainer.

"I don't know if he feels the same."

"You haven't told him how you feel?"

Gina shook her head. "No."

"You should. Don't wait. Take it from me, if you delay in confessing your feelings, you might miss the opportunity and then…" Whitney trailed off, her gaze taking on a faraway look, and sadness dampened her expression.

"Whitney?" Gina wondered if her words were more personal than just advice. Whitney had never named the father of her baby.

"Just tell him before it's too late," Whitney said.

"Is that what happened to you?" Gina tugged on her bottom lip, debating whether to mention the conclusion she'd come to when she and Shane were babysitting Shelby. "Whitney, is Brian Miller Shelby's father?"

Startled, Whitney stared at Gina. "How did you…?"

"Shelby has Brian's green eyes." She touched Whitney's hand. "When you and Brian were in the training session last year I had a feeling you and he were seeing each other."

"You never said anything."

"I didn't want to pry." Empathy cramped her chest. "It

must have been hard for you to have a baby alone. I wish you'd have confided in me. I would have helped you."

A tear welled in Whitney's eye. "I wish I had. I was going to tell Brian that night, but then the fire happened and it was too late." She wiped at her tears. "I didn't get a chance to tell my brother either before he was killed in Afghanistan."

Gina hugged her. "Oh, honey, I'm so sorry. I'm here for you—you know that, right?"

Drawing back, Whitney nodded. "Thank you. I appreciate that. I've felt so alone. But I have my neighbor and her family. They take good care of Shelby when I'm at work."

"That's good, but don't close yourself off to love. One day you'll meet someone who will fill the void left by Brian and your brother."

Whitney arched an eyebrow. "I could give you the same advice."

With a rueful smile, Gina agreed. "Yes. I should take my own advice."

Whitney sobered. "So if your brother didn't kill Veronica, then who did?"

Shifting back to the question of the day, Gina couldn't stop the shudder coursing over her. "I would hazard a guess it was the same person who hurt Marian Foxcroft."

"Probably. She's in a coma, you know."

Sympathy twisted Gina's insides. "I was sorry to hear that. I'll pray she wakes up soon."

"Me, too." Whitney leaned closer and lowered her voice. "I've been looking into Brian's death. For all intents and purposes it does appear like an accident. But I knew Brian. His family died in a house fire. There is no way he'd have ever lit that candle, let alone put it in a place where it would topple over and catch the house on fire."

A chill skated across Gina's flesh. "As much as I hate to say this, I think we have a serial murderer in our midst."

"Dad, stop," Shane said, holding up a hand to cut off his father's diatribe. They stood in the chief's office facing each other. Dad was dressed in his chief's uniform, all his medals and bars reminders of his status. "You don't get to make this decision."

Dad wanted Shane to be released from his obligations here in Desert Valley and return with him to Flagstaff. But Shane wasn't going to bow to his father's expectations or rants. He'd done enough of that in his life. "I've agreed to stay on here until the department's unsolved cases are resolved."

"You did your part by bringing in that criminal," Trent Weston said between clenched teeth. He was a man who expected others to bend to his will.

"I did, but there's more work to be done." Shane glanced at the chief, who sat behind his desk taking in the family drama playing out before him. Shane didn't blame Jones for not wanting to intervene. Family dynamics could be tricky. Shane refocused on his dad. Though he was at his father's eye level, Trent Weston had an intimidating presence that made him a formidable chief of police and father.

"Look, Dad, when it's time for me to leave Desert Valley, I'll be going wherever I'm assigned, whether that's Flagstaff or some other department in the state."

"That's not what we agreed to when you left for your training."

"True, but I've decided that I need to live my life for

me. Not you." Gina had made him realize how much he'd been living to please his family rather than to fulfill his own destiny that God had planned for him.

Dad pressed his lips together and narrowed his gaze. "If you change your mind, you know where to find me."

With that his dad spun on his heel and stormed out. Shane stared after him. Wow, that had gone way better than he'd anticipated.

"Good for you, son," the chief said as he rose. "Now, we've got work to do. If Gina is to be believed and her brother didn't kill Veronica, then we have a murderer still loose."

"I do believe Gina, sir," Shane said.

"Then let's get busy." The chief led the way out of his office.

Shane went in search of Gina and found her still in the conference room with Whitney. When he stepped into the room, Whitney jumped up from the chair. "I'm sure I've got to be somewhere." She sent Gina a look rife with unspoken meaning. "Don't wait."

Whitney grinned at Shane and then she and Hunter left the room.

"What was that about?" he asked as he took the seat next to Gina.

She swallowed as she faced him. Her eyes were huge in her face. Something was wrong. Concern arched through him. He gathered her hands. "What wrong?"

Her fingers laced through his. "Nothing is wrong. I have something I need to say."

Why did that sound so ominous? "Okay."

"You may not want to hear this, but I need to say it before I lose my nerve," she said, her voice trembling. "I know you're going to leave Desert Valley. Probably sooner than later, but I can't let you go without telling you that I, uh, well—" She took a deep breath. "I love you, Shane Weston."

If he hadn't been sitting, her words would have knocked him flat on his behind. She loved him. Joy like he'd never experienced blasted through him, making his chest tight and his breathing restricted, but no inhaler was needed. "I feel the same way," he managed to say past the lump in his throat.

"What?"

He breathed in and let it out slowly as a calm happiness took hold of him. "I love you, Gina Perry. I think I have since that first day I walked into your training class."

A delighted smile spread over her lovely face. "Really?"

"Yes, really." He leaned in and planted his lips against hers. They kissed for several minutes of pure bliss. When they broke apart, he said, "I don't know what the future holds or where I'll end up assigned to, but would you… Do you think you'd, uh, well, be willing to…" He couldn't believe how badly he was botching this up. How did he ask her to leave her life for him?

"Yes," she said.

He stilled, daring not to hope she meant what he hoped she meant. "Yes, what?"

She grinned. Her hazel eyes sparkled. "Yes, I'll go wherever you're assigned."

He let out a relieved sigh. "I'm so glad to hear that."

Then he kissed her again.

* * * * *

With over seventy books published and millions in print, **Lenora Worth** writes award-winning romance and romantic suspense. Three of her books finaled in the ACFW Carol Awards, and her Love Inspired Suspense novel *Body of Evidence* became a *New York Times* bestseller. Her novella in *Mistletoe Kisses* made her a *USA TODAY* bestselling author. Lenora goes on adventures with her retired husband, Don, and enjoys reading, baking and shopping…especially shoe shopping.

Books by Lenora Worth

Love Inspired Suspense

Military K-9 Unit

Rescue Operation

Classified K-9 Unit

Tracker
Classified K-9 Unit Christmas
"A Killer Christmas"

Rookie K-9 Unit

Truth and Consequences
Rookie K-9 Unit Christmas
"Holiday High Alert"

Capitol K-9 Unit

Proof of Innocence
Capitol K-9 Unit Christmas
"Guarding Abigail"

Visit the Author Profile page
at Harlequin.com for more titles.

TRUTH AND CONSEQUENCES

Lenora Worth

For where envying and contention is, there is
inconstancy, and every evil work.
—*James* 3:16

Many thanks to my fellow writers in this series—
Terri Reed, Lynette Eason, Shirlee McCoy,
Dana Mentink and Valerie Hansen.
I loved working with all of you.

ONE

"Next stop, Desert Valley, Arizona."

David Evans took a deep breath and got up to exit the passenger train, glad to finally be at his destination. Now if he could locate the woman he'd come here to see.

There were only two other people left in this car. Two men wearing baseball caps and dark shades. They'd kept to themselves most of the trip from Los Angeles, and so had David. There was something about these two.

They grabbed their carry-on duffels and rushed out of their seats so fast they stumbled upon the car attendant coming up the aisle. Startled, one of them dropped his tattered black bag, causing it to rip open.

Several colorful bundles covered in shrink-wrap crashed onto the floor. Everything after that happened so fast—David's blood pressure spiked, and he felt himself slipping back into the arid mountains of Afghanistan.

The attendant's surprise turned to realization, his gaze moving from the two men to the packages spilling from the duffel.

"Keep moving, old man," one of the men told the attendant. "Don't you have someplace else to be?"

The attendant stared at the bag. "No, can't do that. I'm afraid I'll have to report this immediately."

"Wrong answer." One of them pulled a knife on the frightened older attendant, stabbing him in the stomach. The attendant went down on his knees, shock and fear evident in his wide-eyed stare.

David saw the whole thing from his seat a few feet up the aisle. While the two argued about leaving without the packages they'd dropped, David hurried to help the injured man.

But one of the men pulled out a gun and pointed it at David, his expression hard-edged while his trigger finger twitched. "Get out of here. Now."

David glanced up at the man holding a gun on him and then down at the bleeding man lying on the floor of the passenger train. "I'm not leaving. I'm a medic, and this man needs help."

He braced himself and knelt down beside the attendant, fully expecting to be shot. Which was kind of ironic since he'd just returned from Afghanistan. He'd managed to survive the front lines, and now he might be killed while trying to honor the promise he'd made to a dying soldier.

Before the standoff could continue, voices outside caused the gunman's friend to whirl in a nervous dance. "I didn't agree to this," he said in a growling whisper, his oversize red baseball cap covering most of his face. "Man, if you shoot him, the DEA and every cop around here will be on us. We need to leave."

The man holding the gun glanced around, the sweat of panic radiating off him like hot steam. Then he spouted off to his short but wise buddy, his words as brittle as desert sand. "Get all that up and let's go. Now!"

He kept the gun on David while his nervous helper shoved the packages back inside the gaping duffel. "You better keep traveling, mister, if you want to live." Then he pointed to the moaning attendant. "I'll finish off both of you if either of you talks."

David held his breath and stayed on his knees near the injured attendant while the two men rushed off the train, baseball caps pulled low over their faces and sunglasses hiding their eyes. But the minute he saw them heading for a black SUV in the small parking lot near the square Tudor-style train station, he pulled out his cell and called 911. Straining to see, he memorized only part of the license plate and quickly glanced at what looked like some sort of Aztec emblem centered over the plates.

"I'm a medic," he told the shocked older man after giving the dispatcher the needed information. "I'm going to help you, okay?" He checked the man's vitals and found a weak pulse.

The pale-faced man nodded, his expression full of fright, his pupils dilating as he went into shock. "He stabbed me."

"I saw," David said. Taking off the button-up shirt over his old T-shirt, he quickly used it to stanch the blood oozing from the gash in the man's abdomen. "Lie still while I examine you. Help should be on the way."

The man moaned and closed his eyes. "My wife is gonna be so mad."

David sank down beside the man, hoping to keep him talking. "Hey, buddy, what's your name?"

"Herman," the man said. "Herman Gallagher." Then he grabbed David's arm. "You need to report this to our conductor, too. Drugs. I think they had drugs in those bags."

David did as he asked, and soon the conductor and several attendants were moving up and down the aisles.

David put up a hand to hold them away and kept talking to the man after handing his phone to a young assistant, who stayed on the line with 911. When he heard sirens, he breathed a sigh of relief. Though he was concerned because of Mr. Gallagher's age and still disoriented himself, he'd seen much worse than this in the heat of battle. But right now, he was struggling to fight his own flashbacks.

This trip had sure ended with a bang.

And he hadn't even stepped off the train to his final destination.

He'd come here searching for a woman he didn't really know, except in his imagination. But a promise was a promise. He wasn't leaving Desert Valley without finding her.

When he looked up a few minutes later to see a pretty female officer with long blond hair coming toward him, a sleek tan-and-white canine pulling on a leash in front of her, David thought he surely must be dreaming. Either that or his flashbacks were taking a new turn.

He knew that face. Had seen it in his dreams many times over.

While he sat on the cold train floor holding a bloody shirt to a man who was about to pass out, he looked up and into the vivid blue eyes of the woman he'd traveled here to find. The woman who'd colored his dreams during the brutality of war and made him wish he could finally settle down. Thinking of the worn picture in his pocket that her brother, Lucas, had given him right before he died, David couldn't believe this was really happening.

Whitney Godwin was coming to his aid.

Whitney took one look at the two men on the train floor and went into action. Turning to her partner, a white-and-tan pointer appropriately named Hunter, she commanded, "Stay."

Hunter whimpered, his shiny nose sniffing the air, his dark eyes lifting to her in a definite alert. Did the big dog sense something else around here? Hunter was trained in drug detection, so it was possible. They'd both recently finished an intense twelve-week session in town, so Whitney knew they were up to the task. Yet her heart beat with a burst of adrenaline that shouted, *This is the real deal.*

She took a good look at the injured train attendant and the man helping him. They'd both have to be questioned and cleared. "We'll get to our search later, Hunter."

Turning from Hunter, she spoke into the radio attached to her shoulder. "James, need that bus, stat. We have one injured and one who doesn't look so hot." Then she added, "We need to clear the train, too. Hunter's a little antsy."

"Bus is en route. ETA three minutes," James Harrison, fellow rookie, responded. "I'll take Hawk and have a look around, question some of the bystanders. Ellen's on the way. She and Carly can help with a sweep."

Ellen Foxcroft was also a rookie, and her golden retriever, Carly, was trained in tracking. Her mother, the formidable Marian Foxcroft, who'd always been supportive of the K9 training program in Desert Valley, had recently made an offer to Chief Jones that he couldn't ignore. They'd all been asked to stay here after graduation from the training course to help investigate the high-profile murder of their master trainer, Veronica Earnshaw.

Marian had offered to underwrite their salaries since she wanted Veronica's murder solved right away. Not to mention, she wanted the two suspicious deaths of two former rookies to be declared accidents once and for all. Marian didn't like any black marks on the Desert Valley Police Department's record. But someone seemed to have a beef with Marian, too, since she'd been found unconscious in her home a few weeks ago and was still in a coma at the Canyon County Regional Medical Center located twenty miles west of Desert Valley. Ellen had requested round-the-clock security for her mother's room. They were all on high alert.

"Roger that," Whitney responded to James. While the rookies were still in Desert Valley, they took whatever calls they could to gain experience. James's dog, Hawk, a bloodhound trained in crime scene investigations, would sniff out any evidence. And she'd get Hunter on that, too. "I'll stay with the eyewitness."

Then she turned to the railroad employees and urged them to keep away the anxious passengers craning their necks to see what had happened. Her fellow officers would conduct interviews with the few passengers waiting to return to the train. Maybe they, or some of the passengers about to board for the first time, had seen something.

Whitney leaned over the two men. "Hey, I'm Officer Whitney Godwin with the Desert Valley K9 Unit." *For now.* Just until she could get through this murder investigation and, she hoped, move back to Tucson. Centering her gaze on the young, good-looking one, she asked, "Can you tell me what happened here?"

He nodded and blinked as if refocusing, his hand splayed across a bloody shirt covering the other man's wound. "Two men came up the aisle, heading for the exit." He pointed to his left, indicating the third coach seat from the door. "They had two big duffels, and they ran smack into Mr. Gallagher here." He stopped and sucked in a breath. "A bag ripped open and packages fell everywhere. All different colors but about the same size. Pretty obvious that they were carrying drugs."

Whitney nodded and took notes. No wonder Hunter was champing at the bit. Drugs? "Okay. What happened after that?"

"One of them stabbed Mr. Gallagher." He motioned to the injured man. "That same one saw me moving up the aisle and pulled a gun on me, but when they heard voices outside, the other man talked him out of shooting me. They grabbed their duffels and left. I watched them get into a dark SUV in the parking lot."

He checked the injured man's pulse and talked to him in soothing, reassuring tones. "Hang on, Mr. Gallagher. Help is coming."

Whitney went over her notes to make sure she had everything, his soothing voice calming her, too. He had a distinctive accent, a Southern drawl. "Did they pull a gun on the victim?"

"No. He surprised them. The man stabbed him, probably to keep anyone from hearing. But I saw the whole thing, so he pulled the gun on me." David shook his head. "I guess they thought everyone had exited already, and we both surprised them."

"He's telling the truth," Mr. Gallagher said in a weak voice. "He threatened this young man if he talked. Threatened me, too, but I'm not scared of any criminal. Drug runners are getting mighty bold these days."

"Got it," Whitney said, glancing at the man aiding the victim. Obviously he hadn't taken that threat seriously, either. "And again, where were you, sir, when this took place?"

He looked up at her with deep brown eyes that were now clear and sure. "The last seat on the right, near the door to the next car. I... I'm an army medic. I mean, I'm a former army medic."

"Army medic?" That brought a heavy pain to Whitney's heart. Her brother had been a sergeant in the army. But he'd been killed almost a year ago. Before she could figure out how to tell him about all the changes in her life.

I made it, Lucas. She had so much she wanted to tell her big brother, such as that she'd passed through her second stint of training without a hitch and that she had an amazing responsibility in her life, her baby daughter, Shelby, but now it was too late.

At least her brother had accepted her choice of careers before he'd died. Wishing he could have seen her graduate after her second attempt to finish the rigorous twelve-week K9 training here in Desert Valley, Whitney pushed aside the too-sad thoughts of her brother and got back to her job.

"Okay, that's good. You're both doing great. The paramedics should be here any minute."

Already she could hear another dog barking. Probably one of her fellow rookies coming to help out. They were all stuck here on the big investigation into the murder of Veronica Earnshaw and the suspicious deaths of the two rookies.

Whitney didn't have time right now to think about those deaths, even though she'd been personally involved with one of the victims.

For now this stabbing had to be her top priority. She needed to get the details right or she'd hear an earful from Chief Jones. The chief had her on his radar since she'd gone to him with a theory regarding one of those deaths, a theory he'd found hard to believe. If she messed this up, he might think she wasn't qualified for the job.

The medic seemed calmer now, so she hoped she could trust his eyewitness details to be accurate. He seemed capable and sure, even if he was a bit disoriented.

Then, because she wanted to know, and needed to know for her report, she asked, "What's your name?"

"David Evans." He waited as if he expected her to say something else, his brown eyes bright with anticipation.

Whitney wrote his name in her notes. They'd run a background check on him. "You're passing through?"

With what looked like relief in his eyes, he shook his head. "No. I'm here to stay for a while. Maybe."

Surprised, Whitney added that to her notes. "Welcome to Desert Valley."

He gave her a tight smile. "Thanks. Is it always like this?"

Whitney shook her head. "No. More like routine traffic stops and bar brawls. But...we do get some drug runners through here now and then." She glanced back at her anxious partner. Hunter wanted to get on the move. "Did you happen to see the license plate on the SUV?"

He squinted, blinked. "I... I think. But only partly. The numbers one and five and...and several letters that might be some sort of vanity plate. I can't remember the name, but there was a symbol over the plate—on the back of the SUV. I didn't get the details, but it was small. I got a quick glance."

"Maybe it'll come back to you," Whitney said, observing his clipped chestnut-brown hair. He seemed to be in good shape other than the shock that must have hit him right after he'd witnessed all of this. But he wore a mantle of weariness, too. He looked world-weary and rugged, almost haggard. And tired.

She jotted down what he'd said. "Can you describe the two men?"

"I'm not sure of their race, but both had dark hair, and they were kind of disguised and wearing baseball caps—one was red. The guy who stabbed Mr. Gallagher and pointed a gun at me—he had a thick beard and longer hair, and he wore a black hat. He was tall. The other one was shorter. They had on sunglasses." He gave her their estimated heights and weights. "And…they both had the same kind of dark bag. Old and worn and full of what looked like birthday gifts or some kind of shipment, but it had to be drugs."

"We'll do a thorough check of the train," she said, never doubting he was correct. Mr. Gallagher was right. This was happening a lot lately.

When Whitney heard sirens, she breathed easier. The heat inside the train was stifling even though it was early spring. She wouldn't go home until she and Hunter had sniffed and searched this entire train and talked to the other employees and questioned the few passengers who waited to board. She was relieved that help for this injured man was on the way.

"You did a good job," she told David. "Now you can relax and let my friends take over."

But Mr. Brown Eyes grabbed her arm. "I'm pretty sure those two will try something else. Drug couriers are ruthless, pretty packages aside."

Whitney nodded, suspecting the same thing. "My partner, Hunter, will alert if any drugs have been transported, and we'll put out a BOLO on the suspects."

When they heard the paramedics coming onto the train, David turned to Mr. Gallagher. "The posse's here, sir. You'll be in good hands. I know you're in pain, but I think you'll be fine. The wound isn't as deep as it feels and thankfully, from what I can tell, the knife didn't hit any major organs." He glanced at Whitney. "I'll give them the rundown on his vitals."

"Thank you, son," the older man said. "You're a hero."

"You're welcome, sir," David replied, wearing an embarrassed expression, his face coloring.

Mr. Gallagher nodded. "And thank you for serving our country."

David's eyes met Whitney's, a pain etched there in the dark irises. "Yes, sir."

Whitney got the feeling that he wanted to say something else. Maybe the newcomer knew more about all of this than he was willing to divulge right now.

TWO

David leaned against the back of the old Crown Victoria and waited for Officer Godwin and her K9 partner, Hunter, to return. The ambulance had left, and two other patrol cars were now leaving. The impatient passengers who wanted to continue their journeys were waiting inside the quaint little train station while the K9 officers inspected their luggage piled up outside. As far as he knew, none of them had witnessed the event or the two men leaving the train. Suitcase by suitcase, their luggage was cleared so they could board.

Maybe he should do that, too. He could keep drifting, forget his troubles and…try to find a normal life again.

But he wasn't about to go anywhere until he knew Whitney was safe. Which was stupid, really. She was the one with a gun and a trained canine partner. She could certainly take care of herself, based on what Lucas had told him and based on what he'd seen here today. She might look like a cheerleader, but she was all business on the job.

According to Lucas, Whitney was stubborn and hugely independent. When they'd first met, Lucas had proudly explained that after a couple of years as a beat cop back in Tucson, Whitney had been accepted as part of a training program for K9 officers based here in Desert Valley. But he'd had concerns about the whole thing since he knew the work could be grueling and dangerous. They'd argued before he deployed, but after admitting that no one had stopped *him* from following his own path, Lucas had finally emailed Whitney and apologized, only to learn that she'd had to drop out of the program. David had no doubt that Lucas loved his sister.

"She had some trouble, but she's gonna try again next spring," Lucas had stated a few days before he'd been wounded. "That's Whitney. She never gives up."

Lucas had died a week later. That had been last summer.

It had taken David months to get here. After finishing his deployment and returning stateside, he'd fought against this quest. He hadn't even been home to Texas yet, mainly because there wasn't much left there for him. Now that he was here, he was pretty sure Whitney would be shocked and surprised that he'd followed through on a deathbed promise to her brother.

And yet he couldn't leave her. He kept watching the shadows of her long ponytail, the silhouette of her moving through the train for one last search. He'd watched in amazement earlier as the sleek, powerful dog—a pointer, she'd told him—did just that, pointed near the seats where those two men had been. Hunter had stopped with his nose in the air, his tail lifted in statue-like stillness. Then he'd become agitated and aggressive, growling low while he pawed the floor by the seats.

After Whitney had encouraged Hunter to "Go find," the big dog had sniffed and pawed. They'd found a package wrapped to look like a gift box that had slid under the seat when the bag had torn open. Obviously the two couriers hadn't seen it when they'd dropped part of the duffel's contents. But the lone package they'd left behind would create a lot more than birthday-party memories. Heroin. With a street value of hundreds of thousands of dollars per kilo, according to what he'd heard Whitney and some of the others discussing.

Hunter sniffed out a couple more spots, two sleeping car closets and two bathrooms. David heard Whitney telling one of the officers that drugs had obviously been transported in those areas, too, since he'd alerted on both.

"No telling how long they've been using this route," she'd said to an older, distinguished-looking man she'd addressed as Chief Jones. "We'll have to study the video cameras and the passenger manifest, too. Maybe pick up an image or establish a pattern."

Now David looked up to find her walking toward him with another K9 officer she'd introduced as Ellen Fox-croft, a native of Desert Valley, and her K9 partner, Carly, a golden retriever specializing in tracking.

"Thanks," Whitney said to her friend after they stopped by Ellen's vehicle. "So we know based on Car-ly's alert and Hawk's detection of that dusty shoe print that they got into a vehicle here in the lot, as our witness reported."

Ellen listened to Whitney and then glanced over at David and nodded. "And based on the partial plate your witness here was able to remember, we might be able to find that vehicle soon." She nodded to David and then opened the door to her vehicle to let Carly inside the back. "I'll talk to you tomorrow, Whitney. We'll compare notes."

Whitney agreed and then turned to give David a dark scowl, her blue eyes flashing aggravation. Aside from the frown on her pretty face, she looked kind of cute in her uniform. She was buff but she was also dainty, like a fragile flower. Only she was way too fierce to be a flower. One tough female. David's heart beat an extra thump at the danger she had to put herself through in order to do her job.

Same as her brother.

"Why are you still here?" she asked, suspicion lacing the question. "We've cleared the scene, and I have to file an official report. I have your contact information. You're free to go until we call you in to look at mug shots."

"I'm waiting on you," he said, thinking if he told her he'd stayed behind to keep an eye on her, she'd laugh in his face. David didn't think right now would be a good time to explain that her late brother had sent him here.

"You really don't need to worry about me," she retorted. Glancing back at the train and then at her alert partner, she said, "We didn't find anything else during that last sweep. But we dusted for prints on the seats where we found the one package, and we found some shoe prints, so maybe those clues will turn something up."

David waited while she gave Hunter water and food from two tin buckets she had clipped inside his wire kennel in her police car.

"You did a good job, Hunter," she mumbled in a sweet voice that tickled at David's senses like butterfly wings. "Such a good boy."

Hunter gave her a grateful stare and started gnawing on a rope throw that David guessed was his chew treat after each find. David gave her an appraising glance and realized how tough she was underneath that porcelain doll skin and sunshine-blond hair.

Satisfied, she turned to David. "Where are you headed?"

"I don't know, honestly. I'm on some R & R right now,

meandering around the West, taking in the sights. Maybe volunteering to help here and there. Thought I'd find a place nearby for the night."

So I can stay near you for a while.

Her suspicions hit like sunspots all around him. "There's a bed-and-breakfast in town. The Desert Rose, right off Desert Valley Drive. You might find a room there. Just until you decide which way you want to go."

Then she gave him a no-nonsense stare. "Of course, you need to stick around anyway in case you can help us identify those two. I'll talk to the chief and see if we need to call you in to the station tomorrow."

He nodded, taking advantage of the intro. "Why not now? I can go to the station tonight since I'm in no hurry."

She checked her watch. "We've put out a bulletin on any dark SUVs matching your description, but drug couriers are notorious for switching up vehicles or changing license plates. Look, it's late, and I have to be somewhere. First thing tomorrow, okay? But if you remember anything before then, here's my card."

In spite of everything that had happened, David was almost glad he had a legitimate excuse to stay in town. He pocketed her business card, also grateful for the contact number.

"I did some searches online when I decided to take this trip. I found some information about the Desert Valley Clinic. One article mentioned the need for more funding and more doctors. They use volunteer doctors, physician's assistants, and nurses for the free services they offer." He'd have to sign a waiver to get a temporary license to practice at free clinics in the state. "Thought I might volunteer there while I'm here. Don't want to get rusty."

"And exactly why are you *here* when you could be anywhere in the world right now?" she asked, her eyes scanning the train again before she whipped her gaze back to him. "Because I've never heard of anyone wanting to spend downtime in Desert Valley or wanting to *volunteer* to work with Dr. Pennington."

David braced himself and stored up her pointed notations for future reference. He'd have to be careful with this one. Whitney would keep digging until she had him figured out. "Well—"

But Whitney Godwin was no longer listening to him. She held up her finger and then, giving Hunter a silent command, drew her weapon and took off in a crouched run toward the empty train.

A man scurried toward the train like a lizard, his head down and his back hunched. He wore a burgundy hat and dark shades.

Whitney spotted him when she glanced back while talking with David. She'd have to figure out the medic's angle and his story later. Right now, she intended to nab two criminals. With her gun drawn and Hunter waiting for her command as he trailed along, she hurried around the stopped train and looked up and down the tracks.

Nothing. No one. Had she only imagined seeing someone? No, she'd seen the man, and his description had fit the one David Evans and Mr. Gallagher had given her. She hadn't slept much last night, but she wasn't imagining things. Fatigue weighed on her like a blanket of dry heat, but she kept her cool and went on with doing her job. Being a rookie meant she always had to go the extra mile. Being a female police officer meant she had to work twice as hard as the men around her.

She checked the front of the stopped train again and then walked by the narrow openings between the four small passenger cars, and headed to the car where she and Hunter had found a kilo of heroin earlier.

"C'mon, Hunter," she commanded. Hunter went in ahead of her, doing his job with practiced excitement. He sniffed and moved on, sniffed again, dug around some and then kept up the search.

Could one of these men have come back for the package they'd dropped? Or did they have more stashed elsewhere?

Thinking it was mighty bold of this one to creep back so soon after they'd taken off earlier, Whitney glanced around. They'd allowed the few passengers traveling west to get back on, but some of the passenger cars were still empty.

Easy for someone to slip in and hide.

Whitney moved behind Hunter up the aisle, careful to search every compartment and seat. When they didn't find anything, she shook her head and wiped at the sweat dripping down her brow. It would be so nice to get home and have a long shower. But she had reports to file and other obligations to consider.

And one very good-looking medic hanging around for no good reason. Her suspicions regarding David Evans increased by the minute. His excuse for being here didn't make sense to her practical way of thinking. And yet he'd put his own life on the line to help the injured attendant, and he'd cooperated fully with the police. He'd answered her questions without hesitation.

Maybe she was too tired to have any clear thoughts right now.

"Let's get out of here," she said to Hunter, her gut telling her the criminal was still lurking somewhere near the train.

They exited the train and she did one last sweep,

checking between the sleek cars, looking underneath, turning toward the scraggly woods.

Then Hunter let out a guttural growl and stood staring at a spot at the end of the train.

"Go ahead," Whitney commanded as she drew her gun and hurried down the side of the tracks near a copse of ponderosa pines, dry shrubs and chaparrals. A few spring wildflowers peeked out in bright orange and red, interspersed underneath a scraggly cactus bush, but she was interested only in seeing what Hunter wanted her to see.

Hunter took off, silent but steady, toward the scattered rocks and shrubs.

Whitney followed. When Hunter alerted again, she crouched down near a jutting rock. Too late to call for backup. She'd have to do this on her own. Bracing for action, she whirled out from the rock with her weapon ready only to find a dirty black shirt lying on the ground.

Then Hunter started barking. She heard a click behind her. "Halt the dog and drop the gun."

Whitney did as he asked. "Stay," she said to Hunter in a commanding voice, her insides like jelly. Then she slowly laid her gun on the ground, her mind racing. This could go wrong if she lost her cool. Hunter growled low, but he wouldn't attack without her order.

Could she do this? Could she risk having her K9 partner shot in midair? Hunter was still in training, too. What if he got hurt because of her carelessness?

"Stay," she told him again, her tone firm in spite of her trembling nerves.

She glanced back and found a handgun pointed at her head by a tall bearded man wearing a black baseball cap and dark shades. But this wasn't the man she'd seen running beside the train. That man had been wearing the dark red baseball cap and had shorter hair. Which meant he was probably moving through the train car, looking for any lost packages of heroin. They'd set a trap.

"What do you want?" she asked the man who held his gun pointed at her.

"Keep telling the dog to heel," he whispered in a rasp that burned her neck.

Hunter stood growling, ready to attack.

"Stay," Whitney commanded, her pulse pumping adrenaline through her body. "Stay."

Hunter didn't move, but the big dog's whole body shook with aggression, his bared teeth visible.

"One move from you, lady, and that dog and you both die." He twisted her around and jerked her arm with a brutal grasp, his rancid breath hissing against her ear.

"I'm not a lady," she retorted. "I'm a police officer."

The stench of his sweat assaulted her. Sweat and fear. "And a nosy one," he replied on a huff of air. "Shoulda kept going."

He pushed her deeper into the sparse, dry landscape, kicking up dust that made her want to cough. Whitney glanced around, her breath settling. No one had noticed them on the far side of the big train car, and now the train would soon be leaving the station. She wouldn't let this criminal get to her, but she wasn't going to die here, either. She'd get out of this. Somehow.

She'd acted too hastily and made a rookie mistake. She hadn't been careful, and she hadn't called for backup. Hunter would do her bidding, but she had to find the right moment. She'd like to blame her lack of attention to detail on the mysterious medic who'd appeared here and stayed with her. But Whitney wasn't one for pushing off blame on others. This was her mistake.

The man kicked her gun behind him, then shoved her into a cluster of pines and rock. Praying that someone would see what was happening, Whitney kept thinking ahead. He could be bringing her out here for only one reason.

Trying to memorize all the details around her, she took a deep breath. Black Hat had a tattoo on his lower arm. Some sort of intricate symbol. An arrow and three hanging feathers with what looked like a face in the arrow. Could it be the same symbol David Evans had mentioned seeing over the license plate of the SUV?

"So what's your plan?" she asked in a matter-of-fact tone that belied the tremors running through her body. "Where's your buddy?"

"Shut up so I can think," he said into her ear. "We got surprised today, so I have to clean up this mess before the boss finds out."

"Who's your boss? If you agree to cooperate, we might be able to help you out. Think about it. Your boss won't help you."

His voice shook. "Right. I'm not buying that, so shut up."

Whitney could take advantage of his nervous energy.

She prayed for calm and clarity. She'd been one of the best in her class when she'd returned to training this year, so she centered her thoughts on what she'd been taught. Determined to stay alive, she concentrated on her sweet five-month-old baby girl, Shelby. The baby she'd fought so hard to have. Alone. The baby her brother had never heard about because he'd died before she'd found the courage to tell him.

Whitney would regret for the rest of her life that Lucas would never know his niece. But she would fight for her child's sake, too.

She was at her best when she was cornered and alone. The man shoved her toward the tumbleweeds and scrub brush that surrounded the scant trees and jutting rocks. "Let's get this done and over."

The train now hissed like a big snake. He was waiting for the train to leave. It would serve as a cover when he shot her. So that meant his friend must have made it off the train without detection.

Adrenaline pumped a new energy through Whitney's system. She had to act fast or she'd never see Shelby again.

She went limp so she could use her body to get away from the man holding her. It worked. Her body fell against the man, causing his hands to go up and giving her enough time to slip a booted foot behind his left calf and bring him down. But on the way down, she heard a grunt and then felt a blur of air rushing by her head. The next thing she knew, the man who'd been holding her let out a yelp of pain and dropped at her feet, his gun sliding over dry dirt and skidding to a stop a few feet away.

Surprised, she watched in amazement as a now familiar form crashed over the gunman who'd been about to shoot her and held him pinned to the ground.

THREE

The medic! She'd forgotten all about him. With a grunt, he lifted his right arm and hit the man on the head with a big jagged rock. Which didn't do much in the way of injuries, so it wouldn't keep him down long. But it gave David time to get up and Whitney enough time to react. Flipping the man over, she motioned to David, and he helped her control the man on the ground.

Hunter growled and danced, eyeing her for instructions.

"Guard," Whitney ordered as she scrambled up, her breath leaving her body. David helped her, steadying her until she caught her breath and searched for her radio. The dog stood over the moaning man.

"He'll bite you if I tell him to," Whitney informed the man. "It's up to you, but I strongly suggest you stay still and remain on your stomach."

David glanced around and then spotted her gun. He grabbed it and held it on the man, who was now curled up with Hunter hovering over him. "Are you okay?" he asked Whitney.

She nodded and then reached out to David. "Give me the gun."

David looked uncertain and then shook his head. "I'd feel better if you get him cuffed."

Whitney debated and then nodded while she leaned over the suspect. "Now it's your turn to stay still, or I will let my partner here tear you to shreds."

Panic poured off the criminal on the ground. His eyes widened in fear, his gaze darting here and there. "*My* partner will be here soon."

"No, he won't," David said. "I saw him heading the other way about five minutes ago. He left you."

And the train was finally leaving the station. Once it was well up the tracks in a fading echo, the desert went quiet. Whitney reached for her cuffs, using her strength to hold the man while she tried to slap the restraints against his wrists.

But the man on the ground turned desperate. He rolled and came at her with both feet kicking, causing her to flip in the air before she ever got the first cuff secured. Hunter barked and danced while Whitney felt herself sliding on dry rock, her knees and hands burning with heat and friction, the cuffs slipping out of her grip. The criminal and she both reached and grabbed for the handgun he'd lost before, the weapon out of reach between them. Hunter went into frenzied barking while Whitney fought with a person who had twice her strength.

David grabbed the man and lifted him away before the criminal could get to the gun. This time, David put a booted foot on the man's chest and held her gun to the man's head.

"Don't even think about it," David said, his tone deep and full of rage. "I'll shoot you in the leg and damage you for life. If you doubt me, I can show you which artery I'll hit. You might bleed to death before help can come."

The man spewed out a round of nasty words, but Whitney saw him eyeing David as if he didn't believe him.

She hustled into action, grabbed her lost radio and took her gun back from David.

She motioned to the man. "On your stomach again."

This criminal would not give in. He gave both of them a quick glance and then stared at Hunter before he jumped up, knocked her down again and then sprinted across the rocks with all his might. David threw his body over hers, holding her gun aimed at the man who was now running toward the open tracks.

Pain shooting up her arms, she commanded Hunter to "Bite," and then watched the man getting away, Hunter chasing him.

A black SUV slid up next to the tracks, its tires burning rubber and slinging dirt and rocks. The driver opened the passenger-side door. "Hurry. We'll take care of this later."

The man sped up, but Hunter nipped at his pants and tore part of the left pants leg away before the suspect threw himself inside the vehicle. It took off while he was still climbing inside. Hunter stood with the torn piece of fabric at his feet.

"Hunter, stay!" Whitney screamed at David, "Let me up!"

He rolled away, his gaze following the disappearing SUV.

"Give me my gun!" Whitney lifted herself up and started after them.

But a strong hand grabbed her and tugged her back.

David shook his head. "Let's get out of here," he said into her ear. "It's too dangerous."

"No," she said, disbelief making her angry. "I have to go after them. It's my job, and you're hindering me from doing it."

He held her there, his eyes as rich as dark leather. "They'll kill you."

If he thought that would hold her back, he was mistaken. Whitney pushed up again. Every muscle in her body hurt, and her skin burned with abrasions. "I said, let me go. Now!"

Hunter sensed she might be in danger and growled, his black eyes centered on David.

"I don't like this," she said. "Hunter's reacting to my stress. He thinks you're hurting me."

But David wasn't listening. He glared across the train tracks, watching, waiting, his hand holding her arm. "They've stopped. They might be coming back. They'll ambush you again."

Whitney took in a deep breath and called Hunter to come. She didn't want to agree with the man, but she'd already messed up on so many levels. She couldn't do this alone. Pushing back anger and frustration, she glared at him.

"I have to report in," she said, reaching for her radio as she sank against a rock. After giving the dispatcher her location and a description of the men and the vehicle, she shifted away from David, her body still shaky. "We'll up the search and the BOLO alert."

When she tried to stand, one of her legs buckled. David tucked her weapon into his waistband and then scooped her up into his arms and started walking.

"Put me down," Whitney shouted as David carried her through the heavy brush next to the train tracks. He might be tall and lanky, but the man had surprising strength. She should turn her weapon on *him*.

But when they heard a vehicle's engine revving up down the tracks, Whitney looked up and into David's eyes.

"They're back," he said. "We need to hide and wait for help."

Taking her to a small copse of spindly pines, he gestured to a huge jagged rock, and they crouched behind it, David in front of her as if he were waiting for a battle to begin.

And maybe a battle *was* about to begin. These men were desperate and dangerous.

Whitney glared at him, her breath coming in huffs. "You should have stayed out of this. They know you. They've seen your face. That's why they turned around. They have to eliminate any witnesses."

He inhaled and stared through the bushes. "Yes, they saw my face when they came close to shooting me the first time. I'm trying to keep you from going after them because they know you now, too."

Whitney struggled to find footing, his words sobering. "I don't need your help. I mean it. Let me go."

When they heard hurried footsteps, they stopped arguing.

David glanced at her, relieved. "That's probably one of your patrol officers coming to check on us." Then he gave her an imploring stare. "You heard those men. They'll keep coming. To deal with this problem."

Whitney had the distinct feeling that he wasn't referring to the other bags of heroin.

"You shouldn't have interfered."

David glanced over at the woman who'd practically forced him to get into her vehicle earlier so she could take him in to give a statement and look at mug shots. After she'd been confronted by the same two men a second time, both Whitney and Chief Jones had decided now would be a good time to identify them.

After they'd both been checked over by the EMTs at the scene and she'd gone over the details with Chief Jones and handed over the suspect's handgun and the torn fabric from his pants as evidence, David had been questioned. Then she'd brought him to the police station, where it seemed the whole rookie team had gathered for some sort of briefing.

David had noticed at least five other K9 officers, four men and one other woman, plus several older officers milling around. For a small-town department, Desert Valley sure had a lot of willing law enforcement personnel right now.

And they'd all checked him out in one way or another.

He'd glanced at mug shots for what seemed like hours. He'd also described what he'd remembered about the symbol he'd seen on the license plate of the SUV. "It looked like an arrow, pointing up. And feathers. Three or four, maybe, dangling down." There was something else, but he couldn't remember what he was missing.

"We get a lot of that around here," Whitney's fellow officer, Eddie Harmon, had said with a shrug. "And we don't have an artist on site to sketch it out for us."

"I saw a tattoo on one of the men's arms," Whitney had told David and Eddie. "Could be the same." She'd glanced over at a tall female officer with short brown hair who had an Amazonian-type build. "Louise, maybe you can do some research on tattoos for us, based on the description."

"I'll see what I can find," the woman had replied.

David had gone back to searching the mug shots, but he was glad Whitney had verified what he'd seen. Maybe it was some sort of cartel symbol or a popular Southwestern tattoo.

But he couldn't match any of the faces in the books

to the two men who'd caused all the trouble on the train. Now he wondered if they'd both disguised themselves.

"Go home, Godwin," the chief, a tall man with a paunch and thick gray hair, had finally commanded. "And stay home and rest tomorrow morning. You look a little beat up, and I noticed you've been favoring that left leg."

Whitney had frowned, but she hadn't argued with the man. Instead, she'd made a couple of phone calls and seemed anxious to leave the station.

After the two hours or so they'd spent together, she'd also offered to give David a ride to the nearest inn. "It's on the way," she'd explained. "So get in and don't argue with me."

Now back in the squad car with her, and refusing to apologize for coming to her aid, David said, "I was trying to help. There were two of them, and they're obviously ruthless. They might have killed you if I'd left you there."

"But I'm a trained officer," Whitney replied, her blue eyes popping fire. "I could have handled it."

"You're also a rookie," David said. "And Desert Valley isn't exactly a large town."

She stopped the car in front of the Desert Rose B and B, which seemed to live up to its name. The big Victorian house was painted a blush pink and surrounded by rosebushes. "How did you know I was a rookie?"

David realized he'd made a mistake. But he'd learned to listen and observe during his years on the front lines. "I...uh...heard you talking back at the train station, to that other officer—Eddie. I think he was teasing you about it."

Which was true. David had witnessed how the older officer's teasing seemed to rub her the wrong way. To change the subject, he said, "Let me have a look at your hands again."

"My hands are fine," she said, her expression full of fatigue.

"Let me check," he said, his gaze moving over her.

She reluctantly held out her hands.

"You should have let the paramedic bandage these scratches." He reached for her, taking her right hand in his so he could turn it over and look at her palm. In spite of being tough, she had delicate, graceful hands. "Hard to see your wounds in this light, but you need to wash these scratches and cuts with soap and water and make sure you flush all the embedded dirt and rock out. And if you don't have some antibacterial ointment, you need to stop and get some."

"Okay." She pulled her hand away, wincing. "Okay, I'll take care of it. I have soap and I have ointment."

"And stay off that ankle. It might be a light sprain. You need to—"

"RICE," she interrupted, impatient with him. "Rest, ice, compression and elevation. I know the drill, Doc."

David tried to get her to open up. "I guess you're used to slamming bad guys against the rocks, huh?"

"Not really," she admitted. "Only in training up to now. But I got in a lot of quality experience today, I guess."

"You were amazing." He meant that. He was still in awe of her.

Her suspicious stare mellowed to a confused scowl. "Eddie Harmon—the officer you heard teasing me earlier—is totally harmless and probably doesn't even realize he's insulting me. He likes to pick on me since I'm one of the few female officers around here. And he's not much help with an investigation. He's been on the force for thirty years, and I think he's not really into chasing any-one or solving anything. He hates even issuing tickets."

Glad he'd distracted her, David nodded. That older officer was a fine one to talk. "Explains why he left the scene before the rest of you did. If anything had hap-pened to you—"

She shook her head and gave him an aggravated glare. "He likes to get home in time to have dinner with his wife and kids. Your overly protective attitude is kind of chivalrous but I told you, I had it covered."

"And I told you, I wasn't about to leave you there."

"Would you have left a male officer?"

David glanced at her, hoping to make her understand. But she had him on that one. "Okay, probably yes." Then he shrugged. "But I would have called 911 regardless."

"But because I'm a rookie and a woman, you felt the need to rush in and help me. Don't do that again."

Wow. She sure had a chip on her shoulder. Seemed she also had a lot to prove.

"It's not in my nature to leave a woman alone when she could be in danger. I'm not sorry I stayed."

"Well, cowboy, I do appreciate your assistance, but ideally, there won't be another time for you to play the hero."

"I didn't do it to be a hero." David didn't normally get this involved in trying to defend himself. But normally, he could at least form a complete sentence. "Look, I ar-rived here still reeling from what I'd been through over in Afghanistan. I saw all of this happening in front of my eyes, and I was concerned. Drug runners don't mess around."

She still wasn't happy with him. With a dark frown, she stopped the squad car near the curb and motioned to the Desert Rose. "Go in and get yourself a room. I might need to question you again when I go back over my report, but right now I have to go."

She glanced to Hunter behind a wired screen in the backseat, habitually checking on her partner. "At least we got a good look at their faces." Giving him another serious stare, she added, "I'll be in touch. Take care."

"You take care, too." David saw a flicker of concern pass through her eyes. "Look, if you're worried about those guys—"

"I'm not." Another blue-eyed glare. "I'd like to haul them in, but to do that, I have to go back over everything, including your part in this."

Did she think he *was* part of this? Surely not.

Her next words confirmed that she didn't. "If they see you hanging around, you'll be on their radar. So be careful."

"Same to you. They saw you. Up close." He couldn't stop thinking about that. "What if they come after you?"

"Hunter lives with me. He'll alert."

"And you feel comfortable with that?"

"Yes, I do." She sighed and brushed at the hair escaping her ponytail. "Look, I appreciate your warnings, but…this is my job. I've trained for this, and I worked hard to become a K9 officer. I'll be okay. You watch *your* back, all right?"

"Always." He got out but turned and leaned back into the vehicle. She obviously wasn't ready to listen to reason. And in spite of his misgivings, he wasn't quite ready to blurt out the truth to her. "Thanks for your help today. I'm sorry I overstepped my bounds."

"Relax," she said. "You just got back from what had to be a lot of trauma. It's natural you'd overreact." Then her expression softened. "You remind me of my brother. He was always protective of me."

David's heart did a little lurch. He wanted to tell her that he'd known her brother. But not yet. Not after such a bad start.

He swallowed and looked over at her while he tried to hold it all together. "He sounds like a good brother."

"He *was*." She looked up and right into David's eyes. "He was army—in Afghanistan. He died over there last year."

"I'm sorry." David stood there, wanting to comfort her, understanding her brother's need to take care of her. She was strong and tough, but David saw that essence of vulnerability in her pretty eyes and let go of his courage yet again. "We lost a lot of good soldiers. I'm sorry I couldn't save all of them."

I'm sorry I couldn't save your brother.

Compassion filled her eyes. "I'm sure you tried. You're one of the heroes, David. But you're home now, so take care of yourself."

David decided he had to tell her the truth soon. She'd be angry at him all over again, but he thought she was the kind of woman who'd respect the truth.

He took a deep breath. "Hey, listen, I—"

Whitney gave him a distracted, impatient stare. Then she blinked and stared at the clock on the console. "I'm sorry, but it's late and I've gotta go."

David shut the door and watched as she sped off along Desert Valley Drive. She couldn't get away from him fast enough. Or maybe she couldn't get away from the emotions he evoked in her. Too many bad memories. That was what he carried around, too.

How would she react when she found out he'd promised her brother he'd come here to see her? How could he keep her safe when she was so bent on taking care of herself?

It had to be done. He needed to let Whitney know that he'd tried to save Lucas. And that he'd promised Lucas he'd do this. Tomorrow, once he was settled and acclimated to his surroundings, he'd find her and talk to her.

He wasn't going anywhere for a few weeks at least. She'd get used to having him around. And he'd find a way to tell her exactly why he was here.

FOUR

David went inside the quaint inn, the chill of the dusk chasing him and the memory of Whitney cornered with a dangerous criminal still front and center in his mind.

"Well, you look plumb whipped," the petite gray-haired woman behind the counter said with a smile, her plump hands splayed across the old wood. "I'm Rosa. How can I help you?"

David explained that he needed a room for an indefinite time. "And where can I rent a car?"

The woman laughed at that, her pink bifocals slipping down on her nose. "Not around here, dear. But… I have a loaner you can use. All I ask is that you gas her up and keep her running smoothly."

David couldn't argue with that. "Deal."

Whitney pulled up to the small stucco house she rented from the Carters next door. When she'd first signed up for training last year, she'd stayed in the dorm-like condos next to the K9 Training Center. She'd met Shelby's father there, Brian Miller. Whitney had been a rookie in every way, naive and eager to fit in. When the handsome, charming fellow rookie had started flirting with her in spite of the no-fraternizing policy, she'd fallen hard.

Brian hadn't lived in the dorms, but he'd hung out there a lot. He'd had his own house between Desert Valley and another small town, about ten miles from the training center. He'd told her he preferred to live in his own place since he had a part-time job as a night watchman at a strip mall.

But she understood now, Brian had a house because he liked to take women there, where it was private and secluded. And apparently, he'd taken a lot of women there.

Brian had lied to her and cheated on her, even on the night before the police dance when she'd planned to tell him she was carrying his child. But then Brian had never made it to the dance. He'd died in a fire at his house about an hour before the dance started. Then, about two weeks later, her brother, Lucas, had been killed in Afghanistan.

Now Shelby would never know her daddy or her uncle. Whitney often wondered if Brian would have been happy to hear about the baby. Or would he have turned away from her?

She had no doubt Lucas would have loved Shelby, but he also would have made it his mission to come home and help Whitney out. She'd withheld telling him, and she'd paid dearly for that, too.

What did it matter now? Brian and her brother had both died too young. She knew how her brother had died. But she still didn't understand why or how Brian had died. Until lately, no one in the department had wanted to listen to the one theory that she couldn't shake. Had Brian been murdered?

Whitney glanced around, blinking. Night had settled in and with it, a desert chill. Every time she remembered Brian, the tug of a bittersweet struggle warred inside her soul. She'd loved him immediately. And he'd taken advantage of her completely. Now she had a beautiful baby girl and…because of Shelby, Whitney had turned her life around. She wanted to be worthy in her daughter's eyes, so she'd dedicated her life to Christ and made a pledge to be very careful regarding men. But even after all the pain of Brian's betrayal, Whitney still had concerns about how Brian had died.

In a house fire, supposedly from a burning candle.

His entire family had died in a horrible fire caused by a lit candle when he was a teenager. He'd been the only survivor. So Brian never lit candles in his house. Ever.

It didn't make sense. But whenever she tried to explain that to people, they'd pat her on the hand and tell her the fire had been ruled as an accident. Whitney hoped to prove one day that the fire that had killed Brian had not been an accident. And since another rookie had died from a mysterious fall down the stairs of his home almost two years to the day before Brian died, she couldn't help but notice certain similarities. Couple that with Veronica Earnshaw's murder and the horrible murder of a police officer's wife five years ago and…things were being to look eerily similar.

But she couldn't think about that tonight. She needed to go next door and pick up Shelby. Marilyn Carter had four kids of her own, but she'd insisted on babysitting Shelby.

What's one more, honey? She'll fit right in and she'll learn a lot faster, watching my rug rats running around.

Whitney loved the Carters, and so did Shelby. She paid Marilyn what she could and thanked God each day for the family who had helped her change her life for the better.

She might be starting out with the department, but she loved her job, and she hoped like most of the rookies to move on to a big-city department one day. She wanted Shelby to have what she'd never had—stability.

"C'mon, Hunter," she said. "Here. Let's go find Shelby."

Whitney leashed the big dog and started toward her neighbors' rambling ranch house. But Hunter held back.

"What's wrong?" Whitney had never seen Hunter refusing to go next door. He loved the hustle and bustle of the crazy household full of children. He looked forward to seeing Shelby every day, too. "What's up, Hunter?"

He bristled and started growling low, a sure sign that something wasn't right. Whitney drew her weapon and ordered, "Go ahead."

Hunter tugged her toward the gate to her backyard, his growls now turning into aggressive barking. When Whitney rounded the corner, her heart picked up its tempo. The gate stood open, a broken latch dangling against it, the sound of the metal hitting wood grating on her nerves as a reminder that she'd messed with some dangerous people today.

Someone had broken into her backyard.

Releasing Hunter, Whitney ordered the K9 to search. Hunter took off, growling and barking. Whitney followed, thankful for the security light shining a sickly yellow glow over most of the small backyard. When Hunter alerted near the fence running along the back of the property, Whitney noticed some broken branches on a spindly pine sapling and some splintered areas on the weathered wood. Sneakers? Someone had hopped this fence. Ordering Hunter ahead of her, she quickly checked the house. The back door was locked, but she could tell from the scratches etched near the wood on the old lock that someone had been here and had tried to get into her house. She and Hunter had scared them away.

By the time she'd gathered herself enough to go next door to pick up Shelby, she saw Jack Carter standing out on the porch, squinting into the darkness.

"What's going on?" he asked, glancing at her house, his deep voice full of concern.

"A prowler, from what I could tell," she said, knowing the big, burly mechanic would watch the neighborhood if he thought someone was messing with them. But Whitney wanted to reassure her neighbor. She wouldn't put Jack and the family she trusted with her baby in danger. "Hunter will alert if they come back."

"It's getting as bad here as in the big towns," Jack said. "Want me to take a look?"

"No. I checked everything. The house is still locked tight. We arrived in time to keep them from getting inside."

"What do you think they wanted?" Jack asked, his hands on his hips.

She couldn't tell him her suspicions since she wasn't supposed to talk about an active case. It could get out around the neighborhood that drug dealers might be lurking in the area, and people might panic or, worse, take the law into their own hands. This could have been a coincidence, kids out for kicks. She hoped.

"I don't know," she said. "I don't have anything much of value in there." She glanced back at her tiny little rental home. The home she'd decorated with secondhand items. The home she loved even if it was a temporary place until she got her first assignment. It might be a rental, but it meant the world to her while she was still here in Desert Valley. "But would you tell Marilyn to give me a few more minutes? I want to check inside just in case."

"Sure," Jack said. "Shelby is on her play quilt giggling at the boys. She's fine."

Whitney nodded. She wanted to keep it that way, too. But as she made her way along with Hunter to the front door of the house, David Evans's words came back to her with full clarity, making Whitney wonder about those two men who'd gotten away earlier.

What if they come after you?

"I don't care what you think I should have done," Dr. William Pennington shouted to the scurrying nurse. "Get the gauze and let's get this man's finger sutured so I can get out of here on time for a change."

"I'll take care of Mr. Ramsey's cut," David told the teary-eyed nurse when she headed toward the supply room. The poor woman had been on her feet for over eight hours now. He'd arrived in town yesterday, and this was the first afternoon he'd volunteered here, but he hadn't seen any of the three nurses on staff take a real lunch break.

David enjoyed the work and being able to get to know some of the locals, but Whitney had been right. He couldn't see how anyone on earth would actually *want* to work for this tyrant of a physician. The man obviously thought he was above managing a run-down clinic in a small town. But he sure didn't make it easy to work for him, let alone volunteer.

Wondering if Whitney would make good on calling him in to look at mug shots, David hoped she'd been able to ID the two men without his help. He wanted to have another opportunity to talk to her, but not in a busy police station. He'd have to find a way to see her again and tell her that he'd known her brother, Lucas.

"Go ahead. Be my guest," the nurse whispered as she shoved the supplies into David's hands. David returned to the present, but the nurse was already leaving. "I'm outta here."

David watched her grab her purse and head for the back door, thinking his first day here had turned out to be exhausting. The doctor he'd talked to on the phone had seemed wary about someone offering to volunteer in the first place, but he'd also told David he could use the help. But in person, Dr. William Pennington was a harsh leader who barked orders and scared both nurses and patients. He'd guided David through the proper papers to allow him to practice medicine on a temporary volunteer basis, but he sure didn't seem appreciative of having an experienced volunteer on hand. Maybe he didn't want the staff to outshine him?

David had caught Dr. Pennington staring at him at odd moments. Maybe the man was territorial. His ego was as big as the whole state of Arizona. He stayed locked in his office between patients and talked in low growls on his cell when he paced up and down the hallway.

David intended to show the good doctor that he didn't scare that easily. He needed this work to keep him centered. He had a compulsion to help hurting people, a need that obviously stemmed from seeing too much death and destruction.

Or maybe from being the only son of a now deceased highly successful doctor who had been considered a pillar of the community back in East Texas. Could he ever live up to what his father had expected?

He returned to the exam room, where the doctor was fussing at the frazzled man who'd come in with a work-related injury. "You need to be more careful in that garage, Mr. Ramsey. This is the third work-related accident you've had in the past year."

"Couldn't be helped," the man said. "Wrench slipped. We're always backed up and behind. I got in a rush."

The condescending doctor with the gray-streaked dark hair stared down the grimy mechanic, his rimless glasses giving a clear view of his disapproval. "That doesn't

mean you should get careless. I have my car serviced at
Carter's Garage, you know. I'd hate to file a complaint
with your boss because you failed to do your job correctly by being careless."

"Need some help?" David offered, smiling at the man
who sat with a worried frown wrinkling his forehead.

"Where's Phyllis?" Dr. Pennington asked in a curt,
angry tone, his scowl meant for David.

"I told her I'd help you out," David replied, daring the
doctor to say anything. "She never got her lunch break."

"All of my nurses know to take breaks," the doctor
spouted. "Wait till I see her tomorrow. She also knows not
to leave when we still have a patient. And you shouldn't
be giving orders around here."

"I wasn't giving orders. I told her I'd help you," David
repeated. "I'm here and I know what to do."

"Go home, Evans," the older doctor said, shaking his
head as he glanced at David. "I still don't get why you're
here in the first place." Grunting, he added, "I have my
eye on you."

"I told you when I called," David said, preparing a
care kit for Mr. Ramsey to take home with him. "I need
something to do while I'm visiting, and since this is what
I did as a medic, here I am." He eyed his surroundings,
taking in the dents in the walls, the worn linoleum floors
and the lack of needed supplies. "And it looks like you
can use the help."

"Never enough time or help around here," Pennington
retorted on a snarl. "And I sure can't pay you, so I hope
you don't think your time here will count toward a permanent work situation."

"I'm volunteering," David reminded him, anger sim-
mering behind his politeness. "I don't expect pay."

But he did expect this man and the entire staff to

show some respect to the patients. For the most part, the nurses were kind to anyone who came in. But they were so afraid of the doctor who ordered them around with angry comments and nasty expletives that they all had a serious morale problem.

"You must have some sort of motive, or a death wish," the doctor said to David. He stitched Mr. Ramsey's numbed finger without regard for the man's fearful expression. "Who'd purposely come here? Especially after serving for almost a year in Afghanistan."

David wondered about the doctor's question later when he was about to lock up the clinic for the day. But before he could bolt the front door of the old ranch-style building that must have once been a family home, the door burst open, and he stood face-to-face with Whitney Godwin. And she was carrying a crying baby girl.

FIVE

"David?"

She'd forgotten he'd offered to volunteer here. But it was too late to turn around and leave. Besides, she needed help, and in spite of not knowing David well, she did trust him for some strange reason.

"What's wrong?" he asked, his gaze moving over Shelby.

Getting over her shock, Whitney explained why *she* was here. She had nothing to hide after all. "My baby has a fever. It started last night. I think she's coming down with something, and I don't know what to do."

David replaced the look of complete surprise on his face with one of professional concern. "Okay, okay. Calm down. Let's get her into an exam room."

He guided Whitney down a short hallway and took her and Shelby into an empty, cold room. After he checked the examining table to make sure it had been cleared and cleaned, he turned back to Whitney. "Let's see if we can get her to lie still while I check her vitals."

She cooed at Shelby and tried to lay her on the table, but her daughter started sobbing all over again.

Whitney took a deep breath. She wouldn't fall apart in front of David Evans. If her day had gone according to plan, she would have called him to come back to the station for one more round of looking at mug shots. She was already in hot water with the chief for not calling for backup with the whole train fiasco, but he'd forgiven her when she'd produced the suspect's weapon and that shred of clothing. She'd barely had a chance to look at the mug books herself.

She'd gone back to work today, but the chief had put her on light duty since her ankle was still tender, a fact she tried to hide from everyone. But Carrie Dunleavy, the department secretary, had noticed her limping.

"I made cinnamon rolls," Carrie had said. "Thought everyone could use something sweet with all of this going on. Go sit in the break room and put your foot up. I'll bring you one with some coffee."

Whitney had accepted the delicious roll, but she'd stayed at her desk to make calls to sort real tips from false ones. They needed witnesses to help piece together the lead K9 trainer's murder and to find Marco, the missing German shepherd puppy that had disappeared from the training yard the night of her death.

Whitney might be sore and bruised, but she wasn't one to give up.

Today, she'd been teamed again with officer Eddie Harmon to run down some leads, most of which were either crazy people wanting attention or curious people hoping to make the news, since a reporter from the *Canyon County Gazette* had been snooping around. Tracking those two low-level criminals from the train had taken a backseat.

But Whitney sure would have liked to collar them and find another shipment of heroin to prove her case. If what David Evans had seen was correct, that much heroin would be worth a lot of money on the street. As in thousands of dollars.

When Shelby started crying again, she forgot about her workload and returned her attention to David. "She woke up around three this morning, fussy and crying. I gave her some drops for the fever and rocked her back to sleep. She seemed better this morning when I left her with the babysitter."

David nodded and spoke softly to Shelby. He managed to check her ears while Whitney held her, but Shelby wasn't happy with that, either.

"Is she okay?" she asked, praying Shelby just had a bit of a cold. Was she old enough to be teething? Whitney wished she'd reread all the help books well-meaning people had given her.

"I think she'll be fine," David said. "Let me check a few other things." He gave Whitney a reassuring smile. Then he started with the standard questions. "How old is she?"

"Five months. Closer to six, really."

"Is she eating properly?"

"Yes. Formula and some baby food."

"Any other illnesses or problems recently?"

"No. Nothing." Whitney patted Shelby's little back. "She's usually a happy, healthy baby."

She wanted him to understand, so Whitney started with nervous chatter, trying to explain, trying to show that she was a good mother. "I work such crazy hours, but I have a great babysitter right next door. Marilyn. She has four boys. She thinks it might be an ear infection."

"She might be right," David said, his tone professional and sure. "An experienced mother usually knows her stuff."

And she wasn't that experienced, Whitney thought. She should have stayed at home today. How could she leave her sick child with someone else? How could she do this? Love someone so much it hurt to breathe whenever her baby was hurting?

How could she take care of Shelby and do the kind of work her job demanded?

Tired and bleary-eyed, Whitney had gone on to work after Marilyn had promised she'd call if Shelby got cranky again. When Marilyn called later in the day and told her Shelby had a fever and it was climbing, Whitney had rushed home in time to get Shelby to the clinic.

"She'd never been this sick before," she said, trying to hold tight to her emotions. "Marilyn suggested I bring her here since I'd never make it to the pediatrician's office before it closes. It's about twenty miles west of here in the Canyon County Medical Center."

"You did the right thing," David said, his voice soothing, his eyes on Shelby. He placed a thermometer inside Shelby's little ear. Which the baby didn't like at all.

"She has a high fever," he said after reading the thermometer. "One-oh-three."

Whitney inhaled and wished she could be a better mother. "It was close to a hundred and two the last time Marilyn checked. She didn't want to give her any more medicine until I got home."

"We'll give her something to bring it down," David said. "What's her name?"

"Shelby," Whitney said, her heart breaking with each little whimper.

David took over, checking Shelby and cooing to her in a way that helped Whitney relax. Shelby actually started smiling at his antics. Whitney smiled, too, but it didn't relieve her apprehension.

She felt guilty for spending the day checking leads and trying to figure out angles on Veronica Earnshaw's murder at the K9 Training Center. Whitney wished she could get the case out of her mind. But they all wondered why one of the puppies Veronica had been working with when she'd been killed had gone missing. Chief Jones wanted this case solved. And so did a lot of prominent people who'd helped sponsor the whole puppy program. Today they'd at least tracked down leads on witnesses who'd said they'd seen a puppy running along Desert Valley Road the night Veronica had been murdered. Whitney had reported her prowler to the chief, too. She didn't need a drug lord gunning for her. She had to protect Shelby, no matter what.

Torn between doing her job and taking care of her baby, Whitney tried to focus on the here and now.

"Okay, Shelby," David said, his expression hard to read. "We're going to make you feel better."

Shelby laughed and then reached up for her mother. After Whitney took her, she buried her little head against Whitney's blue uniform collar and started bawling all over again.

Whitney heard footsteps stalking up the hallway. Dr. Pennington charged into the room, his face red with rage. "What's going on here? I was on my way out the door."

When he saw Whitney standing there, he looked shocked, but a cautious blankness wiped his surprise away. "Oh, Officer Godwin. What are you doing here?"

Whitney wanted to drop through the floor. She'd never cared for Dr. Pennington, but she tried to tolerate him since he'd once been married to Veronica Earnshaw. But she refused to succumb to the shame she'd felt after he'd insulted her when she'd become pregnant and had remained husbandless. At least he hadn't spread the word when she'd come to him as a patient last year, since he couldn't break confidentiality.

Straightening her spine, she held Shelby tight. "We're almost done."

"Her little girl is sick," David said on a sharp note before Whitney could say more. "You can leave, Doc. I've got it."

The cantankerous doctor glanced from David back to Whitney. "Stop ordering me around, Evans. You've only been here one day, and this is still my clinic." He tried to take Shelby, but the baby started crying again. "What seems to be the problem?"

"A high fever," David said. "I've checked her ears. She has some congestion in her chest, too."

"She's been cranky," Whitney said, gently holding Shelby still while David listened to Shelby's heart. "She was congested last night."

The doctor scrubbed a hand down his face. "Could be allergies or she might be teething."

Whitney watched in amazement as David ignored the doctor and went about examining Shelby. Most people cowered when Dr. Pennington entered a room. He was a known bully around here. She'd brought Shelby here only because she was so worried. She'd take Shelby to her regular doctor for a second opinion, just to be sure. Right now, she had to trust David and Dr. Pennington.

Together, they checked Shelby over, both silent and seeming determined to make the proper diagnosis. Whitney even sensed a begrudging respect for David in Dr. Pennington's silvery eyes.

"She has an ear infection," David finally announced.

"And she's teething," the doctor said, his tone grumpy but low-key. "We'll prescribe antibiotics and something for the fever."

"Will she be all right?" Whitney asked, more frightened of something happening to Shelby than she'd ever been of dealing with dangerous criminals.

David gave her an encouraging glance. "She'll be better soon. This is normal at five months." His expression changed to something she couldn't quite figure out. He was probably wondering if she had a husband. Whitney hoped he wouldn't ask.

After locking up, David walked Whitney to her police vehicle. While she put a drowsy little Shelby in the baby seat, he glanced in the back. "Where's Hunter?"

Whitney hurried to find her keys. "I left him at my house, and I need to get back." She couldn't thank David enough, but she turned to tell him once again.

He spoke before she could show him her gratitude. "I'll follow you home and make sure Shelby is okay. I mean, until your husband gets home. Or is he already there?"

"You don't have to do that." Whitney's surprise turned to anger. "And I don't have a husband. It's just Shelby and me."

Maybe she shouldn't have told him that. She didn't know him and his reasons for being here were a bit sketchy. He could be the one who'd tried to break into her house. Besides, he probably didn't even have a car.

"I wasn't trying to be nosy," David said. "I wanted to check up on you today, but I got busy here. Any word on those two goons?"

"No, and I can't discuss that with you right now. Sorry I didn't call you with an update."

She whirled and opened the driver's-side door. "As for me, I told you, I can take care of myself. Thank you for checking over my baby, but I have to get her home."

David didn't make a move to let her leave. "Look, I need to talk to you about something important."

Whitney's instincts kicked in, making her wonder what this man was doing in Desert Valley and why he'd volunteered to work at the clinic. But in spite of her doubts, she believed David Evans was a good man. He had come to her rescue yesterday, and she appreciated that. She couldn't be careless like that again. She had to think of Shelby.

"What is it?" she asked David, hoping she wouldn't regret trusting this man. In spite of that fragile trust, she had to be firm with him. "I told you, I'm okay. I've been on my own for a long time. So you don't need to—"

He put a hand on the open door of her car, his brown eyes reminding her of the desert at dusk. "You're right. You don't know me, Whitney. But… I knew your brother. I knew Lucas. And that's why I'm here."

SIX

Whitney dropped her car keys onto the seat. "What did you say?"

David held the door, his expression full of sympathy and regret. "I served with Lucas. I was assigned to his unit."

Whitney swayed on her feet. Putting a hand to her temple, she said, "No. That can't be possible. He never mentioned you."

David held her, his hand on her arm. "It's true. I wanted to tell you right away, but everything got so crazy."

Now she was mad. Pushing him away, she glanced back at Shelby and then whirled, still trying to absorb what he'd just admitted. "So when were you going to tell me, David? You've been here a couple of days now."

He nodded. "Yes...and I've been threatened, held at gunpoint and interrogated at the police station. Not a good time to blurt out something like that. Then today I headed to the clinic to get a tour, but I got busy helping the crowd in the waiting room. I planned on calling you tonight."

"After you *volunteered* in this clinic today," she pointed out. "If I hadn't run into you here, I don't think you would have told me at all."

"I planned on telling you tonight," he repeated. "Look, it's been kind of wild since I got here. I had to get settled and I had to get things straight in my head. This wasn't easy, coming here right after I got back stateside. But I'm here, and I'm willing to explain."

"Yeah, well, you do have a lot to explain."

She'd had more than enough of dishonest men in her life, but she also yearned for any information regarding her brother. Her anger misted into an intense pain that she didn't want David to see. Turning to grab her keys, she said, "I need to get Shelby home and into bed."

"Wait." David held the door again. "Lucas made me promise, Whitney. His last words were about you."

Whitney's anger and despair dispersed like a mirage floating out over the horizon. Tears pricked at her eyes. "What…what did he say?"

David touched her arm again, this time to comfort her. "He said a lot of things, but mostly that you were strong and tough, but he'd feel better knowing someone was looking out for you."

She blinked and took in a breath. "And he picked you for that task?"

David's smile was soft and bittersweet. "Yeah, for some reason he believed in me."

Shelby whimpered and held out her arms. Whitney wiped at the tears in her eyes, but she wouldn't fall apart in front of her baby. "Why don't you follow me home so we can talk, okay?"

David let out a breath. "Good idea. I'll be right behind you."

She nodded, and wondered if that statement meant for longer than tonight. "Lucas," she whispered as she slowly drove home, her heart breaking. "What have you done?"

* * *

Thankful that the rusty yellow vintage Chevy truck Miss Rosa loaned him had made it across town, David stood in front of the tiny fireplace, staring at the un-burned logs Whitney had placed there, while Hunter lay by the table, staring at David. The stucco house was tiny and neat with a minimalist decor that spoke of Whitney's efficiency. A floral couch with deep cushions and one lone blue chair by the hearth. A small round coffee table holding magazines and a green plant centered in front of the couch. A few pretty pictures and decorative mirrors scattered on the cream-colored walls.

On a side table, he spotted a picture of Shelby as a newborn. Then he noticed some sort of colorful contrap-tion in the corner that had all kinds of fun toy attach-ments to entice a baby.

Hunter had his own bed, too, near the fireplace.

The sleek dog stared up at David with eyes that wanted to like him, but David was pretty sure Hunter was waiting for the next command. Or maybe his next meal. David hoped it would be dog food and not his arm or leg.

"We'll get to know each other more," David told Hunter. "Just you wait. We'll be best friends soon."

Hunter didn't move, but his ears perked up.

David took another glance at the baby picture. A little girl dressed in white and pink. Tiny. So tiny.

Whitney had a five-month-old baby. Born in Novem-ber of last year, if David's calculations were correct. If Lucas had known before he died, he'd never mentioned it. Had he withheld that particular bit of information for a reason?

David couldn't judge Whitney, but he sure was curi-ous. To hide that curiosity, he studied the rest of the house and hoped he'd find some clues. Hunter's gaze followed him as he strolled around the long rectangular room.

Across from the fireplace wall, a small kitchen island with two tall stools opened to the white-and-blue kitchen and a side door to the carport.

Down the short hallway where she'd taken Shelby, he'd noticed what had to be two bedrooms with a bath centered between them. Simple and clean.

He figured Whitney was a bit more complex and intriguing than anyone knew, and he had a feeling he'd see a different side of her once she got Shelby all tucked in.

When he heard her coming back up the hallway, he noticed her faded jeans and white T-shirt. Her personal dress code must be efficient, too. But that long, shiny blond hair made her all woman. She probably had no idea that the casual outfit and loose mane of hair made her look attractive. Way too attractive.

She gave him a wary glance as she headed barefoot to the kitchen. Then she called to Hunter. The dog came trotting, his brown eyes giving Whitney an adoring stare. He was an impressive animal with a pretty white coat spotted with tan.

After feeding Hunter and giving him clean water, she turned to David. "I have water, soda and coffee."

"Coffee," he said. It had been a long day.

She reached for the coffeemaker, and he walked over to a bar stool and sat down. "So…you trained here and now you live here?"

She didn't look ready to divulge anything, but she finally said, "Yes. I lived in the dorms—a big condo located near the training center—last year when I first came here to train. But I had to drop out when I got pregnant."

"Did Lucas know?"

Her expression turned somber. "He died before I could tell him. I was in my first trimester."

"Okay, that explains that."

"It was hard, burying my brother when I had a new life inside me." She shook her hair off her face as if to shake away the grief. "But I managed to keep going. I had to, for Shelby's sake."

And she was doing that now, he thought.

"I've waffled between regret for not letting him know sooner and relief that he never knew. Lucas would have moved heaven and earth to come home, and I didn't want him to jeopardize his military career on my account." She stared down at the counter. "But he might be alive today if I'd told him about the baby. He would have found a way to come home."

The torment in her eyes ripped through David's heart. He knew all about that kind of guilt and regret. "You couldn't have predicted this, Whitney. I know it sounds pat, but he was doing what he loved, and he was good at it. He wanted you to feel the same about becoming a police officer."

"I do," she said. "So much so that I came back to try again, and now I'm renting this house from the people next door. The Carters. Marilyn is my babysitter, and her husband's a mechanic. He owns a garage here in town. I owe them a lot. They encouraged me to go to church with them, and I'm glad I did."

"That's good," David said, relieved that she had decent people in her life to help her out. "So you came back to start over, but you couldn't live in the dorms with a baby."

"Right. I'm only here temporarily. We all got involved in a big murder case right after we graduated, so our assignments to police stations across the state have been put on hold. One of our own was killed. Our master dog trainer, Veronica Earnshaw, was found dead near a gate to the puppy yard. Someone shot her. We were all in shock, and then the chief explained we'd been put on retainer by one of our wealthy donors, Marian Foxcroft. You met her daughter, Ellen, yesterday. We were all ordered to stay here and help solve not only Veronica's murder but also the suspicious deaths of two rookies and the murder of an officer's wife five years ago. That officer had been a rookie at the time."

"Wow." David could see the stress and strain in her eyes, but he was glad she'd be hanging around for a while. And he sure wasn't leaving now, either. "How long are you staying?"

"Indefinitely," she said. "I've extended my lease here for another month."

One month. He would probably be gone after that anyway.

"Where do you want to go once this is over?"

She busied herself with measuring coffee into the filter cup. "I'm from Tucson, so I'd like to go back there. But you probably already know about Tucson. My mother and Lucas are both buried there."

He listened, treading carefully. Did those two men from yesterday have anything to do with the murder case? He knew she couldn't reveal details to a civilian, but he wondered if she was in danger from more than one source.

He'd talk about her brother for now since that was why she'd let him follow her home. "Lucas told me he was from Arizona, but he never mentioned Tucson. He said his family moved around a lot."

David had confided in Lucas about his own deceased parents, too. They'd had that in common. But now wasn't the time to mention that to Whitney.

She hit the brew button on the tiny coffeepot and then started putting away clean dishes from the drainer sitting by the sink. "Yes, we went from base to base, but we finally settled in Tucson. Our dad was military, too. He was wounded in Desert Storm not long after I was born and came home and later died of heart disease. He and our mother divorced when I was around ten, and she never remarried. She died of breast cancer about five years ago."

David didn't know what to say. "Lucas didn't talk much about that, but I knew your parents were both dead. He said you were his only close relative."

She took two bright red coffee cups out of a cabinet. "He had a hard time with it since he was the eldest. He was twenty and I was only fifteen when Dad had a massive heart attack." She brought the coffee over, pulled out what looked like homemade muffins and handed him one. Blueberry. "After Mom died, Lucas became the typical protective brother."

David smiled. "You mean overbearing and always bossy but also loyal and fearless?"

She nodded and nibbled on her muffin, then turned to pull some leftover cold chicken out of the fridge. "Yes, you do know my brother. He vetted all of my boyfriends. It got worse when he joined up. I was out on my own by then…but he always worried about me."

"He was proud of you," David said. "He worried about your choice of professions, but he loved you. And he came around on the whole K9 officer thing in the end."

"He told you about that?"

David saw the rush of embarrassment in her eyes. She seemed to value her privacy. "He needed to vent a little. Lucas was like that. He had to figure out things on his own terms."

"Yes, we're alike in that respect," she said with a wry smile.

"I'm gathering that."

"I guess this is kind of weird for you." She stared across at him. "I can't believe he made you promise to come here. And frankly, I can't understand why you *are* here."

"Isn't that obvious?" David asked, the baked chicken reminding him that he was starving. He had to smile at Hunter. The dog lifted his nose in the air. Maybe he liked chicken, too.

"Nothing about this is obvious," she retorted as she shredded the meat and handed him a plate. "Why are you here?"

She had the direct-questioning thing down. He pitied anyone who had the misfortune of being interrogated by her. She stared at him with a blue-eyed vengeance.

David didn't know how to explain. "I made a promise to a dying soldier," he said. "But… Lucas was also my friend."

Her eyes looked like a cloudy sky. "So you always keep your promises?"

David realized one thing, sitting there with her. Lucas might have sent him here, but Whitney would be the reason he'd stay. "I try," he said. Then he bit into the tender chicken.

"Finish eating," she told him. "And then you and I are going to have a serious discussion."

Whitney stared at her reflection in the bathroom mirror. She wouldn't give in to the tears or the regrets or the frustration. Nothing could bring back all the people she'd lost. Her parents, her brother, the father of her child.

And now she had to deal with a man who'd traveled around the world to find her.

Unbelievable. The odds of that same man being all tangled up as a witness to a possible drug smuggling ring were hard to imagine. It only forced them together— for now.

Of all the trains in all the towns…

He had to be on that particular one.

He could have been killed, and then she would never have known about her brother's last hours.

So she looked at herself in the mirror and decided to get over being angry at David. She should be thankful that he'd been so determined to find her. And that, like her brother, he was a true gentleman and a protector.

He's a good man. A kind, caring man who helped save a lot of lives during the worst of circumstances. He tried to save my brother. He tried to help me.

And David was probably feeling a lot of guilt pangs, too.

She could do this. She could go back out there and let him talk, just talk. And maybe she'd finally be able to talk about her life, too. It would be nice to share things with someone who would be out of her life soon anyway. No repercussions. No drama. If she didn't count the facts that he'd known Lucas and that he'd come a long way to honor her brother's wishes.

Time to find out a little bit more about her new protector.

But when she opened the bathroom door, she heard Hunter emitting a low, dangerous growl. Thinking he might have David pinned against a wall, she rounded the corner. "Hey—"

David wasn't anywhere in the living room or kitchen. And the door to the carport was standing open.

Hunter gave her a let's-roll glance and alerted. Something was definitely going on out there.

Going to the hall closet, Whitney unlocked her gun box and hurried to the open door. "David?" she called in a low whisper. "David, are you out there?"

SEVEN

David knew he wasn't imagining things.

When he'd glanced out the back window, he'd seen a shadow in the backyard. A movement there in the moonlight. Maybe a tree? But then he'd heard a commotion, too. Without thinking, he'd opened the carport door and hurried around the corner of the house.

Now he could hear Hunter's growls. Whitney would wonder what had happened. When he heard footsteps, he stopped behind a tree. Then a light switched on, and he heard Whitney commanding Hunter.

"Go. Find."

The dog leaped into the air, barking and snarling as he took off toward the back fence. David saw a dark figure running out from behind a cluster of bushes, and then he heard the old fence creaking and groaning. Hurrying to where Hunter stood barking, David saw a sneakered foot making it over the shoulder-high enclosure.

"Stop," Whitney called as she came running.

David figured she had her gun on *him*. He turned. "It's me."

"I know it's you. And I know you well enough now to think you might sail over that fence right after whoever that was in my yard."

She had him there. "Yep. Hunter saw him, too."

Whitney slowly made her way toward him, her gun held down at her side. "Probably the same person who broke the lock on my gate when I got home last night."

"What?" David whirled to stare at her. "Someone was here? Was it the drug smugglers?"

She let out a sigh. "I don't know. Hunter alerted when we got home. But I checked and didn't find anyone."

"Did you tell your chief or anyone else about this?"

"Yes," she said in a defensive tone. "I thought it might be kids. We have a lot of teens always wandering around here."

"And you had a run-in with drug smugglers that same day," he reminded her. "It could have been one of them."

She stalked around the small yard. "I know."

"We both saw them up close. They might want to wipe that little scene *and* us out of their minds."

"I have Hunter, and I'd never put Shelby in danger but I do have to be alert until we find them." Then she let out a breath. "Shelby. I have to get back inside."

David watched as she took off, Hunter behind her.

He checked the fence, touching it and pushing on it. It was wobbly and old, and that was probably what he'd heard earlier when someone tried to climb over. He could fix that. Her landlord next door needed to do something about this, but David could take care of it and solve the problem for all of them.

After making sure no one else was around, he started toward the house. When he heard a car cranking up down the street, he had a feeling that the intruder was once again getting away.

When he came inside, Whitney was sitting on the couch, her gun lying on the table beside her.

Glancing around, he asked, "Is Shelby okay?"

"She's asleep. Her room is safe."

"Did you report this?"

"I'm the police, remember?"

"Yeah. I can see that. But…you're not safe."

"I have my weapon and a trained partner."

Hunter sat at her feet as if to prove that point.

David wanted to prove *his* point. "Yeah, well, now you have me, too."

Whitney held up one hand. "Oh, no. No, I don't. You've done what you came here to do. You don't have to stick around on my account."

Because no one else had, apparently.

"I said, I'm not leaving."

"You mean, tonight? Or tomorrow? Or never?"

"That all depends. You've got a lot going on. A baby to take care of, drug smugglers hounding you and some big murder case you can't talk much about."

Her blue eyes shot fire. "That's right. That's my job."

"Well, whether you like it or not, you and I are involved in what happened yesterday. Together. We were there together."

"And whether you like it or not, I have to investigate, and I will find out what's going on. You only need to take care of yourself. Not me. I'm not holding you to that misguided promise my brother guilted you into."

David stood in front of the fireplace while she stayed on the couch. "Why are you so stubborn?"

"Why are you so determined to be my knight in shining armor?"

He wanted to tell her that he'd promised. But mainly, he wanted to assure her that he would stick around whether she liked it or not. He almost told her, because even though they'd had some odd, trying moments together so far, he liked her.

But she wasn't ready for a showdown right now. Or anything else.

"I don't want to be anybody's hero," he finally said. "I'm in this, Whitney. Whether you like it or not, I'm on those two criminals' list right along with you. Why don't we work together to bring them to justice?"

She gave him a stubborn pout and then tugged at her hair. "I want justice," she said. "For all of them."

"What do you mean, for all of them?"

She let out a sigh and stood up. "I don't know if the person who came into my backyard has to do with the alleged drug trafficking through this town or…if it has to do with several people I know possibly being murdered. But one way or another, I intend to find out."

A few minutes later, David gave up trying to figure out this case. But he didn't want to go back to the inn just yet. "I guess you want me to leave, right?"

Whitney didn't know what she wanted. Yesterday, David Evans had been an eyewitness to a strange drug-smuggling operation and a stabbing. Today, he had become so much more. The medic who'd tried to save her brother and helped her baby, and a man who'd traveled a long way to honor a promise.

Now she longed to know everything, including his history.

When she didn't respond, he added, "I know you can't talk about your work, so I won't ask you to explain that earlier comment about possible murders, but I'd like to know more about you."

"It is getting late, but… David…we've talked about me a lot. Let's get back to you."

"Are you asking as a police officer?" His brown eyes grew daring. "Or as a friend?"

Surprised, she let out a breath. "Are we friends?"

"I'd like to think so," he said. Settling into the old chair she'd found at a flea market and recovered in a denim blue, he scrubbed a hand down his five-o'clock shadow. "I mean, doesn't being attacked and almost shot make people BFFs?"

Whitney laughed at that. And realized it had been a while since she'd had a good laugh. "I would think so, yes. Best friends forever."

Then she looked up and into his eyes and really saw *him*.

As a man. A very attractive man, sitting here in her living room late at night. She remembered how a scene very much like this one had gotten her into a lot of hot water just over a year ago.

Trouble.

She didn't need any more trouble.

She loved Shelby and thanked God every day for her sweet little girl. But next time she wanted to fall in love by the book. Faith, hope and love. That was what she wanted next time.

And in that order.

"Hey, you don't have to be my best friend," he said, misunderstanding her sudden silence. "I'll settle for being new friends right now."

"I'm thinking," she admitted. "I'd like to get to know you a little better."

He smiled and tapped his fingers against the chair. "I lost both my parents, too," he said, his tone quiet.

"What?"

"They were killed in a car wreck two years ago. I was inside a triage tent at a field hospital, trying to convince a dying soldier that he would be okay. He had a hole in his gut that no amount of morphine or surgery would ever relieve."

Whitney gulped in air and then put her hand to her mouth. "David, I'm so sorry."

"My father suffered a massive heart attack while they were heading down a country road, admiring the wild-flower trails in the Texas Hill Country. The car ran off the road and hit a tree. It's fitting that they died together. They loved each other so much. I was their only child. I became a medic because of my father. He was a surgeon."

Whitney sat there, thinking how blessed they'd both been in their lives—and yet they'd both suffered trag-edies, too. "Did he…know what you'd done? Saving so many, trying to comfort those who wouldn't make it?"

"He knew. He was proud of me, but he kind of planned for me to follow in his footsteps. I wanted to open a fam-ily practice and he fussed at me, telling me I'd be over-worked and underpaid. Then, when I joined the army, he…he changed. He was full of resolve and accepted my choices, but I think he was waiting for me to come home and settle down. He worried that something would hap-pen to me. His legacy was the most important thing in the world to him, and I was supposed to be a big part of that."

"You felt guilty because you weren't there, right?"

She could see it in his eyes. Feel it whenever he heaved a shuddering breath. The same guilt she felt whenever she thought of Brian and her brother.

"Yes. I might have seen the signs, or I could have cau-tioned him to slow down and take it easy. He volunteered a lot—clinics and mission trips and homeless shelters. He had a true servant's heart."

Now she understood what made David Evans tick. Coming here to see her, immediately volunteering at the clinic that always needed extra hands, sitting with the injured train attendant and even staying with her at the train scene until he knew she was safe. David was trying to measure up to his father's expectations. But he also had a servant's heart. He cared about people, and he wasn't like that just to measure up to someone else's legacy. He's made his own legacy by being a good man.

"I think you might be that way, too," she said, seeing him in a whole new light. "And I think your father would be proud that the Evans legacy will live on…in you."

"I guess so." He smiled again. "Didn't mean to be a downer. I wanted you to know that I understand how you feel. It's tough, going it alone. But you and I… We're survivors."

"Yes." They could agree on that, at least.

"I should go," he said, getting up in a slow, lanky way that made her want him to stay a while longer. "But…are you sure you'll be okay?"

"I'm fine, David," she replied, appreciating him more now that they'd talked. "I have security lights, and I have Hunter to alert me. Shelby's window has a solid lock on it. The house is small and secure. And I have the Carters right next door."

"Plus, you are a highly trained police officer."

"Twice trained," she quipped, feeling good about him but a little anxious about whoever kept coming into her yard. But she wouldn't tell David that. He'd sleep on the couch if it meant fulfilling his duty.

He started toward the front door and then pivoted. "Hey, I can at least check on Shelby and see if her fever's broken."

"Good idea. You are highly trained, right?"

"Right." He grinned. "I've seen it all, too."

"Yes, and you'll see everything at the clinic. Be careful around Dr. Pennington. He was married to Veronica, just so you know. He's still bitter because she left him for another man. He hates it here and he'd like nothing more than to get hired on at some big city hospital. And…he's kind of territorial. I'm surprised he even accepted your offer to volunteer."

"I did notice he likes to call the shots, but when I walked in today, he didn't have time to argue with me. I think his entire staff would be glad if he'd find another position," David said. "But don't worry. I'll watch my back."

While he was watching her back, Whitney thought.

She guided him back to Shelby's nursery, which she'd decorated in soft pinks and bright greens. Her sweet baby was sleeping peacefully, her flowers-and-frogs mobile floating over the bed.

Whitney watched as David leaned over the white crib and touched a big, tanned hand to Shelby's brow. Seeing him there reminded her of how she'd often imagined Brian, Shelby's father, there. But David wasn't Brian, and nothing could change that.

David was different. Strong, noble, caring, willing to sacrifice for others. He touched Shelby in a way that showed he cared. This scene touched Whitney in places that had long gone dormant.

Whitney's brittle heart seemed to soften like a dry desert flower opening up to a soaking rain.

Faith, hope and love.

She wanted those things.

Now more than ever.

But first, she had to solve a murder. She needed to find out who killed Veronica and the others. Especially who killed Brian Miller. Maybe Marian Foxcroft was right to want these incidents declared accidents, but Whitney's gut told her differently. Maybe all of these murders were connected.

EIGHT

Two days later, Whitney was once again on the job and feeling better. Shelby had improved after a day at home, where Whitney made some cold calls regarding Veronica's murder, hoping to follow up on some tips that had come into the station. Marilyn had promised to call if Shelby had any problems. Whitney was still learning how to balance work with having a baby to care for, but knowing Marilyn would alert her if Shelby needed her helped a lot to ease her mind.

Now, after a day of chasing down more leads that hadn't panned out, Whitney was back with Eddie Harmon again. Chief Jones liked to pair the rookies with older, more experienced police officers, and that was all fine and good.

But Eddie wasn't the best mentor. He wasn't focused on the job anymore, and he didn't care that someone had shot Veronica. While she'd angered a lot of people and she'd been hard to deal with, Veronica didn't deserve to die the way she had. But Eddie didn't seem too concerned about finding her killer. He only wanted to work the beat and go home early. Still smarting from his wisecracks about her at the train scene the other day, Whitney planned to ignore Eddie and do what she had to do.

"I want you two to interview Veronica's ex-husband, Dr. Pennington, again," Chief Jones said, his towering height intimidating Whitney.

"I thought he'd already been interviewed," Eddie whined. "I can't deal with that sorry—"

"Careful," the chief cautioned. "Let me explain, Eddie." He turned to Whitney, silently assigning her as point person when he gave her a direct nod. "The doctor was interviewed a few weeks ago, but I need you to ask him one more time if he can think of anyone else who had it in for Veronica. I've heard that they argued about a lot of things, that maybe Veronica was making demands on the doctor's finances. We've asked questions, yes, but we need to narrow this down and see if he slips up on something. We keep asking until we hit on something. Or notice something that might be off a little bit."

"Half the town had it in for that woman," Eddie said, his massive hands on his hips.

"Then, you interview half the town," the chief replied, his piercing eyes daring Eddie to say another word.

"We'll take care of it, sir," Whitney said. She turned and headed out, not waiting for Eddie to get in gear.

"Hey, Godwin!"

She turned back at the chief's call, almost running into the always-in-a-hurry department secretary, Carrie Dunleavy.

"Sorry," Carrie said, her brown eyes behind horn-rimmed glasses, a stack of files in her hands.

"That's okay," Whitney replied with a smile. Carrie took care of a lot of details around here. Scooting around Carrie, she said, "Yes, sir."

"What's the status on our eyewitness—David Evans?"

That she could answer. "His background check came back clean. He was deployed for nine months this past tour, and he's only been back stateside for a couple of months. No record, not even a traffic ticket. Grew up in Texas, played football and baseball in high school and was top of his class in college and med school. Made sure he had all the proper paperwork in check to volunteer at the clinic while he's here."

David was one of the good guys.

The chief nodded. "We haven't found any vehicles matching the partial plates Evans remembered, but Louise is still searching for the emblem you and your witness described. No word from the lab in Flagstaff regarding the fabric from the suspect's pants. Hope to hear on the weapon later today."

"Thanks, sir," Whitney replied. "We'll get on with these leads. Oh, and the railroad station manager said we could take a look at the video cameras at the station sometime this week."

"All right. Get out there and get at it," Chief Jones said, waving her away.

The department secretary, back at her desk, called out, "Hey, how's Shelby?"

"Much better, thankfully," Whitney replied.

"You work too hard," Carrie replied with an appreciative smile. "But you're good at it. Sooner or later, the person who did this will slip up. I hope you get a chance to be in on finding out the truth."

Whitney wanted that chance, too. "Thanks, Carrie."

Carrie smiled. "Hey, do you have a date for the dance next month?"

Whitney thought of David. "Nah, I'll probably go solo."

"Welcome to my world," Carrie said on a wistful note. "I'll probably be by myself again."

Hoping to encourage the shy woman, Whitney said,

"Well, you never know. Someone might surprise you and ask to be your date."

"From your mouth to God's ear," Carrie said as she walked away.

Carrie was single like Whitney, so they often compared notes on everything from plants to fashion. Not that either of them looked like supermodels. But it was good to have someone to talk to now and then. Next time Whitney got the female rookies and trainers together for a girls' night out, she'd have to invite Carrie.

As she headed out the door, she refocused and wished Eddie would go ahead and retire, since he wanted to do that anyway. He made it known all the time that he was ready to spend more time with his family. Whitney didn't have that luxury, however. So she had to follow orders.

"Chief Jones is determined to find a killer," Eddie said once he was in the car. His aggravation showed as he yanked the seat belt on the passenger side of the patrol car and made sure it clicked.

"We all want to find Veronica's killer," Whitney countered. "Not to mention investigating Melanie's murder and the two other deaths."

"You mean Mike and Brian?" Eddie shook his head. "Both ruled accidents. Need to let that go, girl."

"I'm not letting anything go," Whitney said. "It's all too coincidental, Eddie. Surely you have to agree with that."

"Yeah, I guess so." He gave her a sheepish glance. "Don't mind me. I should be more encouraging to a rookie. It's just that sometimes all the politics and red tape get to me. It's frustrating to see the truth right there and not find any evidence to substantiate it."

Hunter sat in the back, staring at Eddie as if he was

trying to figure him out. But Whitney could understand Eddie's frustration. Police work was tedious at times.

"We have to do our jobs," Whitney reminded him, hoping to get him enthused and involved. "We don't have to like Veronica, but we do have an obligation to find out who killed her."

"Right." Eddie chuckled. "All you rookies, so eager to please. Does the chief throw you treats, too?" He grinned to soften that remark.

Whitney changed lanes and said, "Let's get this over with so I can make it home at a decent hour right along with you."

He chuckled again, but he did shut up. Eddie liked to get home as early as possible so he could watch sports and boss his overworked wife around. The poor woman had four kids of various ages to take care of. She carted them all over town for sports events and dance classes, and he wanted to be there for all of it. Admirable in a sweet kind of way. He did brag on his children, so Whitney knew he loved them.

Five minutes later, Whitney pulled the car into the big, rambling house that had been rezoned commercial and now served as Desert Valley Clinic. Remembering that she might run into David there, she took a deep breath and made a solemn pledge to herself to concentrate on doing her job.

But when they entered the clinic, it was chaos, as usual. A lot of the people around there didn't have well-paying jobs, let alone insurance. This was the only place they could come. Several patients sat in the waiting room. They all looked up when they saw a K9 officer with a dog coming through the doors.

Hunter sniffed the air but didn't alert, thankfully. She never knew whom she'd find waiting in the overworked clinic. And since the train fiasco had been on the evening news, she was sure everyone around here was a little jittery.

"I hate this place," Eddie said in a loud whisper. "Hot and stinking."

Whitney wanted to tell him to get a better attitude since *his* deodorant had stopped working around noon, but she kept moving toward the reception desk. "We need to speak with Dr. Pennington, please," she said after showing the frazzled woman her badge.

"He's in with a patient," the woman said. "Might have to take a number."

Whitney glanced around. Nowhere to sit. Hunter was good with crowds, but she didn't need a curious child to pet the big dog. "Can we come into the hallway?"

"Sure." The woman didn't seem to care one way or another. Maybe she and Eddie could compare notes.

The woman buzzed them in since the door stayed locked due to the various medications they kept on hand.

They found two well-worn fabric chairs tucked in a corner and sat down.

"Stay," Whitney ordered Hunter with a brush of her hand across the fur on his head. The big canine settled at her feet. Eddie immediately pulled out his cell and started scrolling while she did a visual scan of the long hallway and wondered if David was here today.

When she heard a scream coming from a room down the hallway, she went on alert. Hunter did the same, lifting his head to her for instructions.

But a nurse came out of the room and shook her head. "Sorry. Patient doesn't like needles."

"Who does?" Eddie said, never taking his eyes off his phone.

Then Whitney looked up and saw Dr. Pennington

coming toward them. "What now? I told the receptionist I'm busy."

Whitney stood to greet him. "We have a few more questions. I won't take up much of your time."

The doctor's expression boiled red with anger. "Let's go into my office. I've got patients coming and going. Don't need that dog to bite someone."

Whitney gave Eddie a pointed look, and together they followed the doctor down the hallway to his large office. A bank of windows offered a view of a huge oak tree in the back parking lot.

"If you're going to ask me about the night Veronica was murdered, I told two other officers I was working at the hospital that night."

"You mean the Canyon County Regional Medical Center?" Whitney asked. Dr. Pennington was sometimes on call there, too.

"Of course," Dr. Pennington said. "I was in the ER, and I have witnesses to that. We had a busy night."

"Okay, so we've established that, sir," Whitney said, doing her best to maintain a professional calm. "But... you can help us in another way. Do you know of anyone who might have had beef with Veronica Earnshaw?"

A black SUV pulled up beside Dr. Pennington's foreign sports car in the parking lot. He glanced at the vehicle and started fidgeting. "Look, if you're still wondering who might have killed my ex-wife, go talk to Lloyd Harglow. She left me for him, but that little coupling didn't go very well. She loved his money more than she loved him, and Lloyd doesn't take too well to people who don't fall at his feet."

Whitney had heard Lloyd could be a real pain. But then, so could Veronica. "So you think they could have argued?"

"Argued?" The doctor snorted and started gathering his briefcase and some papers, his gaze moving toward the parking lot again. "They fought all the time. Threatened each other. She'd call me for a shoulder to cry on—not that Veronica ever cried a tear." He scratched his head. "You know, Lloyd's wife hated Veronica, too. For obvious reasons. Veronica didn't care who she stepped on to get what she wanted."

"Okay, we'll speak to both Mr. and Mrs. Harglow again," Whitney said. She was pretty sure they'd both been interviewed, but she'd talk to them if she had to. "Did you and Veronica argue when you were married?"

Dr. Pennington looked affronted. "Like most married couples, yes. Stop fishing for something that isn't there, Officer. We fought, but we always made up."

Whitney wanted to believe him. "Okay. Thanks for your time."

"Glad I could help you." Dr. Pennington glanced around, irritation coloring his features and sarcasm streaming through his words. "Now, if you'll excuse me, I have some business to take care of myself. I have to go."

Whitney glanced at Eddie, but he was busy studying the sports memorabilia on the wall. Useless.

"Thank you, Dr. Pennington," she said. But the doctor was already out in the hallway, barking orders at the nurses. When she nudged Eddie, he seemed to realize the interview was over.

They went out into the hallway, and Whitney looked up to find David conferring with a nurse. "We only have three more patients," he said. "Let's get them taken care of, and you can go home."

David turned and saw Whitney standing in front of Dr. Pennington's office. "Hi," he said, moving toward her. He glanced into the office. "I see he left early again." Then he looked out the window, his gaze turning into a frown.

"Yes." Whitney watched as Eddie went to chat with the receptionist. She hoped he was gathering information. "Does Dr. Pennington do that a lot?"

David nodded, his expression grim as he stared out the window. "According to the nurses, yes. And he left briefly after I got here yesterday. I'm staying late tonight to clear the waiting area."

He glanced back up the hallway and then moved close and pointed toward the window. "Whitney, he got into that dark SUV."

Whitney turned and saw the vehicle peeling out of the back parking area. "Interesting."

"Yes," David said. "Especially since it's almost identical to the one we saw the other day at the train station."

Whitney realized he was right. "I don't know why I didn't catch that myself." Then she shook her head. "But a lot of people around here drive SUVs. This is rugged terrain, and we see all kinds. He took his briefcase with him. Maybe he had a business meeting."

"I could be wrong," David said. "But I'll tell you one thing. I'm going to keep an eye on the doctor. He's good at his job, but why would he come and go like that when we have patients waiting?"

"He doesn't care about the patients," Whitney said. She jotted notes in her pocket pad. "And he doesn't care about Veronica's murder, either." Tapping her pen against paper, she checked to make sure no one was listening. "He did act a little squirrely today. He couldn't wait to get out of here."

"He keeps to his office most of the time," David said. "And he watches the staff. Doesn't seem to trust anyone. Especially me."

"What do you mean?" Whitney asked. "I'd think he'd appreciate a qualified volunteer."

"He appreciates my work, but my presence seems to irritate him. I focus on the patients. That's mostly what I do." He shrugged and checked his watch. "I don't know. He seems to like to issue veiled threats to anyone who crosses him."

"If he threatens you, you need to let me know."

David's stern expression mirrored what she felt. "Well, he seems to care a lot about something other than this clinic. And I intend to find out what it is."

Whitney put a hand on David's arm. "You need to be careful. He could be dangerous."

David nodded. "We both need to be careful. Something's not right here."

Whitney agreed with him on that, the hair on her neck standing up when she remembered the chief had cautioned them to look for things that seemed off. David had noticed this already, and he'd been here only a few days. She hoped he wouldn't get caught in the middle of any criminal activities. But he'd witnessed two dangerous criminals hauling illegal drugs. He definitely had a target on his back.

NINE

David took a long drink from his bottled water and glanced around the empty clinic. The sun was going down, and he hadn't eaten since this morning's breakfast at the Desert Rose. But it had been a hearty breakfast.

Rosa Helena—Miss Rosa—and her staff cooked up everything from muffins and French toast to omelets and pounds of bacon and sausage. David had eaten some of each since Miss Rosa had kept putting food on his plate. Now he could walk back to the Desert Rose and grab something off the snack table, or maybe he'd try out the Cactus Café. It wasn't far from the clinic, and the nurses had recommended it since it had everything from steak and potatoes to fried chicken and hamburgers.

Besides, he could use a good walk to take his mind off Whitney and the events going on around here. For such a small town, Desert Valley was full of interesting, mysterious people. And apparently a murderer. Did everyone here have secrets?

After checking all of the examining rooms and making sure the trash and laundry had been taken care of and that all the instruments were being properly sterilized, David locked the medicine cabinet and the front door and started out the back. It was kind of amazing that Dr. Pennington had left and returned only to get his car and then leave again. Even more surprising, the rest of the staff members had gladly given David the job of closing up tonight.

David didn't like the lackadaisical way this clinic worked, but he had used the opportunity to explore the entire building for any clues to what the good doctor was up to. Maybe he had a female friend he liked to meet during the day, or maybe he had a family stashed somewhere and he made an appearance now and then. He could have a patient who demanded privacy, so he did what he had to do by sneaking away.

But having been thrown into the middle of some already shady dealings with those drug runners, David's mind was going wild with all sorts of scenarios. He couldn't prove anything, but he could watch and listen. Being in a war zone had honed his senses and his intuition enough that he knew to be cautious.

Had he stepped into a different kind of war zone?

He walked along the row of offices and retail shops that the locals called the Town Center and saw the neon blinking lights of the Cactus Café. He could get something to take back to his room at the Desert Rose, or he could eat at the counter and listen in on the conversations going on around him.

He decided sitting at the counter would be entertaining, and getting the local angle would certainly help him. After he ordered chicken-fried steak and mashed potatoes, he sat back and glanced around. The Cactus Café was decorated appropriately in live cacti of all shapes and sizes, along with murals of the town, including what must have been the first train to come through.

"I hear there's a puppy missing," one old man said to the couple sitting in a booth across from him. "The police know about it. I saw one of them K9 cops talking to several people who live near the training center."

"My wife heard at church the other day that Marian Foxcroft is still in a coma. They got a round-the-clock guard on her hospital room. She donates a lot of those puppies, and when that Earnshaw woman got shot, she offered something like a million dollars to keep all them rookies here to help find the killer. Mighty suspicious that now someone tried to do her in, too. I'm telling you, it ain't safe here anymore."

"And then that whole thing with the train the other day. That poor attendant couldn't wait to go back east after he was released from the hospital. They put a guard on him, too. Drugs moving right under our noses. A lot of good that training center is doing if they can't even find drugs coming through here."

David lowered his head when the waitress brought his food. He didn't want to get into any kind of speculative conversation with the locals. If they recognized him as being the eyewitness, he'd get grilled, but he wouldn't be able to provide any answers. So he kept listening and started piecing together information while he ate his dinner.

But before he'd finished his meal, he realized the incident at the train station could be just the beginning. The drug smugglers might lie low for a while, but they'd be back. They wouldn't want to leave any witnesses behind. Someone had already tried to break into Whitney's house, and that meant Whitney was in a lot of danger, just as he'd figured. Add to that her being involved in investigating a high-profile murder case and the danger became even worse.

Would they keep coming until they hurt her or killed her?

David paid and tipped the waitress and then started

walking the short distance back to the Desert Rose. A blue souped-up car driven by a dark-haired man wearing a cowboy hat pulled out of the parking lot. The big motor revved like a growling cat. David eyed the muscle car, thinking he probably should have driven Miss Rosa's decrepit truck to work, but walking was about as quick since the clinic was around the corner from the inn.

When the car moved along Main Street at a slow pace before taking off into the growing darkness, he stared after it, wondering if the man had been following him.

"I'm imagining things," he mumbled. But it didn't hurt to be aware of his surroundings, all things considered.

When he turned the corner, he was surprised to see a patrol car parked in the small front yard of the inn. He hurried up the front steps. "What's going on?"

Whitney turned from the front door. "Miss Rosa called us to report a prowler in the backyard and a blue car idling on the curb."

He glanced inside the house. "I saw that car headed west on Main Street. But Miss Rosa sees things a lot. She thought a topiary tree was someone's head the other night. And she thinks she's seen your missing puppy. But if I saw that same car, she might be right this time. Where is she now?"

"I'm not sure," Whitney said. "I've knocked and called out." Giving him a firm stare that dared him to move, she said, "Stay here."

"I have a key," David said, fishing it out of his pocket.

She knocked again. "Desert Valley Police, Miss Rosa."

They heard a piercing scream coming from inside the house, followed by a round of gunshots.

TEN

David hurried to slide his key into the lock and opened the big door with a bang. He didn't wait for Whitney.

Whitney ordered Hunter inside, giving the dog a hand signal to search. Drawing her weapon, she hurried through the open stained-glass door. Hunter ran ahead, doing his job like a pro.

Soon angry barks carried throughout the house, coming from the back.

"David?" she called as she cleared the formal sitting room and the elaborate dining room on each side of the long hallway. "David, answer me!"

"Back here."

He sounded winded. Hunter's barks grew more frenzied.

She made it to the big kitchen and then hurried out onto the long sunporch that stretched across the back of the house where she found David with Miss Rosa. Then another gunshot rang out.

Whitney ducked down and called out, "David, help Miss Rosa."

David knelt beside a Victorian sofa, where Miss Rosa lay with a hand to her head. The petite woman's wiry gray hair stood out like a feather duster against the embroidered pillow behind her. Hunter snarled near the screen door centered on the porch.

Then they heard a car peeling away down the street.

"Is she shot?" Whitney asked, her breath coming fast.

"I'm fine," Miss Rosa said. "I'm short, so he missed. Is someone trying to kill all of us?"

"She saw the shadow again," David explained from behind Whitney, his fingers on Miss Rosa's wrist. "It wasn't the topiary tree, Whitney. She saw a face beyond the sunporch. He came back, but he ran when she screamed."

"A big man," Miss Rosa said through a moan, her dark brown eyes wide open. "I went out to water my rosebushes earlier. I water them every night. You know, they're very hard to grow in this climate, but I make it work. That's when I saw him, right there by the door." She sat up. "I screamed and doused him with the water hose and then I came inside and called 911."

"I'll take Hunter out for a search, but they probably got away when we heard the car leaving," Whitney said. "Do we need to call an ambulance?"

David shook his head. "She's fine. Just scared." He started talking in soothing tones in answer to the innkeeper's many comments and questions. "Yes, I know I'm your only boarder right now. No, I'm not checking out. Yes, I'll watch out for things around here. Let me go get you some water."

"I'm so glad we have a law officer here," Miss Rosa said on a weak note. "I don't abide Peeping Toms or being shot at. Why did he shoot at us?"

"Just rest," David replied. He darted a concerned glance at Whitney before he headed inside to get Miss Rosa's water.

Whitney grabbed her flashlight off her equipment belt and held it over her weapon. Then she opened the screen door. "Go out," she told Hunter. The dog immediately took off toward the back of the long, narrow yard.

Whitney followed and held the flashlight up to the tall white fence, where the fragrant yellow puffballs of an acacia tree hovered like cotton. Nothing there but a tree that covered the fence corner. On the other side, near a rock garden, a blue palm fanned out, rustling in the wind.

Hunter alerted near the gate.

Whitney shined the scant light down to the rocky dirt and saw a red baseball cap by the fence.

Her heart pumped against her rib cage as realization swept through her. Miss Rosa was seeing things all right.

She'd seen a person. And that red baseball cap indicated that the person who'd been near the sunporch door was probably one of the drug smugglers who'd been on the train earlier this week. She'd surprised him, so he'd retaliated by shooting at her.

They were trying to make good on their threats.

The drug runners were hunting down both Whitney and David.

And it would be only a matter of time before they made it all the way inside one of the houses. Whitney shuddered to think what would happen then.

Shelby.

Whitney called Hunter away and whirled to run back to the inn. She had to warn the Carters.

"All is well here, honey," Marilyn said. "We're inside and eating dinner. Jack is here. I'll have him set the alarm."

"Thank you, Marilyn. The cruiser the chief put on our street should be just outside, too."

Gathering her thoughts, Whitney retrieved her evidence kit from the car so she could bag the red cap. And then she took a quick breath and said a prayer for all of them.

Dear Lord, protect my baby and my friends.
God, please protect all of us.

"Are you sure you don't need to go to the ER?"

"Yes." Miss Rosa got up from her chair on the sunporch. "I'm fine. All I did was scream and fall onto a love seat. Now I have to go and check on dinner." She turned at the door to the dining room and slanted her head in a dainty way. "I have a permit, you know. And from now on I can assure you I'll be packing heat."

David watched her head to the kitchen, wishing he hadn't brought this danger into the quaint old inn. "I should go and help her." Then he shook his head. "And I pray she won't make good on that threat. Miss Rosa with a pistol—that's scary."

"We do have drug people out to get us," Whitney said. "She has every right to protect herself."

"So do we," David replied.

The whole place had been checked over for prints and any evidence of a prowler, and the team had combed the woods and yards nearby, looking for bullet fragments and anything else they could find.

Yet they had nothing except the description of the blue car that both David and Miss Rosa had seen, a vintage Camaro that had been overhauled to get away quickly. That and the red cap, which could offer up some DNA, at least.

Now there was an alert out on that vehicle, too.

"I know, but we can't go into hiding," Whitney said. "I have my work, and you volunteer at the clinic. Do you want to hang out at the police station all day?"

"No." Although that would relieve some of his anxieties regarding her.

He glanced out into the dusk to hide his concern. But

he needed answers to the whole picture since he was knee-deep in this danger. "I know you can't tell me everything, but what's the deal with the missing puppy? And a woman named Marian?"

Her face twisted in surprise. "How do you know about that?"

"The café," he said. "Everyone is talking about the drug couriers and the missing puppy. And Marian being in a coma."

"I can tell you what the public knows. Veronica Earnshaw was our master dog trainer. She loved animals and was very good with them. But she didn't have the best people skills. Shane Weston, one of the rookies, found her dead inside the open gate to the training yard. Gina Perry, another trainer who worked with Veronica, was there with her. At first, people suspected Gina since she and Veronica didn't get along, but she's been cleared. And Shane, too, for that matter."

David held up his hand. "Wait. One of your own was a suspect?"

She nodded. "Briefly. The bullets used to kill Veronica matched those of an antique gun that belonged to Shane's grandfather—a .45 caliber. But thankfully, Shane was cleared since he had a solid alibi."

She stopped and took a breath. "Marian Foxcroft, Ellen's mother, is the woman who funded the department so we could all stay here. She was found unconscious in her home not long after Veronica's death. She's in a coma at the medical center. This case has all of us on edge."

Toying with a rough spot on the arm of the old rocker, she said, "We have briefings almost daily, and we all try to think outside the box."

"No wonder you didn't trust me when you first met me," David said. "You've been dealing with a lot of stuff here and then I pop up, a stranger in town. The Old West is alive and well."

She took a breath and stared out at the growing night. "It gets worse. Marian donated a litter of puppies to the training center. Veronica had been working with them. The night of the murder, she was at the training center, tagging them with microchips. When they found Veronica, they realized one of the puppies was missing. Little Marco. Witnesses spotted someone on a bike picking up the puppy, but it was dark and the person on the bicycle wore a hoodie, so the witnesses couldn't tell if it was a man or woman. We've speculated during our meetings whether Veronica let the puppy go on purpose. The evidence from the crime scene points to that, at least. So we put out flyers all over town, hoping someone would step up and tell us more or maybe bring Marco back."

"And you have to follow every lead, just in case."

She ran a hand over her always neat ponytail. "We're all assigned to the case, so I've been making return calls to eliminate some of the crazy tips that we've received. We need to find that puppy."

David followed the maze. "The puppy might help solve the crime?"

"The puppy could be with Veronica's killer," Whitney said. "So we have to talk to anyone who might have seen that puppy. Marco had been socialized—trained to be around people—from a very young age. He'd naturally run toward someone, so it's anybody's guess who took him. But yes, the killer might have Marco. Especially if Veronica was letting him go as a message or to give us a clue."

David studied the windows behind them. The inn shimmered with welcoming light. Miss Rosa had turned on all the lamps. "So…did you warn Miss Rosa about all of this?"

Whitney lifted her chin. "Yes, I've talked to her about the missing puppy. She said she saw Marco one night, out in her yard. I checked it out, but I think it was probably the neighbor's calico cat. Kind of the same markings as our missing puppy—fawn colored with a black circle on its head."

David wondered who'd taken the puppy. "This is serious. Me being here put her in danger, too. We've got someone covering up a murder and drug traffickers shooting at us. Any more on those two from the train?"

"No, nothing, but I'm pretty sure one of them was here tonight. I turned the gun over to the property room after we disarmed it. It's been dusted for prints, but it takes a while to hear back from the crime lab in Flagstaff. They'll check it and that scrap of fabric from the pants leg for trace evidence."

"Trace evidence?" David was fascinated, but mostly, he wanted to keep her here a while longer. He enjoyed talking to her about her work and asking her questions. Her answers gave him hints of her personality. He'd learned to listen to wounded soldiers who needed to talk, so he used that technique on the woman he wanted to get to know better. "You'll have to explain."

"Blood, DNA, hair or fabric fibers."

"And I thought my job was hard."

"We all have hard jobs," she said, getting up. She tilted her head. "Miss Rosa raves to everyone about what a nice young man you are. How you have manners and offer to help her out a lot. She told me you're overhauling her old Chevy pickup."

"I don't know if that jalopy can be overhauled. But she's a sweetheart. She leaves fresh-baked cookies out on the refreshment bar and folds my laundry straight from the dryer." He stared into the house, making sure Miss Rosa was okay. "I'd hate for something to happen to her."

"She's a character," Whitney said. "She has regular boarders passing through, and they don't want to leave. And I'm pretty sure she'd like to keep you as one of them, so stay diligent. This isn't over."

David stood, too, his eyes meeting hers. Funny how he'd just noticed her heart-shaped face. Here in the growing dusk, she looked young and fresh faced, beautiful.

Whitney Godwin was a beautiful woman.

Whoa. In the middle of all of this, he'd still managed to notice? He needed to rein in that notion. Yes, he'd carried her picture near his heart. But he'd done that to honor her brother. Hadn't he? Lucas hadn't sent him here to make the moves on his sister. David would have to tamp down any attraction he might be feeling. They both needed to be aware of their surroundings, not each other.

He leaned down. "You don't need to worry about me."

Whitney tossed her ponytail and stared out across the salmon-colored roses blooming along the porch railing. "I can't seem to *stop* worrying about you."

"I can take care of myself."

"I don't doubt that but…this situation is growing more and more dangerous." Then she turned stoic again. "Now we need to search for a blue car."

"It took off in a hurry. Must have dropped off the shooter and doubled back."

He didn't want her to leave, but he figured Shelby was waiting. She'd be anxious to get home to her little girl. The image of Whitney holding that cute little baby invaded his efforts to ignore his growing attraction to her.

And before he could stop them, the words were out of his mouth. "Hey, maybe we could get together later in the week," he called as she headed down the steps. "Dinner or something. Low-key, and we'll be careful."

Whitney stopped by her car, surprise chasing confusion in her expression. "Maybe, yeah, sure. Maybe this weekend. If the chief doesn't put me in protective custody."

"If he does, I'm going in there with you," David blurted. "You can't leave me out here alone. We're a team now, right?"

"I'd never leave you alone," she replied.

Then they stopped talking and stared at each other. "We can make jokes but…this is no laughing matter," she said. "I wasn't too scared before, but now… I'm terrified. For Shelby, for Miss Rosa and for you, David."

David wanted to hold her and assure her that he'd take care of this, but…he had no idea how to do that.

Another long day.

Glad to be home, Whitney checked on Shelby for the fourth time. Her baby was sleeping, the little lamb nightlight showing her cherubic face in muted white and yellow. After the scare at the inn last night, she'd explained to Marilyn and Jack that they needed to be cautious, too.

"I don't think they'll try anything with you but… I just want you to be aware. Keep Shelby in for a while."

"I will," Marilyn had said. "We won't go for our afternoon strolls until you think it's safe."

Marilyn and Jack knew the danger involved in Whitney's work, but they seemed to take it in stride. Jack's garage was only five minutes away, so he'd reassured her he could be home very quickly if need be. Marilyn had taken self-defense classes years ago when Jack worked at night, and they had a good alarm system. She didn't seem afraid, but she wasn't someone who'd be careless or take too many risks, either.

Now Whitney went back over her week. She'd tracked down false leads and filed numerous reports. But she kept returning to the conversations she'd had with two possible witnesses early this morning before she'd gone to work.

"I saw that puppy," the woman had told her through a screen door, her hair still in sponge curlers. "He was running down Desert Valley Road all by his lonesome. Cute little thing, too. I almost stopped and picked him up, but when I looked back, I didn't see him."

"Describe him," Whitney said.

"Tan colored with a black blob on his little face. As if he fell into some chocolate."

Marco.

One other witness, a scrawny skateboarder, had told her he'd also seen Marco. "But somebody on a bike picked him up, so I thought he belonged to the rider."

The kid had verified what they already knew.

"I saw someone with the puppy," the kid had said, his foot flipping his worn skateboard up and into his hands. "I mean, it was kinda dark and whoever it was had on a hoodie that covered their head and face. But I do know they took that puppy and rode away on that bike."

Both the kid and the older woman who'd talked to her had told Whitney they had hoped someone would take the puppy to a shelter or maybe turn it in to the police.

But that hadn't happened. And nothing else was standing out. No word from the lab in Flagstaff on the drug couriers and nothing substantial regarding Veronica's murder. Whitney kept wondering if the two were random incidents or if they might possibly be connected.

At their briefing this morning, Whitney gave the report on the two witnesses who'd seen someone take

Marco, and then she reported her findings after talking to Dr. Pennington. She mentioned Lloyd Harglow.

"Dr. Pennington says Lloyd and Veronica fought a lot. She confided in him, apparently. He implicated Harglow as a possible suspect."

James Harrison, one of the rookie K9 officers, looked over at her, his blue eyes full of skepticism. "I interviewed Lloyd Harglow on Monday after the murder. He was at a meeting with city officials on the night Veronica died. After the meeting, three of them went out for a late dinner in Canyon County City. I have several witnesses who corroborated his story." James pushed at his spiked blond hair. "He did admit that their fling went sour after a few months, but he insists he'd never hurt Veronica. He's trying to patch things up with his wife, who has an alibi, too, by the way."

The chief moved on to Whitney and David's run-in with the couriers. "What do you have on the drug runners, Godwin?"

Whitney went back over the occurrences at her house and at the inn. "The drug couriers are trying to scare us. Mr. Gallagher is safe since he doesn't live here but... I did see their faces, and so did the one other eyewitness. The shooter fired two shots and then left," she said, almost thinking out loud.

"But?" Chief Jones pinned her with his stark gaze. "You look as if you have something else on your mind."

Whitney cleared her throat. "Drug runners usually follow through pretty quickly. They wouldn't waste time walking around just to scare someone. Frankly, I'm surprised they didn't get into a shootout with me." Then she glanced at her friends. "I have a baby to consider, sir."

"And I don't have the manpower to guard everyone,"

the chief replied. "You do what you need to keep little Shelby safe."

"Yes, sir."

"They'll keep comin'," Officer Ryder Hayes said. Like James, he had the blond hair and blue eyes that seemed to make some women swoon. Good-looking but guarded, Ryder was still mourning the unsolved death of his wife five years ago. Melanie had been robbed and murdered the night of the police dance. She'd never made it to the party.

Mike Riverton had died from a fall on the stairs of his home on the night of the dance two years ago.

Brian had died in a house fire on that same night last year.

A clear pattern, but one they couldn't figure out. The night of the annual police dance was significant, but how? And why?

"Whitney?"

She looked up to see Ryder and the others waiting for her to respond. "Yes. Drug runners are usually brutal and swift. So far, we've managed to scare them away, and based on the cap we found at the inn, we can assume that was the drug runners." Then she added, "But I wonder if the prowler in my yard could be related to Veronica's murder and not the drug runners. What if someone thinks I know something or have something they want?"

"We've had a lot of reports about people doing that recently," Ellen Foxcroft said. "Snooping, but they don't take anything. Maybe these intruders are just random. Kids out for fun."

"Or the drug runners could be casing places, hoping to find any opportunity," James pointed out. "You got to them and scared them off before they could get to you."

"That could be it." They could easily have killed

Hunter and her and possibly David, too. Something didn't make sense, but she had too much on her mind to piece it together. "In any case, I'll be vigilant, and I've warned David Evans to do the same."

"Do you trust him?" Ryder asked. "I mean, he's new in town, and he happened to be on the same train as those alleged couriers."

She answered without even thinking about it. "I do trust David. He's not involved with the drug couriers. He put his life on the line to help Mr. Gallagher."

Since she'd already reported on his background check coming back clean, she didn't offer any further explanations. But she hadn't told anyone why David was here. She didn't want anyone to think his presence was impacting her work.

Even if it was beginning to do just that.

She'd have to be careful about her feelings toward David. She'd already had one impulsive love affair, and she was pretty sure everyone around here had figured that out. She couldn't afford to mess up her personal life again, so she'd have to keep her comments on a professional level. And her feelings, too.

Just before she left for the day, the department secretary, Carrie, came by her desk. "Hey, the chief needs you in his office, Whitney. He doesn't look happy," she added nervously.

"Okay." Whitney followed Carrie down the hallway.

"Hope you're not in trouble," Carrie said, her brown eyes sympathetic.

Whitney stood near the open door, hoping the same thing. "Sir, you wanted to see me?"

"Shut the door, Godwin."

Whitney braced herself and took a calming breath.

"Have a seat."

"Sir, what is it?"

"You remember coming to me about the rookie deaths and suggesting how they didn't seem so random to you? You were concerned because of the way they each died, especially Brian Miller."

She nodded, but before she could respond, he kept on talking. "And since Marian Foxcroft made her demands and then threw in her generous offer, I've had all of you going back over files and trying to pinpoint something to connect all of this."

"Yes, sir," she said. "But it's only been a few weeks. We've all been taking turns with the case files. I know Mrs. Foxcroft wanted these cases declared accidents, but…"

"But some of you seem to think differently. Especially you."

"How could I not?" she asked. "The two rookies' backgrounds don't match up with the way they both died. Mike was an expert mountain climber, and yet he died from a fall down the stairs. And Brian's whole family died from a horrible house fire. He would never light a candle in his home, let alone leave it unattended. But that's what the fire marshal thinks happened."

"Yeah, well, the police dance is coming up again," Chief Jones said. "I'm not saying I agree or disagree with your theory, but yes, there does seem to be a certain pattern, especially with Melanie Hayes's murder and the rookies' deaths all happening on the night of prior dances. And even though Marian wanted the rookies' deaths ruled as accidents, she's not the chief of police. I am, and I don't want another murder on my hands. If she ever wakes up, I'll convince her of that. I want you to investigate that angle. Talk to anyone who knew them." He leaned his head down then cast his gaze back up to

her. "Can you handle that? And don't leave out Melanie Hayes."

"Melanie? So you agree the same person might have
killed Melanie?"

"What did I just say, Godwin?"

"Yes, sir. Go over her case, too." Whitney would handle it. She'd been trying to get to the bottom of this for a
long time, but she'd tried to be careful since she wasn't
sure who to trust. She'd talked about Brian's death with
Gina Perry a couple of weeks ago. No one here knew for
sure that Brian was Shelby's father, but she was fairly
certain Gina had guessed. Now, at least, she had the chief
on her side, even if he didn't know the whole story regarding Brian and her. "I'll get right on it."

When she left the chief's office, Carrie gave her the
thumbs-up sign. Had she heard the chief's loud voice? It
didn't matter. Everyone who worked at the station wanted
those deaths solved.

Now, home at last and clean from her shower, she'd
just settled down in her pj's to catch up on the evening
news when her cell buzzed. The caller ID showed the
name David Evans.

She almost didn't answer. David was too tempting,
and she had to stay centered and focused right now. She'd
also need to tell him the truth about Brian.

"Hi," she said. Muting the television, she curled her
legs up onto the couch. Hunter was in the hallway by
Shelby's room. On guard for the night.

"Hi. I got Miss Rosa settled down last night. And I
made sure the security lights are all working. This old
inn could use a security system, but she says she doesn't
have the money for that. Or a good hot water heater, either, apparently."

"No hot water? How's that working for you?"

"Let's just say I come clean pretty quickly these days."

She grinned at that. "Should I send a patrol around, just in case?"

"To fix the water heater or to watch the inn?"

She enjoyed his sense of humor. "They could probably do both. Small towns tend to have multitaskers by necessity."

"Miss Rosa would probably feel better with a patrol car in the area," he said. "But I'll be okay. You have enough to deal with right now."

"I'm trained to take care of such things."

"I know. Talk about threatening my manhood."

"So you don't like it when a woman comes to your rescue?"

"Oh, I don't mind at all, but… I've never had the tables turned on me. Takes getting used to, I reckon."

"Maybe Lucas sent you here for that very reason."

"He was tricky, your big brother. He loved to play practical jokes on the whole platoon."

"That sounds like Lucas. Always joking around." She stopped smiling and bit back tears. "I miss him every day."

"I know. He was the best of the best."

"I'm so glad that you're here, David. And that you knew Lucas."

"So you wouldn't mind if your big brother had an ulterior motive?"

She couldn't lie about that. Lucas might have handpicked David for her, but she couldn't go beyond friendship with him right now.

"I didn't like you being here at first, but…it's almost as if he sent me one last gift."

"That's a nice way to look at it."

"It's good to talk about him with someone who was with him on a daily basis. No one here knew him, so they all draw a blank when I mention him."

"They don't know what to say. Death is a tough topic."

"Yes. Yes, it is." She wanted to tell him about Brian, but not tonight. She planned to pull all the files on Brian's death, along with those of Mike Riverton and Melanie Hayes, first thing tomorrow. But for now, she could use a little distraction.

So they talked about random things well into the night, laughing and discussing everything from movies to ice cream to the Arizona weather.

And when her head finally hit the pillow, she thought of what it would be like to have a man like David in her life for longer than a few weeks.

ELEVEN

Friday, David knocked on Whitney's front door and waited. They'd agreed to go out to dinner tonight, but Whitney had decided they should stay in.

"I'm afraid to take Shelby out of the house." Two days had passed with no incidents, but that didn't mean they were safe. If it made her feel better to have her baby in her sights right now, he certainly understood. He also figured the baby would serve as a buffer to keep him from getting too close.

She opened the door with a smile playing across her lips. A smile that left him speechless. She looked amazing in a casual denim sundress and strappy sandals, her blond hair falling around her face.

In her uniform, she was impressive.

In a dress, she was a knockout.

"Come in," she said waving him in with her hand in the air. "I ordered delivery from the steak house. It should be here in fifteen minutes. Have a seat, and I'll go get Shelby."

"Okay." He followed her inside and patted Hunter's head, sensing that she still wasn't sure about this date. "Hey, big boy. How you doing?"

Hunter enjoyed being scratched between the ears.

"He's looking forward to a night of rest," Whitney said. "And so am I."

David sat down on the blue chair, Hunter at his feet. "Long week, huh?"

"Yes. And today was the longest. I've been pulling files all day, hoping to find clues."

That explained things. She was exhausted and probably preoccupied with watching her back. Better that they stayed here, even if it did mean things would be more intimate.

Whitney came back into the living room, little Shelby in her arms. The baby shot a smile toward David, but he was pretty sure Shelby was really smiling at her buddy Hunter. The dog seemed to have a special bond with the baby.

"Need any help?"

She sat down and stretched some bright green baby socks that mimicked real shoes over Shelby's kicking feet. "No. By the way, Chief Jones pulled me aside yesterday and told me to do some asking around regarding a few cold cases."

"That sounds dangerous."

"Not really. A lot of what we do involves pounding the pavement and asking the right questions. It's the boring part of our job, but it's still the best way to follow through on leads."

David watched her with her baby and wished she'd chosen another profession. No wonder Lucas worried about her. But it wasn't David's place to protest Whitney's work. She was more than capable of doing her job.

And yet, he also pictured this same image in a different frame that included him coming home after a long day to kiss his wife and baby.

Whoa. He needed to clear that image right out of his

head. Whitney wasn't his wife, and Shelby wasn't his daughter.

"Just be careful," he said to hide the awareness racing throughout his system.

Whitney finished gathering Shelby's things. "I will. Routine stuff." Then she did a little pivot. "I'm still missing her other white bootie. The dryer seems to eat them."

"Well, she looks great," David said, watching as she put Shelby into her play swing. "A well-dressed little girl." Then he looked at Whitney. "And her mother is a well-dressed woman."

Whitney's smile widened as something like heat lightning sizzled between them.

After they settled on the couch and started munching on chips and salsa, she turned to David. "I need you to know the truth, David. The chief finally gave me permission to pursue something I've had on my mind for a while now. I'm working on my own time tomorrow to find out what really happened to Brian Miller."

David saw the shadows falling across her face. "Who's that?"

"One of the rookies from last year's class. He died in a house fire last summer, on the night of the police dance. It's a fund-raising event we hold every year. I believe someone murdered him. I've always believed that, along with a couple of others. Now the chief thinks so, too."

David let that soak in. "Okay. Does this have anything to do with the dog trainer's murder?"

"It could," she said. "We need to establish some sort of connection between all the deaths with the K9 Training Center in common—the two K9 rookies, Melanie Hayes, who was the wife of a then rookie, and the lead dog trainer."

David could understand that. "Makes sense."

Whitney glanced at Shelby and then looked straight into David's eyes. "I have another important reason to investigate Brian's death," she said. "He's the father of my baby."

David stared back in shock, thinking that now a whole lot of other things were beginning to make sense, too.

"So you had a thing for a fellow rookie?"

"We weren't rookies yet," she corrected him. "We went through training together." She kept checking on Shelby. The baby kicked her chubby legs. "But it was more than just a thing to me. I thought... Well, never mind what I thought. It didn't work out."

David could see it all now. "Did he know about your pregnancy before he died?"

She shook her head. "No. Brian lived in a house in another town about twenty miles from here. He worked part-time as a security guard at a strip mall near his house, so he stayed there most of the time, even when he was training at the center with the rest of us."

She closed her eyes. "I fell for him right away. I was naive, and I hadn't had a serious boyfriend since high school. Brian made it so easy."

Shelby started fussing, her little feet gearing up for a tantrum.

"She's getting hungry," Whitney said. "I can go ahead and feed her, since our food isn't here yet."

David lifted Shelby up out of her little playpen. "And we can finish this conversation while you're at it."

Whitney wished she hadn't just blurted it out, but she had to tell David sometime. Better tonight, before she got involved in searching for answers. Tonight they could have a few quiet hours. Tomorrow she'd get serious about these deaths.

Whitney put Shelby in her high chair and offered her a cracker while she prepared the tiny jar of baby food. "We weren't supposed to fraternize. But going over to his house for pizza and movies didn't seem like fraternizing. It felt so natural, so right. We became an item even though we tried to keep it a secret. I thought I'd found the one, at last."

"But it didn't turn out that way?"

"No." She wished she could sugarcoat it, but Shelby was living proof of how far Brian and she had taken things. "We were halfway through training when I realized I might be pregnant. I did a home pregnancy test, got tested at our clinic here and followed up with a doctor in another town, just to be sure and to set up health care for my baby. When I got a positive confirmation, I immediately went to Brian's house to tell him. And found him with another woman."

David's frown clouded with anger. "What?"

"Yes. Kissing her and telling her pretty much all the same things he'd been telling me. I saw them and heard all of it through the open window by the front door." She smiled while she spooned carrots and peas into Shelby's little mouth. "I left before he saw me through the window. The police dance was the next weekend. We were supposed to meet up there, and I thought maybe if I told him he was going to be a father, he'd…change."

She blinked back the tears that always stayed right below the surface, the tears she refused to shed. "But he never made it to the dance. His house burned down that night."

David stayed quiet for a couple of minutes, but Whitney could tell he was doing the math in his head. "So you decided not to complete the training?"

"How could I?" she said after she'd finished feeding

Shelby. "It was too risky, and besides, I'm pretty sure I would have gotten kicked out anyway." She shrugged. "I had a little money saved up from the job I left in Tucson to become a police officer. I went back to work for the insurance company until I had Shelby."

"So you had a job, health insurance and a place to stay in Tucson. Shelby was born there?"

"Yes." Wiping at Shelby's dimpled face, she tried to explain. "Once I was settled there, I planned to tell my brother. But I kept putting it off. And then, of course, I got the news that he'd been wounded and had died." Putting her elbows on the table, Whitney knuckled her hands against her chin. "I wish I'd told him. He would have been angry and worried, but Lucas would have loved being an uncle."

David finally looked up and into her eyes. "Yes, Lucas would have loved Shelby."

"I've made a mess of so many things," Whitney said. "But I thank God every day for Shelby and for the lessons I've learned. I'm trying to be a good mother to her. I won't be so naive next time, though."

And she needed to remember that pledge each time her feelings for David made her become all mushy and hopeful. Shelby was her first priority now. She had to guard her heart and take care of her little girl.

He gave her a wry smile, followed by a serious look of appraisal. "And yet you're determined to prove that her father was murdered."

"Yes," she said. "Brian might not have been the best choice as a boyfriend but…he would have been a good police officer. And I'd like to believe that whether he loved me or not, he would have been a good father to Shelby. He can't have that chance now, but I can find out who took his life."

"And what if that person comes looking for you, too, Whitney? What happens then?"

She hadn't thought about that, but it wouldn't stop her. "I don't intend on letting that happen," she replied. "Everyone is so caught up in Veronica's murder that I don't think I'll have to worry about them noticing anything different."

She didn't tell him that she'd already pored over Melanie Hayes' file, gone back to the houses near the Hayes ranch and questioned neighbors. But the only thing she'd found out was from a widow who said Melanie often took that path home since she loved to walk for exercise.

That could mean someone had been watching her or knew her well enough to be aware of her habits.

"Unless these deaths are connected to Veronica's death," David said, bringing Whitney back to the present. "You said yourself the same person might have committed all of these murders."

She knew she shouldn't tell him anything more, but she wanted to be honest. "Chief Jones has finally given me the go-ahead to do some more digging. Brian knew a lot of people, and he probably left a few broken hearts in his wake. I need to find out who might have had it in for him, because I know this was no accident. Even if I didn't want to do this, which I do, the chief put me on this case."

"Yes, since you've made it known how you feel."

"The other rookies are beginning to agree with me." She watched as Shelby's eyelids started drooping. "Shouldn't I let him know my suspicions, especially if we all have concerns?"

"Yes. I can't argue with that. You're a good cop. You were right to go to your superior with this."

"Well, everyone pretty much feels the same now that

we've been comparing notes," she said. "None of it makes any sense if the deaths aren't connected."

"No, it doesn't. I get why you're so determined," he said. "You're also investigating this on your own time. Are you obsessed with this because you couldn't save Brian?"

"Yes, I am," she admitted. "I'm obsessed with finding out the truth." She lifted Shelby out of her little chair and held her tight. "I can't seem to find any closure. I'll always wonder if he might have been a good father to Shelby, even if he clearly didn't love me."

David jabbed a chip into the spicy dip. "It won't bring him back."

"No, but it will bring about justice. That's all I have left to show my daughter what real honesty and integrity are all about."

"I can see why you'd want that. So no problem. I mean, you don't need my permission anyway."

But she wanted his approval for some reason. His opinion mattered to her, even if she'd only known him for a week. Reminding herself not to rush into anything, she took a deep breath. Holding Shelby, she glanced at the clock in the kitchen.

"The food is late. I'm sorry."

David stood up and turned to stare into the empty fireplace.

"We won't be able to hang out as much," she told him. "Maybe you should leave and get on with your life."

"I am getting on with my life," he said, pivoting to face her. "But I'm not leaving Desert Valley yet."

"I just told you—"

"I know. You'll be busy." He leaned in, his tone even and firm. "But you won't be alone. I'm going to help you find out the truth, whether you like having me around or not."

Before she could protest, the doorbell rang. Whitney grabbed some cash and hurried to answer it. David took the baby so she could pay the delivery person and take the food.

When the door opened, Whitney was surprised but handed the skinny blond-haired man the money. "Thank you. Keep the change."

The man moved into the room and handed Whitney the big bag full of food. "You two have the cutest little girl."

That innocent comment did not go over well.

Whitney's eyes crashed with David's, embarrassment and awareness hitting her in the gut. "Uh…she's mine. David is just a friend."

The scrawny man watched as Whitney took the food and set it on the nearby table. Then he stepped back and drew a pistol out from underneath his lightweight jacket. "Too bad."

TWELVE

"Shelby," Whitney cried, one hand reaching for her baby.

"Watch it," the man said, the gun aimed at David and Shelby. "Don't make any moves, lady."

In the hallway, Hunter stood and growled.

"Call off the dog. Now," the man said as he walked around the room, his beady eyes darting here and there.

David gave Whitney a warning glance. He knew where she kept her gun, and there was no way she'd be able to get to it.

Hunter started barking, and then everything happened so fast, David could only react, his mind racing back to the many times he'd had to take cover.

Whitney shouted to Hunter to attack. Then she head butted the man wielding the gun, her hand going up to grab his arm. She wrestled with him, the weapon caught between them as she slammed him back against the wall next to the front door.

"Hold her," Whitney shouted to David as Hunter came charging up the hallway. "Get Shelby out of here."

David wasn't about to leave Whitney, but he had to protect the now frightened little girl. Taking the sobbing baby, he dived behind the couch and watched as Hunter attacked the man who was wrestling with Whitney.

The man screamed in pain, the gun went off and then the man slumped against the wall, with Hunter still biting into his leg with a vengeance.

Whitney rolled away, the man's weapon in her hand. David lifted up, his hand over Shelby's head as he ran toward Whitney.

"No," Whitney said. "I've got this. Take her to the bedroom and calm her down." The fear in her blue eyes floored David. "Please, David."

David couldn't speak so he hurried to the nursery. He tried to soothe Shelby. Finding her pacifier, he sat down in the big rocking chair by the baby's bed and rocked her until her sobs subsided. He didn't know if he could ever let her go again.

While he sat, he listened to sirens and dogs and voices shouting over each other. He knew what was going on. Whitney was being questioned and checked over. She'd killed a man right here in her house. And he'd seen the whole thing.

At least he'd shielded Shelby from the worst of it.

"It's okay," he said to the sleepy, tired little girl. "It's okay. I won't let anything happen to you or your mother, I promise."

But even as he made that vow, he wondered how in the world any of them would survive this.

Whitney's heart was beating so fast, she felt dizzy. How could she have been so careless as to put Shelby in danger?

Just another reason why she needed to stay away from David. He made her forget her responsibilities and her duty as a mother. But deep inside, she knew this wasn't David's fault.

Someone wanted her dead. And it was anyone's guess about who that someone might be. Drug runners or Veronica's killer or both? Had she stirred up too much attention by asking too many questions?

Now she moved down the short hallway to Shelby's room, needing to see her daughter, to touch her, to hold her.

"David?"

"We're good," he said from the rocking chair.

Whitney stopped in the doorway. He held Shelby against his broad chest as if she were the most precious thing in the world.

She heard Shelby sniffle in her sleep and felt her heart crush against her rib cage. *Dear God, protect my baby and David. Help me to keep us safe, Lord.*

"David... I..."

"Breathe," David said. "Slow, deep breaths."

She did as he told her, the doorjamb steadying her. "Shelby?"

"Shelby is just fine. She's got her pacifier and she's fast asleep. I think she likes my singing."

"That's my girl," Whitney said, tears pricking at her eyes.

For as long as she lived, she'd never forget this tender scene. This man who'd fought so hard to get to her had taken care of her baby while she'd done what she had to do.

For once, he'd listened to her.

But this scene made him more of a hero than any shootout ever could. At least in her eyes anyway.

She lifted off the wall and hurried to sink down beside the rocking chair. Kissing Shelby, she glanced up and into David's brown eyes. "Thank you."

His gaze held hers. He started to speak, but the sound of boots hitting the hallway floor pulled her away.

"Godwin?"

"In here," she called, standing and wiping her eyes.

David gave her a nod. "We're okay here."

Rookie K9 officer Shane Weston stepped into the doorway, his partner, Bella, by his side. "Hey, you okay?"

The tall, dark-haired cop's expression was hard to read. His gaze moved to where David sat rocking the baby.

"Yes," Whitney said to the question in his green eyes. "David and I were going to have dinner. I thought we'd be safe here."

She gave David an appreciative glance. "David...took care of Shelby for me."

Shane looked at David with a new respect. "Okay, the ME has taken the body away. No ID yet, but we'll know something soon." He shuffled in his boots. "We found the real delivery person knocked out in the bushes by the front door. I guess our man dragged him in there before the cruiser watching your house noticed, took the food and came on in."

"I had alerted the officer that I was having food delivered, so don't blame him. Is the deliveryman okay?"

"Yeah. Probably a concussion. He said he didn't see who did it. Kid's pretty shaken."

"It has to be the drug runners. They're watching," Whitney said. "They knew we were here and they waited for an opportunity. Seeing a delivery person walking up to the door gave them an easy way inside."

"Yep. But they might have come in later, when you

were alone," Shane pointed out. "Good thing you had some help."

Whitney eyed David. "Yes. I'm thankful for that."

"We knew it would only be a matter of time," David said. "They came for me the other night, and now they're following us."

Shane stepped back. "Do you want me to put a stronger detail on your house, Whitney?"

"No," she said at the same time David said, "Yes."

"No? Yes?" Shane looked amused. "Which do I listen to?"

"I'll watch out for her," David said, lifting from the chair to hand Shelby to Whitney. "Whitney's brother, Lucas, and I served together in Afghanistan. And I came here because he was concerned about her before he died. I can watch out for her."

"You don't have to do that," Whitney said. "I can take care of myself. The department is stretched as it is. I don't need a heavy detail trailing around with me."

David studied Shane, probably figuring he'd protest, but Shane just stood there like a solid wall, a knowing gleam in his eyes.

"Yeah, I heard rumors that you'd come all this way to see Godwin," Shane finally said. "But that doesn't mean you can protect her. You're both in danger."

"I'll set up camp in her backyard if I have to," David said. Then he planted his feet apart and crossed his arms over his chest. "Because like I've already told Whitney, I'm not leaving any time soon."

"I told you, you can't stay in my house."

Whitney stared over at David while she fed Shelby a bottle before putting her back to bed. Her little girl was exhausted, and so was she. She was almost too tired to argue with David.

Everyone else had left. A different patrol car sat outside, relieving the officer who'd somehow missed the delivery kid being knocked out cold in her yard. But she still couldn't blame the tired patrolman. These people were sneaky and trained in finding their way into any situation.

"I can't let you go through this alone," David said, his eyes reminding her of rocks at dusk, so dark and mysterious, hard-edged. "Not after tonight."

"What part of 'I'm a police officer' don't you get?" she asked, knowing he should leave. Wishing she could let him sleep on her couch.

No. She had to get that kind of notion right out of her head. Still vulnerable from Brian's deception and death and still all warm and fuzzy from the way David had protected Shelby earlier, she had no business thinking any kind of warm thoughts about the man standing at her kitchen counter. They barely knew each other, but it felt as if they'd known each other always.

David gave her an appreciative glance. "I've seen you in action. But… I know what evil people can do, Whitney. It's dangerous." He pointed to the crime scene tape stretched across the front door. "That hit man forced his way into your house. We've messed in their world, and now they'll keep coming until they eliminate us. And they can do that in awful, torturous ways."

"Are you trying to scare me?"

"Yes," he said. Stalking around the counter, he set down the bottle of water she'd given him. "I can't help but worry about you and Shelby. You both could have been killed tonight."

Whitney knew he was right. And she was so weary. So very weary. "I'm going to check on her one more time."

David picked up a picture of Shelby. "She's beautiful," he said on a strained whisper.

"I know." Whitney peeked out the windows and turned the volume up high on the baby monitor. Hunter followed her around the house, still on high alert. The chief had let her stay here tonight only because of Shelby and... probably because David was here. Chief Jones had also stationed James Harrison and his partner, Hawk, out in the backyard.

She should have felt safe. And yet she shivered.

"Stay," she said to Hunter after she'd kissed Shelby and tugged her blanket over her. His trusting, dark-eyed gaze moved from her to Shelby's bed. Hunter circled and lay down between the door and the bed. "Guard," Whitney said.

Hunter would attack anyone who tried to come into this room. She knew that, but she couldn't stop the shiver that curled around her like a rattlesnake.

Checking the shadows one more time, Whitney planned her own attack on the man waiting in the den. She had to make David see that he didn't have to be her protector.

And yet something deep inside her heart loved how he'd rushed to her defense again by insisting he'd take care of her. Had she ever had anyone fight so much for her and with her?

Not in this way, no. Her brother had been her knight in shining armor, but Lucas had gone off to the other side of the world, fighting an even bigger battle. She'd accepted that and moved on with her goals and dreams, hoping to make him proud.

Then Brian had come along, and she'd placed such high hopes in what she believed to be their love. But that had been only a daydream, a false assumption based on her misguided illusions.

She wouldn't make that mistake again so soon after being burned, even if it seemed her brother had practically handpicked the man who'd come here. David needed to leave Desert Valley and move on to whatever his future held. Now to convince him of that. And maybe herself, too.

But when she walked into the den and saw him folding a baby blanket, her heart did a little heated dance of joy.

Wrong man, but right moves. He'd make a good husband and daddy for some lucky woman. "You're exhausted," she said, an edge of exhaustion hiding the tremors cresting in her body.

"Yes," he said, turning to stare at her. "But I can't leave you alone here."

She sank down on the couch, fatigue weighing on her like a suffocating dry heat while she tried not to look at the chalk lines on the floor where the intruder's body had fallen. "I've been on my own for a long time now."

"I admire that about you," he said, sitting down beside her with one booted foot resting across the knee of his other leg.

He took up too much space. On her couch. In her house. Inside her head. Maybe if she just talked to him. "You've been on your own a while, too."

"Yes. And I don't like being told what to do. I don't like asking for help, either." He shrugged. "What do you want me to do? Just leave? I can't. I'd never forgive myself."

"And why do you need to stay?" she asked, grabbing a pillow to hold so she wouldn't be tempted to touch him. "You don't owe me anything, David. And this obligation you feel toward my brother is noble but unnecessary."

David turned to her, his dark gaze roaming over her with a look of awareness that left her emotionally stripped. "What if it's not about Lucas anymore?" he asked, one finger moving to touch her arm. "What if I want to stick around for you and Shelby?"

Whitney shot up off the couch. "No." She shook her head and tried to ignore the tingle of anticipation David's touch had ignited. "No, that is not such a good idea."

"Why?" he asked, not moving. But his gaze on her, searching, questioning, told her just how dangerous being around him had become.

"You know why. I'm a single mother. An unmarried mother who had my baby alone. No one here knows the truth, but I think some of them suspect. I mean, Brian and I flirted a lot, and it's a small town. I'm sure they know, but…no one's condemned me yet. I'm working hard to prove myself. I have to. Brian and I weren't supposed to be together in the first place, so I guess I'm still trying to protect him, too."

David stood and then moved close to where she paced in front of the empty fireplace. "What's all of that got to do with you and me?"

"Everything," Whitney said, inching away from him. "I have to put Shelby first. I need to help solve this murder case and… I want to find out the truth about Brian's death." She shrugged and crossed her arms over her midsection. "I need to stay focused on my continued training and my job or I could ruin my entire future as a K9 officer."

He shook his head. "I understand your work is important, but it's dangerous, looking for drug smugglers and a killer. Let someone else handle some of those investigations."

"No, because it's *part* of my work, and it will help me

to understand…why Brian had to die that way. I have to know."

"Will knowing change anything?"

"I don't know," she said, anger tamping down the attraction she'd tried so hard to ignore. "Nothing can change this tragedy, but at least I'd feel as if I found justice and the truth. Brian might not have been the man I wanted him to be, but he didn't have to die in such a horrible way, either. I want the truth, and I want whoever did this to suffer the consequences."

Something shifted in David's eyes. His expression hardened into an unyielding acceptance. "You're not over him, are you?"

Whitney's breath went shallow while her pulse leaped. "I have to solve the mystery behind his death. Otherwise, how can I put Brian behind me when I see him each time I look at my little girl?"

David backed away, nodding as he moved to the couch. "Okay, so you're not ready for anything heavy right now. I get that. But… I'm here, and I'm staying until I at least know you'll be safe."

"You can't stay here with…me," she said, relief washing over the regret she already felt. "I've changed since Shelby was born. I'm trying to be a better example, for her sake."

It would be so easy to let him into her life, to invite him to stay here with her and Shelby. But she couldn't do that. She'd turned her life around, and she'd made a pledge to stay smart and in control for her baby and for her own redemption.

"I won't," he finally said. "I'll stay at the Desert Rose but… I'm going to help you with this investigation."

"How do you plan on doing that?" she asked, amazed that he refused to give up. "You're not qualified."

"I'll watch Shelby for you or go with you to some of the places you'll want to check out, and I'll wait in the car or outside. Kind of a bodyguard. I'm good at observing situations. I had to be since I dealt with a lot of things at once during the heat of battle."

"Is that what kept you alive? Being watchful and alert?"

"I don't know what kept me alive but… I intend to live my life to the fullest, with a strong faith that I'm here for a reason. I believe we all have a purpose in life."

Whitney wished her faith could be that sure and solid. "I believe that, too, but I can't have it on my conscience if something happens to you, David."

"And I can't walk away," he said, moving toward her again. "Not now. We're both up to our eyeballs in this. I'm an eyewitness to a possible drug smuggling operation. I was threatened at gunpoint. If we work together, we might solve this thing a lot sooner. And if, after we do find the smugglers or your killer, you still want me to leave, then I will."

Whitney decided she didn't have want to argue with him. "All right," she said, wondering if she'd regret this. "But you can't get in my way, or try to protect me, or tackle any bad guys. Let me do what I'm trained to do, okay?"

"Okay. Unless someone is trying to harm you," he said. "Then… I'll do whatever it takes—"

"David."

"As a last resort," he finished, a soft, sure smile lifting his lips. "Deal?" He reached out a hand as if to shake hers.

"Deal," she said. "I could use some neutral eyes to help me go over the particulars. But you can only tag along when I'm on my own time. You can't be part of an active investigation."

"I'll tag along whenever I can," he said, his eyes holding hers. "And you'll have a partner with you when you're out there, right?"

"If you want to call Eddie a partner, yes. At least he looks intimidating." She glanced toward the back of the house. "I have Hunter and I trust him completely. We've trained together for weeks now. I also trust my fellow team members. They're all good people."

"Okay, so we agree I have to keep out of your way and let you do what you need to do."

"Yes," she said. She put her hand in his, and they shook. "I have to put it off for a couple of days anyway. I shot a man, and we have to clear that up first. Chief Jones says I need to see a counselor first thing tomorrow."

"A good idea," David replied. "Trust me on that. You'll have flashbacks and nightmares for a while to come."

Whitney didn't doubt that. She'd never forget that moment when she thought her baby might be killed. And she'd never forget David.

He tugged her into his arms. "Don't push me away, Whitney. I'm not like Brian."

Whitney should have pushed him away right then and there, but instead she hugged him close. "I know you're not. Lucas must have thought highly of you to send you here like this. So that means I care about you, too."

"I appreciate Lucas and his misguided mission," David said, "but this has gone beyond honoring Lucas. You might think you're too tough for someone like me but… we've both been through things that no one else can understand. For now, we need each other."

They held each other for a couple of minutes, and Whitney realized she hadn't been held or hugged like this in a long time. David was right. She did need someone she could trust.

"I miss my brother," she said. But right now being in David's arms did not feel so brotherly. It felt right. Too right.

"Me, too," David replied. He held her with no demands, and he didn't try to make any advances. Could he see her fear, and feel it in his heart, too? "I miss his goofy laugh and his bad jokes. I miss how he talked about you all the time. Almost as good as being here with you."

Whitney absorbed some of his quiet strength and thanked God for David's sweet concern. But she prayed for her own strength and willpower to hold her steady so she wouldn't give in to these erratic, disturbing feelings she felt each time she was around him.

Pulling away, she looked up and into his eyes and saw the same hopes and fears she felt centered there in his powerful gaze. For a brief moment, she wanted to throw caution to the wind and kiss him. But…she had to control that impulse.

"You should go," she finally said. "You're worried about Miss Rosa, too, right?"

"Yep. You're right. I can't protect all of you."

"I could get in trouble for letting you ride along with me," she pointed out, making one last attempt to dissuade him.

"You could get in trouble if I don't ride along with you," he reminded her. "I can't see how anyone could argue with that."

After David left, Whitney checked the entire house to make sure all the doors and windows were locked, and she also checked in with James. As she was passing through the laundry room near the kitchen, she spotted Shelby's white bootie lying in front of the door to the garage.

"There you are," she said, lifting the bootie up. She must have dropped it when she'd taken it out of the laundry.

She turned one last time to stare into the backyard before she went to bed, and saw James and Hawk making their rounds. Blinking, Whitney moved through the house, intent on sleeping with her gun nearby.

Then the house phone rang. No one ever called her on that line, and it was strange to get a call this late at night. Her pulse puttering, Whitney picked up the receiver. "Hello?"

"We're watching you. Cute baby. Cute little booties."

Then the line went dead.

A chill ran down Whitney's neck and shivered toward her spine. Had someone been inside her house even before tonight?

THIRTEEN

On the way home, David shifted the ancient gears of the yellow Chevy, thinking he stood out like a school bus moving along through traffic. Checking the rearview mirror, he wondered if he was being watched right now. He glanced toward the Desert Valley Clinic and saw lights on.

Whirling the old truck into the parking lot, he thought he'd check around, just in case. But after what had happened hours earlier at Whitney's house, he planned to be very careful.

The front door was locked tight, so he walked around back to one of the big windows and saw Dr. Pennington in an exam room with a teenage boy. The kid was dirty, his pants torn, and he was bleeding from his left leg.

David checked the back door. Locked. So he knocked loudly.

Dr. Pennington opened the door, a surprised frown on his face. "Evans, what are you doing here?"

"I saw a light burning. Thought I'd see if everything was okay."

"Just get in here now," the gruff doctor said, motioning to the last exam room near the door while his gaze scanned the parking lot. "I've got a problem."

David turned toward the examining room. He might not like the doctor, but David had an obligation to help him as needed.

The doctor waved a gloved hand toward the young man writhing on the table. "He needs stitching, and I need you to assist."

David noticed the kid's fearful glance, his face twisted with pain. "What happened?"

Dr. Pennington gave David a stern stare. "We don't ask questions around here. We just do what we can."

"Looks like a knife wound," David said, memories of his first day in Desert Valley still fresh. "Should we report it?"

"Already did," Dr. Pennington replied on a tart note. "But the kid won't say anything. Can't press charges if we don't know what happened. He's afraid to talk."

He shot the kid a hard stare. The teen looked frightened and then lowered his gaze.

David took mental notes while he helped the doctor clean and stitch the deep gash slashing across the kid's left upper leg. This boy needed to go to the ER at the hospital. "Did you get into a fight?"

The teen ignored him, his jaw tight, his dark eyes darting here and there. He looked as if he could be high on something. Or maybe the doctor had given him something.

"He probably can't speak much English," Dr. Pennington said under his breath. "We do what we can, when we can. Best to keep your nose clean. Ask too many questions around here and you might live to regret it."

David couldn't decide if the scared kid was Latino or Native American or a mixture of both. But he had a sneaking suspicion the kid could understand everything they were saying.

When they were finished, the teen sat up and grabbed his bloody, dirty shirt. That was when David noticed the tattoo on his scrawny back.

It looked exactly like the symbol he'd had trouble remembering from the train attack. Was it the same? Or could it just be a coincidence?

He glanced at the tattoo, and then he looked into the black eyes of the teenager. The kid shot a furtive glance toward the doctor, who had his back turned.

Then he stared into David's eyes, a hidden plea shouting through his scared expression. David had seen that kind of plea in the eyes of children caught in the throes of war. Too many times.

"Where do you live?" David asked, hoping to encourage the boy to talk. "I'll give you a ride home."

The teen shut down again, his gaze moving back to the floor.

When Dr. Pennington turned around, the kid had the stoic, angry expression of someone who didn't want to be messed with.

And David had the distinct impression that the good doctor knew exactly what had happened to this teenager. So why had he insisted David stay to help? Maybe to give him a warning? Or to show him what happened when people saw things they shouldn't see?

"Hey, I heard about last Friday night. I'm so glad you're all okay," Gina, a junior dog trainer, said into the phone. "What can I do to help?"

"I need to run some errands," Whitney said. "I was wondering if you'd mind watching Shelby and Hunter for a couple of hours."

"Sure," Gina replied. "I'm on light duty myself these

days, so I'd love a break. Want me to come to your house?"

"I'd feel better if you kept her at the training center," Whitney replied. "Hunter can have some play time, and Shelby should nap most of the time. Think Sophie will mind?" Sophie, the new lead dog trainer, was Gina's boss now.

"No. I'll keep Shelby in the apartment upstairs, where it's quiet and relatively safe. Now tell me about the other night."

"It was scary," Whitney replied, the nightmare still fresh in her mind a few days later. "But it was over so quickly, I'm still trying to absorb what happened. Killing a man is something I'll never forget."

"I can't even imagine. You run your errands and don't worry about us. But first, tell me more about what happened."

Whitney gave Gina some of the details of that night. Although Gina wasn't a K9 rookie, she was an excellent trainer who'd worked with Veronica Earnshaw. She was also newly engaged to rookie Shane Weston, but they hadn't announced that publicly yet, so Whitney knew to keep it to herself. Gina had tried to help piece together some of the details of Veronica's life.

"I've got some things to do today, so I appreciate the help. The Carters are pretty traumatized by what happened, so I'm letting them off the hook today."

She planned to do some checking on the rookie deaths, at least. She'd put it off for a couple of days, but now it was Tuesday and she was getting restless. "I talked to a counselor Saturday morning, so that helped. But we're so shorthanded, I should be back on the job soon."

"I get it," Gina replied. "Hey, Shane said you and the medic seem to have a thing going on."

Whitney forced a chuckle. "He saw us together the other night right after this happened. We were both still in shock." Then she decided to be honest. "David knew my brother, so he's a good friend. He's checked on me all weekend, and he came by Sunday night for a visit."

"Since you've told a few people why David's really here, everyone is talking about how he promised Lucas he'd come here and find you. It's kind of romantic."

"Everything is romantic to you," Whitney pointed out. "You're in love."

"Yes, I am."

Whitney avoided any further discussion about David. Thankfully, Gina wasn't one to pry.

"I'm glad David was with you," Gina said. "But I sure don't like this coming on the heels of Veronica's death. First Ellen's mother gets hit over the head. Now someone's trying to get to you and David. And we still don't know what happened to little Marco. We need to find that puppy. I can't wait until the end of all this."

"You went through your own scare," Whitney said, thinking of the horror of Gina's troubled brother coming to Desert Valley and trying to kill her. But Tim was getting some much-needed help now.

"I'm okay," Gina replied. "Just glad it's over. I'm concerned about you now, though."

Whitney refused to be a coward. "I intend to catch the drug traffickers."

"Be careful," Gina warned. "You have a big target on your back after that train incident. Not to mention everything else we're dealing with."

"I will," Whitney replied. "I'll meet you at the training center."

"Okay. Hey, if you and the medic are growing close, more power to you."

"Thanks, Gina."

Whitney ended the call, wishing she could ask Gina for advice. Gina and Shane were engaged, and that was exciting. While she was happy for them, she wasn't ready to give in to having a man in her life again so soon after losing Brian.

But you never really had him, she thought.

She couldn't get involved with anyone until all of these dark clouds hanging over her head went away, starting with proving that Brian's death had not been an accident.

She dropped Shelby and Hunter with Gina and Sophie, giving her baby a big kiss and hug and a promise to be back in two hours. Then she headed toward the Desert Rose to pick up David. Today she planned to go back over the burned remains of Brian's house, hoping to find anything that might give her a clue to what had happened the night of the fire.

Even though it had been over a year, the charred husk of the house hadn't been cleared yet. It was in an area that didn't get much attention from the county. Brian had liked the isolation of his little house near the river. She wondered if his land had been claimed by any relatives.

She'd gone back over the short list of people who knew Brian, but she still had no answers on old girlfriends or angry friends who'd realized he was a player. Brian had been a loner and he never talked about his friends or family much, so it would be hard to pin down anyone on that account.

When she pulled up to the Rose, David was sitting in one of the rocking chairs on the porch. He hopped up and hurried to get in the vehicle. "Miss Rosa is watching out the window on the pretense of making sure the patrol car comes by every thirty minutes. She thinks we're going for a romantic drive through the desert." He shrugged.

"I didn't have the heart to explain we can't do that since we'd probably never make it home."

Whitney ignored the horror of that. "Does everyone around here think you and I are—"

"Yes," he said. "Miss Rosa wants you to find a good papa for your beautiful little girl."

A heated blush colored Whitney's face. The day was warm and getting warmer, but this heat came from within. "Why can't people understand I'm okay with being a single mother?"

David shot her a solemn frown. "Don't worry. I set her straight. Told her we're friends since I knew your brother." He stared out the window. "That is the standard response these days."

Whitney could tell her outburst bothered him, but his excuses to Miss Rosa bothered her. She didn't want his landlord to get the wrong idea. "It's not you, David."

"Right, it's you. You're still in love with a man who wasn't willing to make a commitment to you. A man who's been dead for almost a year."

This day wasn't starting off the way she'd planned. "I'm not in love with him. It's just that one thing after another has happened, and I haven't really had time to… mourn him. Not just his death but…the truth that was right there in front of me."

"Yes, so I get that maybe this quest to bring about justice will help you to heal and get on with your life."

"I'm trying to do that," she retorted. "I was on my way to finding out which police station I'd be assigned to when Veronica's murder took precedence, and then you showed up. Cut me some slack."

He looked sheepish. "I'm sorry. I've been on 'go' since I got off that train. I think we both need to relax and chill a little, don't you?"

"Sure, if we forget we've got drug runners gunning for us." Then she pointed a finger at him. "When we get to the house, just remember, you can't do anything or touch anything. It could mess with the chain of evidence and get it all thrown right out of court."

David let out a groan. "Maybe I should have listened to you and stayed out of this."

"I can let you out here," Whitney said, slamming on the brakes at a traffic light.

"No." David sat up. "Hey, we're both still on edge. Let's start over."

"Good idea." She smiled over at him. "I enjoyed the chocolate you brought over Sunday night."

"I'm glad you liked it."

Thirty minutes later, Whitney pulled up to the burned-out shell that had once been Brian's house, relieved that they hadn't been followed. Staring over at the blackened remains of the small cottage, she remembered laughing with Brian, kissing him, giving in to all the impulses he brought out in her.

"Hey."

She didn't even realize she was gripping the steering wheel with a white-knuckled intensity until David's hand on her arm brought her back to the here and now.

"What?"

"Are you sure about this?"

"Yes," she said. "And I'm glad you're with me."

He looked relieved. "I wasn't sure you wanted me here."

Whitney took the keys out of the ignition. "I don't talk about Brian with anyone. It's too hard to explain, and I would hate the looks of pity I'd be sure to get." She eyed him. "Kind of like the way you're looking at me now."

David came around to meet her near the back of the

SUV. "Hey, I don't pity you. I understand. I mean, I've seen all kinds of death, and in battle you learn to harden your heart against all the pain and suffering. You hide your emotions for so long, you forget how to feel. I think you're trying to do that. So I don't pity you. I admire you, Whitney. You're strong and brave and…you love your little baby. You faced down the world, accepted your lot in life and decided to overcome a bad situation and turn it into something good."

"Are you trying to make me cry?" she asked, touched that he could read her so easily. Touched that he saw how hard she'd fought to find her way alone.

"No." He pushed a hand over his clipped hair. "I'm trying to give you a compliment, but you're so shut down, you can't even accept that, either."

He was right. She didn't accept praise very well because she'd never thought she deserved praise. "Thank you," she said on a husky whisper. Then to add some levity, she asked, "Are we going to argue all day?"

"No." He nodded toward the skeleton of what was once a house. "Let's get this over with."

Whitney wanted nothing more than that. She hadn't been back here since the night they'd heard the report. She and her fellow rookies had watched as the fire department had gone over the house, searching for the source of the fire. When the fire inspector had found a burned-out cracked glass candleholder with the name of a prominent brand scorched but still readable on the glass, the department had deemed it as the source, since it had been located near what remained of the front window curtains.

Now the debris had been cleared and piled in the front yard. The house had been stripped down to the bare bones. It was an eyesore. And months had gone by. Almost a year. What was she doing here?

"I'm not sure what I'm looking for," she told David, her tone quiet. "It's a long shot, but I just needed to start here to get my bearings."

The house was located on a secluded, rutted road away from the surrounding neighborhood. Brian hadn't been much on yard work or decor, and the cute little stucco house had been simple and neat, with just enough room and privacy for a bachelor.

And the many women he'd brought here.

"It shouldn't take long to do a walk-through," she said, her shades pulled down to avoid the glaring midmorning sun. And maybe to hide her eyes. "I'm sure vandals have taken anything of value that was left."

She studied the blackened beams and singed carpet, went over what was left of the furniture and appliances. The fire had started up front, which was odd in itself. "If Brian had bought a candle, he wouldn't have put it near the door. Maybe on the coffee table or even in the bedroom. Why by the curtains?"

"What else was near the curtains?" David asked, scanning the worst of the burned areas of the house.

"Nothing," she said, memories charring her brain in the same way the fire had scorched this house. "He had a table near the door where he placed the mail and some of his gear. It was near the hall closet, where he kept the lockbox for his gun. But that's over there." She pointed to the other side of the hallway, where the front door had been burned to a crisp. "That's away from the curtains. The remains of the candle were found near the window."

"Maybe the fire blew it off the table, or he threw the candle over there when he found the house on fire."

"I don't think he had time to do that. He was supposedly getting dressed for the police dance." She took a deep breath. "They found him just inside the bedroom door. He died of smoke inhalation." She closed her eyes, hoping he had passed out before the heat became too intense.

"Was his K9 partner here with him?"

"No." Whitney closed her eyes. "He'd left him kenneled at the training center. He did that sometimes when he knew he'd be out late." She touched the scorched remains of the couch. "His partner went to a police department in Winslow."

David moved through the tiny living area to stare into the bedroom. "Did you come here with him?"

"Yes," she said, glad she hadn't kept this a secret from David. Maybe because he hadn't questioned or judged her, she felt she could share things with him. "I came here a lot. Stayed here a lot." Then she stared over at David. "Obviously."

"And no one knew? I mean, could someone who was jealous have done this deliberately?"

"Possibly. He went through a lot of women. I'd heard rumors that he and Veronica flirted with each other while she was still married to Dr. Pennington."

"Wow." David stopped, his hands on his hips. "It's still weird that I found him at the clinic the other night stitching up that stab wound. And that the kid had the same sort of tattoo we've been seeing everywhere lately."

David had called her Saturday morning to tell her about that strange encounter. But the police department didn't have a report of an officer being alerted about the injured teen.

"Doc's known for helping those who can't pay and for going above the law to keep from having to deal with the police and the immigration officials. The teen could have been here illegally or…a drug mule."

"He seemed out of it, kind of high. I almost felt as

though he wanted to say something to me, but he looked scared. I mean, really scared."

"Probably afraid he'd go to jail or be shipped back across the border," Whitney said. "Sometimes things are different here. Like when you were in battle and had to make snap decisions. Dr. Pennington does that a lot, too, I think."

She moved around, memories distracting her.

"The tattoo could match all the other symbols we've been seeing," David said.

"The doctor should have done a better job of reporting this. The department lets him get away with a lot."

"Okay, I'm reporting it to you," David said. "Just for the record."

"I've got it," she said, her eyes scanning the area by the door. When she saw something glistening near a pile of burned rubbish out in the yard, Whitney hurried over. With gloved hands, she pulled back the debris.

"I found something," she said, her heart lurching with both dread and hope.

Before she could say anything else, David threw his body over hers and held her down.

FOURTEEN

"David?"

"Sniper," he said, his breath coming in huffs. "I saw a flash up in the hills, just past the house."

Whitney lay still, believing him. "Can you see anything else?"

He lifted his head and scanned the hills off to the right of the house. "Hard to say." He moved his body a fraction. The whiz of a bullet hit about a foot from where they lay.

"I guess that answers that," he said, squinting toward the distant hills. "We're pretty much trapped."

"I can't breathe," Whitney said, the security of him protecting her bringing out more emotions and awareness than she cared to admit. "Let me up."

He moved away, his gaze focused on the hills. "We can make a run for your SUV."

Whitney weighed that choice with calling for backup. "Okay, I'll cover you. Can you get in and drive close so I can make it to the vehicle?"

"Yes."

She rolled and centered herself behind the pile of rubble, sweat now pooling between her shoulder blades.

David took the keys. "Ready?"

She nodded. "It's not locked. Just get in as fast as you can."

They counted to three, and he took off while she fired a round toward the hills. When return fire pinged all around her, she twisted to check on David. She heard the roar of the truck's motor and breathed a sigh of relief.

Through another round of fire, David brought the truck to a skidding stop close to the burned-out shell of the house and opened the SUV door. Whitney fired another round and crawled toward the waiting vehicle.

Soon she was inside, and David was spinning out of the deserted yard. The shooting had ended.

"Did you get the bracelet?" he asked after he made sure she was okay.

Whitney held up the tarnished piece of jewelry and let out a breath. "Yes. Held on to it while I fired shots."

David's expression showed relief and appreciation. "Is it yours?"

"No. I've never seen it before. But I can tell you this—Brian didn't allow me to leave any jewelry or clothing here. He didn't like clutter, especially feminine clutter."

"Maybe someone dropped it on her way out," David replied, his eyes on the silver charm bracelet. "And...if she lost it out here, the investigators obviously missed seeing it."

"It seems that way," Whitney replied. Holding the tarnished, dirty bracelet up in the light, she added, "Whoever wore this could also be the same person who set this fire. Possibly the person who just shot at us, too."

"So you've accomplished something," David replied. "And we didn't die doing it, thankfully. What now?"

"I bag it and tag it," she said, careful that she didn't break the delicate thread that might hold the truth. "And... we report that we were shot at once again."

"It's escalating," he said, taking her hand in his. "We need to stick closer together."

Whitney saw the reasoning in that comment, but she couldn't be around David 24/7. Too tempting.

"The chief has just about run out of people to cover us," she said. "We might have to be on our own for a while."

She should have felt some sense of relief and accomplishment after finding the bracelet, but being shot at so soon after killing that man in her house had ruined that buzz. Instead, she felt sick to her stomach and full of even more questions and doubts.

Who had dropped this bracelet?

And would she ever be able to find that person, or would she have to leave this as evidence and never find her answers?

Tuesday morning, Whitney reported to work again, went to Chief Jones and showed him the bracelet she'd found. "This is it, Chief. This bracelet seemed out of place at that house."

The chief's heavy eyebrows winged up. "Seriously, Godwin? That's all you've got? Some lookie looker combing over the ashes could have lost that piece of jewelry there."

"I'm sending it to the state lab for testing," she said. She couldn't tell him that since she knew Brian from experience, her gut was burning with the knowledge that someone had accidentally left the bracelet. "I wish I could find the woman who lost this."

"It's a long shot," the chief said. "But I guess we have to cover every angle. Send it on and keep me informed."

"Yes, sir." She'd already reported what the neighbor had told her about Melanie's habit of walking the same trail home on a regular basis, and now she added that she planned to go back over Mike Riverton's files, too. "And I'll go back over the fire report on Miller's house. Maybe we'll hit on something."

"You're dedicated, I'll give you that," Chief Jones said. "You'll make a top-notch investigator." Then he took off his glasses and gave her a fatherly stare. "If you don't get shot."

"It's hard to guess when they'll strike next," she admitted. "But I appreciate the patrols you've set up at the inn and around my neighborhood."

She left the chief's office and placed the envelope on her desk until she could get it to the lab. Then she went on with her day. After going over reports and checking for any new details regarding Veronica's death, she glanced up and realized it was lunchtime.

She met Ellen Foxcroft, the other female rookie, on the way to the break room. "Hey, how's your mother?"

"Still in a coma," Ellen said, her fatigue evident in her blue eyes. "We've still got guards at her door. I'm worried that whoever did this will return and try something else."

They walked into the break room and found Carrie Dunleavy, the police department secretary, sitting at a table, munching on some chips. She looked up through her horn-rimmed glasses. "Hello, ladies. I brought brownies. Well, actually, they're blondies but...still good."

"Hmm, sounds yummy," Ellen said. "How ya doing, Carrie?"

"Can't complain," Carrie replied, her shy smile making her look cute. "How's your mom, Ellen?"

Ellen repeated what she'd told Whitney while Whitney heated up some soup and found her sandwich in the refrigerator. Ellen grabbed a banana and her yogurt and sat down across from Carrie.

"How are you?" Ellen asked Whitney, a concerned expression on her face.

"Okay," Whitney replied, not mentioning being shot at or finding the bracelet. "I'm doing all right, but I did go over some of these reports on Veronica's death. I thought maybe I'd hit on a clue or find a good tip."

"And what about this new man in your life?" Ellen asked with a soft smile.

Carrie looked up with interest and then shoved the plastic container of caramel-colored brownies toward Whitney. "Tell us. We want details."

"I guess word gets out around here," Whitney replied. Grabbing one of the moist dessert bars, she said, "You've all heard David knew my brother and served with him in Afghanistan. He's a medic. He was with Lucas when he died, so he came here to meet me."

Carrie sat up, her eyes going wide. "Wow, so it is true. That's so romantic. I mean, I know you lost your brother, and I'm so sorry, but for his friend to come here to see you—that's so sweet. He must have been close to Lucas."

Ellen gave Whitney an apologetic glance while Carrie blushed a bright pink. "I didn't mean to stir all of that up."

"It's okay." Whitney replied. "He and Lucas were close. Lucas convinced him to come and see me. But David and I are just friends. Nothing more." She shrugged. "He won't be here for long anyway."

Carrie's embarrassment changed to curiosity. "Is that the guy who came to look at mug shots that night? He's a hunk."

Whitney and Ellen both laughed. "Yes, he is," Whitney said, unable to deny it. "He's a nice man and a good medic. He'd make a great doctor one day."

They moved on to other topics. When Whitney finished and cleaned up her lunch, Carrie came to the sink and touched her on the arm.

"I'm glad you have a new friend, Whitney. Maybe one day I'll find a friend like that."

Then Carrie turned and hurried out of the break room.

Whitney again told herself that the next time she had one of her girls' night get-togethers, she'd invite Carrie, too. The secretary worked hard for all of them, and she really cared about the whole team. But it didn't look as though they'd have any downtime for a while.

It was a shame that they were all so closed off and private, but being a police officer did that to a person. She thought of David and how her feelings for him were changing from friendship to…something more. Something she wasn't sure she was ready for. Would she ever be able to hand her heart over to anyone again?

"Is this the symbol?" Whitney asked David on Wednesday morning.

David looked at the photo and nodded. "It looks like it, yes."

Hard to believe he'd been in Desert Valley for almost two weeks now. He'd grown closer to Whitney and he'd settled into a routine at the clinic, but he was tired of being stalked by bad people. He couldn't leave until he knew with certainty that those drug couriers wouldn't hurt Whitney or little Shelby.

"David?" Whitney waited for him to say something else. When he didn't, she prompted him. "Does it look like the one you saw on the teen in the clinic?"

"Close. Yeah, I'd say they were almost the same."

"It matches the one I spotted on the courier's arm," Whitney said, making notes.

"And I saw it on the SUV," David replied. "I'd say we've established it as some sort of emblem or totem."

He glanced up at Louise Donaldson. Louise was an older patrol officer who now seemed to be mostly on desk duty, according to Whitney, so she'd been doing research to help. She'd already confirmed that neither the 911 dispatcher nor the department had received a call from Dr. Pennington regarding a knife wound. He'd lied to David about reporting the kid's injury.

"Here's what I've found online," Louise said. "Dealing with criminals around here, I come across a lot of emblems and amulets. I've found some tattoos like the one you're describing, so let me pull them up for you to compare."

"Louise is good at this," Whitney had told him when she'd called him last night. "She can unearth all kinds of things. She's found her niche in doing background checks and research on cases for us."

Tall and solid, Louise wore her brown hair in a no-nonsense short bob that only made her brown eyes look even bigger. "So…you think this is it?"

"I can't be one hundred percent sure," David admitted while he studied the symbol, "but it's close." He'd looked at a lot of feather symbols, but this one stood out. "I guess the tattoos could vary, but the arrow with the three feathers was definitely on the kid's arm. And it looks like what I glimpsed on the SUV, too."

"The kids love to get symbolic tattoos," Louise said. "Thinks it makes 'em look cool. It could mean they've been inducted into some sort of drug smuggling operation, too. Young mules and couriers who'll likely die young. Probably why the kid was so scared. And the doc, too. If either of them squealed, they could both be buried in the desert."

David thought about how Dr. Pennington had acted. "The boy was scared. The doctor just seemed aggravated. But he did lie about reporting it, so maybe he was afraid he'd get caught in the middle of things."

"He works too hard," Louise replied while she scanned some other templates of local tattoos. "That can make a person ornery." She chuckled and nodded. "I'm counting the days myself."

Whitney and David studied the arrowhead symbol again. "It has three feathers," Whitney said. "That could mean something. Three branches or territories maybe?"

Louise bobbed her head. "Good guess. In Native American folklore, the feather represents honor and bravery, strength and power, and it's only given or worn to reflect those things. In this case, someone could be using it in an unscrupulous way that has no honor, but it could wield a lot of intimidation and power. In Spanish, it could mean *tres plumas*. Simply *three feathers*. That term has been around for centuries in one form or another."

"I've seen enough," Whitney said. "David?"

"This could be it," he said, still unsure. "It's close." Then he looked up at Whitney. "Will it help, or is this just a common thing around here? We didn't find a tattoo on the man you shot the other night."

"And we haven't identified him yet," Louise reminded them.

Whitney studied the screen, her long blond hair falling against her shoulders. She rarely wore it down, but today she'd left it pulled back just enough for some of the silky strands to cluster around her face, and it was distracting him big-time.

"It's a beginning," she said. "Since we haven't been able to identify the two men from the train or the one I shot, we can try to connect this symbol to them. And meantime, I'll call the state lab to push them along on the evidence we sent to them—the torn pants material and the weapon. Maybe they've heard something on our John Doe, too."

David thought of something else. "I could check the clinic records to see if Dr. Pennington's treated anyone else—say, someone who suffered a dog bite or stabbing—in the time I've been around."

"If he treated one of our guys, he probably wouldn't have left any trace of a report or record behind," Whitney said. "He seems to do things his own way."

"Or...he's being threatened," Louise pointed out.

David wasn't buying it, but Whitney looked thoughtful. "Don't go Rambo on me, okay?"

"I'm not planning on getting into trouble," David replied. "But I can check records and look around."

Louise's inquisitive gaze moved between David and Whitney. "What about train schedules? Have you confiscated the passenger log from that day?"

"Yes," Whitney said. "But the names don't match the description of these two, and no one along the route remembers them. We can't find them on any video surveillance, either. I figure they use fake IDs and heavy disguises and change things up at each stop they make. It's frustrating."

Louise read over the reports. "Let me see if I can establish a pattern. You know, match reports on drug smuggler arrests from other towns to what we know about ours. They might change things all the time, but sooner or later, they'll mess up."

"You are amazing," Whitney said to Louise. "I owe you a good cup of coffee."

"And a piece of cheesecake," Louise replied with a smile.

"You've got it. I'm ordering lunch, so I'll get it now." Whitney glanced at David. "Want to hang around? I'm eating lunch in to be safe."

"Sure," David said. "I don't have to be at the clinic until the late shift. Doc requested I work during some of the after-hours shifts."

She glanced over a menu from the Cactus Café. "They deliver, and this time we'll make sure it's the right person." After she'd placed their orders, she turned to David. "Hey, you ever thought about staying here and *working* at the clinic?"

David's gut burned with anxiety and awareness. He'd stay in a heartbeat if he knew she'd be staying here, too. But she'd made it clear she wanted to go back to Tucson.

"I'd have to think about it," he replied. "But hey, I'm wide-open for suggestions."

Surprise made her cornflower-blue eyes widen. "I guess you do have a lot of options."

David wondered if she thought of herself as one of those options.

FIFTEEN

Whitney accepted that part of her job involved waiting. It took time to get evidence back and to get lab reports, too, since they had to send everything to Flagstaff. But she was growing impatient. She had hoped to be in Tucson by now, living in a new place and getting adjusted to a bigger police department.

Instead, here she sat with a man who'd appeared in her life at the worst possible time.

Or...had David come at the best time?

The minister had talked about timing in church Sunday. He'd mentioned waiting on God's time. But that was hard to do, Whitney decided now, Hunter at her feet. Her impulsive, impatient nature had caused her to move too quickly with Brian. And she'd made mistakes in her first days as a rookie because of both of those things, too.

She had to be careful with David.

But when he smiled at her and settled his loose-limbed body into the chair across from her desk, she had to wonder if God hadn't timed this one just right.

She was beginning to care about David. A lot.

Would God send him here only to take him away?

Or should she jump at this opportunity to find true happiness?

"What are you thinking?" David asked, his eyes scanning her face.

She couldn't tell him that. "Shrimp tacos," she said instead. "Can't wait to eat lunch."

He smiled. "I don't believe that, but we'll go with it."

After their lunch had been delivered, he leaned in and asked, "Do you feel as if we're still being watched?"

"Yes. I can't relax even stuck inside the police station. It's creepy, but what can we do?"

"Keep plugging away," he said. "Hope we find the people running drugs through Desert Valley."

"And the person who might have murdered four people," she said. Then she twisted her napkin. "This isn't a very fun lunch, is it?"

"Well, we tried a real date, and you know how that ended."

"Yes, I do." The thought of something happening to Shelby terrified her. The Carters were being diligent by keeping their children close and watching over Shelby, a patrol car parked on the curb.

David tapped his fingers on the old desk. "Hey, we need to talk about us."

"What about us?" she asked, glancing around, her heart doing odd little bumps and beats.

"Whitney, I…like you. A lot. I wonder what it would be like not to have to look over our shoulders for criminals chasing us, to be friends, to get to know each other more. To be together without any threats hanging over our heads."

Her shivers of apprehension turned to shivers of delight. That would be amazing, so nice. Wonderful. "I don't know," she admitted. "I've made so many mistakes."

"Hey, this isn't a mistake," he said, his brown eyes turning as rich and dark as the mocha brownies Carrie had brought in this morning. "My feelings for you can't be wrong. And I think you feel something for me, don't you?"

Whitney swallowed, her throat dry. "I—"

"How's it going?"

Whitney glanced up to find Ellen grinning at them.

"Good," she said, her gaze clashing with David's. "Kind of lying low."

"Okay," Ellen said. She nodded at David, grabbed an apple and kept going.

Whitney looked into David's eyes. "I have to eat and get back to work," she said on a hurried whisper. "Hunter needs a bath, so I'm taking him by the training center this afternoon. They have a huge shower that all the dogs love."

"Okay, then," David said, disappointment shifting through his gaze. Grabbing a taco, he bit in and chewed. Then he put it down and wiped at his fingers. "Dinner Friday night, at the inn. Bring Shelby and Hunter if you want, so you won't worry about anything. We should be safe with a patrol car on the watch."

"All right," she said, barely able to eat. "Another real date?" Then she shrugged. "I mean, if it is, maybe it should just be the two of us."

David's expression heated up at that comment. "Ah, something tells me the rookie is beginning to like me."

"I do like you and… I'd like a real date with you," she admitted, relieved to be honest with him.

"This will be as real as it gets," David said. "And ideally, no one will try to shoot us."

"C'mon, boy. Time for your bath."

The welcoming sound of yelping puppies echoed around Whitney and Hunter as they headed for the vet office.

Whitney moved through the big training yard and entered the building near the puppy yard, her mind on poor little Marco. The missing puppy might be just fine, but she couldn't help but worry. It was well over a month and a half since Veronica's murder and still no sign of the puppy. She hoped someone who loved animals had found the little shepherd. Since Veronica put ID chips in all the puppies she trained, it was possible that Marco had one a vet could easily read. But no one had reported finding him.

Hunter spotted the door she was about to enter and glanced up at her with a hopeful expression. He seemed to enjoy getting a bath now and then, and he really didn't mind visiting the vet too much since Tanya Fowler, the center's veterinarian, always gave Whitney treats for him. Whitney liked to bathe him here in the big industrial tub and shower located in the hallway of the vet's office. Easier than trying to get him clean in the tub at home. Since he got into all kinds of things while on duty, it also saved her having to scrub down her bathroom.

"Hey, Whitney," Tanya said, her eyes lighting up at the sight of Hunter. "Hi there, Hunter. How ya doing?"

Hunter sniffed Tanya's knuckles but stayed by Whitney.

"Hi. He needs a bath," Whitney said. "Is it too late for me to give him one today?"

Tanya fluffed Hunter's coat. "Nah. Just lock up after you're done. You know the drill. Sophie's out in the yard, so she'll be around."

Sophie Williams had worked under Veronica's iron fist, and after Veronica's death, she'd immediately been promoted to lead trainer. She was doing a good job. But the pressure of the job and the implication that she'd killed Veronica had made her a little distant lately. Whitney didn't believe for a minute Sophie had murdered

Veronica, even though the two colleagues had had their moments.

Veronica had not made life easy for anyone around her, and Sophie and she had gone a few rounds, but Sophie was dedicated to her work. From what Whitney had heard and seen, Sophie had been genuinely upset when they'd found Veronica. Whitney couldn't see her being involved in such a heinous act.

"I'll let her know I'm here," Whitney said.

"I'm on my way out there, so I'll tell her you're inside," Tanya said.

"Thanks, Tanya."

"You're welcome," Tanya said, her strawberry blonde curls swishing around her face. "Still no word on little Marco, huh?"

"Nope." Whitney guided Hunter toward the open shower and turned on the gentle spray to adjust the water temperature. "I've canvassed just about every neighborhood near where he was last seen. Someone took him. I wish we knew who and for what purpose. To keep him? To sell him?" Or worse—as some sort of memento because maybe it was Veronica's killer who had taken him, Veronica's killer who witnesses had seen on the bike?

"I hope he turns up," Tanya said. "Good to see you. I'll keep my eyes open for little Marco."

"Thanks," Whitney said. "C'mon, Hunter. We need to hurry up and get home to Shelby."

Hunter's ears perked up at Shelby's name. He loved the baby almost as much as he loved working. Soon Whitney had him lathered up and enjoying a good, clean blast of warm water on his short, lush fur. "Nice, huh?"

After giving Hunter a good rinse, she heard a door opening and figured Sophie was calling it a day. "Wanna say hi to Sophie?"

He glanced around and then growled low.

"Hunter? What's wrong, boy?"

Whitney felt it, too. The hair on the back of her neck stood up. Afraid to look around, she hurried to finish up with Hunter. "It's okay, boy," she said to calm the dog. "Stay."

Hunter kept looking beyond the hallway, out toward the puppy-training-yard door.

"Sophie, is that you?"

No response.

Grabbing a huge towel, Whitney turned off the spray and quickly toweled Hunter. The big dog shook off the moisture but became more agitated with each second that ticked by.

"Stay," Whitney commanded on a gentle note. She thought she heard a sound. Footsteps? A door creaking open down the hallway?

"Who's there?"

No one answered, but Hunter kept growling. Whitney commanded Hunter to calm down, but she drew her gun all the same. Leashing the still-damp K9, she whispered, "Search."

Hunter did his job, moving toward the door to the puppy yard. They passed storage closets and kennels, but Hunter stopped at a closed door near the open yard outside. Whitney held her weapon in front of her, her other hand on the knob. But before she could turn the knob, the door opened with a swish of force that sent her flying backward. She hit her head on a metal cabinet, the pain jolting through her while Hunter's barks echoed throughout the building.

Suddenly, the door from the inside training area opened, and Sophie hurried up the hallway. "Whitney?"

Whitney blinked, dizziness overcoming her. She saw

a dark shadow dressed in black pushing out the door to the yard, Hunter snarling and dancing around her as the door slammed shut. Then she passed out.

"Whitney?"

She opened her eyes to find Sophie leaning over her.

Touching her head, she asked, "What happened?" Then she realized she was no longer at the training center.

"Someone knocked you down," Sophie said. "Stay still. You're at the clinic in an examining room."

"Hunter?"

"He's safe. He wanted to go after them, but I held him back. The whole team is searching the yard and buildings."

Whitney tried to sit up. "Shelby?"

"We've sent Ryder to check on her. It's okay. Just stay still."

Whitney tried to sit up again, but another door burst open and she heard voices, then a man issuing an order.

"Let me check on her."

David. Of course he was here. He'd been on his way to the clinic earlier.

He came into focus, concern marking his steely expression. "Hey, how you doing?"

"Head hurts."

She shouldn't be so glad to see him, but she was. Or maybe she was still dreaming.

"You might have a concussion," he said, his fingers moving gingerly over the back of her head. "We'll get you checked out."

"I'm okay. Home. Shelby."

"Soon," he said, his tone gentle, his eyes full of concern.

Whitney nodded and closed her eyes while everyone around her went about their work. David probed and checked and examined and asked her questions, his hand gentle on her head.

"I want to go home," she told him. "I can't stay here, and I'm not going to the hospital. Shelby needs me." She grabbed his shirtsleeve. "David?"

An hour later, David had her lying on the couch at her house. "I'll be right here monitoring you," he said. "You need to stay up for a few hours."

"David," she said, taking his hand. "I can't get myself killed. Shelby needs me."

"I know," he said. "Shelby is safe. I'm here. But we need to step things up. The person who knocked you against that shelf got away. No place is safe around here."

Then he leaned down and whispered in her ear. "Which is why I'll be here with you all night long."

Whitney didn't argue. This had escalated beyond the breaking point. They'd been threatened in both their homes, shot at over and over and now someone had breached the training center.

Drug traffickers or someone trying to sabotage the investigation involving Veronica's death? Either way, Whitney realized this might not be over for a while.

David waited until the clinic was quiet.

After making sure Whitney's concussion was mild enough that he could leave her with her neighbor Marilyn Carter, he'd agreed to work the late shift at the clinic today. Now he understood why Dr. Pennington had asked him to do so. The doctor had left early again tonight. David had bent the rules a lot in the middle of the battlefield. Having to make snap decisions meant the difference between life and death. But here, it was a whole other kind of triage.

The place was a mess. Nurses coming and going, quitting and coming back, a doctor who was brilliant at his job but not so diligent with protocol or his bedside manner, and too many sick, hurting patients who didn't have insurance or the money to pay. He almost wished he could just take over and get things in order.

But...that couldn't happen, could it? He didn't think Dr. Pennington was going anywhere soon. David wasn't sure he had enough fight in him right now to do more than try to help the patients.

David had a small window of opportunity to do a little snooping, and then he'd get back to Whitney. He carefully checked the medicine cabinets and made sure no drugs were missing. Everything looked in order there. He'd ventured into Dr. Pennington's office a couple of times, but the doctor kept things tidy so nothing could look out of place. Besides, he wasn't even sure what he was looking for.

David moved silently down the empty hallway, careful to watch the parking lot as he entered Pennington's office. The big mahogany desk centered inside had several folders stacked on one side, an ink pad and calendar in the middle and some textbooks on the other side. On one wall, a set of bookshelves housed more textbooks and medical tomes along with hunting pictures and a few scattered artifacts. Apparently Dr. Pennington loved the great outdoors.

David moved past the bookcase and tried opening the top-right drawer of the desk, but it was locked.

That figured.

Then he pulled open the bottom drawer and was surprised to find a handgun hidden underneath some prescription pads and other papers. Well, that didn't make the doctor a criminal. This clinic could be a dangerous place if a drug addict showed up, demanding supplies. Having a weapon on site was probably a good idea.

Still…it was unusual to find in a doctor's office. David didn't touch the handgun, but he did note the details. A semiautomatic with an ivory handle. Nice weapon.

He picked up one of the folders and read over it. Nothing there. They'd treated an older man for dementia and suggested he find a specialist. Dr. Pennington had even called a colleague to give the referral. It was all right there. The other reports were in order, too. At least the man kept accurate records when it came to the everyday patients. But David was more concerned with the doctor's nefarious activities.

Frustrated, David couldn't pinpoint anything out of the ordinary. Maybe Dr. Pennington was just harried, but David's gut told him there was more to the doctor's mysterious ways than just being busy and under stress.

Maybe the doctor had a drug habit. The way he came and went with various people, his temper and mood swings, even his erratic behavior could point to that.

David got up to recheck the drug cabinet but then he realized that if the doctor had a serious problem, he wouldn't take from the cabinet. He'd leave the clinic to meet his supplier. That had to be it. He could be buying drugs for personal use.

Deciding he'd have to start watching for more signs, David went back to the office. He looked up to find a vehicle pulling up behind the clinic, its headlights shining right into the office window. He grabbed a report and walked out just as the back door opened.

The doctor stood there glaring at him with an accusatory expression plastered on his face. "Evans, what are you still doing here?"

SIXTEEN

An hour later, David knocked on Whitney's door.

"Hi," Marilyn said, opening it with Shelby in her arms. "She's awake and waiting for you." Marilyn chuckled and tickled Shelby. "We all are."

After Marilyn had made it safely next door, he sank down in the chair beside Whitney sitting propped on the couch. Shelby played in her little fun kiddie bed nearby. "I'm sorry I had to leave for a while."

Whitney gave him a wry smile. "I think you had cabin fever after staying here last night and part of today."

"I did not. I've enjoyed being your…private doctor."

"I have to admit, I've enjoyed having you around. So has Shelby. Even Marilyn beams when you enter a room."

"I need to talk to you," he said, relieved to see the color back in her face. Happy that she liked being with him.

Whitney settled against the couch and stared up at him. "Is everything okay?"

David saw Hunter positioned in front of Shelby's room in the hallway. The big dog gave him a curious glance and then laid his head on his paws. That was becoming an endearing sight.

And so was Whitney. She wore her hair down. It

looked damp, so she must have just washed it. She had on a long DVPD black T-shirt and dark gray leggings.

"Everything's fine," he said. Then he moved to the couch and pulled her close, his fingers automatically moving over her head. "Just…a long day. I wanted to get back here. Right here."

Whitney hugged him but pulled away. "I'm fine. No more headaches and more energy today. But you don't look so hot. What's going on?"

"I think I might have something figured out," he said after checking her pupils.

Whitney pushed his hands away. "Stop examining me, David, and tell me what's going on."

He told her about almost being caught by Dr. Pennington. "I made up some excuse about looking over a patient file," he said. "I think he bought it, or maybe he pretended to believe me."

"What did you find?" Whitney asked.

"Nothing," he admitted, fatigue weighing heavy on his shoulders. "But I have a theory. I'm beginning to wonder if Dr. Pennington might have a drug habit."

Whitney gasped. "Have you seen him taking drugs?"

"No, nothing I can prove. The medicine cabinet is safe." He sat up and hung his hands together over his knees. "But he comes and goes at the oddest times. Sometimes he leaves in his sports car. Other times someone picks him up, and they leave for a while."

"Same vehicle as the one we saw?"

"I can't ever tell enough about it to compare it to the one we saw near the tracks, but I did manage to check it out a couple of times. No emblems."

"A dark SUV doesn't mean he's taking drugs."

"I realize that, since Dr. Pennington doesn't seem concerned about his friends pulling up to take him away. He trusts me way too much, too. I'm supposed to be a volunteer, but he's letting me handle a lot of responsibility that I really shouldn't be handling. If he's suspicious or scared, he sure doesn't act like it, and really, he keeps everything just within the law at the clinic."

"Maybe he's setting you up," Whitney suggested, a trace of fear in her words. "He could turn you in for something trivial just to make a point or get you out of his hair."

"Yeah, that did occur to me." He shook his head. "I'm gonna keep at it, though. His actions are too erratic to be normal."

"David, you don't have to do this. Maybe you should reconsider volunteering there."

"I have to find out what he's up to," he said. "Something's off, and with everything that's happened, I can't help but be involved."

Whitney propped herself up on her pillows again. "I wish you'd come to town under different circumstances."

"Yeah, me, too." David smiled at her. "I'm sorry."

She pushed at her hair. Her skin shimmered with a fresh-faced glimmer. "For what?"

"I rushed in here and unloaded on you without even asking you about your day."

"My day was boring," she said. "I rested as ordered, chatted with Marilyn since she sat with me all afternoon while her wonderful husband took care of her four children. Sleep a little, had a shower and talked to Gina about her hush-hush wedding plans."

She glanced toward the hallway and then moved her gaze to Shelby. "And enjoyed spending some quiet time with Shelby." Then she stared into his eyes. "I wanted to see you. Isn't that silly? I mean, I keep seeing that guy I shot, and I think about what could happen to Shelby or you. Then I think about the spot where I was attacked. That's almost the exact spot where Veronica died."

Seeing the distress in her eyes, David gave in and moved closer. Without hesitation, he wrapped her in his arms.

"Let's take a deep breath and talk about something else," he suggested while he enjoyed the sweet floral scent of her hair.

"Good idea," she mumbled. "Still nothing on the bracelet or the shooter, and I can't pinpoint anything from the fire report. I went back over Mike Riverton's file one more time, but I didn't find anything new. He was an expert mountain climber, and the official report has him falling down the stairs in his house."

"Let all of it go for a while," David said. "Have you eaten?"

"No, you?"

"No."

"Pizza?"

"Please." Then he lifted her chin with his index finger. "But we're still having our real date tomorrow night so don't try to get out of it."

"I won't. I can't wait."

"Miss Rosa is going all out."

She grinned up at him. "I'm glad you're here. I mean, I have friends from church, and the other rookies are my friends, but…it's different with you. I trust you, David."

"Is that because I knew Lucas, or in spite of it?"

"Both," she said, getting up before he could hold her close again. "Pepperoni or sausage?" she asked as she grabbed her cell phone.

"Both," he retorted with a wink.

But in spite of his high hopes, he had a feeling they

wouldn't ever be able to relax completely until all the mysteries surrounding them were done and over.

"Godwin, I need you and Harmon in my office right now," Chief Jones shouted up the hallway on Friday. Whitney stopped and let out a sigh. All day, she'd tracked down tips and had phone conversations with everyone from kids messing with her and pranking the whole department to people telling her Marco had been taken by aliens who landed in the desert on a regular basis. She'd spent hours going over the reports on Brian's house fire and Mike Riverton's fatal fall down the stairs at his house again. And while she hadn't cracked anything, she had discovered that both Brian and Mike had something in common besides being rookies.

They'd both had blond hair, and they'd both been killed on the night of the police dance and fund-raiser.

These observations were known facts, but when she put them together and added that Melanie Hayes had also been killed that same night years before, things got weird all over again. But it was the blond hair of the two men that had her establishing a certain pattern.

Did the alleged killer have a thing for blond-haired cops?

Or did the killer hate all blonds? If so, why kill Melanie Hayes? Then she'd realized the obvious.

Ryder Hayes had blond hair, too.

Did they have a serial killer on their hands?

But one thing stood out more than anything else—this person had to have inside knowledge of the whole department. Even the frequency of Melanie's route home. Even the layout of Brian's house and the exact spot on Mike's stairs that could cause a fall.

She'd reported all of her findings earlier, but she hadn't

discovered anything else that outstanding. She'd only reinforced that the killer had an established pattern.

"We might want to beef up security at the police dance this year, sir."

Chief Jones had agreed with that.

Now Whitney only wanted to go home and get ready for her big date with David. She'd even arranged for her friends Gina and Ellen to babysit Shelby and watch out for Hunter. Leaving her baby and her K9 partner with trusted colleagues made her feel better about going on this date. And it gave the Carters next door a break.

Turning, she gritted her teeth. "Yes, sir. What's up?"

"Louise has found something," the chief said as he stalked up the hall toward her. "Might be nothing, but she's been checking on passengers up and down the train line. We've put out an alert, and someone in Las Vegas saw a couple of suspicious-looking men boarding with large dark duffels. Two coach seats, no checked luggage and disembarking in good ol' Desert Valley in about an hour. Sent us an alert. We've established probable cause with our last find, and we're using a K9 for the search in a public place, so no warrant necessary. You know the drill. Don't harass the passengers, but do a sweep, get permission to search any private compartments if needed and see what you find in the storage areas."

Whitney glanced at the clock and then back to the chief. No way she'd be able to meet David on time, if at all.

"You got something important to do tonight, Godwin?" the chief asked, overly animated.

"No, sir. Nothing as important as this."

"Good. I'm sending you to search the train, and I'll have Weston and Harrison there with their K9 partners for backup."

"Why me, sir?"

"This is your case," the chief said. "You've been cleared to go back out there. Are you ready?"

"Yes, sir."

She hurried Hunter toward the patrol car, her cell phone in hand. Can't make it tonight. Work. The text to David would have to do for now. This could be the big break they'd all been waiting for on this drug case.

David read the text again.

Work. Tonight of all nights?

Well, he didn't have work tonight, because he'd made it clear at the clinic that he had plans.

Glancing around, he took in the bistro table Miss Rosa had set up on the long back porch for the two of them. A new security light made the whole yard glow, and the new gate had a solid lock on it. Plus a patrol car was parked in the alley.

"What do you think?" she asked now, her hands on her plump hips. "It's been a long time since we've had anything so romantic going on here, so I tried to make it special."

"It's very nice," David said, taking in the lush pink and yellow roses trailing down from a glass vase in the center of the table, the white cloth and silver utensils, crystal goblets and fine china. A latticework screen standing a few feet away kept the table secluded and private, while a ceiling fan whirled in a gentle motion overhead. "You've outdone yourself."

"Then, why so glum?" Miss Rosa asked. "The food is ready. Baked chicken with herbs, a salad, my famous cheesy potatoes and strawberries I hand dipped in chocolate. We're good to go."

"Not all of us," David said. "My date has to work late tonight."

Miss Rosa pursed her lips. "Oh, no. The nature of the job, honey." Patting him on the arm, she said, "I don't sleep well anyway. We'll wait for her and heat it all up, no matter how late."

Wait for her.

David wondered if he could do that. Wait for her, worry about her, try always to watch over her. He'd insult Whitney if he kept up with that. He couldn't protect her in the way Lucas had wanted him to. Whitney was too independent and stubborn for her own good, but those traits also made her a good police officer. Those traits attracted David to her but made it hard for him to give in to the attraction.

She wasn't the kind of woman who'd want to settle down to domestic bliss. And he wasn't even sure if he was that kind of man. He'd barely had time to think anything through over the past few months. He'd come here as a courtesy to a dying soldier, only to be thrust into the kind of adrenaline-filled world he'd left. He wasn't ready to rush headlong back into danger and death at every turn. He wasn't a coward, but he wasn't sure he wanted this kind of life forever.

Not with the woman he had so easily fallen for.

It might be time for him to leave Desert Valley.

He turned to Miss Rosa. "Thank you so much. I'll let you know if I hear from her."

But he wouldn't hear from her tonight, and he knew it. Whitney loved her work, and he appreciated that about her. But she was also obsessed with another man. A man whom she could mold and shape in her dreams to make him perfect, no matter how much he'd hurt her in real life. A dead man. Her child's father.

David couldn't measure up to that.

"I'm going for a drive," he told Miss Rosa.

The older woman reached out her arms. "I need a hug."

David hugged her tight, accepting that she saw he was the one who needed the hug. "Thank you, Miss Rosa, for everything."

Miss Rosa stood back and patted his arm. "You're a good man, David. She's a blessed woman to have you in her life."

David wasn't so sure about that, but he smiled down at Miss Rosa. "I'll see you later."

Then he hopped inside Miss Rosa's old pickup and headed north.

To buy a train ticket out of Desert Valley.

David turned onto the two-lane road leading to the train station, his mind whirling with what he had to do next. Traffic was light. As he rounded a curve, he spotted a familiar car up ahead.

The blue Camaro. The drug traffickers.

Disregarding everything he'd thought or decided since he'd seen Whitney's text, he started following the blue car. Keeping his eyes on the souped-up vehicle, David called 911 and reported seeing it. Whatever was happening, he planned to hang around and make sure Whitney was safe.

SEVENTEEN

Whitney pulled into the almost empty parking lot. She'd called Gina and Ellen to update them on the change of plans, that she was working instead of…going on a date. Whitney was grateful that Ellen, fellow rookie and a brave officer, would be at her home tonight, watching over both Gina and Shelby while Whitney was out.

"Be careful, Whitney," Ellen said. "We'll be fine here."

Eddie Harmon grunted beside her. "I had plans to go to a movie with my wife and grandchildren."

"I had plans, too," she shot back. She said goodbye and thanks to Ellen and pocketed her phone. "Let's check this out, and hopefully we can be done with these people."

Hunter stood on the seat, staring out the back window.

They exited the vehicle, and she leashed Hunter. "All right, let's get on with it." After she and Hunter had cleared the checked luggage compartment, she alerted the train conductor to leave all the exits shut except the one through which she and Hunter would enter.

"Harmon, you stand guard at that exit," she told Eddie. "No one on or off, understand?"

"Got it," Eddie replied with a grimace. They'd both put on bulletproof vests, just in case.

"Only a few passengers this trip," the conductor told

Whitney. "I've alerted them to stay seated and to cooperate." He nodded for her to enter the open exit.

Whitney took a deep breath, the dust whirls moving through the sagebrush kicking up particles that tickled her nose. If this went the way she figured, she wouldn't have to dig through too much luggage. On the other hand, she really wanted to catch some drug couriers.

"Go," she commanded Hunter. "Search."

Hunter tugged at the leash and started doing his job. Lifting his head, he sniffed the hundreds of different scents in the stuffy train, moving by some people and stopping for a couple of seconds near others.

Whitney searched the faces of the half-dozen or so passengers. She didn't see anyone who looked like the two men she'd encountered the last time she'd been here, but then, she hadn't expected to see the same ones. They were either in hiding or dead. Their boss wouldn't be happy that they'd failed.

They moved on to the last two seats on the last row. According to the tip, the two suspicious men should have been in these seats. How had they gotten off the train without her seeing them? Hunter sniffed the seats on both sides of the aisle and then stopped, his whole body going rigid near the two seats in question.

"Find," Whitney urged, watching the exits.

Hunter pressed his front paws down and sniffed under the seat nearest the aisle. He barked and turned to stare at Whitney.

To make sure he wasn't giving her a false alert, Whitney encouraged him again. "Search."

Hunter crept down and pawed under the other seat, moving his snout over the floor area.

Whitney told him to stay, and then she let go of his leash so she could get down and check underneath the seats. She saw two black canvas duffels stuffed together. Dragging one out, she settled it across the seat. Hunter's excited frenzy increased, and he started pawing at the duffel.

Whitney opened it and found what she'd been looking for underneath a barrier of clothes and plastic garment bags. Party boxes. Not as many as before, but enough. She pulled out the other duffel, with the conductor and another staff member watching.

After taking out one of the packages, Whitney opened it with a box cutter and took a picture of the powdery white substance. Then she alerted Eddie Harmon so he could vouch for her find, called it in to the department, sent pictures and requested backup.

"Already there," the dispatcher reported.

"Do I have permission to remove this evidence from the train?" she asked the chief after she'd been patched through.

"Go ahead," Chief Jones said. "We'll alert the DEA to meet you at the site. Get those drugs off that train, but keep your eyes on them."

Whitney and Eddie carefully removed the duffels with gloved hands and tagged them as evidence. Then, after Eddie had pulled the car up alongside the tracks, they loaded them into the trunk of the Crown Victoria and took yet another picture. Both Shane Weston and James Harrison were doing a sweep of the other cars and the surrounding areas. They'd have to wait here for the DEA, but at least these drugs wouldn't make it to the streets.

But where were the couriers?

"I'll guard the stash and watch for the DEA," Eddie said. "The drug runners might still be hiding out somewhere in another car."

"Right." He made sense to Whitney, and he was actually doing his job. She commanded Hunter to go, and they headed back onto the train. Now she started asking passengers about the two people who were supposed to be on the train along with the duffels, all the while checking each person for disguises or nervous twitches.

"I saw only one person sitting near that spot," an older lady replied. "He was tall, with dark hair, and he was wearing a cowboy hat and dark shades. But he got off at the stop before this one and never got back on."

After several passengers had verified that, Whitney figured someone had tipped the courier. But why hadn't he taken the duffels? Maybe someone else was supposed to board the train to retrieve them?

The passengers were beginning to grow restless, but she couldn't let this train leave until all the cars had been cleared. When Hunter alerted at one of the closed bathroom doors, Whitney motioned for the train employees to back away. The bathroom appeared to be occupied.

"Police officer," she called out. "Anyone in there?"

Hunter seemed to think so. Or he smelled the scent of someone who'd been here recently.

Whitney jiggled the door and it fell open. The bathroom was empty. Deciding one of the couriers had managed to get to the bathroom and hide before she got on the train, she figured he'd somehow managed to sneak out before all the doors were shut.

They didn't find anything or anybody, so she thanked the officials and exited through the one open door where she'd started.

Then she heard gunshots.

David heard shooting.

Whirling outside the train station gift shop, he looked for the man he'd followed into the ticket office. David was almost certain he recognized the man as the same one driving this car once before. Where had he gone?

The man had parked the blue Camaro. David noticed the tattoo on his left lower arm. The arrow pointed up, with the three feathers dangling below the arrowhead. The tattoo looked almost exactly like the one he'd seen on the SUVs and on the injured teen. He was pretty sure this man was disguised but…he looked a lot like the taller of the two who'd attacked Whitney the first time.

When the shots rang out, David spotted two K9 officers hurrying toward the front of the train.

And then he saw Whitney moving through one of the cars.

He had to warn Whitney. But the rapid fire of more gunshots going off had everyone around him scurrying for cover.

Running out of the train station, he saw the Crown Victoria pulled up close to the track on the other side, facing the train, and Eddie Harmon crouched down beside the open trunk. Sweat pouring off his face and shock in his eyes, Harmon had his weapon trained on the sparse woods past the train station. And he was bleeding from the shoulder.

Harmon spotted David and waved him back. "Get out of here."

"Hang on," David called back. "I'm coming to check on you." Lifting up, he searched for Whitney. Another round of shots whizzed through the air.

"Get down," Harmon called, his face pale. But he was watching the woods. Holding his shoulder, he shook his head. "I'll be fine. Go find Whitney."

"Where is she?" David asked. Off in the distance, he heard sirens. An officer and a K9 ran toward the train station. He recognized Ryder Hayes and his K9 partner,

Titus. Then another K9 officer and former soldier Tristan McKeller walked up with his yellow lab, Jesse. Tristan had a high-powered rifle with him.

"Don't know," Harmon called out in answer to David's question. "But...we got a sniper or two out in those hills past the train tracks. Got me good before I knew what was coming."

Almost the same spot where they'd taken Whitney last time. Would they get away with yet another shipment?

David prayed he was wrong and asked God to protect Whitney.

But he didn't plan on waiting, so he skirted the train cars. When he saw her running up the side of the train with her gun drawn and Hunter beside her, he eyed the woods and then eyed the distance between Whitney and Eddie Harmon.

If he could get to the other side of the tracks, he'd be able to watch the woods and maybe locate the sniper. And distract him enough to get Whitney to safety.

When another shot rang out, followed by Harmon's return fire, David crouched low and took off. He slid in beside Eddie Harmon as another shot whizzed by and hit a rock about ten feet away.

"Might be more than one," Harmon shouted into the radio. He didn't even bother fussing at David. "I can't see anyone. I'm in possession of the confiscated packages. Injured but still up."

In spite of his protests, David did a quick check of Eddie's shoulder. "A through and through," he told Eddie. "Are you okay for now?"

Eddie nodded, his face white and sweaty. "I've had worse mowing the yard. Hurts like a scorpion sting, but I'm good for now."

David lifted up to look for Whitney. He heard Hunter

barking and saw her crouched down the way, between two cars.

He couldn't get to her. David didn't mind the danger for himself, but he'd be a hindrance if he tried anything and distracted her too much.

A hindrance. This situation only reinforced his earlier decision to leave. He was a medical professional, and even though he'd been trained for combat, he did not want to stand in the way of the woman he cared about because she was an officer.

But when Whitney made it back to the open door of the train car, which still held several passengers, he watched as she ordered Hunter, "Guard." When she left Hunter in front of the open door and started running toward the woods, he realized she was going to backtrack to get to the shooter. Alone.

David gave Eddie Harmon a determined glance, turned and took off back across the track. He couldn't let her go out there alone, and Harmon was pinned down and injured. David did know a thing or two about rescuing people under fire, but he only hoped he wouldn't witness Whitney getting gunned down.

He hurried around the train and came up on the perimeter of the area where the sniper seemed to be embedded. The arid area around the tracks consisted of sagebrush and cacti, ponderosa pines and deep gullies and dry, gutted washes.

Whitney was a sitting duck out there on her own.

Whitney pressed against the hot train, bullets whizzing past her head while the fumes from the idling engine engulfed her in an oily smelling fog.

She could hear return fire, thankful that Eddie was okay and apparently firing back.

But she had two train cars between the police vehicle and her, and she had to make sure Hunter didn't get caught in the cross fire. He'd guard the passengers unless she told him to move, and he'd make sure no one left that train car or got into it, but he was still exposed.

She lay against the dusty earth, watching the rocks and trees off in the distance, assessing that one man had gotten off the train earlier while the other one had hidden in the bathroom and slipped out undetected. Then she heard barking and voices calling out commands. Her team was organizing a perimeter. Now if they could figure out how to subdue the shooter without getting anyone killed.

David made it to the back of the train without getting hit. He'd been careful to belly crawl slow and steady against the dry shrub brush and the hard brown sandstone. His jeans scraped against rocks and cactus shrubs, and his elbows ached from scratches and slides, the burn of raw skin reminding him of being pinned down on a vast mountain on the other side of the world, injured men moaning and crying out all around him.

For a moment, he was back there, praying and trying desperately to save one of them.

David shut his eyes to the burning that pricked at him with a piercing agony worse than any cactus thorn. Here, with Whitney caught in a trap, he realized why he couldn't take that next step and give in to his feelings for her.

He didn't want to live through this kind of pain ever again. If he stayed, he might have to do this over and over, even if it was in his nightmares.

When he heard more gunfire, David forced his eyes open and saw that he wasn't in Afghanistan and there were no wounded, crying soldiers around him.

There was only the hot desert sun and one brave woman trying to protect everyone.

He wasn't going to let her do it alone, no matter how reckless and stupid his actions might seem. But he wasn't going to die, and neither was she.

God had brought him here. God would see him through.

He clung to that hope as he watched the distant woods and finally saw the glint of the sniper's gun. David slid along beside the tracks, finding rocks and shrubs to shelter him. Careful to look before he reached, he checked for rattlesnakes hiding in the rocks and crevices.

In what seemed like hours but had only been minutes, he made it into the outcropping covered in shrubs and bushes across from the last car of the train. Squinting into the sun, he saw several officers converging up the way, but the sniper—or snipers—were holding them in a standoff.

He was about to make his move toward where he thought the sniper was hiding when he saw Whitney doing the same thing he'd been doing—crawling her way toward the woods.

Not good.

David had to make a move before the sniper spotted her.

He reached a worn trail near some saplings and tumbleweeds and slid up behind a jutting rock formation.

And heard the click of a gun behind his head.

EIGHTEEN

"Godwin, talk to me. What's the status?"

Whitney had to answer Chief Jones. "I'm on the ground near the middle train car," she replied. "One, possibly two, shooters to the northwest through the woods. Hunter is guarding the occupied train car. Eight passengers inside, sir."

"Hang on, Godwin. We're gonna get you outta there."

"Yes, sir."

Whitney squinted into the woods. Sweat poured into her eyes and she blinked. Once. Twice. Then she saw it. Two men walking toward the train.

Her heart tripped over itself as she spoke into her radio. "Sir, we have a situation."

"You mean worse than the one we're already in?"

"Yes, sir." She lifted up and tried to get a good look. Pulling down her dark shades, she slid up against the locomotive and watched the dust kicking up behind the two crouched men.

David!

They had David out there.

"Godwin, report!"

"They have a hostage, sir." She swallowed and described David. "I think it's David Evans."

Chief Jones shouted down the line. "We have a hostage situation. Stand down."

Wondering how this could be possible, Whitney watched as the man holding David at gunpoint marched right up to the edge of the woods and stared over at her, using David as a shield.

Whitney crouched on one knee and held her gun out. "Let him go. Now!"

"I don't think that's gonna work," the man said through a dry cackle of laughter. "We tried to warn you."

The man had a dark beard and wore a cowboy hat. He must have been on the train at one point. The witnesses had described him. Whitney felt sick to her stomach. The drug dealers had tried to outsmart her. But they hadn't planned on Whitney getting a solid tip.

"Look, your beef is with me and the police department," Whitney said as the man drew closer. "Let him go."

"Can't," the man replied, the gun digging into David's ribs. "I have my orders."

"And what orders are those?" she asked, her gaze on David. He looked calm and dangerous. She hoped, prayed, he wouldn't try anything. His eyes moved over her with an urgency that told her he'd do what he had to do—to save her.

She could hear the discussion over the radio. "We have a visual, Godwin. Keep 'em talking."

"What do you want?" she asked the man, her eyes moving over him, taking in details. She spotted the tattoo right away. Just as David had described it and exactly like the one she'd seen, too.

Her heart jumped and skidded, making her feel lightheaded. Whitney blinked and took a deep breath. She had to stay calm and in control. But her mind was screaming, *Why David?* Why did he somehow always show up at the worst possible time?

Maybe there would never be a good time for them. He was used to rescuing people in danger. And that meant her, too.

She wanted him in her life, but not like this. Not ever like this.

The man chuckled and yanked David back against him. "First, I want you to call off the marksman who's got his rifle trained on me. If he shoots me, your friend here goes with me."

Whitney closed her eyes to that image. "How can you be so sure?" she asked, certain that team member and former soldier Tristan McKeller had a high-powered rifle trained on them right now. The chief would do everything he could to save David, but if he ordered Tristan to take the shot…it could go wrong. So wrong.

"We can talk," she said. "Give us a name, and you might be able to get off easier. Who's in charge?"

"I'm not making any deals," the man said. He glanced back behind him.

"Is your friend out there?" Whitney asked, holding the man and David in her gaze. "Is he the other shooter?"

"What do you think?" the man asked. "We want what we left on the train, lady. And we need you to bring it to us."

"You mean the drugs. The duffels full of heroin? You sure didn't hide that very well. Your boss must be fuming by now."

Again, he looked over his shoulder. Was he running scared or running out of options?

"Tell your people to bring the bags. Then, nobody gets hurt."

"You want us dead, right?" David said. "Kind of stupid. Now everyone knows who you are."

"We should have killed both of you the first time," the man shouted.

"If she goes, I go with her," David said, his eyes on Whitney.

She at least agreed with that. She wouldn't let them take him.

"Shut up!" The man yanked at David again, but this time David shoved back, a full-on slam with his entire body.

Whitney gasped as the man hit David on the side of the head with the butt of the gun, but it gave her one quick instant to do what she had to do.

Taking a glance down the track, she called out to Hunter. "Attack!" Then she looked into David's eyes, saw the blood running down his cheek and screamed, "Get down, David."

David stepped back, knocking the man away with a grunt as he elbowed his attacker and then fell to the ground and rolled away. The man screamed his rage, lifted on one knee and turned with the gun toward David. But Hunter was already running, leaping, barking in a snarling frenzy.

Whitney cringed, her gun lifted, a silent scream trapped inside her throat. She called out, "Drop the weapon."

The man kept turning toward where David lay, but David rolled and grabbed at the man's leg, bringing him off balance as he fired. The shot hit the rocks as David brought him down.

Then Hunter leaped into the air, his teeth exposed, and bit into the man's bare arm. The suspect screamed and writhed, but Whitney didn't call off her partner.

"Hold," she told Hunter.

"Suspect subdued," Whitney said into the radio, running, her gun still drawn. When she heard shots firing all around them, she didn't care.

She was headed straight for David.

"I'm okay."

David kept telling Whitney that, but she didn't seem to believe him. He was sitting in the back of an ambulance, but he didn't plan on going to the hospital.

Another ambulance had already taken Eddie away, but not before Whitney had run up to the big man and gave him a hug. "Eddie, you're my hero," she'd told the embarrassed-looking officer.

"I might be your hero, Godwin," Eddie had replied on a hoarse chuckle. "But… I am definitely retiring at the end of this year. I've had enough."

Now Whitney stared at David, her blue eyes alert in spite of the lines of fatigue etched around them. "I still can't believe you did that," she said, anger warring with admiration in her tone. "What were you thinking?"

"I didn't know what else to do," he said, memories of getting reamed out by her and the chief and several other officers still burning through his brain. "I followed the blue car here, and then I heard shooting."

"You could have been killed," she said, her tone low and quiet. "How many times do I have to explain this to you?"

"I'm here and I'm fine," he replied. "I was a distraction, so it all worked out."

"This time," she said, her blue eyes holding him and making him want to tug her close and hold on to her forever.

But David couldn't do that. Not now. Not today.

He didn't tell her why he'd been in the train station, and in all the excitement of arresting the man who'd held David, she hadn't asked. Yet.

"Well, yes, it did work out. The DEA has carted away the suspect and the drugs. No one was killed, thankfully, and the train is back on track, so to speak."

"But the other one got away," David said, wishing he could have exposed both of them. "When Tattoo Man showed up and held me, I'd already decided I wasn't falling for his tricks. I would have taken him."

"I don't like your recklessness and bravery," Whitney retorted. "Your man, better known as Ramon Catez, is with the DEA now. If he talks, we might get somewhere." She shook her head. "But…he seemed really scared. I don't think he'll talk at all. He knows the consequences if he does."

David wanted to pull her close and kiss her. But with so many people walking around, including that pesky reporter Madison Coles from the *Canyon County Gazette*, he didn't dare make a move.

"Can I go now?" he asked, knowing he'd have to tell Whitney he'd decided to leave Desert Valley. Or maybe he'd leave without any more words. That might be the best way to handle this.

"You should be checked out."

"I'm fine. Just a black eye." He winced when he touched the spot on his temple where Catez had slammed him with the handgun.

"I'm sorry about our dinner," she replied. When she heard the chief calling her name, she said, "I have to go. I'll call you later."

"Better yet, come by the Rose," he said, wanting to hold her one more time even if he didn't have the guts to tell her the truth. "Miss Rosa is saving dinner for us."

"I'm starving," she said. "Maybe I'll do that." Then, after a quick glance, she touched her hand to his wound. "Thank you, David."

While he appreciated her gratitude and her attitude, David wanted more. He signed off on not going to the ER and got back in Miss Rosa's yellow truck without buying a train ticket.

But he was going to have to leave, and soon. He just didn't know how to say goodbye.

David sent Miss Rosa to bed, promising her he'd heat up the dinner she'd prepared. But he didn't have an appetite.

So here he sat, staring out into the late-night moonlight, wondering how he was going to get back on that train and leave Whitney.

What else could he do?

He had fallen for her in a fast and easy way that scared him. Was he reacting to everything they'd been through? Or did he really love her? Lucas had talked about her so much and David had carried that picture of her for so long, he felt as if he'd always known her. And yet he wanted to know more.

He'd been here only a couple of weeks. It didn't make any sense. Was he projecting all the pain and sorrow he'd experienced, including the death of her brother, onto her, expecting her to fix all of his problems?

Or had Lucas sent him here for this very thing—hoping that he and Whitney would fall in love?

Help me, Lord. Help me to see what I need to do next. He prayed about his past life, asking God to release him from this tremendous guilt that pulled at him like quicksand. He prayed for his future, wishing he could find some hope.

David felt as if he were traipsing around in a vast wilderness, searching for something. Searching for someone.

He closed his eyes, thinking he'd never felt so lonely in his life.

And then he heard a gentle knock at the door.

Getting up, he walked through the dark hallway of the big house. The other guests had gone to bed long ago, so the old house was quiet now, its Victorian sofas and velvet curtains hushed in a muted gray wash of color. David looked through the side window by the stained-glass front door and saw Whitney standing there.

She'd come.

He opened the door with a smile and a bittersweet heart. "Hi."

"Hi. Am I too late?"

He didn't know how to answer that, so he did what he should have done sooner. He pulled her inside, shut the door and kissed her. Then he whispered, "No. You're right on time."

The food was amazing.

Whitney bit into another strawberry, her mind on that kiss instead of her full stomach. She'd eaten out of nervousness and relief. Her nerves were frazzled and frayed, but she'd learned something in today's standoff.

She was a survivor. And she so wanted to be the best police officer she could possibly be. She'd also realized that she'd been holding back in all the other areas of her life because she was afraid to take a chance again.

Lucas knew her so well. She could imagine her brother handpicking the perfect man for her.

And that man had trekked across the world to show her what Lucas had seen all along. That she needed someone solid and good in her life.

She was falling for the medic.

But…now that she'd come to that conclusion, something wasn't right. David's actions tonight were subdued and quiet. Not his usual good-natured teasing and flirting.

She stared over at him. "You're tired. I should go."

"No, don't." He got up, came around the table and pulled her up. "You look so pretty."

She grinned and touched a hand to her hair. "I changed in a hurry. Gina and Ellen insisted I needed to come see you."

"Ah, so I have Gina and Ellen to thank for this midnight supper."

"Yes. Shelby was asleep and Hunter was tired, so they both insisted on staying so I could see you. Told me to put on a dress and some lipstick and get over here."

"I like your friends." He touched a finger to Whitney's nose. "And I like this dress."

Whitney giggled at that, thinking she felt young and carefree in the blue maxidress in spite of being exhausted. But David made her feel alive in a way that no one else ever had.

She reached up a hand to his face, touching his swollen eye. "I was so scared today when I saw that man holding a gun on you."

He put his hand over hers. "You were as cool as anyone I've ever seen. You handled the situation."

"My heart was about to come out of my chest," she replied, shaking her head. "I need to explain to you again, David. You don't have to protect me."

He pulled away, and she realized this was the *something* between them. It wasn't in his nature to ignore someone in danger. He'd been trained to help people who were in danger or injured, to minister to them and keep them alive. How could she ask him to give up the very essence of his being? They'd clash at every turn.

"I know you can take care of yourself," he finally said. "But I'm still having some flashbacks about…seeing people die while in battle."

"So you have to step in. You haven't learned how to tamp that down yet."

"No, I haven't."

He turned to her, his eyes dark in the moonlight. "Old habits die hard."

"But this isn't a habit for you, David. This is what you're trained to do."

"Yes. I need to refocus that training on medicine. In a hospital. In the clinic, anywhere except…when I'm near you."

She moved toward him, hoping to make him see what she felt in her heart. "Lucas did this. It's his fault. He sent you here as a proxy for all his worries. He was my big brother, my protector, but he hovered and worried. I needed to breathe. I had to find my own way. And I did, in spite of everything."

"Yeah, and you're not ready to give up your independence. I don't expect you to do that. Not for me."

"So where does that leave us?" she asked. "Can't we try? Once this is all over, I could be moving on anyway."

"Is that what you want?"

"I want a lot of things, but I have a job that I love, and I want to be the best at it. I also want a life away from work. I want to be a good mother to Shelby. I'm still struggling to find that balance."

"And I'm still struggling to find my footing back on solid ground. It's a long process."

"Should I go?" she asked, wanting to stay.

He looked into her eyes, a war exploding in his dark

gaze. Then he pulled her into his arms. "No, don't go. Not yet."

He kissed her again, the moonlight washing over them in shades of pale gray and shimmering blue. Whitney gave in to the thousands of emotions flowing through her. Fear, heat, need, want, hope and despair, faith that this could work, doubt that they'd ever make it. She was willing to make it work, willing to give him time, willing to do whatever it would take to make it right this time. With this man.

The right man for her.

They moved over to the white wicker love seat and sat together, touching, holding on, whispering. They talked about their best dreams and their worst fears.

"Do you think Lucas would approve of us being together?" he asked, his hand holding hers.

"I'd like to think that," she admitted. "If not, then why did he make you promise to come here and find me?"

"He worried about you."

"Yes, but he had to know you wouldn't walk away once you got here."

"What if I can't live up to what he expected of me, of what you might expect from me?"

"I don't expect anything," she said. "I want someone in my life who I can trust and enjoy being around."

"Do I fit that bill?"

She kissed him to show him that he fit perfectly. But in her heart, she felt him pulling away. Had today been the last straw for him?

"I have to get home," she finally said, wishing she could do more to ease his pain. "Tomorrow, I write up more reports and keep looking for that other suspect and his boss."

"And what about Brian?"

That question threw her. "I'll keep investigating the house fire and hope I can come up with a clue or connection that can give us a break."

"What if you never find the answers?"

So this was between them, too.

"I have to find the answers."

"But…what if you can't? Are you willing to live with that?"

She'd never thought beyond finding the truth. Was she willing to let it go and get on with her life? "I don't know," she said, trying to be honest. "Can *you* live with *that*?"

"I don't know," he said. Then he added, "But it's not about me. I didn't know Brian. It's about you and your feelings for him."

David wanted her to let go of those feelings. Could she?

She left him standing on the front porch. She was more confused than ever but also more sure than ever.

She wanted David in her life. Now she'd have to hope he'd want to stay in her life.

Whitney went home and lay in her bed, asking God to guide her on all of these conflicting, life-changing decisions.

Back at the Rose, David stared out into the moonlight, his heart heavy with the sure knowledge that he'd kissed the woman he loved for the first and probably the last time.

NINETEEN

Monday, David went to the clinic, intent on telling Dr. Pennington that he was done. He'd tried to find evidence of any wrongdoing on the doctor's part, but so far, he couldn't pin anything on Pennington.

The man did his job, and the patients seemed to keep coming back in spite of his brusque manner. After carefully watching Pennington, David couldn't say for sure if he was using any kind of drugs himself. No erratic behavior, no dilated pupils, no signs of wear and tear or needle marks. But he could be involved in selling illegal drugs on the side. The man drove a nice sports car and lived in a fancy house on a swanky canyon road.

He also apparently had friends in high places, since he bragged about having dinner with politicians and business leaders around the area.

Whatever was going on with the doctor, David didn't need this kind of disruption in his life.

But when David had walked into the clinic three hours earlier, the place had been in chaos. He'd dived right in, handling an elderly woman who had developed pneumonia and a toddler with an allergic reaction to a bee sting. Then he'd examined patient after patient, which had kept him hopping until late in the day.

"You should get paid," one of the weary nurses told him as she was heading out the door. "Better yet, you should apply to practice medicine here permanently and take over this clinic."

David could see himself doing that, but he had to stick to his plan. He couldn't stay around and watch Whitney while she still carried a torch for another man. And he certainly couldn't deal with the dangers she faced every day. He knew if he remained here, these issues would push them apart.

And yet, he wanted to stay. He had sensed that she wanted the same but...how could they make it happen?

Maybe if he stepped away and gave her some time, they could try again when things settled down. That would give him time to accept her line of work, too.

David went about his business, clearing away supplies and sterilizing instruments. By the time he was done, Dr. Pennington had left. Deciding he'd write a note and leave it on the doctor's door, David did one last check of all the clinic rooms and then headed down the hallway to the doctor's office.

Whitney was glad this Monday was over.

She'd been questioned over and over by the chief and several DEA agents about her handling of the train incident. Not because she'd done anything wrong, as the chief pointed out. But because she had to explain why David Evans had gotten caught up in the middle of things yet again.

"He saw the blue Camaro that followed him and that we know was seen near the Desert Rose Inn," she'd told the chief.

"So he followed the car to the train station? Why was David headed that way?"

Good question. She didn't have an answer, and she hadn't thought to ask David. She'd just been glad he was safe and that they'd had a wonderful couple of hours together.

The man they'd arrested wasn't talking, however. Ramon Catez had a long rap sheet and was known to hang with alleged drug dealers and unscrupulous characters. But he refused to give up the goods on whoever his boss was. He'd rather rot in prison than face the person in control, apparently.

The lab had found DNA on the red cap and the torn pants fabric. The torn fabric from a pants leg connected Catez to the first drug run, and the red hat they'd found at the Rose had been matched to his partner through the DNA found on both. But the other man was on the run and was now wanted for questioning. They still didn't know who was running the whole show. The man she'd shot had been identified, but he was a petty criminal— a junkie they couldn't connect to anyone.

Now, with that question of why David was at the train station burning inside her head, Whitney headed home with Hunter in the back of the old squad car. She hadn't seen David or heard from him since Friday night. She'd purposely given him time to think about what was happening between them.

And herself time to absorb being with him. Still amazed that she'd fallen for him, Whitney cautioned herself to take things slow. If David decided to stick around, they didn't have to rush anything.

She'd turned onto Desert Valley Road when she noticed a red car parked near a rutted side road up ahead. The vehicle didn't look familiar, but it caused all of her instincts to kick into overdrive. When a scrawny teenager got out of the car and waved her down, Whitney pulled over but left Hunter in the patrol car.

"What the problem?" she asked, taking in the teen's demeanor. "Did your car break down?"

"Yes." He nodded. "It's out of gas. But someone went to get some for me." He shrugged. "I got kind of scared, waiting here by myself. Glad you came along."

Whitney glanced around. "Okay. I can wait with you."

He nodded, his dark eyes darting here and there.

Then Whitney noticed something familiar about the young man. He had the three-feathers tattoo on his left arm.

Drawing her weapon, she said, "You need to show me some ID."

The boy's frightened eyes widened. "They made me do it," he said on a shattered breath. "I'm sorry, lady."

Then she heard another vehicle approaching from the rutted road into the woods. A black SUV, coming right at her.

"Get out of here now," she shouted to the boy, her weapon drawn. Then she hurried back to her own car, but not before the ping of bullets hit the ground around her.

The boy took off running into the woods. Whitney radioed for backup and gave the boy's description while she retreated from the approaching SUV.

She skidded onto the main road and started toward the police station. She looked up to see a silver sports car passing by, and she glanced over and into the startling blue eyes of Dr. William Pennington.

Still shocked by his hostile glare, she watched in her rearview mirror to see where the doctor was headed. He kept going on into town.

Did she follow him or try to get away from the SUV?

She rounded a curve about two miles away from the

station and looked in the rearview as the SUV suddenly came up on her tail.

Grabbing the mic to the radio, she reported in. "Suspicious vehicle tailing me. Headed back your way. Send patrol."

Then she checked the rearview again.

And saw a man with a gun hanging out the passenger-side window. He fired a shot as she rounded the curve. She heard the spray of bullets pelting off the back of the car. Hunter started barking.

"Down," she screamed, hoping to keep her partner from being shot.

They'd thought they were through with the drug traffickers.

But they were back.

Whitney knew they'd kill her this time.

And they'd go after David, too.

She had to warn him to be careful with Dr. Pennington.

Because from the look she'd seen in the doctor's eyes and with this SUV chasing her, she knew without a doubt that the doctor had to be the mysterious drug boss who'd been playing all of them.

David hurried into the swank office, notepad in hand. But he couldn't find a pen. When he didn't see one on Dr. Pennington's desk, he opened a drawer. Nothing there except prescription pads. Where did the doctor keep all of his expensive gold pens?

Turning to the bookcase and credenza, he searched for something to write with, his thoughts on what he should say.

Sorry, I'm done. Best wishes.

Sorry, Dr. Pennington, but I have to leave Desert Valley.

What could he say?

That he'd fallen for the one woman he couldn't have? That Whitney's brother had asked him to check on her, he'd gone above and beyond that duty and he never wanted to leave her?

That he suspected everyone around him of being involved in drug trafficking and a conspiracy and murder? And that he couldn't stand by and watch Whitney put her life on the line the same way he'd seen her brother do?

He dug through a narrow drawer on the credenza, his fingers grasping for a pen. At about the time his hand hit on something, his phone buzzed against the pocket of his jeans. Ignoring the phone for now, he felt around again.

A small object.

David tugged at the drawer, but the object had jammed against the top of the bookcase. Slipping his hand inside, he managed to lift it out of the way so he could open the drawer wider. When he had the drawer all the way out, he stopped and took in a breath.

A small plaque of some kind or maybe even a paperweight. Black with gold etchings. An arrow pointed upward, three feathers dangling below its tip.

The three feathers.

Why hadn't he seen this before?

The doctor had obviously hidden it way back in this drawer a long time ago, and since he didn't like people walking into his office, he must have thought no one would ever find it.

And yet, he never locked the office door.

Absentminded or too confident for his own good?

None of that mattered now. David had to get this to the police.

He lifted the square plaque with the tail of his shirt and started toward the supply room to find a paper envelope, and maybe a pen, too. When he got there, he stopped. The door was shut. He hadn't locked it up yet, and he didn't remember closing the door earlier when he'd grabbed the notepad from in here.

David glanced around, the hair on the back of his neck sending a definite warning that he wasn't alone.

He had two choices. He could run as fast as he could toward either door, but he'd already locked the front door. He could make it down the hall to the back but…someone could be out there waiting.

Deciding he'd faced down worse, he didn't choose either of those options. Instead, he opened the supply closet door and barreled inside, hoping he'd knock over whoever must be waiting there. It was his only chance of making it out of here alive.

It worked.

He surprised the man lurking against the door, knocking him down while David landed on top of him, the heavy black glass plaque slipping out of his hand to hit the floor with a heavy thud.

They rolled. David pinned the man down, then stared into his eyes. "You were on the train that day," he shouted, recognizing the shorter, chunky man who'd been wearing the red baseball cap. The man the police had been trying to find.

"Shoulda killed you then," the man spat, struggling to flip David over.

But David held him down, sheer adrenaline giving him the strength he needed to end this. The man eyed him, then glanced over at the plaque. Seeing his intent, David lifted one hand and stretched it toward the sparkling black glass.

While the man he was trying to hold did the same thing.

David had his hand on the heavy, squared-off glass, grunting as he gathered it into his grip. Lifting it, he stared into the eyes of a man he'd never forget.

But before he could bring it down on the attacker's head, a voice behind him halted his hand in midair.

"Don't do it, Evans," Dr. Pennington said in a gruff shout. "I'll kill you myself. And right about now I have someone taking care of that annoying K9 officer, too."

Whitney heard the shot and then felt a thud right before her car started skidding out of control. They'd hit a tire!

She held tight to the wheel, letting the car do a spin so she wouldn't run off into a ditch on the other side of the road. If she stopped, they'd shoot her on the spot.

"Hunter, hang on," she called to the barking, snarling dog. "Hang on."

She righted the car, faced the SUV head-on and then checked her weapon while holding the steering wheel with one hand. Help was on the way, but she'd have to hold these guys off until someone showed up.

She'd tried to call David to warn him to get out of the clinic. He shouldn't go back to the Desert Rose, either. Too dangerous. But he hadn't answered.

Praying she wasn't too late, Whitney ducked as another round of bullets pierced the glass in front of her. Diving down in the seat, she prayed for her life.

And for backup.

The dark SUV hovered on the road a few yards away. Whitney peeked again to make sure no one was sneaking up on her. When she heard a car door opening, she watched as a tall man dressed in black started toward her, his gun raised.

She didn't have time or a way to let Hunter out to attack the man. And she didn't have time to do anything to protect herself. Except hold on to her gun and shoot for all she was worth.

She hit the button on the driver's-side window to let it down enough that she could shoot out of it. Then she waited for the man to come closer, her breath steady and sure even if her pulse was jumping like a live wire. She thought of Shelby and how much she loved her little girl. She thought of her work, how far she'd come and how Hunter trusted her and kept her safe. And then she thought of David, a man who'd walked into her life out of the blue and captured her heart immediately.

Thank you, Lucas.

She had too much to live for to die here on this dry stretch of road.

"Drop the weapon," she said to the approaching man.

His chuckle hit the silent woods.

When she saw his shadow cast over the still car, she lifted and started shooting through the open window. And she didn't stop until her weapon was empty and she heard sirens approaching.

David let go of the heavy object in his hand and fell away from the man underneath him. He wasn't surprised to find Dr. Pennington holding a gun on him, but the tremor of fear that shot through him had him glaring up at the man. "You wouldn't hurt Whitney. She's doing her job."

"And her work is interfering with my extracurricular activities."

David had to be cool. He had to get to Whitney.

"What took you so long? I mean, that was you or some of your underlings who've tried to kill us over and over, right?" he quipped, accepting what he'd seen all along.

He should have acted sooner, taken matters into his own hands. But his focus had been on Whitney and watching over her instead of keeping closer tabs on the man who ran this clinic. Now that one mistake could prove to be fatal. "What do you plan to do?"

Dear God, don't let them hurt her.

"I think you know the answer to that," Dr. Pennington said while his goon got up and yanked David to his feet. "I kept you close to watch you, Evans. Even showing you what can happen when someone disobeys me. But you had to be the noble medic, home from the horror of war. And I had to be careful. Didn't want this to happen here, but... I'm all out of options. People who always do the right thing really get on my nerves."

David took in the situation. No way out of here unless he fought his way out, but then he'd get shot, and that wouldn't help Whitney. But he sure didn't plan on going for a ride with these two, either. They'd fight it out here and end it here, one way or another.

And he had to trust God and trust Whitney.

See us through. See us through.

If he made it out of here, he'd tell Whitney he never wanted to leave her again.

"I can see how that might annoy you," David replied, his gaze flickering to the strange piece of glass he'd stumbled upon, which now lay forgotten on the floor. "So... did you kill Veronica Earnshaw?"

Dr. Pennington looked surprised, his expression turning to mock hurt. "Do I look like a killer?"

"You look like a lot of things to me," David said. "I wouldn't put it past you."

The doctor shook his head. "I need to vet my volunteers better from now on. You're way too nosy for your own good, Evans."

"I like answers," David retorted. "And the truth."

"I didn't kill Veronica. I loved her." Dr. Pennington's gaze went to a faraway place, hollow and distant. "She used me, of course. Ran around on me, taunted me, made me feel like less than a man. I got angry at her but... I didn't kill her."

David saw a glimmer of redemption in those cold blue eyes. "Then, why do you want to kill Whitney and leave her baby without a mother?"

"Shut up," Dr. Pennington shouted. "You both saw too much. Someone had to have sent you here. DEA? The locals? Who?"

David shook his head. "Are you serious? I only came here to see Whitney since I knew her brother. We served together in Afghanistan. And... I wanted to help out here to stay busy. That's it."

"You saw my men," the doctor shouted. "You're messing where you don't belong."

"We saw two criminals doing what they do best," David said, pushing backward while he talked. "Killing us will only bring the whole police department down on your head. No one sent me, but you were kind of obvious, so this won't end here."

Dr. Pennington started pacing. When he whirled around, he noticed David's foot by the shimmering black plaque. Reaching down, he yanked it up and held it in David's face. "Where did you find this?"

"In your office," David replied. "It reminded me of Ramon Catez's tattoo." He glanced at the man beside him. "I'm guessing he has one, too. Do you make all of your couriers get this tattoo as a symbol of their loyalty? That young boy you were stitching up, did he fail one of your tests?"

"You have no idea how hard I work," the doctor said

in reply. "Veronica was a demanding woman, even after she left me."

"So this is her fault?"

"The Three Feathers used to mean something to me," Dr. Pennington said. "I have that tattoo on my back. I've helped a lot of the indigenous people around here. I received this plaque because of my work."

"What happened to you?" David asked.

Pennington shook his head. "I don't know. Power. Money. I needed more. I found a way to get it and to give others a means for a better life."

David felt sorry for the doctor, but he wasn't going to forgive him. "Stop this, Doc. Do whatever to me, but don't kill Whitney."

Dr. Pennington's smile twisted in anger. "It's too late, Evans. She's probably already dead."

David couldn't believe that. He wouldn't believe it.

He looked around and decided he'd get out of here and get to Whitney. And this time he didn't care who thought he should stay out of her way.

He whirled and shoved the shorter man into a rack full of supplies and then ducked and head butted the doctor, slamming him down. The doctor dropped his prize possession and groaned, but David caught it up and rammed it into Pennington's skull. Then he flipped around, grabbed the gun, turned just as the other man started after him again. David shot the man in the leg.

The doctor moaned and tried to get up. David fisted him in the face and knocked him back down. Then he called 911 and reported what had happened.

"Somebody needs to come and collect these two," he said. "And…you need to find Officer Whitney Godwin and make sure she's okay."

David turned, only to find Dr. Pennington rising up

like a ghostly phoenix, a pair of scissors in his hand. He rushed at David, a dark madness in his steel-cold eyes.

David backed up as the back door burst open and Whitney ran toward him, with officers and K9s on her heels.

"Bite!"

Hunter did his job. The big dog leaped into the air, landed solidly against the startled doctor and knocked him to the floor. Then Hunter sank his teeth into the doctor's arm. Dr. Pennington screamed and dropped the scissors as they went down. Hunter held him there on the floor.

Whitney rushed up the hallway.

"David," she shouted. "David, are you okay?"

"I am now," David said, grabbing her close.

All this time, he'd been the one anxious to save Whitney, but she'd been the one who'd saved him. By letting him into her life and her heart.

"I'm fine now," he said as he took her into his arms.

He'd never let her go again.

TWENTY

Two days later, Chief Jones stood staring out at the whole department. Whitney sat with Hunter curled at her feet, her fellow rookies gathered with their own partners at their sides, too. She'd been cleared for duty yet again after the incident out on the road, but she had one more afternoon of free time after this meeting. That free time had been ordered by the chief.

She'd wounded the man who'd tried to kill her out on the road.

He was still at the medical center, being heavily guarded. And based on the DNA evidence they'd gotten back from the Flagstaff lab, they'd managed to confirm that the red cap belonged to the man who'd attacked David in the clinic, which could prove he was the other man who'd been involved in the train smugglings. They'd also found the young man who'd been with the stalled car—the same teen David had helped stitch up—hiding in the woods, afraid, hungry and covered with bug bites. He'd signed on with Dr. Pennington's drug ring to earn money for his impoverished family, but soon he'd found out the doctor would never let him leave. Whitney had made sure he got the help he needed from the proper authorities to hopefully turn his life around.

She'd had help with her life from the local church, so she knew this boy could be saved from a life of drugs and crime.

Chief Jones gave her one of his rare smiles. "Let's give Officer Whitney Godwin a big hand for nabbing a local drug dealer and busting up his ring."

Everyone clapped, and even stoic Ryder Hayes gave her a nod and a smile. Wishing she could find out who'd murdered his wife, Whitney vowed to keep working toward that goal. But she had to decide what she was going to do about her need to find Brian's killer. She didn't want that to come between David and her.

While the chief went over the details of Dr. Pennington's elaborate drug activities and assured them that the doctor would be tried and put away for his crimes, Whitney's thoughts went back to David.

"I can't leave you," he'd whispered to her when she'd found him at the clinic.

Had he been planning on doing that? It didn't take much police work to figure out he'd been headed toward the train station because he was planning to buy a ticket. So later that night, when he'd come to her house and held her close, she'd asked him outright.

"But you were going to leave me, right?"

He'd nodded. "Yes, and then I saw the blue car and followed it. Even after all of that, I still thought leaving would be the best thing for you. And maybe for me, since I wasn't handling things very well. I thought if I stayed I'd be in the way. Hindering you at every turn is not a good way to begin a relationship. And in this case, it was kind of dangerous, too."

"No, not exactly good but…you are my hero, no matter what."

"Do you want me to stay, then?"

"Do you think you can learn to live with me being a K9 officer?"

He'd stared down at her, his hands touching her hair, his eyes full of an endearing fear mixed with a dollop of hope. "I don't think I have any other choice, Whitney. I love you."

"I love you, too," she'd told him, tears in her eyes, joy in her heart. "But…are we rushing this? Should we step back and see how we do?"

"We've been through the worst," he'd said. "It can only get better from here."

She wanted better.

Whitney loved him. This feeling far outweighed the feelings she'd had for Brian. Brian had been good-looking and charming but…she could see now what she'd denied before. All of the signs had been there, in the way he flirted with everyone from Carrie to Gina and Sophie and even Veronica. In the way he'd always demanded they stay in at his house rather than taking her out on real dates and showing her the hundreds of different ways he could love her.

And he'd done the flirting right in front of Whitney. He'd chosen her over the others because she'd been the one to cave.

She didn't want to cave. She wanted to love. Really love a man who'd done nothing but try to protect her. A man who shared her values and who believed in faith and hope and love even though he'd been through war and disaster and death.

If she let David go, she might lose the best man for her. The one man who could match her and allow her to be his equal. Her soul mate.

"I don't want you to leave," she'd finally told David. "I don't want you to go."

So he was staying here until this case was solved, and then they'd decide where they'd wind up. "I don't care if we stay here or go to Tucson," he'd told her. "I want to be with you." Then he'd kissed her. "And I'm going to learn to trust you and God when it comes to your line of work."

He also told her he really wanted to take over the Desert Valley Clinic and get it in top shape. "That way, if we leave, it'll be ready for the next doctor."

Whitney couldn't think of a better plan.

And she couldn't wait to spend the afternoon with David.

After Chief Jones had gone over the particulars of the drug case, he moved to the investigation of Veronica's death. "We're hitting roadblocks, but we're not gonna give up. We've canvassed neighborhoods looking for Marco, the missing puppy, and we know someone is breaking into a lot of the homes around the training area. They have to be looking for something. And so are we. Marco. That little puppy might hold the clue to whoever murdered Veronica."

Chief Jones stopped and glanced around. "I also want everyone to be aware about the upcoming Canyon County Police Dance and Fundraiser in May. We've established that for the past two years on the night of the dance, a rookie has died. Both deaths occurred at their homes and right before the dance. I've had some of you investigating these incidents, and these mysterious deaths are a matter of concern for all of us."

He looked at James Harrison, who sat near Whitney. "Especially you, Harrison. You've got the markings— blond hair and good looks. That seems to be the pattern." He winked, but his tone was serious. "I suggest all of you be alert on that day and be careful about being alone. Get dressed with the doors locked and the lights on and your partners on guard."

"I could try to draw out the killer, Chief," James said with a shrug. As if it was no big deal at all.

Whitney breathed a sigh of relief when the chief disagreed with that idea. "Harrison, you're already a target. Don't push your luck. All of you, be aware. We've got enough to deal with, and I don't want to lose another good officer."

After the meeting broke up, James leaned over to Whitney. "I want to do something, but I don't know what else can be done."

"I know what you mean," Whitney said. "I feel the same way." They headed out toward the parking lot. "I'll be watching out for you, Harrison."

"Thanks," James said.

Whitney glanced around and spotted David waiting for her by Miss Rosa's bright yellow truck. Hunter's ears perked up.

"Let's go," she said to Hunter, her smile meant for David.

He kissed her hello as the others filed out.

Whitney didn't care what the others saw now. She was done with secrets and hiding. She planned to tell her friends the truth about Brian being Shelby's father. But right now she only wanted to spend a nice afternoon with David.

"How'd it go?" he asked, his expression free of the weariness she'd first seen in him. And he looked great in his faded blue T-shirt and old jeans.

"Okay. We haven't made a lot of progress on Veronica's murder, but at least we got a drug ring off the streets."

"You did that," he reminded her with pride.

"You helped," she shot back.

"Right." They both laughed, and he pulled her close. "Wanna get out of here?"

"Yes."

"You two are so cute together," Carrie said as she walked by with a container of leftover cookies she'd brought to roll call. "Whitney, enjoy your last afternoon off before you get back out there."

Whitney nabbed two oatmeal cookies. "I will, Carrie. Thanks." She sure appreciated what a great baker the department secretary was.

David nibbled on his cookie, and then he nibbled at her ear. "How about a long hike along the river?"

"I'd love that."

They got into the old truck, and he turned to kiss her again. "And…later we can pick up Shelby, and I'll make dinner for you."

Words that made her swoon.

Later, as they sat on some boulders near the gurgling water, Whitney turned to David. "I won't quit trying to figure out these deaths, but I want you to know I'm going to back off a little regarding what happened to Brian. I need to work with the team, and I'll talk to the chief about that, too. I can't do it alone, and you can't help me. You have a lot to do while we're still here."

He took her hand in his. "I'll rest easier knowing you're not setting yourself up as a target. I like the team concept."

"I like the you-and-me concept," she said.

He kissed her again. He seemed to like doing that, and she sure liked his kisses. Then his brown eyes went to dark chocolate. "I know we're not supposed to rush this but…one day soon… I'm going to ask you to marry me."

Whitney's heart was already rushing. "You are?"

"Yes, and after that I'm going to go about adopting

Shelby so...so that... I can be her father. If that's okay with you, I mean?"

Whitney wasn't a crier. She never cried. She hated crying and she pushed tears away. Far away.

But now she couldn't hold them back. Tears poured down her face, and all the angst and fear and despair she'd held back for the past year came tumbling down in a flood of emotion, only to be replaced with a flood of joy. She'd lost everything...but here in David's arms, she'd found herself.

"Do you want that?" he asked, his fingers catching her tears.

"I do," she said, bobbing her head. "I do want that."

"Okay, then," he replied, his hands moving over her face. "Okay. We'll make it happen, and when I ask you, we'll have dinner at the Rose, and Miss Rosa will make us something decadent and I'll get down on one knee—"

"And I'll say yes. I'll say yes, David."

"Sounds like a plan."

They sat and talked about the future while the sun turned the desert and woods shades of pink and burned orange. Then they held each other and watched the sun set over the river—with the promise of rising again tomorrow.

* * * * *

Officer Zach Jameson surveyed the throng of people congregated around the ticket counter at LaGuardia Airport. Most ignored Zach and K-9 partner, Eddie, and that suited him just fine. Two months earlier he would have greeted people with a smile, or at least a polite nod while he and Eddie did their work of scanning for potential drug smugglers. These days he struggled to keep his mind on his duty while the ever-present darkness nibbled at the edges of his soul.

Eddie plopped himself on Zach's boot. He stroked the dog's ears, trying to clear away the fog that had descended the moment he heard of his brother's death.

Zach hadn't had so much as a whiff of suspicion that his brother was in danger. His brain knew he should talk to somebody, somebody like Violet Griffin, his friend from childhood who'd reached out so many times, but his heart would not let him pass through the dark curtain.

"Just get to work," he muttered to himself as his phone rang. He checked the number.

Violet.

He considered ignoring it, but Violet didn't ever call unless she needed help, and she rarely needed anyone. Strong enough to run a ticket counter at LaGuardia and have enough energy left over to help out at Griffin's, her family's diner. She could handle belligerent customers in both arenas and bake the best apple pie he'd ever had the privilege to chow down.

It almost made him smile as he accepted the call.

"Someone's after me, Zach."

Panic rippled through their connection. Panic, from a woman who was tough as they came. "Who? Where are you?"

Her breath was shallow as if she was running.

"I'm trying to get to the break room. I can lock myself in, but I don't... I can't..." There was a clatter.

"Violet?" he shouted.

But there was no answer.

Don't miss
Act of Valor *by Dana Mentink,*
available May 2019 wherever
Love Inspired® Suspense books and ebooks are sold.

www.LoveInspired.com

WE HOPE YOU
ENJOYED THIS
LOVE INSPIRED® SUSPENSE BOOK.

Discover more **heart-pounding** romances of **danger** and **faith** from the Love Inspired Suspense series.

Be sure to look for all six Love Inspired Suspense books every month.

Love Inspired® SUSPENSE

www.LoveInspired.com

SPECIAL EXCERPT FROM

*When a guide-dog trainer becomes a target of a
dangerous crime ring, a K-9 cop and his loyal
partner will work together to keep her safe.*

Read on for a sneak preview of
Blind Trust *by Laura Scott,*
the next exciting installment in the
True Blue K-9 Unit miniseries, available
June 2019 from Love Inspired Suspense.

Eva Kendall slowed her pace as she approached the training facility where she worked training guide dogs.

Using her key, she entered the training center, thinking about the male chocolate Lab named Cocoa that she would work with this morning. Cocoa was a ten-week-old puppy born to Stella, a gift from the Czech Republic to the NYC K-9 Command Unit located in Queens. Most of Stella's pups were being trained as police dogs, but not Cocoa. In less than a month after basic puppy training, Cocoa would be able to go home with Eva to be fostered during his initial first-year training to become a full-fledged guide dog. Once that year passed, guide dogs like Cocoa would return to the center to train with their new owners.

A few steps into the building, Eva frowned at the loud thumps interspersed between a cacophony of barking. The raucous noise from the various canines contained a level of panic and fear rather than excitement.

Concerned, she moved quickly through the dimly lit training center to the back hallway, where the kennels were located. Normally she was the first one in every morning, but maybe one of the other trainers had gotten an early start.

Rounding the corner, she paused in the doorway when she saw a tall, heavyset stranger scooping Cocoa out of his kennel. Panic squeezed her chest. "Hey! What are you doing?"

The ferocious barking increased in volume, echoing off the walls and ceiling. The stranger must have heard her. He turned to look at her, then roughly tucked Cocoa under his arm like a football.

"No! Stop!" Panicked, Eva charged toward the man, desperately wishing she had a weapon of some sort.

"Get out of my way," he said in a guttural voice.

"No. Put that puppy down right now!" Eva stopped and stood her ground.

"Last chance," he taunted, coming closer.

Don't miss
Blind Trust *by Laura Scott,*
available June 2019 wherever
Love Inspired® Suspense books and ebooks are sold.

www.LoveInspired.com